THE SWALLOWS OF
LUNETTO

A NOVEL

Joseph Fasano

A MAUDLIN HOUSE BOOK

MAUDLIN H❂USE

maudlinhouse.net
twitter.com/maudlinhouse

The Swallows of Lunetto
Copyright © 2022 by Joseph Fasano
ISBN 978-1-7370222-5-1

for Laura

I

I

She lived in an ancient village in Calabria, where her father was buried among the cherry laurels. Each morning she would drift down from the villa and look out at the gray waves of the sea, holding herself still against the west wind. Always she had woken from the same dream, and always at the coldest hour. She had sat up in the linens, in her own arms, then parted the muslin curtains, looked out at the same moon in the cypresses. She couldn't have said what she was looking for.

Surely she had said a name in her sleep. That much she remembered. That, and a voice saying, *Listen: we are the secrets in someone else. We are the voices of each other.*

What it meant she didn't know. She'd woken and dressed in the half-dark, made her way through the quiet streets to the shoreline, stood there where she'd once stood with her sisters—her sisters, who seemed to her like the shore itself, fragile and sun-warmed and what everyone loved—more like young boys than sisters—while she herself was the deep sea with its fevers, dark and wild and unkeepable, shaping and unshaping the battered land: the land, which thought it was the master, but was really in the darkness' arms.

Always she carried the same basket, woven from the hollow reeds of the river. She hooked it under her arm in the sea wind and stared out at the gray waves in their breaking. What was the name she said each evening? Always she woke and half-remembered: the sound of it like small birds in the rafters, like horses kneeling before their riders, like someone praying in the dark. Always she woke, and she almost knew.

Her basket was empty. When she'd stared at the waves a long while, she turned back and swung her leg over the sea wall and stepped back into the streets of the village.

She wore a long cotton dress dyed an uneven green like the shadows of the olive groves in summer. Her hair hung in a dark braid over her shoulder, and always her mother had smiled at her and told her such hair was untamable, like the chaos of the deep before the world was made, and maybe it was best that it was so.

She worked in the shipworks in Lunetto, riveting the great ribs of the cargo ships that were launched, each spring, into the Tyrrhenian Sea. The women and men who worked beside her had sleepless eyes and patches in their overalls, but they had the ancient cheerfulness of the Southern air, and when their wages were lowered the previous autumn, they simply walked out into the shipyard and lay down, singing songs from their youth while injustice passed. We have faith, Alexandra had thought, as she'd lain among them, but she couldn't have said what it was faith in. Simply that injustice would pass them by—as wealth, as happiness, as promise had done. In three days, the managers were hopeless, and the wages were restored to what they'd always been, and the singing stopped, and the machines sang on.

Had she been in love? Once. He was a shy, gray-eyed youth from Messina, and she'd loved the new world and the old in him, the way he'd wander home from the car factory in Scilla and make his way to the little shed behind his father's house, where he kept his wild-eyed falcons, letting them go and watching them return, as though the ancient things were still alive in this world. When she'd brought him home to the villa, her mother and sisters had watched him, this feral thing breaking his bread with his greasy hands, and when dinner was finished her mother had pulled her aside and said, "Alexandra, listen: this one is no father at all; he is not yet ready to be a story."

But why should you not let go of what was never there? Still, it had stung, and at night she had lain awake in her linens, the muslin curtains blowing across her body, and she'd felt his hands that had let go of all those wild birds, and she held herself and rocked herself like the gray waves, and she did not know what the pain meant.

She'd gone afterward, once, to Scilla, to speak with him after his day shift at the factory. But she'd waited beside the chain fence when the whistle blew, and she couldn't find him among the sea of denim work-coats, the faces darkened with oil. Turning up her collar against the evening wind, she'd drifted back and tucked herself into the train car, watching the poplars pass as she gave to sleep, and although she had promised herself not to think of him, he was there with her, in her deep sleep, for the last time, his heart like a falcon on his naked chest. She had stroked that heart, slowly, in its feathers, and she had told herself, as only a dreamer might, that if you had to choose between a god and a mortal—touch him, she told herself, touch him—why would you not choose this world?

Only once had she tried to draw him. He'd sat for her on the sill of her room, his eyes as heavy as the cypresses behind him, his thin fingers twirling a cigarette that he ashed into the denim cuff of his trousers, and she'd sat at her desk and smoothed the large, clean newsprint she'd buy each week for three days' wages from the office of the Gazzetta on the Via Ferrini, its fresh scent that always told her there were more things than Lunetto in this world. *What is it to love a home?* she'd asked herself, often, in the darkness. Perhaps to leave it is to love it; perhaps that is the greatest way of all. She'd sat on trains to Scilla, to Catanzaro; she'd taken trains in the evenings after her double shifts, if only to smell the shore of Palma as she passed it by, if only to feel the tracks swaying under her, to see the world freshened with every seeing, but always she'd returned to Lunetto. *I love it here,* she'd thought. *I do.* But then she'd stare down into the blank grayness of her pages and draw places she had never known, never seen, places she told herself it was enough to visit in the pages themselves, but which she knew, she knew she would have to see. She knew she would have to touch them. She knew she would have to go.

All she knew was a soft voice in her telling her to look. At the sea. At the light on her sisters' faces. At the way the wind shifted the cypresses or the sparks settled on the great steel ribs of the ships and then lifted again, briefly, into the wind. *Look*, something told her. *Just look. And go where it leads you.*

She had drawn since she was a child—first the sea, with wild, swirling leviathans ascending from it; then the leviathans alone, each with a face more fantastical than the next; and then, in recent years, the sea itself, simple and endless and impossible to get right. She had drawn faces from her youth—a priest's, her own, the boys sitting on the docks by Santa Maria. When she'd told herself which ones she could learn from, she'd folded the others into her father's sea-chest in the cellar, pausing a moment to tell them she would be back, and she had gone on working. She had drawn the villa, the sea wall, the harbor darkening suddenly beyond the drop-off, where the fishing ships would have labored in her nonno's time, before the shipworks came and told them they could make their own lives; before the great quake of 1908, in her father's twelfth year, had taken the nets from their hands. She had drawn her sisters, who could never sit still, and her mother, who always could; tucked beneath her winter clothes in her wardrobe was a single portrait of her father, which she'd done, as she'd promised herself she would, from memory alone—like the sea, simple and endless and impossible to get right. Why should she not have tried to draw her falconer?

"Can I see it?"

He'd finished his cigarette and ashed the last of it into his cuff and leaned back against the window.

"Later," she would always say. "Later."

Hers was an ancient family. They had come, they were told, from an old line of the Roman tribes that had mixed blood with the Gauls when they had sacked Rome, and her father had sat with her in the evenings and told her that's how it is with all of us: we are the conqueror and the conquered; we are the law and its shadow; we are the eternal, glittering city, and the furies that will burn it to the ground.

She was thinking of her father as she watched the sea, and as she drifted, now, through the market stalls of the village. They had buried him in the foothills among the cherry laurels, and she thought, less often now, of his stories, of the strange thing her mother had said to her about that first love: he is no father; he is no story at all.

But what could she have said to her mother? She had lain awake, for three days, when her father had died, cradling her own body in the darkness. The great stories live us, she had told herself, and it has never been the other way around.

Summer had come humbly to Calabria, and she made her way through the market stalls with her basket, filling it with fresh bread and onions, bergamotti and olives from the foothills.

Since childhood she had been told what her life might be, and for years now men had come to the villa, jasmine or fiordalisi in their pungent arms, and stood there in their polished shoes on the threshold, waiting as though her life were an answer. None of them, she told her mother. None of those questions are my life.

Yes, her mother would whisper, *yes, but there are changes in you as there are changes in the deep sea, and you cannot know them. You cannot hope to know.*

The first time she saw him, he was leaning on a storefront on the Via Borghese, crossing his arms and uncrossing them, his dark hair glinting in the summer sun. When the young men had gone to war in great waves, they had come back, often, in ruins: this one with a patch over one eye, that one with a folded sleeve where his youth had been. For years now there had been travelers in Lunetto, lost boys and nameless men in the piazza, broken souls with vacant stares on their faces, but the streets had been quiet for a while now—no sirens, no guns in the mountains—and she had never seen a man like this in her village, standing alone in the summer light, a gold cross glinting on his pocket, his face shrouded in a black, unfitting mask.

The piazza was waking with early morning, the Sunday grocers laying out their wares. Now and then, a child would pass on a bicycle and stop short and stare at this strange, masked figure, but he would only cross his arms again and wait awhile, as though he were familiar with the little game, and soon enough he'd be standing alone again in the sun.

Or not quite, not quite alone. He was cocking his head from side to side, speaking, it seemed, to the grocer before him. He shoved himself forward from the storefront and stood before the grocer's bins of fresh fruit. He laid his hands over each one, slowly, as though he were blessing the afflicted—the price, Alexandra guessed, he was asking the price, but the grocer came and stood beside him a long while, and he nodded in his black mask gravely, and she could not hear what they were saying in the wind.

She stepped forward through the stalls, keeping her eyes on the pair of them. When she was close enough to hear them through the morning din, she leaned back on the storefront and listened.

"And this one?"

"Like oranges, Signore."

"No. *Dimmi.*"

"Come, Signore. Oranges smell like oranges. How many would you like?"

"And these?"

"Olives, Signore."

The grocer looked down at his olives, like a child looking at something for the first time. He lifted one to his nose and sniffed deeply.

"Like the hills up in Albanella, Signore."

"The hills of Albanella?"

"Sì, Albanella." His lips moved as if he'd said it again, to no one at all, to someone waiting beside him. "My family lives there, Signore. These are their olives."

"Is it very beautiful?"

The grocer seemed to come back from a long way off.

"It's just an olive, Signore."

"I mean Albanella. Is Albanella beautiful?"

"Sì."

"Sì?"

"Come, Signore. How many?"

The figure said nothing. When the wind shifted his mask, he slid a step to the left and laid his hand over the next bin beside him, but the grocer only shook his head and lumbered away and sat on the curb in his cotton smock, fishing for a cigarette in his pocket.

"And these?"

Alexandra stepped forward and stood beside him.

"*Carciofi*," she said.

He turned toward her sharply. The sea wind shaped his face in the fabric—silk, no doubt, draping into his collar—and only his eyes shone through it; the thin, crescent slits seemed to have been cut with tremendous care. When he blinked the breeze away, his eyes flashed deep brown, amber, like the honey in her high cellar windows when it was found out suddenly by the light.

"You're not blind," she said.

"Why should I be blind?"

Alexandra turned toward the grocer, laying her braid back over her shoulder, but he waved her away.

"Why ask this man what these are?"

"Is that what I'm doing?"

The morning light shifted in the arcata, and she thought she could feel him smile behind the silk, a sharpness honing in his cheekbones, but he turned away and laid his hands on the fruit.

No, he was not asking what they were, he told her. Only what they were like.

"What they are like?"

"Close your eyes."

She squinted at him.

"Close them," he said.

She did, and she felt something alight in her palm.

"What is it?"

"An almond," she said.

"No. Smell it."

She opened her eyes.

"Come," he said. "Play."

"*Non sono credulone.*"

"Who said you were a fool? Play."

She closed her eyes slowly, lifted the almond to her nose.

"It smells like an almond."

He told her not to be ridiculous. To tell what it smelled like. To tell herself.

His scent had come closer, and something moved in her. She thought to open her eyes, but she did not.

"It smells like vanilla."

"Vanilla."

"Yes."

"And where does it smell like?"

"Where does it smell like?"

When she opened her eyes, he had turned away from her, and she could feel his eyes were closed, his chin lifting as he breathed the sea wind in the piazza.

"It smells like home," she said.

"Home."

He lifted it to his mask and set it in her palm again.

"Or not quite," she said. "It smells like the shore at Palma."

She waited for him to answer, but he said nothing. Very slowly he lifted the almond from her palm and laid it down again among the others. He went there once as a boy, he told her, before all this, before the war, before everything.

"Palma's beautiful," she said. "My father used to take us."

"When everything was better," he whispered. She could not tell if it was a question.

"I don't know. I wouldn't want to be a child again."

"You wouldn't?"

"What's a child? A child is powerless."

He seemed to consider it, his eyes half-closed as he looked over her shoulder toward the sea.

"Maybe," he said. "Maybe a child doesn't know it's powerless."

"Oh, yes it does."

His eyes found her again. He seemed to have decided he was done with his little game, or perhaps that it had never been a game at all. "Andreas," he said, bowing slightly. He had come a long way from the North, from Milano, when the Repubblica had fallen. *Ma non abbiamo bisogno di parlarne,* he told her. It is hard to stay in one place when everything has fallen apart, fallen into rubble, nothing but rubble, again and again, as it was sure to do.

"A German name."

"*Sì,*" he said. "My father was a traveler. He loved the Germans as much as Il Duce."

She cocked her head.

"You should be careful what you say, don't you think? Even now."

"Nonsense."

She glanced back for the grocer, but he was not there.

"You don't think it's dangerous?"

"Life is dangerous." He touched his face.

"I'm sorry," she said.

"Come." He waved vaguely at the sea. "Let's walk."

She'd told him her name as they climbed over the sea wall, the wind shaping the mask against his face, her dress snagging and unsnagging on the masonry. There are some wounds, he told her, that you cannot look at yourself, but others you can spare the world. A face so changed is not a face to show anyone who has not chosen to look.

"I was there in the Piazzale Loreto," he said.

They were walking along the sea, her basket slung over his shoulder, and when the farthest fog parted they could see a pair of cargo ships maneuvering past each other out in the morning light.

"Where they killed Il Duce?"

"No, just where they strung him up. They killed him up near Dongo. Shot him against a wall. Like a dog."

She shook her head. "Ugly."

"Yes. The whole thing is ugly. But what isn't?"

"It must have been terrible in the Piazzale."

She could hear him breathe deeply behind his mask.

"Maybe. It's hard to say."

"How?"

He seemed to consider it a long time, brushing something from his cuffs, but he only told her it was not something he could explain. You see those men hanging up there on the girders, and you feel the thrill of it—*il brivido*—the thrill that maybe all your pain is hanging up there, right there in the wind, and nowhere else at all. That it's so simple.

"But it isn't so simple," she said.

He dragged a toe of his black shoe in the sand. She looked back at the mark he'd made as they walked on, the sea rising to fray itself in the seam and fall back again.

"No," he breathed.

They walked together as the tide rose, and she spoke of the British ships appearing one morning on the horizon. Many in the village had not prayed in a long time, she told him, but they prayed that the Germans might pull back to spare them. She'd stayed up some nights thinking about how strange it is to pray in language like that. Tedeschi. Britannico. Us. Them.

"But you did?"

"Of course."

When they'd walked to the breakwater, they stood a moment and looked at each other. The sea wind was pressing his mask against his face, but he did not look away.

"Come," she said.

They walked on past the breakwater and up to the beach where the sand turned to small stones washed up from the depths of the harbor—sea-glass; jasper; the little flecks of volcanic rock that had settled ages ago on the sea floor, and that had washed up in the big storms of winter. He held the silk of his mask taut when the wind rose, and they walked on past the stones and down between the tidepools where the water was still cool with morning. A single plover rose up from the surf and flared its wings once and then settled in the kelp along the margin.

Its wings twitched as it settled, and it seemed to have come a long way. She asked him how long he'd been in Milan.

"Only for what happened at the Piazzale, and after. I'd been with the Divisione Julia at Klisura when the Greeks broke through, but they sent me back to Bologna. I went up to Milano much later."

"Is it true what's been written? What they did to them after? Mussolini and his mistress."

"Worse."

"Ugly," she said. "Ugly."

"History is ugly."

She turned to him.

"That's just a thing to say. Nothing is history until it's over."

"You think so?"

"I just mean history is us. We make it."

"Maybe," he said. "Maybe."

A pair of shearwaters dove low and passed them and circled up and settled on the far side of the dunes.

She told him her family had stayed in the village when the British came across. Some prayers, even faithless ones, can be answered, perhaps because they are faithless. The Germans had pulled back, and those left in their houses had known it wouldn't be much, but of course they'd been afraid. They'd heard the guns up in Aspromonte.

"I could go my whole life never hearing a gun again," he said.

They were silent a short while, his shoes flickering when he stepped clear of the water. Finally she asked him about Milan.

"It wasn't Italy," he said.

"What about the partisans? Were the partisans Italy?"

"I don't know. Maybe none of it was. Do we have to talk like this?"

She turned to him and watched him breathe through his silk, the light from the sea flashing off the cross on his pocket, and they stood together as the wind calmed. His eyes were not honey at all, or not quite like the honey in her cellar, but more the harbor itself—the sands inside it flashing with morning—the edges just as shallow, the center just as deep. When he looked away, she lowered her eyes and nodded, and they walked on.

His family was from Puglia, he said. Brindisi. By the sea.

"Still?"

He shook his head slowly. Two of his brothers had fallen early—the younger two, he said, but he didn't name them. The oldest had disappeared in Russia, in the snows, in all those snows. They hadn't known for a long time—how can you ever be sure?—and perhaps even now they did not know.

"I went back after the Piazzale to find my mother. She was alone."

He looked out at the water. His father was gone when he was very young, he told her. His mother had not even had his father. Sometimes he'd lie awake in the mountains and feel his father was the war itself. Something he could not explain.

"Did you find her?"

"Yes. It isn't easy to tell."

"Nothing is."

He turned to her as they walked, the black silk of his mask tucked into his collar. He nodded and dragged his toe in the sand again, like a child drawing something for the tides to take away.

"It's hard to be home when everyone wants to see you again."

"Why come here, though? Lunetto isn't much."

For Palma, he told her, for places like that. When you've seen enough of things, sometimes you just want everything to be simple again.

"You were there?"

A few days ago, he told her. He'd just stood there, in Palma, where they'd torn down the hotel, and that was that.

"So you're passing through?"

"Who isn't?"

He knitted his fingers in the small of his back. He was wearing a blue cotton shirt with its top button undone, a weathered belt with its buckle near his hip, and his khaki trousers were pleated and cuffed.

"Let me ask you something," he said. "Why should you want to walk with me?"

"Why not?"

"*Non hai paura*?"

"Why would I be scared?"

The shearwaters rose up from the dunes again and circled and flew out over the water.

"I've been scared plenty of times," he said. "In the mountains when the Greeks broke through. You could hear them rolling their guns up into the pass in the dark. You knew you were going to die. It wasn't a question."

"Is that where you were hurt?"

When he did not answer, she said she was sorry—*mi dispiace*—but he looked at her and told her no, don't be. There was a strange comfort in it; you could lie there in the dark listening to the machine of your death, and for one brief moment you weren't a question. Nothing in your life was a question. You knew you were dead and that was that. When a shell comes, you don't hear it, he told her. You just die and you become the darkness. But then there's the pain that comes after, and you know you're alive, and you have to be the questions again, all the questions.

"Was it very painful?"

"What isn't?"

He turned to her, and when she felt him smile, she thought she could see the full outline of his lips when the wind pulled the silk against his skin, and she told herself not to look. She told herself it did not matter. But she knew it did.

"There were many Calabrese in Bologna," she said. "They say it's beautiful."

"Not after the Americans."

"It's a shame."

He told her The Repubblica had to end, one way or another.

"Not that way. It's a shame."

The wind had shifted, and he turned to her and slung her basket onto his other shoulder. Then he looked out over the waves where the shearwaters were.

"Yes," he said. "A shame."

The sun had come up full and warmed the sand. She'd slid off her rope-soled sandals and slid them into the basket on his shoulder, and she was thinking of the mornings she'd gone down to the beach and stared at the soldiers' boot prints in the sand, the water rising up to touch them in the half-dark, as though they were merely an error—something in the school book of a child that could be scrubbed, suddenly, away.

They'd turned back when they'd reached the jetty, and she was pointing to the girls' school of Santa Maria Maggiore.

"It wasn't such a bad place to learn why God hates you," she said. "It looks so sad sitting there like that, doesn't it? But sometimes I think everything looks sad on a Sunday. Don't you think?"

"*Sì. Qualunque cosa.*"

"Even me?"

He didn't answer. When she turned to him, the wind had shifted the silk hem from his jaw, and she saw the slightest glint of his clean-shaved face. He reached up slowly and smoothed the silk again.

She asked him if he'd seen the shipworks, where the great ships are welded and rigged and launched out into the sea. Yes, he told her, and he'd heard of the times they'd been burned in the war, so many of them, up and down the coast. That was something that could haunt your dreams, all those ships burning in the dark, burning all night with nowhere to go, all those flames blowing back into the cities and the streets, and no one with anywhere to go.

"It's true," she said. "I used to sit up there on the wall, watching them burn up and down the coast. *È stato terribile.*"

"But not Lunetto."

"No," she said, "they never touched us."

She tucked her hands into the pockets of her dress and looked out at the surf. She could have said more, but she knew what she'd said wasn't true; even if you're spared, no one survives untouched; even if no one undoes you in the light of day, and perhaps especially then, no one can keep you from what happens in the dark.

No, she did not want to talk about the shipworks, about the fires, about any fires. She was thinking of the last time she saw her father, how she had been shown into the high-ceilinged room in her church clothes, the swallows flitting in and out through the windows, her father lying quietly in the lamplight. Of his hands folded on his chest like a hymnal. Of his shadow like a small boat. With nowhere to depart from. Nowhere to go. Of the darkness rising around him like a harbor. She had not known what to say to him, and she'd only knelt there with her mother's hand on her shoulder, the little candle burning beside him, and she'd felt, yes, like the sea her mother had always said she was, shifting in her own arms, in the darkness, until all the dead inside her had no names.

"They tried to lower the wages when the British came," she said. "As though the war were over."

"The war is never over."

"This one is."

"For now."

"You think we'll fight again?"

He told her no one could know. The country had been a mess in the North, rotten from inside, broken from outside—revolt in its heart, bombs in its skies—and in that way, maybe in that way, it was like its people, like anyone. How can we do that to ourselves? In the days before they'd killed Il Duce, he'd seen partisans hanged in the streets—when he said it, he tilted his head slightly, and she knew he had closed his eyes—and then he'd seen it the other way around: fascisti being hanged in the streets. Like dogs.

"It's not like that down here."

"It's not so easy," he said. "I was in Bologna when Il Duce lost Rome. We heard about what happened down here."

"The celebrations?"

He nodded.

"Why would the people not want their country back?"

"Was that not their country?" he asked. "What their young men died for?"

"*Ma dai.*" She waved at his medal. "No one says a thing against the men. This is still Italia."

"Maybe." he said. "But would they not stone a fascist?"

"Stone? *In che secolo vivi?* No one stones anyone."

"But they'd shoot one."

"Impossible. This is Calabria. We make bread and we pray."

Something had quickened their step, and she was searching the shape of his face for something she could not see. The wind tugged at the braid she'd tucked into her collar, and she felt her lips part twice, silently, before she asked it.

"Fascista," she said. "What does it mean to you?"

He tightened the ribbons over his ears, smoothed down the fabric over his face.

"Nothing. Not anymore. Something from another world."

"Good," she said. "Then we should leave it there."

He shook his head. He seemed to be thinking about something a long while, brushing something from his cuffs again. Then he looked out over the sea and said it.

"What about the Gemetti boy?"

She asked him where he had heard of him, and he told her the grocers, who know all. She nodded and looked out at the waves and then shook her head.

"No," she told him, "it would not go well with him."

He asked her to tell him, and she did. No one in Lunetto had forgotten the name Gemetti. He was a tall youth who had stood on a peach crate in the town square, two years before the war, and howled down the pacifists, the republicans. He'd said fascism was the only way to cleanse the heart, to restore the Mare Nostrum, to fulfill the destiny of the heavens. That was his language: fulfill, cleanse, restore. It was merely a boy speaking his heart, a boy powerless before words and ignorant of their power, and most of them had only turned away from him, left him to the Balilla, who had taught him. But no one could have imagined what would come to pass. The young men of Lunetto had gone to war, she told him, and some of them had come back only in letters, only as ghosts, only in their names folded neatly in the pages their mothers pressed to their breasts, nightly, weeping in the deep rooms of their houses. Matteo, Vincenzo, Giuseppe. She'd stood there on that beach and told herself to say their names. The lost. Say their names, and never forget what's real. But it was impossible to think anything but that it was real, this world, this waking, this place where the mothers stumbling through the piazza, and their heavy veils, and their sleepless eyes, promised it would never be anything else; it would never be anything but real.

For years they had heard no word of Gemetti—Leonardo Francesco Gemetti—after he'd left Lunetto, after his little speech, long before the war was a war. He'd gone up North somewhere, were the rumors, to a place where he didn't have to wait to make his name; his younger brothers had followed him, a year later, but they'd never come home. So many of Lunetto had not come home. Gemetti, his brothers, how were they any different? Their mother had sat, daily, on the fountain, throwing her breadcrumbs to the pigeons. She was hopeless, entirely hopeless. The youngest priest sat beside her in his cassock, stroking the old rings on her fingers. "Soon," you would have heard, if you'd passed them by, "soon, Signora Gemetti." But when no word came for two more years, his mother had told the priest, at last, that her son was gone, that the word had come that he had joined his brothers in the other world, and the priest had given the final word in his sermon: leave them, my brothers and sisters; pray for them that even the restless may have rest.

She was still shaking her head now as they shuffled through the kelp along the harbor.

"It was a long war," she said. "Maybe it's not over yet."

"What was he like?"

"Gemetti? I didn't know him. Just one of the boys of San Pietro."

He smoothed the silk over his face. She told him *i ragazzi e le ragazze* did not attend school together in Lunetto—San Pietro over there, Santa Maria Maggiore over here, with the schools for the younger ones, San Filippo and Santa Rosalia, down by the shipworks on the harbor—

that it was an old place, with old laws, old customs, only some of which oldness she adored. The mayor's youngest son had been a partisan in the North, way up where there were still things to be done, where a young boy might go with a reckless quest in his heart, and he had been among those killed. In a way no mother should ever have to survive. At the hand of a countryman.

"In Bologna," he said.

"What does it matter? If it wasn't one son, it was another."

"Thirty."

"What?"

"Thirty sons."

She looked at him and then looked away, voices from the piazza blowing down to them on the wind. Why, she asked, why would he want to know such things, but he only said a soldier has learned to look. Not look away. She thought about that. She looked at his eyes and saw things he had seen. Things she could not explain. Things which once seen cannot be unseen.

"You haven't seen enough?" she asked.

But he only shook his head and said, "Tell me. Gemetti."

It was Gemetti's face the people of Lunetto had seen in the newspapers—his face, his grin, his name in clear, bold ink—and they'd stood in their houses and looked at him looking up at the shoes of the thirty partisans he'd ordered strung up in Bologna, each of them unblindfolded so he could see his own death from within, and the youngest of them, the *sindaco* of Lunetto's own son, no older than sixteen.

His mother had sat no more on the fountain, and the priest had knocked each morning on her locked door, and by night she had roamed the streets alone, each night gone down to stare at the sea through her black veil—as though it had something to tell her—and the door had only opened in the daylight once, just once, when she could keep it closed no more.

When she was done telling him, she said it was perhaps best not to think about such things. After such a war. That there were things to be done now, and they could do them. That they couldn't bring back the dead.

"Sometimes," he said.

She shook her head. It was a treachery, she told him, for a people to suffer for too long, a treachery against itself. Everyone knows that. There are things that can be built now with our own hands. Again. Afresh. Anew.

"I hope so," he said.

She shook her head.

"It's a shame," she said. "People say they can forgive, but they send their boys off to do things they could not forgive in themselves."

He looked at her, but he said nothing.

"These boys," she said, "maybe they were just lost."

"Maybe they were not boys."

She nodded. "Yes," she said, "they did what they did. But maybe it doesn't have to be forever." She looked back toward the village of Lunetto. "Maybe nothing does."

The wind had turned back and was blowing up the beach and over the sea wall. He shifted the basket to his other shoulder and offered to walk her home, and she said yes, good, he would stay. *Mangeremo*, she said. You must eat.

"No, grazie."

"Just to sit with us. *Per favore.* My mother, she loves a man with a good story. *Solo un momento.*"

"I can't."

"You can." She smiled. "You can."

II

When the British had crossed the Strait of Messina the autumn before last, she had stood behind the sea wall and watched them come, the gray ships rising on the horizon. The Germans had pulled back to let them come, and the people of Calabria had gone on living, laying out their olives in the markets, launching the great ships into the harbors.

When the soldiers had come ashore peacefully, they had wandered through the village streets, the piazza, handing out cigarettes and chocolate, shooting the pigeons in the belltower. Alexandra had watched them with her sisters.

"They are not so rough," Clara had said.

"Too bad for you."

"*Ma dai*, Bea. What use do I have of any of them now?"

"We'll see if it lasts."

Clara had held up her ring in the sunlight.

"It lasts. It definitely lasts."

"But look how young they are." Beatrice was leaning back against the stone fountain.

"He's not so old, *diavola*."

"He's thirty-nine."

"Thirty-nine is nothing. Tell her, Alexandra."

Alexandra was watching the soldiers shoot the pigeons. When a bird fell, it would sometimes twitch its wings where it had fallen, beating at the air madly, as though it didn't know it had fallen.

"Let her be happy, Bea."

"He doesn't even fight. He's too old."

"Noble," Clara said. "You mean noble."

"You mean fascist."

Clara had laughed.

"Devil. He's no more fascist than these men."

Another pigeon fell from the belltower.

"Alexandra," Bea said. "How's your English?"

"Better than your honor," Alexandra whispered, in English.

"What does that mean?"

"Nothing."

"Come," Clara said. "Let's talk to them."

"What the hell were they teaching you at Santa Maria, Alexandra? Just English? Gallo was no teacher at all, was she? Lastra gave me the real things, beautiful things, like Stesichorus. You remember that, Claretta? *Where monster Geryon first beheld the light.* That one always got me. Monsters. All men are monsters, *sì,* Clara? That's what they should be teaching."

"I'll eat my shoes if you believe she believes that, Alexandra."

"I do believe it," Bea said.

"Then you love monsters."

"Why can't I?" They were crossing the square toward the men. "Why can't I love monsters?"

When they reached the catedro, Clara leaned back against the stones and whistled to the soldiers. A pair of them turned toward her and smiled.

"Look at the little one, Bea. You can have the little monster."

"I don't want any of them. And you'd better be careful."

"Alexandra, talk to them in English."

"I'm not talking to them."

"Don't be a coward. I heard what you said about honor."

The men had shouldered their carbines and crossed the piazza, toeing aside the pigeons that had fallen.

"Ciao," the taller one said. "Tom speaks Italian." He had clear blue eyes and hair the color of the chestnuts in the mountains. Beatrice was thinking of the dark brown cover of her volume of Stesichorus.

"No, ma'am. Mi dispiace."

"For what are you sorry?"

"We don't speak Italian," the little one said. In truth, Beatrice was thinking, he was not so little. He hadn't shaved in days, though. What was it like to be so far from home? What was it like to cross the water from one place that wasn't home to another?

"We forgive you," Clara said. She nudged Alexandra. "Tell them that in English."

"They won't know it's a joke."

"Nonsense. Tell them."

When Alexandra had said it, the tall one looked at her strangely.

"You're very beautiful, aren't you? Bella, bello. What's the word, Tom?"

"Beautiful is the word."

Someone barked from the far side of the piazza, and the tall one clucked his tongue.

"Excuse us, ragazze." He reached out to touch Alexandra, but she grabbed his wrist. He bowed reverently with a smile, the sea wind lifting the heavy question of his cowlick as he left them.

She was standing alone when he came back. Her sisters had gone off to watch the soldiers unloading the boats in the harbor, but she stood looking up at the pigeons, watching them fall into the square below.

"It's just a game," he said.

She hadn't seen him standing at her shoulder.

"It's a ridiculous game," she said. "Shooting birds."

"No, I mean all of this." He waved his hand vaguely. "It's just a game."

"Maybe to you."

"No, not to me. It's bloody serious to me. But they send us here and there like it's a game. Only who loses if they lose? Not them. Us." He shook his head and looked up at the birds. "What's that?" He was pointing up at the belltower.

"What?"

"That. Just up there."

Suddenly something had seized her from behind. The one she'd been speaking with slid in front of her and backed her into the alley beside the cathedral. She was kicking wildly but someone had lifted her from her feet and a hand was clasped tight over her mouth. All she would let herself remember in the days to come was the breath of the one who pressed her against the cold stones, the stale smell of his uniform, his body. She didn't remember the hours afterward, when she'd wandered with her dress torn through the back streets, nor how she'd washed her face and stared into the mirror, nor the strange figure who had helped her back to the villa, but she remembered waking in her own bed, the muslin curtains blowing over her, the swallows flying in and out of the windows as they'd done when she'd knelt before her father's body, his hands folded, as hers were now, in the dark.

On the third night she rose and walked down to the beach and stared at the soldiers' boot prints in the sand. She was wearing her father's nightshirt and a pair of soft, cotton trousers, and she slipped off her shoes and waded into the water and swam out a long while in the moonlight. She had not thought she was coming back. Her clothes were heavy in the crashing surf, and when she'd swum beyond the break she lay back on the water and floated where the sun, by morning, would fill the harbor. The water was swelling and falling, her dark hair billowing from her shoulders, and when her ears slipped below the water she could hear a strange sound in the depths and she knew it was the chains of the great ships raising their anchors in the channel. She did not understand what it was doing to her, but when she closed her eyes she remembered when she'd heard it before: she'd lain awake, some nights, on her bedroom floor, her ear pressed to the cool tile as she listened, her father's voice trembling the whole house as he spoke about the end of his country. She was a child then, and she didn't understand, but it had soothed her when she couldn't sleep in the evenings, and she lay back in the waters and heard it again, and she could hear it still when she swam back and lay on the beach, and she could hear it still when she curled alone in the nights to come, and she could hear its absence in the rumbling of her mother's voice as she sat with her sisters on the terrace, staring at a strange figure in a black, silk mask, her mother filling the wine glasses slowly as she laid her hand on the shoulder of her guest again.

"You were in Milano?"

"Sì, Signora."

"Mama, let's talk about something else."

"Nonsense, Alexandra. This man has seen great things. You've seen great things, haven't you?"

He lifted his glass of wine and considered it. He had tried, skillfully, to pinch the silk under his chin and pull it taut and wet his lips with a glass of water from below, but this seemed to him only dignified because it was necessary, and to do it with a glass of wine might seem theatrical. He set the glass down and looked at the women before him. It seemed they were trying not to look at him.

"It's hard to say what I've seen, Signora. I was in the Piazzale, yes, but maybe we who were there know least what we've seen. When you've been told what you've seen it's hard to know."

The Signora sat down and looked at her daughters.

"I see."

"No, Signora. Mi dispiace. Please don't misunderstand. I just mean something like that is perhaps beyond words. It's a monstrous thing. And such things are only given a shape later. In the story we tell."

"I see."

"And a story is a difficult thing. It can perhaps give shape to a shape that is not there."

Clara reached across the table and lifted the fresh loaf of bread and broke it in two. She cut a slice from it and leaned back in her chair, dipping the bread in a little dish of olive oil, a sprig of rosemary on its rim.

"Maybe," she said. "But it could be there. The shape could be there."

He felt his mask shift slightly in the wind.

"It could be," he said. "I don't know about these things. Forgive me."

"Was it very scary, in the mountains?"

"Beatrice," Alexandra said, "certainly we can talk about other things."

She had regretted bringing him the moment she'd stepped with him through the little gate off the Vicolo Basso and seen the rows of cypresses leading up to the villa, the dark cypresses standing grim and vigilant like the figures of her mother and her sisters.

"Yes, Signorina," he said. "It was."

"Bea," she said. "Call me Bea. What were they like, the Greeks?"

"I can't say, Bea. They were just men with guns."

"Beautiful," the Signora said. "He has such a beautiful way of saying things, doesn't he?"

"I don't know," Clara said. "What's so beautiful about men with guns?"

"But he means they were just like him. Just like us. Isn't that what you mean, Signor Vinetti?" She did not wait for an answer. "Of course it is. He means they were all the same, up there in the mountains. All that snow and those boys with guns. No one any different. That's beautiful. It makes you *think,* Alexandra. Doesn't it make you think?"

Alexandra knew how her mother spoke when she was nervous.

"Yes, mama."

"I don't know," Clara said again.

"Well, you don't have to know," the Signora said. "None of us has to know. Because we weren't there, were we? Only you, Signor Vinetti, isn't that right? Only you were there." Again she didn't wait for an answer. She had cinched forward and was reaching for the bread, pouring out a dish of oil. "Yes, only you. Tell me, what do you think will happen now? This is no time for a king, I think. We have monarchists in the South who say no, but I think a change is good. It must be good. Anything is better than what we've had." She crossed herself with a piece of bread. "Anything."

"Not anything, mama."

"Let the man answer."

He looked out at the cypresses and then back at Bea, who had spoken.

"I think some things could be worse," he said, "but not this. I think we're all too tired to fight again. The Democrazia Cristiana will have their way."

"And you think that's good?" Clara asked.

"Who can say? Your mother is right. It's better than what we've had."

"Maybe."

He nodded.

"My daughter, Signore. She has no manners."

"Don't pay her any mind," Clara said. She took a loud bite of the bread. "I have perfect manners."

"More water," Alexandra said. "You must be thirsty."

"The wine is fine, grazie." He waved his hand over it, as if to keep it where it was, then glanced back quickly over his shoulder. "I should be on my way, Signora."

"Of course," the Signora said, "of course." She opened her hands. "But let us give you a little something, Signore. *Per favore.* Just a little something to eat."

"Mama, don't—" Alexandra said.

"You know what I think?" The Signora had waved away her daughter's words. "I think everyone wants a role in the tragedy. Isn't that right, Signore? Everyone wants to say they've suffered. And maybe they have. Maybe they have. *I've* suffered." She laid her palm on her chest and bowed strangely. "But you don't hear me complaining about it. My Franco. My husband." She crossed herself and brushed the breadcrumbs from her chest.

"Mama," Bea said.

"Signore, you can let someone else speak, can't you?"

"Mama," Clara said, "we are letting you speak. But don't talk about Papa. Please."

"Why should I not talk about him? This is his house you're in. All of it. He gave us all of it." She looked at her guest. "I'm sorry, Signore. You know what my mother always told me? Grief comes in waves, she told me, great big waves, and you never know when they're coming. I start to talk and there they are. But I'm not ashamed." She touched her chest again. "I'm not ashamed. That's what I think. Everyone wants to be part of the tragedy. Well, we will all get our chance, I say. Just wait. We will all get our chance. Isn't that right, Signore?"

He nodded. Alexandra watched Clara squint at their guest. She tapped his hand where it rested beside the wine glass he hadn't touched.

"We don't have to talk about that, Andreas. Tell her about Bologna, please, and then we'll let you go. Mama, you were there when you were a girl."

"A girl. Look how my daughters speak to me, Signore. A girl. I was never a girl."

"Mama."

"No, I never was. I tell them this, and they never listen. I was old from the beginning. I always knew what the world was."

"The Basilica di San Francesco was one of my favorite places, Signora," he said. "Did you see it?"

"Of course. You see my daughters? Their manners? They get them from my father's blood." She crossed herself. "His brother was in Bologna and we all went up to visit. He'd been in that terrible Abyssinian war. The first one." She waved her hand over the table. "None of you were here. This is a long time ago. A long time. He was like a father to their father, Signore. So we went to see him. And my God what manners. He would sit there and drink and drink. Finally my mother had enough. Bless her, *Madonna*. We went each morning to the Basilica and I remember just lying there in a pew as my mother prayed. I remember looking up at the birds." She looked up and brushed the crumbs from her chest. "Funny what we remember, isn't it, Signore?"

"It is."

She looked at him gravely.

"It's gone, isn't it?"

"No, Signora. They've built it up again."

She shook her head and looked at her daughters.

"You see," she said, "this is our country. These are our people. We build it up again. Isn't that right, Signore?"

"I think so."

"San Francesco." She touched her chest. "He preached there, at the Basilica, long ago. He came through and he preached there. And I lay there with my mother in the same place and looked at the birds. Maybe they were the great great great great granddaughters of the birds he preached to." She laughed. "Who knows? It could be, couldn't it?"

"It could."

"Tell them, Signore. That's right. It could. My daughters are without faith. But I tell them, all the time I tell them, do you know what builds things up again?"

"Mama."

"See, Signore? See how they treat me?"

Alexandra tapped her mother's hand.

"Mama, we treat you fine. Let Signor Vinetti tell us about Bologna."

"Yes," Bea said, "tell us." Her eyes found his, and she looked away. Suddenly she stood. He turned around to see a man standing on the pathway between the cypresses below, holding his hat in his hands.

"Carlo," Bea called, "come."

The figure below nodded and vanished under the terrace, and they heard him climbing the stairs in the house. When he had stepped out onto the terrace, he stood awkwardly by the open doors, fiddling with the brim of his hat. The Signora rose and brushed the crumbs from her chest and gathered him in her arms and led him to the table.

"Carlo Russo, I give you Andreas Vinetti. He is a great hero of the war who has paid a price, a deepest price, and I know you will make him feel at home. I know it. Russo, Vinetti."

He seemed to consider the cross on their guest's pocket, then nodded and pressed his hat against his chest and bowed slightly.

"You have our thanks," he said. "All of us."

There was a slight silence on the terrace before they heard their guest say, "Grazie."

"I was in Belgrade under Ambrosio myself. *Che beffa.*"

Alexandra gestured for Carlo to sit.

"No more talk of the war, *gentiluomini.* It ruins a perfectly good day. Come, Carlo. Sit."

He hung his hat on the arm of his chair and smoothed down his hair with both palms.

"Signora Bianchi, *la mia fonte di gioia,* my mother said she missed you at mass today. *Dimmi,* how are you?"

"You see what manners are?" She touched his face. "These are manners. I'm fine, Carlo. Tell your mother not to worry. I go when there is no one to see me speak to my husband like a madwoman."

"No one thinks that, Signora."

"I do," she said. "Sometimes I do."

"Carlo," Alexandra said, "what news from Piccolo?"

"Nothing. He knows what happened last time. He won't do a thing."

"He'll cut our pay again. He thinks they don't need us now that the war is over."

"He doesn't think that."

"Maybe not," Bea said, "but he thinks we think it."

Carlo shook his head. He considered their guest again, briefly, and then seemed to have told himself not to look.

"Listen. I tell you how I see it. Piccolo wants peace as much as anyone. No more anyone against anyone. Three sons he lost. Three. In this damned war. *Perdonami*, Signora. This war. I wouldn't blame him if he were bitter."

"And why shouldn't he be?" Clara said. "But we won't take the brunt of it. He's lucky the communisti won't get what they want."

"They could. Who knows?"

"No," she said. "Angelo says it couldn't happen. Too many are afraid. One extreme won't heal another."

"That sounds like Angelo," Bea said.

"And? He's right, isn't he?"

"Maybe," Bea said. "But maybe not. Maybe we'll just get one—I don't know—one extreme after another. Back and forth. It could happen." She wet her lips with her glass of wine.

"You don't know anything," Clara said.

"Clara."

"Mama, please. She speaks of my husband as if he doesn't know. He's just as smart as anyone."

"He is," Bea said. "I know he is. But maybe he doesn't know what will happen, that's all."

"Of course he doesn't," Carlo smiled. "And he can't be blamed for that. No one knows."

"That's right," the Signora said. She touched his face again. "What manners. No one knows."

"Signor Vinetti," Carlo said.

There was another pause.

"Andreas. Please." He'd lowered his voice strangely.

"Andreas, we bore you with our business. How long are you with us?"

"We bombard him with questions," Alexandra said. "He's here now."

"Are you looking for work?"

The men looked at each other.

"No, grazie. I'm just passing through." He looked at them a moment. Then he told them Palma, maybe he'd see Palma.

Alexandra turned to him.

"I thought you'd gone already."

"I'm going back. It's the right weather for it, no?"

"Palma," Carlo said.

"Only to pass through. Then back to Brindisi, of course. To see my mother. She hasn't had it easy."

The Signora crossed herself.

"Madonna," she said. "How we've suffered."

"Mama."

"You won't have a train this afternoon," Carlo said.

"Probably not."

"That's not so bad, *compagno*. There's much to see here. If you like Palma you'll love Lunetto. Alexandra will show you."

"Go with them, Carlo," the Signora said, "after you eat." She turned toward him. "Carlo's father is *il sindaco*, Signore. Maybe they can arrange something for you."

"No," he said. "No, grazie. That isn't necessary."

"Necessary," the Signora huffed. "Neither was your sacrifice necessary. Neither was ours. Neither was anything."

"Mama."

"The Signora flatters my father," Carlo said. "He is not so influential,

Signore. Merely the mayor of a provincial town who does what he can."

"He does plenty."

"Thank you, Beatrice. I'll tell him you said that. Every night he paces the floor. He doesn't sleep."

"What they did to your brother was an abomination," the Signora said. She crossed herself twice. "And these men call themselves Italian. Call themselves countrymen. What they do to their brothers, it is an abomination."

"Mama."

"No, Alexandra. Your mother is right." Carlo looked at their guest. "I am a forgiving man. But my brother—Christ, it kills him. And my father—this hate, it rots him from inside. What can I do?"

"Thank God they have your mother," the Signora said. "She is a guide." She laid her hand on Carlo's. "A guide. Today they know nothing about that, about guides, but your mother knows. She is of a different time. She will be their guide."

"Thank you, Signora." He leaned back and slipped a cigarette packet from his left breast pocket and shook one out and lit it. "Thank you."

Clara reached over the table for the cigarette, but her mother swatted her away.

"I think you're right," Carlo said. "She'll try. But Matteo, he's far gone. Far gone. He doesn't know where to set it down." He shook his head. "Andreas. This is a German name?"

Alexandra had been looking out at the sea, thumbing the shapes of the waves on her thigh, but she turned back and tapped her guest on the hand and stood.

"Come," she said. "Carlo's right. There's much to see in Lunetto. Let's walk."

"Lunch," the Signora said. "He must eat."

"Thank you, mama." Alexandra brushed something from the table. "But Signor Vinetti hasn't seen Lunetto at all."

"Go to the piazza," the Signora said. "The market, Signor Vinetti. Eat."

"What a shame," Clara said.

"Yes, Clara. It's too bad, isn't it? But he was kind to walk me home."

Clara shrugged. She reached for the cigarette again, and Carlo shook her away.

"Yes," the Signora said, standing. "He was a perfect gentleman to walk you home. What manners. Go. Walk. Alexandra, take him down to the beach. Where are your things, Signor Vinetti?"

He paused.

"At the station, Signora."

"Good. Go, walk. Then fetch them. Alexandra, go with him to fetch them. Bring them back here, Signore. Please. It would be our honor."

"I'll walk him to the station, mama. Thank you." She tapped his elbow. "Let him decide."

"Good," the Signora said, "very good."

Clara lifted her piece of bread and waved it in a small circle above her. "Ciao, Signor Vinetti."

"Ciao, Signora. Ciao, Beatrice."

Carlo stood and extended his hand.

"I hope to see you again, Signor Vinetti." His voice softened, and he leaned in slightly. "There are things that can be done for you."

He nodded at Carlo, but his eyes were lowered, and he said nothing. Alexandra gathered his arm and walked him out through the open doors and down through the house and its shadows. When they reached the garden she looked up once at the terrace and then led him out toward the hedges, the cypresses standing on either side of them like dignified figures in the sun.

III

When they'd brought the thirty prisoners out into the square of Bologna the autumn before last, he'd looked at the corporal standing before him.

"How many have we today?"

"This is no today, sir. No yesterday either."

"Come," he'd said, "don't play games."

"No games, sir. Thirty."

"Thirty? You joke."

"I wouldn't joke, sir."

He'd said nothing more. Then he'd said he was glad; the caporale's jokes were shit.

"Yes, sir."

"Thirty?"

"Yes, sir." They had planned to kill the *capo,* the caporale told him. At the catedro. "Fools," he said. "The priest gave us names."

"Thirty."

"Yes, sir."

The caporale had saluted and turned to go.

"Mazzaro."

"Yes, sir."

"Don't call them fools. It's sloppy."

"Yes, sir."

He knew he was young to be a tenente, and the caporale was probably his age, or older, but he stood tall in his polished boots and looked at this soldier before him, and his orders from the capitano were sealed orders, and the world was in the master hands of a clockmaker, and everything worked as it should.

"Bring them here," he'd said.

When they'd strung them up, the crowd had mostly cheered, and he had stood before them and given his speech, something he'd heard countless times in the Balilla, something about the clockworks of the universe, the chaos that will not rise from the depths.

He hadn't known the photographers had been there, and he hadn't seen among the faces any face he remembered from Lunetto, certainly not the face of the Russo boy, who had been nothing to him once but a face among the faces of the younger boys of San Filippo. Perhaps he had not looked at any face at all, even when he looked, even when they looked back. Perhaps, he thought. But how could one be blamed for that? One soldier? How, in a world in which to see such things was a sentence of death upon your own heart and your fellow soldiers the same?

His mother had sent him the clippings, three weeks later, from the Roman papers, the local syndications in Lunetto. What had he done? What had he done with their name?

He'd stood over a blank piece of paper, trying to explain it to her clearly, but he only crumpled the paper, again and again, and threw it out into the sewer, and stared down at the empty page before him. Nothing would rise up from that blankness. Nothing would rise up from those depths.

He had not come from Brindisi, nor from Puglia. He'd been raised in Lunetto all his days, and he had indeed been wounded on the Greek front, but the shrapnel had passed clean through his left thigh only, and when they'd shipped him back across the Adriatic he'd spent weeks in the hospital at Bologna, listening to the guns in the mountains, holding his hands over his ears, not knowing which guns were in his dreams.

When the British had come up through Calabria and taken Rome again, it had all seemed over. Il Duce was alone in his prison cell, and there were celebrations as far South as Reggio, the *sindaci* holding back the carabinieri, the peasants dancing in the town squares. But the blackshirts had been an answer, and although the questions in this life might be beautiful, might be worth dancing over in a town square, who wants to give up on an answer?

Not the Germans, certainly not the Germans. They had spirited Il Duce from his captors and installed him in the North, in Salò, deciding it was the true Italian Repubblica, though of course its true capital was Berlin.

Who, the crowds had seemed to say to the Führer, *who wants to give up on an answer?*

Not Leonardo Gemetti. He was seventeen when he'd stood on the peach crate in the piazza of Lunetto and shouted down the pacifists, the *traditori*. His voice had only broken a summer earlier, and he'd distrusted it not to squeak when he needed it most, like the rickety wheel of his father's wagon, always failing him in the coldest of mornings when he shouldered the yoke of his childhood and dragged it into the market to earn his life.

Always his mother had sat him at the table, his eyes flitting from one brother to another, and fielded her sons' questions about their father. Yes, those were his papers. Yes, a long time ago. Yes, German. Finally she had brushed her hands against their faces and touched her eyes as she'd wandered off into the shadows. He was a hero, she told them, *un eroe,* and that's all you need to know.

"But mama, Enzo had protested once, "tell us."

She'd turned back and raised her hand in the threshold.

"Why," she'd sobbed, "why do you make me live this shame again?"

The boys had grown silent at the word *shame,* and like a weed its silence had grown among them. Each of them knew better than to tug at it, and instead they'd clung, each year more wildly, to that other word, *eroe,* hero, knowing it was not the whole story; knowing, in their bones, what Gemetti meant—something that may or may not have happened; something that had left them in the shadows; something someone had tried, without hope, to love.

But there was never a time when he hadn't heard about heroes. He'd sat at the Balilla meetings with Enzo, staring at the great maps on the stained walls, the lecturer with his funny, upturned mustache. *Credere,* he would hear the boys resounding, *credere, obbedire, combattere.* Always there were new ranks to aspire to—the ranks of a brother, of his *amici,* the ranks of a father's faded papers—and the halls of San Pietro had echoed with the polished boots of *avanguardisti.* The schoolmasters were always dry and uninspired—at least the Balilla could amuse you—but then there was Signor Giordano, with his patient way of explaining everything, his warm look as he'd guide you to the back room and show you the books he had once loved. *Tell me,* he would ask you, as he smelled the books, *why are they back here, Leonardo?*

Because they are no longer necessary.

Sì, the Signore had always said, though Leonardo could never tell what was in his voice, that same vague ache that seemed to trouble his mother's. *Sì, Leonardo, sì.*

Once only he'd stood at the back of the class and asked how Il Duce was like Caesar. *La dottrina del fascismo* is confused, isn't it? If a nation can guide another without the need to conquer, then why do we need to do anything, and didn't Caesar know when not to fight? Giordano had only waved away the question, but later, by the chain fence of the schoolyard, the boys were waiting to clarify. *So,* Lupo had sneered at him, *bastardo, is this the time? Codardo, is this a time to fight?*

In Bologna he had gone so far as to write to the offices of Vittorio Emanuele and *il comando supremo* about his brothers, from whom he had had no word for nearly two years. When he'd finally been told, he'd sat in his hospital bed, running his hand over the ink of their names—Paolo and Nicola, with their soft, sharp eyes—and he'd lain awake for two days and nights, remembering the rubble of the Greek guns, the men howling out around him. When the Greeks had taken Klisura Pass, he'd seen men, brave men, throw themselves onto the rocks below, rather than be taken prisoner. A man who hadn't seen such things might have said it was God who had allowed him to crawl back to the support line, but he had only lain back in the transport car as it trundled down the frozen roads of the mountains, and he'd known it was luck, *solo fortuna*, and he'd laid his hands over his face, and he'd ridden the shame.

In the hospital at Bologna he'd tried to stand on the morning after the surgery, but he'd stumbled forward with a crash in the half-dark, and when the nurses came to kneel down and lift him, he'd sworn at them until they left him on the cold floor.

Something, he thought, something had to be done.

And so something had festered in him—a gangrene of the mind, he would later call it, as though the right phrase could throw it away. There was order, there were orders, there were always orders. Put your head down, Gemetti. *Credere, obbedire, combattere.* Think of your brothers. Think of them.

When, exactly, the news of the thirty had gotten back to Calabria he couldn't say, but his mother had written a letter to him in Bologna, her handwriting smaller and more tentative than he'd remembered it. "My son," she had begun the letter. And he knew she knew.

When the partisans had shot Il Duce by Lake Como, two years later, he had indeed gone to the town square to see the bodies strung up on the girders—Il Duce, his mistress, his henchmen—even given them a kick or two when they were taken down, and when Bonomi had denounced the fascists, and when Parri had done the same, he had paced the streets of Milano, like so many others in their sleeplessness, asking what to remember, asking what to forget.

But what right had he to forget? What right, he asked himself, to be done with it? Fascism, he'd said, when he'd stood on the peach crate in Lunetto, fascism was the only way to cleanse the heart, to restore the Mare Nostrum, to fulfill the destiny of the heavens. A boy's language, no doubt—a boy to whom *patria* was an aching word, a boy to whom the Balilla had seemed everything—but all that had happened had filled him with silence, and the language that replaced it was not that.

Certainly he had plenty to go in fear of. The only way, Bonomi told the people, was to root out the fascists among us, to slay the ones who drew us into this madness. Certainly they were hiding among us, ready to put down their roots again, deep into the fatherland's soil. Root them out, Bonomi had told the country. Root them out. Before they bloom again.

Still, Leo wanted to see his home, if only for a moment. You're afraid, he'd thought. Yes, I'm afraid. I always was. But fear is what you have now. Fear is what you have no right to set down.

So he had gone home. Home. Was it that anymore? Paolo and Nico in the wreckage of Durrës, Enzo in the endless snows of Russia. And what about the sons of the *sindaco*, the ones who lived, the ones who would be the death of him? *Carlo fears God*, his mother had written him. *You are nothing but a boy to him, Leonardo, a boy he never knew at all, a wayward son. He knows how terrible this has all been. How confusing. How no one could have known. Come to me, Nardo. He forgives us. He is not like his brother.*

And what about his father? his letter had said.

Merciful, merciful, Nardo.

And what about Matteo, mama?

He is not here, his mother's letter had ended. *Come to me for one week only. If you want to come, I can keep you safe. Just let me see you. Only me. Please, my son, let me see you. Show me you are not an illusion. Show me I still have this one dream. Do not make me leave my only home.*

What could he have written back from Milano? If he had never known his father, and was never going to, he had told himself a mother like theirs was more than enough—their mother, who had always played both roles in earnest. Cross her, and you were sure to get the slipper; flatter her, and you were sure to get the same.

For years now he'd thought of the boy standing on the peach crate in the piazza, of the tenente standing in Bologna. Don't, he thought. Don't you dare say that wasn't you. He'd lain awake, how many years now, and spoken to them. In the nights. In the darkness. That boy. That man. Don't, he told them. Don't. You have no idea what the world is.

You have no idea. But he'd held himself on the train back to Lunetto, and he'd looked out the window at his country, at the poppies quivering among the poplars in the first touch of whatever summer would do to them, and he'd said, *Look at you, guardati, you coward. You don't know. You still don't know.*

Four days he'd been in Lunetto, pacing the floor of his old room, where his mother had hurried him from the station.

How could you have not known, mama?

No one speaks to me, Nardo. No one.

Mama, but he's here now, isn't he? Matteo's here.

Rest. Rest now, Nardo.

Why didn't you tell me, mama? Why did you lie to me, mama?

My son, look at me. I wouldn't lie to you.

How could you not have known? When did he come home, mama?

I told you, Nardo. Why don't you believe me?

Why did he have to come back now?

There are no reasons. Everything is terrible.

Don't say that. Look at me, mama.

Nardo. Please believe me. Why can't you believe me, my only son?

She had slumped down on the long-worn threshold, one hand bracing against the doorframe. The room had swirled, and he had told himself this was not his life, but when he'd crossed the room and knelt before his mother, he'd known that this was all of life he'd ever known.

I do, mama. I do believe you. I do.

On the fifth day, he had woken late and lain alone, staring at the sunlight in the Via Finetti. He knew where his mother was, always, if she wasn't in the catedro—down in the kitchen, in the shadows, reading the letters of his brothers, reading the letters of his father, reading the letters of ghosts. *I can't,* he said aloud, *I can't stay here.*

Surely he was not the only one to hatch such a cleverness. There must be others who had thought of it. There must be, he told his mother, that morning, sitting on his boyhood linens, while she fitted the black silk she had tailored.

"Nardo, you come back to me. Only one hour, I beg of you. *Solo un'ora.* Just to breathe, just to know you're home again."

"I have to see it. I have to be here, mama."

And to let them see, he almost added. *To finish it. To let it be done.*

"Yes, Nardo, and who will question a hero?" She was pinning his *Croce al Merito di Guerra* to his left breast pocket. "Who would dare question *il mio eroe?*"

He had told her he wasn't a hero. Many times he'd said it, many times, but she would always touch his thigh and shake her head.

"You've saved me," she'd tell him. "You've come home."

IV

Alexandra was leading him along the Via Borghese toward the station, and they watched those who passed them turn to stare at his silk and then look away, quickly. He was searching for faces he knew, but he saw none. *You've grown, Lunetto,* he thought. *Good, good, grow.*

On their way through the arcata, only one figure had stopped them, a *vecchio* she knew only as Gino. He laid his hand on her shoulder and asked something, with his eyes, of the cross on her companion's breast. When he was satisfied with the answer, he placed his palm on the medal and whispered a blessing they could not hear, then whispered that a hero's life would be difficult, *molto difficile,* then shook his head and bowed once and was gone.

The streets were quiet with the Sunday afternoon, the pigeons scattering from the campanile as the bell tolled.

"Grazie," he said.

"For what?"

"I don't know. You all talk to me as though I were just anyone else."

"Aren't you?"

He smoothed the silk over his cheeks. *Grazie,* he wanted to say again, but he did not.

"I'm sorry about your father."

"No," she said. "I'm sorry about my mother. I let myself forget how they ask things."

He rolled up his sleeves in the afternoon heat.

"Where's your sister's husband?"

"Angelo. He's gone over to Messina. His mother's not well."

He thought for a moment. Then he asked.

"No," she said. "He didn't fight. Not this time. He was in Abyssinia when all that happened again, but he didn't fight this time. Something about his knees." She shook her head again. "My sister's not easy to love, but we love her. We do. Angelo's mother is not charmed."

"*Capisco.*"

"She thinks marriage is all there is. Finding a man. She doesn't understand there's so much more."

She glanced at him and then looked up at the belltower. The bell had stopped tolling, and the pigeons were settling again on the stones, shaking the light from their wings, in a way she had never been able to shake them on her pages.

"There is, isn't there?"

"Of course," she said.

The sea wind turned up his collar and let it fall again. A silence had slipped between them.

"Is it true what you said about the Basilica in Bologna?"

"What did I say?"

She smiled. "That it was your favorite place. I thought maybe you said it to please my mother."

"No."

"Tell me about it."

He breathed. "I liked what your mother said about the birds. It's true. The swallows nest up in the rafters, and you can hear them up there in the dark before the sermons in the mornings. I liked what she said about San Francesco. It does make you think."

"She's always saying that. Whether or not she does it is another question."

He turned to her and then looked away.

"*Non dovresti dire questo di tua madre.*"

"Only as a joke," she said. "She's the most precious thing in my life."

They turned left on the Via Castellano, and they made their way along the eastern edge of the piazza, shuffling between the grocers' stalls and the children weaving in and out on their bicycles. He picked up an orange and handed a grocer a folded *am-lire* note and held out the orange toward her. She shook her head and he rolled it up his sleeve and popped it in the air with the inside of his elbow and caught it.

He told her it was a strange thing about hunger. About those birds. How you would lie back in the Basilica and hear them up there in the dark, or even see them up there in the sun, while people knelt down in the shadows to pray. Why do people pray like that, in times like these, when they must know?

"Because they hurt," she said. "Because they don't want to hurt anymore."

He held the orange up into the sunlight. He told her how right her mother had been, how he'd sit there for hours listening to those birds, listening to the sound of their wings inside the sermon.

"I don't know if I can explain it," he said. It was as though you could hear something—something that was inside every sermon, every word, just the wild hunger inside all things, those little birds hunting up there in the dark.

"What did it sound like?"

She reached for the orange and held it to her nose and sniffed it.

"Like birds," he said. "But I know what your mother meant. About lying there in those pews, looking up at them. I've done it myself. You can lie there and look up at them and think about things like that. Or just close your eyes and listen to them passing by and think about why hunger came into this world at all." He shook his head. "There isn't any answer to that."

She reached up and plucked something from his hair and blew it from her fingers. They'd walked to the far side of the piazza, and they sat together on the edge of the fountain. He watched her brush the dust from her hem.

"You know what's strange?" she said. "I remember the summer before the British came up. Every day we'd read in the papers about how terrible it all was. And it was, I'm sure it was. But that didn't mean I wasn't alive." She looked at him.

"Go on."

She crossed her ankles and looked up toward the belltower. When she spoke again, her voice was soft but steady.

"I was alive, that's all, and there were things happening. There were good things happening. And yet we were supposed to be miserable. So many were suffering, so why should I be happy? Why did that have to be my time of happiness?'

"What made you so happy?"

She turned to him and closed her eyes.

"You can imagine."

When she opened her eyes, he saw the deep green in them, and he tried to think of what it had been like for others to look at them.

She turned away and looked up at the belltower. A woman passed by and stared at his silk and then looked away. He did not know her, but he thought of Brindi, of Bombasi, of the Parri brothers he thought he had seen on the Via Castellano. Let them look, he thought. Let them all look.

"Maybe home isn't a place to be happy," he said. "Just a place to work."

"Don't be ridiculous. They can be the same thing."

"Really?"

She breathed. "I tell you, something comes over me when I'm working, when I'm just up there with everyone on the scaffolding, with everyone but alone, with my mask down and the sparks flying, this tremendous thing just taking shape in our hands. Something bigger than any of us. Can you imagine that?"

"I think so," he said.

"It's not that I want to build ships forever. That's not a life. Or maybe it is, I don't know. For some it is. But I just mean there's something in it that feels right. All I know is I want that feeling in whatever I do. *Capito?*"

"Sure."

"You laugh."

"No. *Capisco.*"

"There's only one other thing that gives me that feeling."

"What's that?"

She lifted a hand and plucked something from her fingernail and then turned toward him.

"I'll show you later." She breathed. "Maybe."

She looked up at the pigeons in the belltower. "Home is not so bad," she said. "It has work. And bread. And what else?"

"An older sister."

She laughed loudly.

"*Daivolo.*" She looked at his mask and looked away. "Don't say it."

"*Mi dispiace.*"

"*Va bene,*" she said, "say it again."

"An older, wiser sister."

She laughed.

"*Ma dai,*" she said. "We shouldn't be mean. She hasn't had it easy." But she laughed again.

"She seems sweet."

She was shaking her head. "*Va bene,* let's be good." Her eyes found his, and she could feel him smiling. "It must be nice," she said.

"What?"

"To smile." She turned away slowly. "Sometimes I forget I can do it."

She felt him grow quiet.

"It must be hard," she said, "being so far from home."

He cocked his head.

"What's home anymore? It's all different," he said. "Maybe we can't ever go back."

She looked at him.

"You really believe that?"

"I think so, maybe. Yes. But maybe we're not supposed to. Maybe that's just the way it's always been."

"That we can't go back?"

"That we're not supposed to be able to," he said.

She looked up at the belltower again.

"Now that's something mama would never say," she said, "or Claretta. Never." She looked at him. "Sometimes I feel so alone in Lunetto. Did you feel that, when you were home? Alone?"

"Of course."

"Like there's no else who would ever think the things you think."

"And even if you think them, you'd have no home anymore."

Her eyes widened.

"Yes." She shook her head and searched his eyes. "Did you ever feel like—like maybe you were born in the wrong place?"

"I know I was."

"No."

"Yes. I know it."

"How do you know?"

"I just do." He breathed through his silk. "It's hard to say. I used to lie awake at night and think—I don't know—"

"Say it."

"That I was born a long way from where I was supposed to be."

She laid a hand on his arm and then lifted it quickly.

"*Mi dispiace.*"

"No," he said, "say it."

"Me too. All the time, me too."

Her eyes were searching his again. She squinted and looked up at the belltower.

"It's easy for you to say it, though."

"Why?"

"Because you're passing through."

"And you? You're here forever?"

"Don't be ridiculous," she said. "Just until I die of boredom."

He felt himself laugh. She turned toward him and smiled, then looked out into the piazza.

"Andreas," she said, "Andreas the traveler who made a bored *ragazza* laugh once."

"Just that one time," he said.

She looked up at the belltower.

"Just that one time," she said.

The birds flew away from the bell and settled again.

"What were the Americans like?"

"I didn't see much of them," he said. "It's hard to explain."

She asked him to try. He closed his eyes and opened them and looked out at the piazza. He told her he didn't know. That it had been a mess up there, in the North. He was just a boy. That's no excuse for anything, but he was just a boy. Then he spoke very quickly. He told her he'd come to realize nothing was simple. Nothing. That the world was something we try to make simple, and in doing so, we can do terrible things.

He took up the orange and slid his fingernail down its skin, then drew his finger upward again until he'd scored the shape of their country. He scored a line across the middle and pointed to the top right corner. He was there in '41, he told her. After he was hurt. It was a mess. "You know how it was," he said. "When the Britannici came up in '43, this was all Il Duce had left. They stood by him, some of them, but after that nothing was simple anymore. Nothing."

"It never was."

Yes, he told her. It had never been. Nothing was as simple as he'd thought it would be. Things happened, things he didn't think he could ever explain. He would go to the Basilica each morning, and he would just sit there, watching the birds. As her mother had done. It was impossible that her mother had done the same in her own time, but he didn't understand those things. How such things happen. Such common things between us.

They were quiet. After a while he told her the Piazzale had been terrible. "Even that kind of vengeance is terrible," he said. "Especially that kind."

She knocked a knuckle on his knee and held out her hand for the orange. When he gave it to her, she ran her fingers over what he'd drawn in it and looked at him. Then she scored around it with her thumbnail and peeled the orange and laid his drawing on the fountain. They sat eating in the sunlight, pigeons bathing in the fountain behind them, children running in and out of the *arcata,* and he lifted the slices she handed him and slipped them under the silk one by one.

"It's good," he said.

She nodded, but she did not look at him as he ate. She was watching the birds scatter from the campanile again when the bell tolled.

"Come," she said. "Let's get your things."

When they reached the far end of the catedro, he turned down the alley along its southern wall, but she touched his elbow gently.

"Let's take another way," she said.

They walked for a while in silence. The spire of San Pietro rose up high above the houses, its red brick heft still shining in the sun. It was true what she'd said about the sister school of Santa Maria Maggiore, its brown brick façade standing cold and dignified on the opposite side of the harbor, how sad it looked on a Sunday. He thought of boys sitting on the docks to watch the girls clasp their books to their chests and cross over from Santa Maria to the Via Borghese.

Ciao, a boy would call to them. *Cosa hai imparato oggi?*

Non per parlare con te, they would always answer.

What could you say to that? What could a boy do but watch, in silence, then look at the others, smiling, as if it didn't matter? But even a child could feel it in the silence: Everything matters, everything in the world.

"Carlo's good to my mother," she was saying, guiding him toward the Via Madonna.

"He wants to marry you."

She shook her head and said no. Beatrice. But such things were complicated. Always.

They crossed the Via Madonna, and she waved at the priest as he crossed over, shaking his head strangely, toward the catedro. When they'd reached the far side of the Via Madonna, they could see the station ahead. He had felt his own voice echoing in his chest when he'd spoken with her, and he let himself think about it. It had deepened and settled since the afternoon he'd stood on the peach crate, long ago, and although he was not sure she'd been there, she or anyone, he asked himself who could still hear that boy in the man he'd become, and he told himself no one, everyone, and he told himself the world in which they now walked had become a world in which no voice lasted long in the chaos at all.

And yet when he'd walked among the market stalls that morning, glancing at the faces through his silk, he was sure they could see. Though his hair was longer than it had ever been, though his shoulders had broadened, though his step had lengthened, he was sure of it: if they could not hear, they could see. When he had seen Brindi and Bombasi, faces he could not have forgotten from San Pietro, from the Balilla—Bombasi's like an apparition thinned and harrowed by the years—he had lowered his head and hurried from the square and climbed over the sea wall and stood a long while by the waves. Shame, he'd thought, what is shame? Perhaps it is not something a man can ever name. And perhaps that is its perfection, the way it works so wholly, so perfectly. Perhaps it had taken his name for him, and he could never have it back. He'd thought about that. He'd closed his eyes by the sea and thought of his shame like a life outside his own, walking the streets of Lunetto, its face bare and its name naked and its eyes telling the whole story, every last word. Then he said *no*. Aloud. His shame was living his life for him, so why should he not be there? Why not just be naked and be done with it? You couldn't know how the story ended, anyway, so why not just do the thing you had to? Why not just let the story begin?

But he'd stood by waves that morning and told himself why: because that was no life at all. Let the shame go on living my life, he thought, and I will live this one, whoever's life it is. I will be the one standing in this wind, feeling it lift my hair and rinse me. I will be the one smelling the spices in it, the almonds and the oranges and the olives. I will be someone hearing the children's voices in the wind, and if they have secrets to tell me, even me, then I will be the one to hear them. I will be the one who can still hear them and believe all these riches are for him.

"My mother's not done with you." They were standing at the station, her breath fresh with the orange. "Carlo's right," she said. "You won't have a train until tomorrow."

"I'll meet you," he said.

"Don't be silly. Let me help you carry them."

He looked away. He knew he'd done everything wrong. When she asked him again, he looked at her and watched her eyes narrow slightly, a single eyelash slipping down her face, and he heard himself say yes, soon, but he wanted to go to the catedro. Alone.

The wind was playing with his silk again, and he tucked it back into his collar. She'd taken her hair from its braid as they walked, and she ran her fingers down through it once and then pushed it back over her shoulder. It was as dark as his darkest nights in the mountains.

"Of course," she said. "We'll be there."

She turned to go, but he watched her stop and turn toward him. He was still standing where she'd left him.

"It's number 12."

"I know."

The wind was sifting up from the beach through the piazza, whirling into the Via Madonna, and it lifted her hair and blew it forward in a dark wave over her shoulders. When she turned away from him, he watched her gather it and begin to braid it over her shoulder, and she did not look back again until she reached the piazza.

V

He turned and made his way to the far side of the station and leaned back against the wall. You're a fool, he thought. You're just trying to die.

He thought of Paolo and Nico. Then he thought of Enzo. How does someone just vanish? Then he shook his head. You know damn well he didn't just vanish. Maybe for you and for everyone else it feels like he did, but it damn well didn't feel like just vanishing to him. You know that. It was hell and he knew it the whole time.

Maybe she knows. No, he thought. Don't fool yourself. It's not that easy. Your house is just up the Via Finetti on the other side of the tracks, and your mother is waiting there to hear how god damned stupid you are. No. You can't. And you are stupid, aren't you? You don't have to tell anyone that. Not her and not Carlo and not your mother. Carlo. When you figured whose brother he was, I bet your face was a hell of a sight. Don't think for a moment they can't see just because you think they can't see. That's exactly why they can. That's how it always is. You don't have to tell anyone what a fool you are, least of all your mother. Probably she already knows. A mother always knows, doesn't she? She knew when Enzo was dead, didn't she? Probably before Enzo knew it. Why wouldn't she know the same about you? Shut up, he thought. You're not dead yet.

He looked back toward where she'd gone. Don't, he thought. Don't tell yourself it isn't her. How many times? How many times did you sit on those docks by Santa Maria and see her cross over with the others with her silence and her sisters and her dark hair—it was shorter then, wasn't it? *Sì*, always—and how many times did you look away? Once, that one time she didn't look away. She was never like the rest of them. Everyone knew that. She never went to the catedro or the *feste* by the harbor or anything at all. Giuseppina, Maria, Alessia, but never Alexandra. Never Alexandra Bianchi. *Lei è strana,* they always said. *Strana. Bellissima ma strana. Move along. For your own good. Leave that one alone.*

What are you supposed to do now? If you go back there you know who's going to be there. Carlo. And then his father and then Matteo and then your death. No. You know why you'll go there, why anyone goes anywhere ever. *Stai zitto.* What are you going to do? Exactly what you said. Go where you said you were going. You said you were going there and maybe something in you already knows. You don't know anything but maybe you know that. Maybe you do. Go.

He sat in the catedro and listened to the wind in the belltower. The pews were empty after the morning service, and he did not know if they would fill again. *Lascia che ti vedano. Let them come.*

His mask had started to itch in the summer heat, and he pressed the heels of his palms to either side of it and untied the ribbon at the back carefully. He leaned forward and laid his head between his knees and let the silk fall into his hands. He felt the wind sliding beneath the pews from the open door behind him, and he let it cool his face and freshen him. When he breathed it deeply, he could smell the fruit and the spices in the market of the piazza. A thousand years, he thought. A thousand years. Clove and nutmeg and mulberry and the blood of the hunger that turns the world. And what have you done but add to it? What have you done but give it one more taste of the world?

He tied the ribbon and smoothed down the back of his hair and sat upright. In the second pew from the altar, he saw her. She was sitting with the young priest with her head in her hands, his hand on her shoulder, and other than a few children playing in the apses and an old beggar kneeling beside the Madonna, they were alone.

He rose and made his way toward her and stood waiting for the priest to leave, but the priest turned to him and said, *Speak with her. Per favore.* The catedro was quiet, and the priest whispered a few more words and then gathered his cassock and slid out of the pew.

She was dabbing at her eyes behind her black veil, and she waited for him to sit beside her.

"Mama," he said.

"*Ero preoccupata.* When you say you are coming back, you must come back."

He nodded.

She told him he didn't know. That she had raised him to be a man of his own word, and yet she did not know even what he spoke in his own heart. That even he did not know.

"*Mi dispiace,*" he said. "*Io sono qui ora.*"

She laid her hand on his thigh. Yes, she said. You are here.

They were quiet a long while. Finally she told him he didn't know what it was to be a mother. To have everything you make be your word.

"My sons are my only word," she said. "And now I have done nothing but to help you hide. To help you silence that word so that it cannot be known. But it is. It is known." She shook her head. "And I cannot lose another son. I cannot. But what is my life if my son is a lie even to my God?"

"Mama, no."

"Yes," she said. "I am your mother. Listen to me. This priest sits with me every day now, every day, and he is not even my son. I call him father, and yet he is a better son to me than my son. My only son."

They sat together in silence. Finally she raised her hands and opened them and laid them back in her lap. Like a book she had decided not to read.

She told him every day she was in pain. But that she could carry it. Her pain meant nothing to her. It was the pain of her sons that plagued her. Both the living and the dead. She told him she was afraid for the dead, but she was more afraid for the living. That the living are truly the dead, and if they do not repent they must return to their lives again and again, and then their lives would be the same. The same lives. In every moment. And so it would be for those who loved them. Or for anyone they loved.

"Five days," she said, "five days you have been home, five days you have been alive again, and yet why has my joy turned to pain? *Perché?*"

He did not speak, and she told him what the priest had said. To repent here. In this place. Because a life that has repented only in its own home has not the common bread of the feast. Because to come home is to atone. To stand there before all of them like any life. That might show its face and ask forgiveness for its life. As each life is a great crime for which there is no atonement but openness.

He shook his head.

"You should not have told him, mama. We can trust no one."

"No, Nardo. You would not take that from me."

She looked at him, and when he lowered his face, she lifted his chin. She told him she wanted her son to be the one to tell himself the truth of his life. Only him. So he could stay.

"No, mama."

She looked away. No one, she told him, no one was ready for their life. As she had not been ready for hers. Then she said she could not hide him from his father's heart. Nor in it.

She crossed herself.

"My son, it is time. This priest, Nardo, he is a good priest. He will not make you see your own life, not before you have seen it yourself." Then she said that in perhaps that way he was not a good priest at all.

"*Non posso*," he said. "*Non capiscono.*"

"That is what men have always said of God's servants. That they do not understand. And of God the same."

He lowered his head.

No, she told him. Hear me. That is what men have always said of God. As though to serve were to not understand. But to serve is the greatest proof of understanding. To know you are in your father's house and everything you do is a testament for or against him.

She turned toward him. Her eyes were dark green behind her veil, and when she closed them he felt himself disappear.

"If you do not make it right you cannot stay," she said. "You know this. Will you make me leave this place? Will you make me leave the only home I have ever known?"

"Mama. They will kill me."

"Then why do you go out as you do? Why do you ask for your

death?"

She opened her eyes, and he lowered his head.

"You can fix this, Nardo. You can. He tells me so." She waved vaguely at the altar. "They can forgive. All of them. If you admit it all."

He said nothing. She laid her hand on his thigh, and he let her stroke the long-healed scar the shrapnel had left in him.

"Mama."

"Let me speak, *mio figlio*. Let me tell you something. I do not know what will happen with us, but I have asked God to forgive and protect you, and I know I will go to Him long before you do. I trust that. And then there will only be you to carry this story. Only you."

"Mama."

"Let me speak."

Her hands were very still. She told him that although some men believe a story that has no teller survives out of time, it is not so. A story may come back in another life, but it is never the same. Once the telling is broken, it is never restored.

"Let me tell you about your father."

"Mama."

"No, Nardo. Let me speak."

She did not move. Very slowly she opened her hands on her lap, and he slid his hand between them and let her hold it.

She told him what he already knew. That his father's name was his name. That the papers her sons had found had been true—Léonard Gemetti—and in a way that is ancient she had given Léonard's name to him, her second son, though she had given them all their father's name—Gemetti, that ancient name that had come North on Roman roads and then down from the shadows of the Alps, down into the valleys, down into the French fields to sing itself so strangely on their father's tongue. She had given them that name, she told him, because this father was not there to give anything himself. His father was never there, she whispered. Even when he had sometimes returned, when he spent those brief times with them as he did. As she was sure her son remembered. Even then he was not there. She said she'd stood there in that very place and let them lower her son into the water, and she'd said his name aloud for the first time, and for the first time she'd known truly who was not there.

He shut his eyes tightly.

"I have loved all my sons equally," she said, "and in losing them I have lost a part of my life I cannot have back. But in each one I have lost something greater than myself and greater even than them. Do you know what that is?"

He shook his head.

She told him she had lost a promise she made to herself long ago. That she would never let her sons carry in them the silence of their father and believe it was their lives.

He had not stopped her, but she raised a hand and told him to let her speak.

"When I knew in my heart about your brothers, I prayed each day that I might hold you in my arms again, as I did when you were a child. So we could begin again. And in that new beginning I would lean over you and tell you the story of your father so that you did not have to become it. *Diventalo*. Because in this life I know only one truth, and I have had to be its witness. We become the thing that is most silent in us. And if what is silent in us is a shame, we become what we think we must become to give shape to that shame. To deliver it into this world." Then she said that until we give this shame a shape, we carry it around like a stillborn in our hearts, and we feel we are nothing until it comes to pass.

She asked him if he could understand. He looked down at his hand in her hands.

She told him sometimes the Lord Himself lays His hand on our hearts and does not recognize even the book of His own works. But although she too had believed she could hide his face, her son's face, as she had hidden his father from him and his brothers these many years, she understood now there is nothing we can hide in this life. There is nothing we can forge. In the book of judgment, all will be written in the blood of our lives.

"Mama."

"Your father did not leave you, Nardo. He did not leave me. You have his goodness in you, also. I tell you this so that when I tell you what I have to tell you, you will not think I mean to condemn him in you, or you in him. Do you hear me?"

The children had left the apses, and the priest was gone. His mother's voice was nearly a whisper.

"Yes," he said.

"Good. I know you can. If it were easy for me to say these things, I would have said them long ago. But perhaps this is the beginning. Who can say?"

She looked down and said his father had come to her in the autumn of her sixteenth year. His home was in Alsace, and he was beautiful as the sea is deep. She said those words. The sea is deep. He had fought in the Great War, she told him, and he had seen terrible things in his time. As his sons would see in theirs. But he did not pity himself what he'd seen.

She turned to him and told him he knew from his own war what it is to live in a country that is two countries. It is no country at all.

Though she closed her eyes and asked if she could go on, she did not wait for an answer. She told him that is how it had been with his father. To be split. The Germans had taken his father's homeland many years before, and although his blood was French and French was the tongue in which he confessed his sins to his own mother, the land in which he was forgiven was a Reichsland, and so he was made to say he was German. Tedesco. And when the Great War came, his gun was a German gun, and his orders were German orders. But his heart was a French heart.

"But we found his papers, mama. You told us how it was. He fought with the Germans. He told Enzo."

She turned to her son and told him she did not have to tell him what happened next, but she would. In the summer of his father's nineteenth year, they had driven the French back to Reiningue, and they had taken prisoners. "Your father never did tell me the true name of his home town," she said, "but he did not have to. It was Reiningue. I never made him say it. When he told me the story, we were looking out at the sea here in Lunetto, and he told it as straight as he could, as I am trying now. He looked out at the sea and told me what he did. I told him he did not have to tell it, but I knew his not having told it was the reason he could not go home. That perhaps if he told it he might be able to return. If he told it to himself."

"Mama."

"Let me speak."

She told him his father had been given his orders at Reiningue. A country can be split down the middle, she told him, but not the country of a man's heart. It cannot survive it. When his father had shot the prisoners as he'd been told, he had not thought he would survive it. A man can obey any command, his mother told him, but the command of his own heart. Though it says to him he should die he cannot die. And so his father had done what he had done.

"Mama. *Non qui.*"

"If not here, then where? Let me speak."

He lowered his head. His breath was hot inside the silk of his mask, and he would not look at her.

She told him his father had made his way all night along the Doller until he'd come to the little house where his officers were quartered west of Mülhausen. "I remember those names as though they were the names of my sons," she said. "Doller. Reiningue. Mülhausen. Perhaps they are."

He was still looking down at his hands.

"Your father was carrying with him three French rifles slung over his back and his own gun, the name of which I do not recall. Because that is no son of mine."

She shook her head. She told him when his father had reached the house he'd stood in the garden in the dark and whistled for the officers to come out. There had been a sentry at the door, but his father had shot him. The officers had heard it all, and they would not come out. Who would come out to meet his own death? They had thought they were safe that far behind the line, and that one sentry would do. Who would imagine such a thing could be done? Who if not even the one doing it?

His father had shouldered open the door and shot the sergeant where he sat and then looked up at the lieutenant and his aide standing with their arms raised against the far wall. "One was no older than your father," she said, "and your father told him to lie down on the floor, and he did. He said he would not shoot him. *Io prometto.* All the years to come I believe your father trusted himself with his promise. His word. As I trusted him to keep his word that he would stay. Each time. His word. He trusted that the boy believed it. And the boy did believe it. He believed it until he was shot."

Her son looked at her and told her it could not be, but she merely looked at him and said it was. It was. This was the world.

Like him, she said, the young one had not believed he would die, but the lieutenant did believe it. "I have tried to understand that. What it meant to your father. That the boy was shot because he did not believe it and the lieutenant was shot because he did." But there is no order in such things, she told him. You can find an order in them, but it would be a false order, and that is the worst lie of all.

She told him his father had said all these things to her while she was sitting on the sea wall looking out at the sea. Right there. In that town. Their home. "And your brother Enzo already inside me, like a secret I was not certain I could keep. *Un segreto.* And your father turned to me and asked me if I could be with such a man as he was and had been and would always have to be."

He'd tried to slip his hand from hers, but she held it.

She told him she'd loved his father, and love has no reasons. That in that way it is like hate. She told him if she had known then that she was carrying not only this man's son but also the silences in him, she would still have done what she had done. She would still have lived her life.

The catedro was still, and when he looked out at the relics in the apses, the gold and the glasses and the stone faces, he heard his mother saying grief can take from us everything in this world, but she would not let it take from her that last thing. She would not let it make her regret her life.

"Your father did not lie to me," she said, "but to fail to tell something is the same as a lie. As I have done to you. He spoke his first son into me before he had told me who he was, and so the word he spoke into me to give your brother breath was not a truth, and for that reason your brother never knew himself. It is a mystery I cannot explain. I had thought it would be different with you and the others, but it was not. Your father made you with the silence in him, and to that silence he returned. He did not leave you or me any more than he left himself." She looked at her son and told him to listen. She told him a heart is a country, and it cannot abide its severance from itself. When his father had chosen death, in that far place he had gone to, she did not mourn him. Not in any way she could understand. Because she knew her life could not hold such sorrow. And even his father's voice she could not recall.

"*Me lo ricordo,*" he said. "*Ricordo la sua voce.*"

"I know, Nardo. He spoke very strangely, and very slowly, but perhaps you do not remember that. Perhaps we are only imagining it now."

"No. He did. I remember he did."

She let go of his hand and slid her arm around his shoulder and lowered his head into her lap.

"My son. What you have done is not your story alone. I know you had your brothers in your heart when you did it, and I know our lives are a mishearing of our ghosts. I know what a soul can believe its ghosts are asking it to do."

"Mama."

"Hear me. I do not know if you can be forgiven, but I know you cannot stay hidden from your own self. It is the only way, Leonardo. It is the only way."

He knew she could feel him weeping. Very slowly he lifted himself, but she lowered him into her lap again and smoothed the medal on his chest, tightened the ribbon of his mask.

He told himself not to ask her what to do. Then he asked it.

"You are a man, Leonardo. No one can tell you that. But I know your life is not over. Perhaps it has not yet begun."

The priest was walking toward them. He closed his eyes and listened to the footsteps and then looked up at his mother. In all the telling, she had not wept.

"Tell me," she said, "about this woman."

"*Chi*?"

"It is not me you lie to," she said. "Remember that."

He nodded.

"Never in twenty-five years has my son smelled this way."

He looked down at the floor, the dark wood scuffed from the soles that had come and gone, those who had lifted themselves, suddenly, from their prayers.

She turned his face toward her and leaned forward and kissed the silk of his mask through the lace of her veil.

"I will not ask you," she said, "because you have not yet asked yourself. But I think you are old enough now to understand what I have said. What you do not ask yourself you do not live. And what you do not ask yourself cannot be an answer, even when it says yes to your life."

He nodded.

She told him to go. "You are a man," she said, "and now you know. Tomorrow I will be here, as I am now, and every day the same. Until you understand what it is you must do. Until you understand truly why you have come home."

He said nothing.

"Go," she said. "*Lasciami*."

The priest had nearly reached them, and he pulled himself up and lifted his mask briefly and kissed his mother's hair and stood up and stared at the priest.

Father, he nearly said. But then he was gone.

VI

Alexandra was sitting on the terrace again with her sisters. Carlo had left them, and the Signora was asleep in the house. The wind had backed into the east and was blowing out toward the sea again.

"I don't understand you," Clara said. "What kind of a thing is that to bring home?" She waited for an answer. "Admit it. You see something strange and you can't let it alone. He's not just something to draw, you know."

"What does that mean?"

"It means whatever you want it to mean."

"*Regazze*," Bea said.

"*Stai zitta*, Beatrice. You know your sister as well as I do. But this is not just something interesting, Alexandra. You're going to have to see it. What are you going to do then?"

Alexandra said nothing.

Clara slid one of Carlo's cigarettes from above her ear and lit it. "*Va bene*," she said. "He's not a thing. But what is he?"

Alexandra leaned back in her chair. She watched the smoke curl up into the wind and drift out toward the sea.

"I bet it's bad," Bea said.

"What?"

"His wound."

Alexandra shook her head. She took the cigarette and drew deeply, closing her eyes.

"Can you imagine what it was like?"

"What?"

"Being up there in the mountains."

"Papa didn't have to imagine it," Clara said.

"No, and neither did he." She turned toward Bea. "He lost his brothers."

"All of them?"

"Yes. Three."

Bea crossed herself and then looked at Clara.

"*Mi dispiace.*"

"Don't apologize to me," Clara said. "You can fear whatever you want."

"It isn't fear."

"What is it, then?"

Bea reached for the cigarette.

"*È fede*, Clara. It's faith. There, I've said it."

"*Va bene.*"

"Clara," Alexandra said. "Please."

"*Sono razionale.* You bring home a man like this and your sister sits here believing in God." She pinched her fingers in the air, and her sister laid the cigarette between them. They sat smoking in silence, and when Clara heard something stir in the house she stubbed out the cigarette on the heel of her shoe and flicked it off the terrace into the garden.

The doors to the terrace opened slowly, and the Signora was straightening her hair with one hand, waving at the air with another.

"My daughters smoke like *deliquenti*. All my daughters."

Alexandra stood and helped her mother with her hair.

"*Ci dispiace, mamma. Pensavamo che le finestre fossero chiuse.*"

"What does it matter what windows are closed? Windows. All my windows are closed. Are yours, my daughters? Wide open. Wide open to the iniquities of this world."

Clara laughed loudly.

"*Sì*," the Signora said. "Laugh. You'll see."

"Come, mama," Alexandra said. "Sit with us."

"And where is Signor Vinetti?"

"He's coming, mama. Sit."

"Good. Very good." She settled into her chair and seemed to compose herself a long time. She seemed to be asking herself if she could ask something. Then she asked it.

"*Sì*, mama," Alexandra said. "He can eat."

She kissed her mother's hair and stepped back through the open doors into the house. The mezzanino on which she stood was hung with tapestries from another time—dark scenes of battles and huntresses, doves and foxhounds faded by the years—and she closed her eyes and breathed them in and tried to remember what her life was like when it was simpler. But she knew it had never been simple. Never. And a child is merely a sleepwalker in a deep house of shadows.

She opened her eyes and made her way down the stairs to the little kitchen just inside the doors to the garden. *What does Clara know? That's not why you brought him here. She doesn't know that. And if it is? It isn't, but so what if it is? So what if I think it's interesting? That doesn't take anything away from him at all.*

In the icebox she found a small tin of gelato still lingering from the birthdays of her mother and Beatrice not two weeks before. She opened it and scooped some with her thumb and held it against the roof of her mouth to soothe her. *Vaniglia.* She felt herself mouthing it, as she'd done in the piazza. *Vaniglia. Vaniglia. They never make it of the oranges anymore. Those oranges, those belle clementine from way up on the Altipiano di Gioia Tauro. Va bene, you'll just have to do what you always do. You'll just have to make it yourself.*

Shaking her head she slipped the tin back into the icebox and found the carafe her mother had poured from since she was a child and filled it with water from the basin and looked out at the cypresses along the path. They were not at all like her sisters, she thought, not at all like her mother. They were straight and ancient, and whatever the wind did with them, they were not afraid.

She pinched the rims of four glasses and carried the carafe up through the house and out the doors to the terrace. When she set it on the table, her mother was speaking about her father.

"He's always different in your dreams," Bea said.

"Yes, and in this one he was even more different. My God how different he was."

"Mama," Clara said, "you shouldn't go to sleep when you're upset. This is what happens."

"Tell us, Mama." Alexandra poured her mother a glass of water and kissed her on the hair again. The Signora reached up and stroked her daughter's face.

"Thank you, *la mia colomba*. I will."

Alexandra sat waving the smoke away, although there was no smoke at all.

"We were in Palma again, Papa and I. In the dream." She sipped her water and squinted. "We must tell Carlo these pipes are sour. *Non hanno un sapore aspro*?"

"No, mama," Alexandra said. "The water is fine. Drink."

"We'll tell him," the Signora said.

"Yes, we'll tell him. Tell us your dream."

She sipped the water and set the glass before her and grasped it with both hands. She wore four large rings, each one a simple band of silver; they had come down through the hands of her family and her husband's family, and Alexandra thought now of the names engraved inside them, the countless hours so many lives had spent rubbing those names in the darkness, thinking of what a name can do, can undo.

"I will. You know I will." She looked into her glass and told her daughters that her dream was of Palma. Just as it was when they were young, when they were there. She turned toward her youngest daughter. "Not you, Beatrice, *la mia colomba*. *Mi dispiace*."

"Tell us, mama."

She said she was sorry their father had never taken the three of them there, together, the five of them altogether, but that in her dream they were together. All of them. Only it was all different, as it is sometimes in dreams. Their father was so young and strong, and they were sitting in the quiet cove by those three great rocks in the water.

"Do you remember those, Claretta?"

"No."

"*Le mie figlie*. You have no memory."

"Tell us, mama," Alexandra said.

"The three rocks there in the water by the cove where the beach is just stones and the cliffs rise up to the left and there are little houses in the village above us. My God what houses. Just little things. But you can smell the *pane di pescatore* when you walk the roads in the mornings. Remember that, Alexandra?"

She nodded.

"Papa was so young and strong," the Signora said, "and we watched him walk out into the water and climb onto those rocks, the tallest one with the point at the tip of it, and he stood up there and called for us to come in. My God I can still smell the *pane di pescatore*."

"Did we?"

"*Che cosa?*"

"Did we go in?"

"*La mia colomba*, of course we did. We all went in, and when we were sitting on the rocks Papa looked at us and said, *these are my daughters, these three rocks. There is nothing stronger.* My God he was so beautiful to say that."

"But I wasn't there yet, mama," Bea said.

"What does a dream care about that? Papa knew you were coming, so he said what he said."

"I don't know about this dream," Clara said.

Alexandra turned to her and said it was a good dream. *Un bel sogno.*

"I don't know," Clara said.

The Signora looked at her daughter. "Tell me. Tell me what you don't know."

"I'm sorry, mama. It's a beautiful dream. But a rock is just there, just stuck there where it is. Where can it go?"

The Signora closed her eyes. As though someone had struck her. Finally she spoke. "You have no heart, *niente cuore*. You search for meaning in a dream. It means your father loves you, that's all."

"It's a beautiful dream," Alexandra said.

Clara shrugged.

"*Le mie figlie*," the Signora said. "You have no past because your windows are wide open. Wide open to the iniquities of the world."

"Tell us, mama," Alexandra said. "Was there more?"

"No. There was no more."

"Come, mama. There was more."

Her mother looked up from her glass of water and smiled softly. "Of course there was more."

"Mama," Clara said.

"Alexandra, I will tell you my dream. And you, too, Beatrice Maria."

"Mama."

"We were sitting on the rocks, and your father leaped out into the sea and swam away from us. He went down into the water and came up with three bright stones and came up again and gave one to each of us. *Lentamente.* Then we just sat there for so long, looking out over the water. When the sun began to set, we saw ships on the *orizzonte*, far out there where the big winds are. You remember the big winds? Of course you do. These were the same winds. And although the light was dim, we could see after a while that they were burning. The ships were burning."

"This is a good dream," Clara said.

The Signora did not turn toward her. "They were great ships with many oars on either side, like the old ships—remember the old ships Papa told us about? *Gli antichi?*—and they'd come close enough for us to see the oars, but beyond that we could see nothing. *Niente.* Just tremendous ribbons of flames rising up from each ship and going up into the big wind and waving in the air and up into the darkness when the night came. My God what flames. But we were not afraid. I tell you, we were not afraid. The boats came into the cove and lit up our faces. *Mio Dio che luci.* I turned to you and to Papa and I saw our faces all lit up with the fire. But we were not afraid. When I looked back at the ships, the oars were burning, and I saw the oars thrown into the water, but I did not see the men who threw them. When they struck the water, they made a sound I can't explain. Like someone whispering. I don't know. I turned back to ask Papa what they were whispering, but you were all gone. Papa, too. It was just me alone on the rock, and when I looked back at the water the ships were gone and the sky was on fire."

"My God."

"Mama," Alexandra said.

"No, *la mia colomba*. Some of my daughters find my dreams uninteresting, but I know they are trying to tell me something. I know Papa is trying to tell me something. And some of my daughters may wish to listen."

"Mama," Clara said.

The Signora turned toward her.

"Not again," she said. "I tell you this one last time. Even in jest, not again."

Clara sat back in her chair. Her sisters had never seen her lip quiver, not in many years. She reached across the table and poured herself a glass of water and sat drinking it, looking out to sea.

"Mama," Alexandra said, "Signor Vinetti is coming. Should I tell him not to—?"

"Nonsense. He is a great hero and we will celebrate him. My God what he has given up."

"Did he fight with the Repubblica di Salò?" Bea asked.

"I don't know. And I don't think we should ask him."

"Yes," the Signora said. "These things are messy. My God how messy. He will tell us what he wishes to tell us." She sipped her water. "But of course how could we help but be curious?"

"I know, mama."

"When does he come?"

"Soon. He's in the catedro."

"My God what faith. He goes through what he goes through, and yet he has faith. *Mi chiedo se potrei.*"

"Yes you could, mama. You have."

The Signora touched her daughter's face.

"Thank you, Beatrice. We all have." She set down her glass. "Clara, *la mia colomba*. Come. Let's be together. You help me with the genetti. You always loved them."

Clara was still looking out to sea. Alexandra rose and kissed her mother on the hair and gestured for Bea to follow her into the house.

The wind had turned again, and it rattled against the doors as Alexandra shut them and led her sister down the stairs, like a sleepwalker through a woken house of shadows.

VII

He'd stood at the fountain in the piazza, dipping his hand into the water and rubbing it under the mask to freshen his face, then tucked himself into the shadows beside the catedro. The pigeons flew out of the campanile, and he counted the tolling of the bells. Three. Four. Five. He could not even imagine his life. He looked up at the bell and closed his eyes and opened them again. The world was still there.

He walked swiftly through the thin crowd of the piazza, their faces turning away from him, and when he heard children playing in the shadows of the *arcata*, he remembered the *naca* festival in Lunetto he'd woken early for, each year, as a child. His mother would call to him in the dark, and always he'd slept in his clothes so he would be ready. Always he'd dreamt of his father returning from the country of death, a father stepping into a house, a dark house, to find a son sitting with his mother, a son who had gone off to great battles and saved that house and made his name on the far shores of the world. When he had shaken himself from his dreams he would slip from his bed and find his shoes and run down the Via Finetti and join the crowd gathering in the shadows of the *arcata*. In his tenth year they'd let him take his part, and he'd stood on the left side of the other bearers and taken the weight of the empty cradle on his shoulder. The people had built it from the wood of the black pines that grew up in the Sila plateau, and he'd thought of those trees twisted in the high, cold winds as he'd carried the empty cradle with the others. They'd carried it all down the *arcata* and then over the sea wall and down the beach to the sea. When they'd laid it like a small boat in the tide, a bridegroom much younger than the pines would always walk out into the water with his new bride, and they would stand on either side of it, walking it out in their wedding clothes, out past the break and then into the open water. They would stand there with the water to their shoulders and speak their vows again over the cradle, and then they would push it out to sea. That it might not come back. Not until they were ready.

The sun was bright now in the piazza. A grocer at the far end of the *arcata* was half-asleep in the shadows, and Leo bought a loaf of bread from him and a tall green bottle of olive oil, stoppered with a cork carved into the shape of a shield. "For the soldiers," the grocer had said, handing back the lire. "*Per lei.*"

He climbed over the sea wall and walked alone along the beach. The sun was strong over the Strait, and children were running up from the waves and back again, paying him no mind. When the children's voices rose up on the wind, he told himself not to think of his brothers, of his father, of anything his mother had told him in the catedro. *No*, he said aloud. *No.*

He slipped the bottle of oil into his back pocket and tucked the bread under his arm and pushed back his hair the wind had tousled. There was a time when he had kept his hair very short, and when they'd released him from the hospital in Bologna, in the summer of his twenty-first year, the first thing he'd done was to find a barber and sit back in the chair and close his eyes and wait for his life to be restored to what it had been.

"*Quanto corti, Signore?*"

"Short," he had said.

"You must tell me. It can all go wrong."

"It's all gone wrong already."

The barber had hummed deeply.

"I see. It's a shame. My son is in Jugoslavia. In the mess." He was cleaning his glasses. "Where did you fight, Signore?"

"On the Albanian border. At Klisura."

"Very bad."

"The Germans saved us."

"That is no way to put it."

"There is no way to put it. There are only the facts."

The barber had seemed to consider it. "How did they let you let your hair get so long? Do they not have barbers in these hospitals of ours?" He shook his head, as if in answer to his own question. "It's a shame. *Una vergogna empia.* You know what I think, Signore? That this is the end. It's all rotten from within." His scissors made a swift, whispering sound as he worked. "It is all decay. It begins with the little things. Not cutting the hair. It sounds *senza senso* but it's true. What kind of civilization leaves its wounded men lying in beds with their hair uncut? Think about that. Truly think about it."

"*Non è questo il peggio.*"

"No. It's not what's worst. It's a *sintomo.* Do you understand that? A sign of the illness. That's all it is. We are sick from within, and it is starting to show."

"*Come?*"

"How are we sick or how is it starting to show?"

"Both."

"Madonna. You know better than I do. You and my Dominic, who go to war. War is not a sickness, Signore. But to treat our sons like a wheel of a great machine, that is a sickness. That is decay."

"Maybe we are."

"Madonna."

"No," he had told the barber. "Maybe that's not so bad. We're part of a machine, and the machine works. It runs."

"Madonna. This is the sickness." His scissors were working more swiftly now. "We are not a machine, Signore. I beg your pardon but I speak my mind. Italia is not a machine. Maybe Germania, but never Italia." He huffed. "And not even Germania, in truth. A country is not a machine. And neither are its people. We are made to think it is a virtue to be such a thing, but it is not."

He nodded.

"Hold your head still, Signore. I know you know. I hope you do. Men can kill other men and still not lose their souls. But they have to believe they have them to keep."

Leo's eyes were closed.

"Is this good, Signore? The sides like this?"

He did not sit up to look in the mirror.

"*Sì. Continua.*"

"You know what I think, Signore? I think a people is only as good as its ability to contain the great thing. To contain death." He blew the clippings from the back of Leo's neck. "And that is not something a machine can do. A machine does a job, *sì, ovviamente*. But there is no mystery in that. These young men who are like machines, they think it is their work to keep death out. *Per tenere fuori la morte.* And so they fight." He breathed. "There is no dishonor in fighting, Signore. Sottotenente. I should call you Sottotenente."

"No."

"Good. Signore. You are young to have this rank, no?"

"No."

"Very good. When we believe a thing, it can be true." He laughed. "But a man who has fought is no child, *sì*?"

Leo said nothing.

"Very good. You understand. Then I shall call you Signore. I would hate for you to misunderstand. To fight is not a dishonor. But these men fight because they think death is at the gates. That it is trying to get in." He blew the hair away. "But it has never been that way. *Sì*, in part. *Ovviamente.* But it is only half the story, *sì*? Where else is death?" He tapped the back of his scissors against the chair, but Leo said nothing.

"Death is inside us, Signore. Each of us. And we fight because we do not admit it. We do not admit that it is already in our house."

"I see."

"You laugh."

"No. Go on."

"I tell you this as I tell my Dominic. Because you go to make history with your own hands. You understand? I have my theory about this. *La mia teoria.* Would you like to hear my theory, Signore?" He'd held Leo's head. "Don't nod. I know you do. I will tell you. Those of us who do not have our shadows have no way to live. You see? *È semplice.* To deny it is a dangerous thing. If you do not allow that it is in your house, you will see it everywhere else in the world. And then your war with the world will be endless." He ran his hands through the top of Leo's hair. "Like this, Signore?"

"Shorter. Please."

"Very good. I do not say such things to everyone, but you men who have fought, I think maybe you understand. I think maybe you wish to understand."

"*Può essere.*"

"Ah, yes. Maybe. Maybe it is your right not to understand. Maybe you have done enough for us already."

"No."

"Very good, Signore. It is never enough. I agree. So you see what I mean about the shadow? About knowing it is in our house?"

"I don't think so."

His eyes were still closed. He had not felt someone touch him in so long, except the nurses, and he had told himself not to think of them as they touched him. Now, as the barber's hands ran through his hair and kneaded his temples and touched his shoulders, he felt his throat thicken, and he told himself not to think of home. He told himself not to think of anything at all.

"Il Colosseo, Signore? Have you seen it?"

"*Ovviamente.*"

"Good. Then you will understand me. Why did we build it?"

"We didn't."

The barber laughed.

"True. We did not. Not you. Not me." He tapped the chair. "But not so true, *compagno*. Do you not think a people can do something altogether?"

"*Può essere.*"

"Of course you do. This is why you fight. If we win this war you will say we won it. We. And you will be right. Although you were only one small part. *Una ruota.* And it is no different with the dead. We can do things with them together. That is simple."

"I see."

"So we built the Colosseo together, all of us. And why did we build it?"

"To see men die?"

"You joke, but you are right. Only you don't know what you've said. To see it. To bring it into our house, where it already is." He stepped back. "This looks good, Signore. Your *fidanzata* will love it. You have a *fidanzata*?"

"No."

"Too bad. But it is not wasted. You will look like a gentleman who believes in civilization." He ran his hands through his work. "Civilization. This word is like a curse now. People do not know what it means."

"*Cosa significa*?"

"You joke, but I am serious. All of this is serious. In your wound you know how serious it is. Where were you hurt, Signore?"

Leo pointed to his leg.

"*Fortunato*," the barber had said. "*Fortunato*. I am sorry to say it this way, *compagno*. About the seriousness. But it is true. It is very grave. We built the Colosseo not to keep death out but to admit it. To bring it into our house. *Come un leone*. Like a beast by its tail. And to say *here, stay*. So it could show us the horrors, Signore. The horrors that are in our house. So that we might see them in ourselves."

"And then?"

"Only those who have done it can know."

He had opened his eyes. The barber was looking at him in the mirror.

"*Aspetta. Non finito.*" He ran his hands through Leo's hair and leaned him back in the chair. "I tell this to my son, my Dominic. And he tells me no Emperor could think such a thing, no one who could build the Colisseo." His scissors worked lightly. "No. *Ovviamente*. Of course not. But I tell him, I tell him how it is. An Emperor never knows himself, I tell him. And that is why he is an Emperor."

He paused.

"Would you like to hear the rest of my theory, Signore?

"*Sì. Continua.*"

"Very good. I will. An Emperor, he is the mind of the people, Signore. No more, no less. And the people cannot know itself. Perhaps a person can, but not a people."

"But they built it so they could see themselves?"

"No. They built it without knowing what they did. We built it. We built it so we could see that part of ourselves over which we thought we could have mastery. You follow? Of course you do. But it was an illusion. *Un trucco.* We can never know that part of ourselves. But to build it was a great triumph, as doomed as it was. Because we tried, Sottotenente. We tried."

He lifted his towel from his belt and rubbed the hair and ran his fingers through it.

He laid his hands on Leo's shoulders.

"*Finito?*" he asked.

Leo had opened his eyes and sat forward in the chair. The figure he saw in the mirror had light brown eyes and short, black hair, the slightest wave breaking left to right from the part-line. He looked very tired. He closed his eyes again and held his breath, but when he opened his eyes again, that figure was still looking at him.

"*Finito,*" he said.

VIII

"Clara, look at me."

The Signora was alone with her eldest daughter on the terrace. Clara's eyes were wet when she turned toward her.

"What is your anger, *la mia colomba*? Tell me."

"I'm sorry, mama. I don't understand myself anymore."

"Maybe there is nothing to understand. Maybe there is only someone to listen to."

Clara looked out at the sea again and nodded. She turned back toward her mother and folded her hands in her lap.

"Angelo," she said. "Why didn't he bring me?"

"I don't know."

"Is he ashamed of me?"

"Clara, no one is ashamed of you."

"I am, mama. Sometimes I am."

The Signora nodded.

"I know what I'm like," Clara said. "But it's only because I want everything to be right. I can't explain it."

"I know."

"I want everything to be right, and I can't suffer it when I see things going wrong. I see things as they are. I'm not like my sisters, like Angelo. I see things as they are, and I say yes or no."

"I know, Claretta."

"No, mama. Maybe you don't. Bea and Xandra never cared a damn about the Balilla or the rest of it, and I'm glad, I'm glad they didn't. None of that touched them. Even when they brought some of that *merda* into Santa Maria, they never listened."

"Do not swear, *la mia colomba*."

"I know, mama. *Mi dispiace*. I'm glad they never listened. I never listened either. It was all *merda*." She waved the word away. "It was all junk. But I don't know about all of this madness now. I think maybe a little order isn't so terrible, *sì*?"

The Signora shook her head.

"I know, Claretta. But not in that way. Not in that way again."

The wind had shifted. Clara looked out at the waves and laid her hand on the railing of the terrace and tapped her ring against the stone.

"Of course."

The Signora poured a glass of water and tapped it on the table until her daughter turned toward her.

"Tell me, *la mia colomba*."

She gestured toward the glass, and her daughter lifted it and took a small sip and set it back on the table. It was cool against her hand, and she did not let it go.

"That dream of yours. I'm sorry, mama. It hurt me because I know I'm like that. I know."

"Like what?"

"A rock. I know that about myself. I can't be moved."

The Signora shook her head.

"Nothing is so simple."

"I am. And I'm not ashamed of it. To be simple is not wicked. Chaos is wicked. Angelo's mother hates me because I'm not soft. She thinks I have no heart."

The Signora reached across and touched her daughter's hand. "You do have heart, Clara. *Mi dispiace*."

"No. She's right. You're right. But not in the way you think. My heart is just different, mama. His mother thinks I'm no good for him, that I'll ruin him. But maybe I am the one holding him together. Have we thought of that? Maybe that's what we need, all of us. Less fire. Like in your dream."

"I see."

"I'm sorry, mama. I know I'm not the daughter you wanted."

"You don't know that."

"I do. But I know you love me. And you know I love you." She shook it away. "But I worry about my sisters. I do. I'm rough with them because I know what this world can do. And now she comes here with this man, and his life is what? A chaos?"

"You don't know that."

"I do. I can feel it in his heart. You can say I have no heart but I can feel what's in the hearts of others. Always."

"I know, Clara. I know." She had closed her eyes and was nodding slowly, as if to calm her daughter. Clara shook her head.

"Mama, I want her to be happy. I do. I want Beatrice to be happy. I want you to be happy. I want Angelo and Carlo and the whole damned world to be happy."

"Clara."

"I'm sorry. I do. But I'm afraid of what she's brought into this house. This man. Whatever he's seen, whatever's been done to him, how can he not have chaos in his heart?"

"And if he does? He is like all of us, Clara."

"No. Not all of us. I have pity for them. I do. I have pity for all these men, these boys who were sent to die and come back as though they were alive. And maybe they are, maybe they are. But it's not so easy to build it up again, as you say. These men."

"*Questa è la guerra*, Clara."

"That is war? Can you hear yourself, mama? Maybe it is, but he wears it like a ribbon of honor on his face. Can you imagine what's in his heart?"

"Maybe you mistake shame for honor, Clara."

"They are the same. Those who wear their shame loudly are just as proud as the prideful. *Sempre*. And they know no story but their own."

The Signora shook her head. Her daughter looked at her, and they knew what was going to be said. Both of them. The Signora took up her daughter's hands and told her this is how it was. For thousands of years. And for her father the same. For her husband. She told her men come back from their wars and they hold their children in their arms. With those same hands that did terrible things. And they remake their lives.

Clara slipped her hands away and straightened her ring.

"I don't accept it. Thousands of years." She wanted to say what can be changed should be changed, but she did not. Instead she said some men can do that, can remake their lives, but not all. She said we forgive them too soon, always, that there is no limit to what the forgiven can do.

The Signora leaned back and closed her eyes and breathed very slowly. When she opened her eyes, they seemed very young and very far away.

"You speak of love as though it were one thing only. We don't know what love is. None of us."

Her daughter looked at her.

"I know, mama. Angelo doesn't. His mother doesn't. And maybe I don't either. But this man you let into your house, as though he were a toy, what does he know? What does he know except how to burn down a world? Like the ships in your dream, mama. Like what Papa said."

The Signora nodded.

"I see."

"I know you do, mama. I say this to help you. To help my sister. What did you tell me, when I was just a nothing? *Devi guadagnarti la fiducia.* You must earn it. I will not give him anything he hasn't earned."

The Signora nodded again.

"*Capisco, figlia mia.* I will speak with her." Her daughter knew what was coming. "But this man is *un soldato*, Claretta. And I have asked your father what to do with him—"

"—mama—"

"—I have asked your father what to do for him, and we will feed him this once before he goes."

Very slowly she stood and smoothed her blouse. She picked up the glasses and motioned toward the carafe, from which she had poured out water and wine for those long dead, her father and her mother the same, their names etched deep in the rings on her fingers. She lifted the carafe and handed it to her daughter and let her daughter embrace her.

"*La mia colomba,*" she said. "Come. We have much to do."

IX

Alexandra was lying alone in her bed, letting the muslin curtains blow across her body. What did Claretta know? *E Beatrice? Abbondanza.* And her mother? *Abbondanza.* Plenty. What does he pray for? *Per cosa prega?* To have his life back? To look in the mirror again and see his life again, his only life?

She rolled to the side and looked out the window at the cypresses. His mother, she thought. He prays for his mother.

She closed her eyes and let herself think of her mother's dream. Palma. It was beautiful, wasn't it? Maybe you never saw it. Maybe that's what her dream was saying. Maybe there's something you forgot to see.

She let her lips form the name Palma, *il covo,* and she and thought of the ships in her mother's dream. The ships out in the harbor and the oars burning in the darkness. The oars thrown into the water. What did they whisper? What was the sound they made? She thought of her own dreams and the name she'd woken with on her lips, and she thought perhaps it was the same thing the flames had whispered in her mother's dream. *But it is never that simple*, she almost whispered, *is it? It is never that simple at all.*

She lay on her back and watched the shadows play on the ceiling, the shapes they made and unmade. Who is this man, she thought, his eyes like the honey in your cellar? You've never seen his face, and yet what do you see in the shape of it? Forget that. *È ridicolo.* You have your home and your work and you have your life. Your work. Piccolo is a fool, she thought. He thinks he is powerful, but the workers are the power. We play him like the little instrument he is. And that's the way it should be. The world shaped by the hands that work on it. The Maker shaped by the hands of what He's made.

And what have you made? What life? What home? What did he say—about being born a long way from home? *Sì.* Home is something we make, *sì,* Papa? What we make again? *Può essere.* Maybe. But we have this. We have our work and our life and we have a good man buried up in the cherry laurels and what would he say? What would you say, Papa? *Step into your life,* you would say. *I, too, once stood at the gates of the chaos of my life, child. Go in.*

She sat up and pushed her braid over her shoulder and tightened it. Her father had always said such things to her, said to her that even the dead deserve shelter, even the living who are dead because of what they have done, and she thought now of her father's eyes as he said those words, slowly, when he'd woken, some far fire flashing through his eyes like the Austrian guns he would never stop seeing in the dark. That word itself had held such dark magic for her—*Austriaci*—as though in its utterance it could conjure up a world of swirling sabers and steel, great banners flashing in the sunlight, but she knew it had never been like that for her father; there was no honor in that war, he had told her, nothing but endless snows and broken boys, and it was merely a place where a boy might go to step into the winter, into the fire, to abandon the last scraps of his childhood in his own cold brothers that the guns had buried on the far side of the dark.

Papa, she said. Her mother was right to think of him as young and strong in her dream. She was. He had been broken so many times, first by war and then by the wars within him, but he had prevailed. That's all there is, to prevail. He had made a life with nothing but a baker's hands, a fisherman's hands, and maybe that's all there is. The bread of life. The common bread of the heart. Break it. Let it be broken. Taste it. Taste and see.

She lay back again and let herself think of the last time she'd spoken with her father. There are some things, the years had taught her, that you can never set right. There are some words you cannot have back, ever. All those nights her father had woken from his sleep, from his visions, from the black cough that had settled in his lungs at Caporetto, she'd walked him to the kitchen and sat with him and listened, even when

Clara had waved him away, even when her mother had gone on sleeping. His visions had gotten darker and darker—the end of his youth, the end of his country, the end of the world—and finally, when he'd told her the *fascisti* were the healers, that the blackshirts were the only way to cleanse Italia of its shadow, she had let that fear in him overwhelm her; she had wanted to crush it out of him; she had told him he was an old and broken *sciocco,* a fool who did not know how the times would change, a fool who had no grace to change with them. She had struck him, then, with the strength of all her fourteen years, then stared at his astonished eyes in the lamplight. *Sciocco,* she'd said again. *Sciocco spaventato.* She had thought that he would stand, then, and strike her— something he had never done in all their years—but perhaps it was his dazed look that had crushed her. How could she have imagined what would come next? How could she have imagined that her father would weep, that he would hang his head and then look straight at his daughter, that he would tell her it was true he was afraid, afraid, that there were things he'd done, in some long ago, that he could never make right in this world or another. *Prigionieri,* he'd only whispered, *the prisoners.* But then he was quiet as the night itself. *Sciocco,* she'd whispered again, so as not to waver, then left him there, staring into his little glass of water, as he'd once stared into the open depths of the sea.

How could she have known what she would never hear? How could she have known what he was saying? How do you hear the voice of the end and know?

Eight years, she thought. Eight. She closed her eyes and listened to the wind in the cypresses. She'd never spoken of it with her mother, never with her sisters, never with her own self. *Prigionieri, prigionieri, prigioneri.* What did you mean, Papa? What were you asking me to hear?

She opened her eyes and thought of this man. Vinetti. She heard him saying what he'd said about Clara, and she closed her eyes and tried not to smile. It's true, she thought. We are. We're born a long way from home.

What did he pray for? Alone there in the catedro. I'm certain of one thing only, she thought, and that is that Andreas is not his name. But that's not a crime, is it? To lie like that is not a crime. Remember what Papa said. Remember that. There are those who lose everything in their fight to live, and we have no right to take from them the world's last gift, which is nothing but the wish to forget. Remember that. He is just like any soldier.

She rolled to her side and laid her hand on the cool linens of the bed. Go ahead, she thought. Go ahead and think it and get it out of the way. You're not a fool, so you have to think it soon. Think it now and get it out of the way. She did think it, but when she imagined him standing under the thirty figures hanging in the piazza of Bologna, she knew it could not be him.

You don't know anything. Remember that. You don't know anything about what's possible in this world. Shouldn't you be afraid? Why would you be afraid? That's your problem. You're never afraid. No, you always are. You can close your eyes. Like a dreamer. You can lie to yourself any time you want, can't you? I know, Papa, I know. Go ahead. If it's that bad, then go ahead and think it. Think about what Papa told you. Think of how it is for them, for the ones who obeyed. Who have no home because they didn't say no. Think of it. What did you say, Papa? If you have ruined your life here, in one small place, you have ruined it everywhere in the world? Yes. Think of what it would be for them. To be a long way from home. Anywhere you are. No, you don't know. You don't know that. You don't know what home is. And neither does he. And neither does He. And neither does Claretta.

Clara, she thought. What can we do with her? She loves me, and this is the shape of her love. This is the shape it takes. Don't pity her. Where there's pity there can't be love. That's not true. You don't believe that. Pity her if you wish. She can use it. She thinks she's pregnant, and she thinks Angelo isn't coming back. Think of how terrible that would be. To hold yourself in the night and feel your child in you and know you're alone. With only your own hands to make your world. That isn't true. You have us, Claretta. You have me and Bea and mama and all of

Lunetto. If you only let us be there. Why can't we let anyone be there? Why can't we let ourselves be?

She rose and turned and looked out at the cypresses. But you don't have to do that, she thought. You don't have to do any of that, Clara, because you're not *incinta,* and you know that. You're afraid of it, I know, but that's only because you want it more than anything in the world, and we're afraid of what we want. She closed her eyes and asked herself who she was speaking with. Which sister. Then she opened her eyes and looked at the cypresses and thought how terrible it must be when we stand up at last with all the things we've asked for and it does, it does, the new life comes.

She sat at her desk and smoothed down an empty sheet of newsprint and reached down to a small bucket of stones she'd gathered from the beach and placed one on each of the four corners of the page. Sometimes the wind would drift in and shift the newsprint, slightly, even with the stones, and then it was as if some hand other than hers had had a part in the drawing, and always those were the ones she liked most. She would tuck most of them away in the cellar, but the ones the wind had drawn with her she nailed to the wall over her bed, or over the door, or on the wardrobe, and she would lie back sometimes and hang her head from the bed and look at them upside down, and then she would take them down and work on them again because of what she'd seen.

The wind was calm. She leaned back in her chair and ran her palm across the page and took up a piece of her charcoal and sniffed it. She made them from the grapevines that grew along the sea wall by the harbor, and once each month she would cut fresh vine and shrag the bark and pack them into a tin can in the garden, in which she'd taught herself to poke just the right number of holes to keep the fire burning slowly. The fire was always of willow or pine, or sometimes of the cherry laurels if she had gone up to visit her father, and she would place her kiln beside it for an hour or more and then sit with her mother on the terrace as they spoke of whatever the scent of the fire would bring to them.

Don't make them of the laurels, la mia colomba.

Sì, *mama*, sì.

She closed her eyes and tried to let an image come to her, but for months now she had tried not to think of cities in rubble, places in flames. Each night during the war they had sat by the radio in her mother's room and taken the news about Torino, about Genova, about Roma, about places laid low by fires from the skies into which they had once looked for God. When the bombs had rumbled Messina, across the Strait, when they had spared not even the schoolchildren of Gorla, not even the fishing villages of Calabria, they were sure their shipworks would be next, and then they themselves; they were sure, finally sure, they were no longer in a world led by either hand of *Dio*—neither the left hand of faith nor the right of reason—and her mother had simply switched off the radio and said *no, la mia famiglia, we will listen no more. We speak of this no more in your father's house.*

Those were the lean years, certainly, but the shipworks had gone on clanging, and the wages had stayed where they'd made them stay, and though the market stalls were empty of spices, though the bounty of scrapfish was an absence, there was still the bread they made with their own hands, the grains from the traders in Albanella, the *carne* the grocers bartered for, each Sunday, with the *agricoltori* in their hidden worlds in the hills.

No, there were other ways to suffer. Lunetto, Lunetto had been spared.

She laid down the charcoal and made her way to her wardrobe and slipped her green dress over her shoulders and threw it back onto the bed. She stared at herself in the long mirror on the inside door of the wardrobe. She'd let her hair grow long for two years now, and when she took it from its braid and combed it out with her fingers, it hung nearly below her breasts. She had kept it short since she was a child, only above the shoulders, and she'd loved it that way. But then there was what happened in the shadows of the catedro, and she had not wanted anyone to take anything from her again. For three weeks after it happened, she'd drawn nothing at all. She'd spoken about it to no one, not even her mother, though her mother had sat beside her in the nights and read to her, or touched her hair, or said nothing at all. Once only her mother had left a blank page on the desk, when she'd left her asleep, but when the page was gone in the morning, her mother had understood that there are some things we don't look at until we're ready, and some we never look at at all, and the house had settled into a fresh, blank silence about the things this daughter made or didn't make, the lives she chose or no.

Three weeks she had not drawn, but in the fourth week she'd risen from a restless sleep and begun to draw the sea, its terrible question, the simple expanse of it, which she could never get right, and she'd learned you can look into a thing long enough that you vanish entirely, and the waves of the page swallow you wholly, and then it was if you could move with the heart of the world. No one can take that away from anyone, she thought. Not that, not the heart of the world. They cannot take away the gaze that will take you out of here. They cannot take away the voice that whispers *look*.

She tilted her head and stared at herself in the wardrobe mirror—her broad, solid hips, her modest breasts, her shape whose changes she had not drawn since long ago. She could not remember when she'd stopped seeing only herself in the glass, when she'd begun to become nothing but the shapes she would draw, a strange and silent part of them, a light on the waves, a glint through a bird's wing, a shadow of a boat on the sea. She could not have said when she'd decided to let her hair be, but then it was there, covering her breasts in the mirror, and she told herself she did not know what it was, but she would not let anyone take it from her at all. That's an absurd way to think, she'd told herself, standing before the mirror some mornings. They didn't take anything from you at all. And to cut your hair is not to lose anything that you didn't give away to become what you are. But always when she thought of the hair lying in clippings on the floor, she closed her eyes and held her breath and closed the wardrobe slowly.

She showered with the casement open and kneaded the water from her hair and sat on the edge of the tub working the sand from under her toenails. She was proud of her broad, peasant feet, of the way they seemed to hold onto the earth, the good earth, and she told herself that although she was scrubbing the earth away, it was not something that could ever leave her. *Mi dispiace,* she sang to it. *Tornerò a te.* I'll return to you.

When she'd finished, she lay naked on the bed. Mama was right, she thought. Perhaps I'm the earth, but we are all of us the sea, all of us. Only some of us know it. And we who know it know we are the sea and the dead are the changeless shore we touch and they cannot touch us without being lost in our changes.

When she opened her eyes, she knew she had slept a short while. The sun had fallen, and she sat up and hurried to the wardrobe. She heard his voice on the terrace above, and she heard the voice of her sister. Andreas, she thought. What is your name?

When she stepped onto the terrace, she was wearing a yellow top and the cotton trousers in which she had swum out, once, into the sea, as if she would not come back. She wore her rope-soled sandals and a single, silver bracelet on her left wrist, and she'd dried and brushed out her hair so that it hung long and sleek over one shoulder.

He stood when he saw her.

"Alexandra."

"Signor Vinetti. Sit. Beatrice—"

"—Everything's ready. Don't worry."

"Grazie, Bea. Where's mama? *Dov'è Clara?*"

She sat in the chair farthest from him, and Bea gestured toward the carafe of wine, but she waved her away gently. They had broken the loaf he had brought them, and Beatrice sat dipping it in the oil.

"Caffè with the Russos," Bea smiled. "Carlo asked them to bring me."

He felt something sway in him.

"Are they coming?" he asked.

"*Ovviamente.*"

"The Russos, Bea," Alexandra said.

"Oh. No. I don't think so." She turned to him. "But you'd like them, Andreas, some of them. Matteo is just home from—*dove era lui?*"

"Germania," Alexandra said.

"But what did they call it?"

"*Un campo,* Bea."

"That's it," Bea said. "A camp. Something like that. It was—"

"Bea," Alexandra whispered. "Please."

"It was terrible, Andreas. He wouldn't fight with the Repubblica, so they sent him up there. He won't talk about it, but Carlo says he stayed after it all to try to find Bombasi and some of the others. Sabbatini, I think. *Sì?*"

Alexandra shook her head. She was squinting at the black silk of the mask.

"The festa was incredible," Bea crooned. She'd been drinking the wine. "Alexandra didn't go. She's always working. The *sindaco* is a little—well, you know. Go on, Andreas."

"Matteo is—"

"*È tragico,*" Bea said. "But who wants to talk about that? Go on, Andreas. Tell us. Andreas was telling me about France."

"Oh," Alexandra said. "Have you been there?"

"No, but it means a great deal to me. To my family."

"Tell us."

"He was."

"I'm sorry. Go on."

He watched Alexandra turn away. Don't be sorry, he thought. Ever. But he hadn't said it. He looked down at his hands and said he'd thought he'd told her about his father. That his father was German.

"You said he had a fondness for them."

Sì, he told her, but there are some things we don't know even as we say them. Then he told her his father was from the North, from Alsace. *Elsass.* That he hadn't known him.

She looked at him and said perhaps he could go there. Now that he was free. Because he was a long way from home.

Her eyes searched his, but they told him nothing.

"Yes," he said. "I suppose I am."

"No," Bea said. "We're keeping him." She poured herself another splash of wine, then leaned back and tried to drink it delicately. "People are so sad when they talk about that place. *Elsass,*" she said. "Not you, Andreas. Or not just you. Everyone."

Alexandra looked at her sister. Who talks to you about such things? she wanted to ask her. But she told herself not to.

"Yes," she said. "It's split right down the middle."

He looked at her. He could not understand what was in her voice.

"*Diviso a metà?*" Bea said. "You mean French and German?"

"French and German," Alexandra said. "This and that. Anything and nothing. A truth and a lie. It's at war with itself always. Like all of us." She had not taken her eyes off him as she spoke. He looked down into his hands, and when he looked up again, she was looking out at the sea. They could hear Clara and the Signora talking in the garden below. He listened for men's voices, but he heard none. From the kitchen below, he could smell pasta, pomodori, cannellini, but he had learned, somewhere among the fresh bread of ruined cities, how not to let those scents do what they could do to you, not to let them tell you you were home.

"Beatrice," Alexandra said, "can you leave us alone a moment? I want to prepare Signor Vinetti for Clara." She winked at her sister.

"There's nothing you can say about her that you can't say in front of me. I already know it all, and I'm sure he does, too."

"I know, Bea. But you can keep them downstairs a moment. *Solo un momento. Per favore. Per me.*"

Bea set down her glass quietly and stood behind him and lowered herself and kissed him on the head. "*Lo teniamo,*" she said. "We're keeping him." She stuck out her tongue and winked and went out and closed the doors behind her.

Alexandra turned toward him.

"What is your name?"

He felt something rock in him. She looked out at the sea again, and when she spoke her voice was as steady as the waves were not.

"You understand that you can lie to yourself all you want in this life," she said, "but to make someone else lie to herself is not something that is easily forgiven."

"Alexandra."

She looked at him and told him he was in her house. With her own mother. That this was a very serious thing, and he did not know what he was doing. She cocked her head to the side. As though to ask him if it was true. If he had any idea.

He said nothing.

She turned away and told him her sisters were different. Each from each. But that her respect for her older sister was more than he could understand. Ever. Despite what they'd said in the piazza. Her sister was afraid of things she could not name, and that was why she was afraid of them. Because they had no names. "I do not pretend to know which fears are the right fears." She lifted her chin and breathed the wind and did not blink. Then she turned to him and asked if her sister had a reason to be afraid.

"I don't know."

"You don't know."

"I shouldn't—" he said, "—I shouldn't be here."

"No," she said, "probably not."

He lowered his eyes and lifted them again.

"What do you want me to tell you?"

"It doesn't matter," she said. "Tell me why you're afraid."

"Who said I'm afraid?"

"Tell me why you're afraid."

He didn't answer.

"You think I don't know," she said, "what happens with *soldati?* You're in the house of a soldier."

He shifted in his chair.

"Just let me go. I can go."

"Yes," she said. "You can."

He looked out toward the sea, then closed his eyes.

"I don't—I don't want to cause any trouble. I didn't know anyone was going to talk to me."

"You didn't think anyone was going to talk to you?"

"No."

She shook her head.

"I think you mistake me for someone else," she said.

"Who?"

"Someone who runs away."

The doors to the terrace opened. Bea was half-stumbling in front of her mother and sister.

"*Mi dispiace*, Alexandra. I tried."

The Signora looked at her. Then she looked at the two on the terrace. "Nonsense. Tried what? Signor Vinetti is our guest. *Del massimo onore*. You wouldn't keep him from his hosts, *la mia colomba*, would you?"

Alexandra stood. "No, mama. Of course not. Come, sit. Clara, sit."

He was watching her as she went out through the double doors into the house and down the stairs toward the kitchen.

"Signor Vinetti," the Signora said. "We have you to ourselves now."

"Yes," Bea said. "*Tutto per noi.*"

"Signor Vinetti," Clara said. "You'll forgive me. *La mia indiscrezione.* But I believe in being forthright. We hope to have you for dinner, and we are aware, of course, that this may cause some trouble for you. If you would like to take your dinner in your room, we would understand."

He looked at each of their faces in turn.

"No." He had said it very softly. "*Posso cenare con lei.*"

"What manners," the Signora said. "A man of the world has the most excellent manners."

Clara smiled.

"Good," the Signora said. "Very good, then. Now we know." She clapped her hands. "The moon will be full tonight, Signor Vinetti. Did you know that? Of course you did. *Ovviamente.* You're a man of the world. My God what a man of the world."

"Sit, mama."

"Where is your sister?"

"She'll bring everything up."

"Good. Very good. Signor Vinetti, I did not see your things. Did you not fetch them?"

He leaned forward and gave a small bow.

"No," he said. But he did not explain.

"Stolen, then? My God what a world. That is not our town, Signor Vinetti. Please don't believe that is Lunetto."

"I do not believe that is your town."

"My God what manners. *Perfetto.* Ah, Signore. You have nothing to fear. I will have Carlo bring something tonight. Something for our guest."

"No," he said. Then he added, "grazie." She'd begun to stand, and Clara looked at him.

"Grazie," he said again. "It isn't necessary."

"Necessary," the Signora said. "Madonna."

"What about Papa's things?" Bea said.

"Beatrice." Clara had turned toward her sharply.

"*Sì*," the Signora said, but she seemed to be considering it. "*Sì.* Of course, Signor Vinetti. Papa has everything you will need." She stroked his hand, but her eyes did not meet his. "You are a son of this country, and you have given so much. What can a father not give to you?"

He told himself not to lower his head.

"Grazie, Signora."

"*Bene*," she said. "*Adesso lo sappiamo.* Now we know."

She rose to go, but the terrace doors opened behind her, and Alexandra stepped out with a large double-handled pot and her wicker basket over one shoulder. She was carrying a small, blue towel between her teeth, and she let her mother take it and lay it down on the table, and she laid down the pot and slung the basket off her shoulder. She reached into it and laid a small bowl of soft cheese on the table.

"Ricotta forte," she said. "A taste of Signor Vinetti's home."

"Beautiful," the Signora said. "What an idea. Puglia. Brindisi. Beautiful. In all my years, my daughters, I have never seen *il mare Adriatico*. Not once. Tell us, Signore."

Alexandra lifted a stack of shallow earthenware bowls from her basket and laid the basket under the table. She handed the stack to her mother, and her mother took one and passed the others around, thumbing something from the lip of one of them. A long wooden ladle hung from the lip of the pot, and he stood and took up the Signora's bowl and served her.

"It is very beautiful," he said. "Have you seen it, Clara?"

He served the others, and Alexandra sat where she'd sat earlier and held out her hand for the cheese. He handed it to her, and she reached for the bread and spread the cheese on it and began to eat.

"*Sì*," Clara said.

"How'd you know?" Bea asked.

"He didn't know, Bea," Clara said. "He's being polite. What manners," she smiled at her mother.

"No, he knew," Bea said. "How did you know?"

"*Una supposizione.*"

"No." She'd finished her glass of wine. "You can tell. Clara's the traveler. Clara's the worldly one."

"She is," Alexandra said. "And Angelo too. And I'm sure they have much left to see." She patted her sister's hand.

"Have you traveled much, Signor Vinetti?" The Signora waved her own words away. "My God what am I asking? Of course you have. Forgive me. My manners get away from me. They have a mind of their own. Of course you have. Just listen to how you speak. You've been everywhere, everywhere."

He ladled himself some of the *pasta e fagioli* and sat stirring it silently. He could feel them waiting.

"No," he said. "You're right to ask, Signora. To see the world the way we did, as soldiers, is not really to travel. It's all the same."

Alexandra was waiting for her mother to say how much this made her think, how beautiful it was, but she did not. There was a sudden silence on the terrace. The wind had fallen, and the moon was rising over the vicolo. They could hear the cypresses settling in the garden below, the first crickets in the shadows.

"I can only imagine, Andreas," Bea said. "I can only imagine."

They talked amongst themselves while they ate, and they told themselves not to look at him in case he struggled. He would pinch the silk between his forefinger and thumb and pull it taut and lift his spoon under it and eat. Like a machine, he was thinking. He could hear the words of the barber in Bologna. We are not a machine, Signore. That is the sickness.

Well, he thought now, try it. Try not being a machine.

He listened to them speak about the shipworks and the wages, the shore at Palma and their father. He listened to them speak with their different voices, each of them a world inside a world, and he tried to balance his gaze between each of them, but always it drifted back to her. Once only he saw her trying to look at his face while he pulled his mask taut and dabbed at his lips, but when she felt him looking, she turned away swiftly and reached for the bread and asked her sister about Brindisi, about Messina.

When dinner was over, the moon had come up clear over the water. Bea had nearly fallen asleep in her chair, and her mother stood and rubbed her shoulder and told her it was time to rest. *My little clown. Mia figlia.* Clara took up the dishes, and she told him to sit when he rose to help her. The Signora asked him about the genetti, but he knew they were tired of trying to speak with a man behind a mask, knew the disappointment of those who'd found they would not be hearing the stories they'd told themselves they'd hear, the stories they had told themselves alone.

"Grazie, Signora. I think I'll lie down, if I may. *La cen eccellente.*"

"If you may. God what manners. Of course you may. (yours tonight. Alexandra, you'll find Papa's things for S You'll stay with me, *la mia colomba*. Clara, we'll have th' row. Do we like genetti, Signore?"

"*Lo adoro.*"

"*Perfetto,*" she said. "Tomorrow, then, tomorrow. Alexandra, you will show Signor Vinetti to his room."

She turned to Beatrice.

"Come, my most foolish daughter, *è ora di riposare.*"

The Signora gathered the dishes into the basket and gestured for Clara to lift it, and the three of them were gone through the double doors, leaving the wake of their scent, the wine and bread on the table.

"Come," Alexandra said. "Your room."

X

Hers was a modest room on the east side of the house, down by the heavy scents of the garden, and the swallows were flitting in through the casements and out again to hunt the insects in the full moon. Alexandra left him staring at her drawings, and when she came back she was carrying her father's clothes. She laid them on the bed and touched them.

"A sweater, too. For the wind."

She stood with her hands in her pockets. The moon shone in the yellow of her top, and he could smell the rosewater in her cotton.

"They're beautiful," he said. "You made them all?"

"Of course."

"I like this one."

He was pointing to the largest of the drawings. She'd pasted together two sheets of the newsprint and drawn an expanse of the sea, a storm building in the offing, something like a boat in the distance that was no more than a smudge of a thumb.

"Grazie," she said. "I don't like to talk about them."

He turned to her. After a while he knew she was waiting for him to speak.

"It's not what you think," he said.

She said nothing.

He looked straight at her and told himself not to look away. He knew he was ruining it all.

I'm sorry, he wanted to tell her. But he knew it meant nothing.

"Sit," she said.

He sat on the bed and looked away. He did not know what she would do. Or if she would turn and leave. But she stayed.

After a long while she spoke. She told him he didn't know how serious it was, and when he asked her what it was, she said life. Life. He thought to tell her yes, he did. But he said nothing.

She turned and walked to the door and then came back and sat on the bed. Not close. But not far. She told him he was in her house. Her house.

He could smell the soap with which she'd washed her hands, her hair. He had known you could ruin your life, but he had not known if you could ruin it for good. But now he knew.

"*Posso andare,*" he said, very softly. I can go.

She shook her head. Then she rose and walked to the door and stood before it a long while, facing away from him. She touched the latch and let it go. She thought of herself standing before the mirror, in the darkness, letting down her hair and gathering it up again; of a flash of black; of the wind in the silk of his mask, dark as the darkness of the harbor. *Look,* she'd heard something whisper in this room, so often. Then she turned and pressed her back to the door and sat down against it and looked at him.

"Talk," she said.

He looked at her hands as he spoke, a dark hint like ashes under her fingernails. He thought of the wind over the sea, the house he could not go back to. Very slowly he unpinned the medal from his breast pocket and laid it on the bed beside him. Then it was as if he was hearing himself speak. He told her about the battle in Klisura Pass, and everything he told was true. He told her about the wind and the snows. He told her how he'd lain in the transport clutching his leg all through the night, and all through the night he was sure he was going to die. As a dog might. With not even a witness. This man before her, speaking like a child. He told her how he'd prayed with the words he'd learned as a boy, and he'd wondered if he was going to see his father again after it was over, because he'd done as he should do, and if perhaps his brothers were already there. Wherever that was. Then he was silent. Go on, she said. He looked down at his own hands, and he did not look up. He told her about his nights in the hospital at Bologna, how he'd heard about his brothers, one by one, and how something had gone out inside him, with each of their deaths, like a child blowing out the candles in a cathedral. As though the world were something we could wish out of being. Swiftly and without our knowing. He said those words. Wish out of being. As a child might. Or a man. He told her he had asked his brothers if they would fight, young as they were, and when they had vanished he had not known what to do. My own brothers, he said. My mother's sons. He told her about his mother wandering the streets of her village, and though he did not tell her which mother was his own, he'd known there were countless mothers wandering the streets with their losses, and because the world thought they were all the same, the world paid them no mind. Which is a tragedy beyond speaking. Because the mothers are the blood of the world. He told her all he had seen in Bologna, and he told her of the thirty lives hanging in the piazza, and though he did not tell her who had carried out the orders, he did not have to. She knew he was afraid to stop speaking, and although his voice was low and quiet as the swallows flying in and out of the windows, he told her he had to go on speaking, and she nodded and said yes, go on. He told her how he'd been two years in the Repubblica, how it had gotten darker and darker, *più scuro e più scuro*, and when the Germans ate with them in Bologna he heard stories of things he would not say even to God if God did exist. He told her how something terrible had grown in his heart, and he did not know if he would ever be quit of it. In the autumn of his twenty-fourth year, he had no heart left to speak of, and when he'd gotten very drunk one night he'd climbed the rubble of the Basilica to the very top where the swallows used to be and stood high above the piazza. Like these swallows, he said, lifting his hand. Where the thirty had hung, he said. On the Basilica, he had looked down at the cobbles below, and he'd known there was only one promise we can keep with ourselves and with the world at the same time. He told her he had thought about it for a long time, all night, but he knew in his bones he was his mother's only son, and he did not think the end of her story was his story to tell. He knew he could not take her hope from her, and even if he were to come home without hope for himself, he could at least give her some hope that he was not who they said he was. And if he was that man, then he could at least give the world its defeat of him, and he would not take even that out of its hands.

When he was done speaking, she was leaning forward with her head in her hands, and she was very still. He told her he was sorry, that he knew he had made the same mistake again. He knew he had come into another's life, as though that life were also his story to tell, and he knew the world was not here to forgive him or take away his pain. He told her he would leave, that he could not stay in that house in the clothes of her father and not give up calling himself a man.

She sat up and shook her head. He knew what she was going to say, and she did say it. She told him it was not his right to say which stories are his to tell.

She looked at him and shook her head. The words, if they were words, came to her in great waves, dark and constant as the harbor: No story is yours, they said, and to think you are the only one telling it is a worse sin than anything you've done. Anything. And even when we take ourselves away, we are the silences in someone else's story. *Riesci a sentirmi?* We think it is a virtue to tell all, but perhaps the one before you is asking for silence. Perhaps that is compassion.

She was not sure which parts of it she had said aloud. She lifted her hand and looked at it and laid it down again and told him it takes two people to make any story between them, and there is only one hell in this world, and it is for those who are so broken and so childish that they must tell themselves they did not make their lives.

"Do you understand?" she said.

He nodded. Very slowly she rose and stood with her back to the door, looking out at the cypresses through the windows. Then she looked at him. She crossed the room and stood before him breathing. He could not hear her breath. *Perché*, she said.

She lifted her hands and held them on either side of him. Breathing. He could smell charcoal on her fingers. He knew what she was going to do, and he told himself to look at her. He felt her hands slide behind him and finger the black silk ribbons, and he thought of the barber's scissors whispering about death and the sound of the swallows flying in the darkness of the Basilica when the church of the world was already in ruins. He told her no, but he was not sure if he had whispered it aloud or merely thought it. No, he said. But he had not raised his hands, and the swallows were flying in over their hair and out again, and when she pulled the ribbons and let the silk fall, she backed away into the shadows with one hand over her mouth and pressed her back against the cold wood of the door.

"No," he said.

She shook her head. His face was untouched by anything but the years. He was clean-shaven, his eyes in the moonlight the same unchanged brown. His nose was strong and his lips were full, and she told herself to go. Go. But she did not. The bones of his cheeks had sharpened since some wild boy had stood on a peach crate in the piazza, shouting such wild and boyish things, some boy who had sat with the others on the docks by Santa Maria, some boy who had glowered at all of them through the newsprint from Bologna. And yet he was that boy.

"They will kill you," she said.

"I know."

"His brother will—"

"I know."

She shook her head.

He lowered himself from the bed and sat on the floor and leaned back against it. He told himself not to move toward her.

"I'll leave," he said. "I'll leave now and I won't come back."

She shook her head.

"Your mother. The woman in the streets is your mother."

"I know."

"Say your name."

He lowered his head.

"Say it aloud," she said.

Very slowly he lifted his face and looked at her.

"Leonardo," he said. "Gemetti."

She did not move. She shook her head again and looked out at the swallows flitting in and out of the room.

"You don't know what you're doing," she said.

"No," he said. The mask was lying in his hands. "I never have."

"I don't pity you. You can't make me pity you."

"I know."

She touched the latch of the door.

"Please," he said. "They'll hear us. This is my life."

"Yes, this is your life."

He looked down at his hands.

"My mother," he said. "I'll take her with me."

"You'll take her from her home?"

"She has no home. Not now."

"No. No one blames her. Not her."

He looked at the mask and tied the ribbon and laid it on the floor beside him.

"Then I'll go alone."

She shook her head. He knew he was not ready to hear what she had to tell him, but he made himself look at her while she said it, and he did not look away. She told him that if he thought he could ever be free, he was mistaken. *Sbagliato.* She told him that as long as someone is banished from his home, he will never have one in this world. If you have ruined your life here, in one small place, you have ruined it everywhere in the world.

He could not look at her.

"What am I supposed to do?"

"I can't tell you that," she said. "This is your life."

He took up the mask and folded it three times and slipped it into his breast pocket. He could smell her rosewater in the air. Don't ask, he told himself. Don't ask for anything ever again in this world.

But he asked her if he could stay. Only for tonight. Though he did not look at her.

She closed her eyes and breathed deep and then looked at him.

"Tell me one thing," she said.

She watched him look up, but she could not remember what she'd thought to ask him.

He looked away. Then in her own silence she asked herself, Do you believe you make your life? Or do you believe all you have done is out of your hands?

"I'm so ashamed," he said.

She said again that she would not pity him, but she heard her voice falter.

The wind had shifted in the cypresses, and when she closed her eyes she listened to the curtains blowing out into the garden, the weight of them swaying from the house now, as if someone, in her long, soft clothes, had chosen to leave. Then she heard herself speaking. She could not say later which words she'd said aloud, which were hers and which she merely remembered, but she thought she'd said there were forces in us greater than anyone can imagine, that although perhaps in ancient days these forces had been the gods, they went by other names now in this world. But that did not make them any less powerful. She thought she'd said that even when they were called the gods, these forces were not our lives. And they never had been. They were a part of us only, and whether the world is written first in our hearts and then in the world, or whether it is the other way around, it does not matter. We shape the world with our hands, and we can decide. We can choose, she said. But she thought she'd said more. She thought she'd said there are those who are truly powerless, but even they have that last freedom. Even they can choose what is written in the book of their acts. Which is the world. Even they can turn the page in the book of their acts and stare at the blankness of the world and begin again. Even if that beginning is doomed. For her mother was right that faith was nothing but the act of creation, of building it back up again from the rubble. Even if it will fall to rubble again and again, and then forever. For our work is our freedom. To be here in the work of our lives, which cannot last. To try in every moment to see what it is we are losing. And to see what we have done. And to know that perhaps nothing can be atoned, but even if there is no Maker in the heavens, even if there is nothing to confess to, there is still the light of morning. There is still the promise of tomorrow; there is still the soft voice of tomorrow, which is nothing but the wreckage of yesterday, the terrible wreckage of yesterday, saying what in the world have I done.

When she was done speaking, he nodded. She closed her eyes and lifted one hand in the air and held it there strangely. A plea or a reprimand, he could not say. Very slowly he watched her open her eyes and shake her head in the moonlight. She turned toward the door and lowered the latch and then turned back again, the moon in the folds of her cotton.

"Say it again," she said.

He was still sitting where he'd spoken.

"We make our lives."

"Then I will come to you. Lock the door. I will come to you."

XI

She did. He had not slept at all, but he lay in the bed and heard her whistle from the cypresses, and then she was standing by the open window. She climbed in and stood at the foot of the bed and did not look away. He could not understand his life.

"You're cold," she said.

He had not changed into her father's clothes, but he was wearing the thin wool sweater over his shirt, and it smelled of mulberries and the cypresses and the salt air of the sea.

She crossed the room to the door and checked it. Then she turned around and looked at him.

He asked about her sister, how she could hate him even before she knew. He asked if she knew.

She shook her head. "Clara doesn't hate. Indifference is the opposite of love." She breathed. "And she is not indifferent to my life."

She stepped forward slowly and found his medal on the floor and laid it on the night table, running her thumb over it strangely.

"*È una—*"

"I know what it is," she said.

She walked to the wardrobe and straightened one of her drawings, running her finger along its edges. When she sat at the foot of the bed, she did not turn toward him. After a long while he asked her about her father.

"No," she said. "No."

He said he was sorry, and she told him he did not even know what he was sorry for. Not yet. She leaned forward and held herself and rocked slightly in the moonlight.

"Lunetto," she said. "So Lunetto is your home."

He did not answer, but he closed his eyes and thought of his mother making her way up the Via Finetti and opening the door and lying down in a house alone. Three folded notes in the dresser beside her. His father's watch beneath them. He opened his eyes. The cypresses clicked against the window, and he pushed himself up and laid his shoulders against the coolness of the wall, the papers shifting above him.

"Lunetto," he heard again.

After a very long time she began speaking softly, and it was as though she was speaking to no one at all. She said he'd been a baker, her father, and before that a fisherman, out in the Strait of Messina. Out where the waters were deep. She said his eyes had failed him and he'd had to give up the sea, which he loved so much.

She moved as though to look back at him over her shoulder, but she did not.

Perhaps, she said, perhaps that's why he had taken them to Palma. To see it again. To be in another time.

"Palma," he said.

The casements shifted in their hinges, and the drawings riffled softly. He asked if her father had been to war, but when she shook her head, he did not know what it meant. Then she told him yes. In the Alpini, she said. In the mountains.

For a long time she said nothing more. He looked out the window and watched the cypresses and felt the nakedness of his face. Then she was speaking.

Her father had been in the Alpini, yes, and he'd had a coldness in his bones his whole life when he'd come home. He'd come home, but no one comes home all the way. No one.

She did turn. Then she turned away from him again and shook her head, the wind riffling her drawings on the walls around them.

She was speaking of her mother. "She's alone without my father," she said. It seemed a question had slipped into her, a question he had not asked, and she lifted her chin and said no, perhaps it was better this way, not the other way around. That her father would have been lost without her.

"*Tuo padre é stato ferito? Ai suoi tempi?*"

She told him yes, her father had been wounded, but not in the way he thought. Not that way. He had had such nightmares. Each night. Of a time before she was born. But all he had wanted was for her mother to sleep. To rest.

"This was his room," he said.

She nodded.

He knew she was going to say more, and he watched her shoulders rise and fall as she breathed, the ceiling creaking above. She was still turned away from him, and he knew she was looking at her hands.

She told him her father had never spoken of it. His wound. That there were only the sounds of his dreams in the nights and then his long hours of coughing and his sleepless eyes in the mornings. Toward the end it was as though her father had forgotten. At last. Or if he had not forgotten, he had set it down. As though he was sure it would come back in the next life. Then she said perhaps he had. Perhaps he had come back to it.

He knew she was waiting for him to ask, and he did ask. What does a father dream of at the end?

She paused a moment, as though to decide. Then she breathed. She told him about her father's last dreams, about his days fishing as a boy, out in the Strait, out in the winds. How he would wake in the nights and gather his daughters and tell them all, speaking slowly about the nets he pulled up from so deep, the birds swirling over him, speaking to each one of them in turn, as though she were the only one there. He would speak about the wind and the rain, about the storms that came up in summer and the true storms that came in winter. He would catch his breath, time and again, as he spoke, but she had never seen her father so happy, never, as when he spoke of those dreams.

She knew what he was going to ask, and she told him no, she never knew her grandfathers. Something is lost without knowing them, she told him, but maybe something is gained. You can make of their world what you wish. Then she shook her head and said no, the wish is never the way. The way is to know.

She rose and left by the door, and he was certain she was not coming back. Then she did. She was carrying two glasses of water, and she brought one to him and stood beside him and told him to drink. He did. Then she sat down on the night table and told him to tell her about his brothers.

"*Li conoscevi?*"

No, she told him, she had not known them. Something darkened her face, and she touched her chin strangely and whispered a name and then said it again.

"Carlo."

"No," he said, "I never knew him."

His voice had wavered, and she shook her head as though to ask him what it meant.

"And the other brothers—"

"One," she said. "One other."

"Does he come here?"

She searched his eyes.

"Matteo—" she said, "—*Gesù Cristo*, you knew him."

"No," he lied. "No."

She searched his eyes again and then looked back toward the door, tapping her foot softly as she turned back to him. The wind had slid in through the casements and shifted and softened again, and her drawings were very still around her.

"Carlo," she said, "he knows how to forgive. And his father." She breathed. "But Matteo—"

"*Per favore.* Anything but that. *Per favore.*"

She laid her hands on her hips and stood and paced the room, shaking her head slowly.

"*Per favore,*" he said.

"*Gesù Cristo.*"

"*Per favore.*"

He'd sat up and was tapping a heel on the floor. She closed her eyes and stood still at the center of the room.

"What are you going to do?"

"Why do you want to help me? Why are you helping me?"

She looked at him.

"Is that what I'm doing?"

He lowered his eyes and shook his head. When he looked up again, she was pacing.

"I'm helping you not to die," she said. "That's all. You're a fool and you need that much."

"I don't want to—"

"It doesn't matter what you want. Not now." She planted her feet and looked at him. "What are you going to do?"

"Talk. I'm just going to talk to you. And then I'm going to go."

"Is it that easy?"

"No. But that's what I'm going to do."

She leaned against the far wall, her face turned away from him. When he stilled his leg, he could hear footsteps on the mezzanino above, and then the stairs creaked and a door opened and closed somewhere in the villa. His heart was in his temples. Very slowly she made her way to the wardrobe and sat down in front of it, shaking her head as the casements swayed. Twice she parted her lips, as if to speak, but no words came. When she spoke again, her voice was low and strange, and it seemed to come from far off.

"*Gesù Cristo*," she said.

"Che cosa?"

"Everything. Everything."

She opened her eyes. Her voice was barely a whisper. "I'm sorry about your brothers. I can't imagine that."

He looked at his hands and told himself to take it. He told himself not to ask again about the Russo brothers, about the ones who lived, about the one whose face he had known from his days in San Pietro, the one whom perhaps, yes, he'd been searching for in all this mess to bring something trembling in him to an end. Be here, he thought. You had that one lie left. Look at her. Don't you dare lie to her again.

"I can't either," he said. "I still can't."

He was keeping himself very still. She rolled her head against the wardrobe and looked at the door, then ran her thumb in a small circle on the floor beside her. The villa was quiet. She closed her eyes and breathed very deeply, as though she had decided, and then she turned to him and said *dimmi*. Tell me.

He told her how his youngest brother would tease the older. In the family without a father, the older brother is king. But when you're a king, he told her, you get the revolutions. As it was with her mother. He asked her what she'd said about indifference.

"*È l'opposto dell'amore.*"

Yes, told her. He thought so, too. It is the opposite of love. And where there is no respect, there is no sacrilege. So they'd teased Enzo.

She looked at the empty glass on the night table and told him to go on.

His brother Nico would weave long lanyards of leather, as long as an arm, a leg, would paint them blue and green and sometimes the slightest shade of yellow, the most delicate pattern of any snake in any world or any dream. As though they were the real thing. As though the devil could take a pleasing form. Then he'd lay them in his brother's bed.

"*Terribile,*" she said.

No one was there with my mother, he told her. When they died.

She looked at him, and he knew she had said his name to herself before she'd come back. "No," she said. "The priests were there."

"Until I did what I did."

"No. Even then. She couldn't have been alone. Not in Lunetto."

He lifted a hand to his face, but he felt there was no mask to straighten.

When he lowered his hand, she was looking out the window. Very slowly she looked at him.

"In the photograph," she said. "In the papers."

He closed his eyes.

"Yes," he said.

"You were grinning."

His eyes were still closed. He felt himself disappear and come back again.

"Please," he said. "I know."

Then he opened his eyes. Hers were the deep green of the sea. He could hear the wind in the cypresses, and beyond them the sea and the ships blowing their horns in the harbor. He thought of her father alone out on the Strait, hauling up something from the depths, something he could never hope to touch, something he could never hope to lose.

He told himself he had to ask it. About the boy and his brothers. Russo. Ask it, he thought. Ask it.

She shook her head.

"No," she said. "There are limits to knowing. To torture yourself is also an indulgence. We suffer our changes. We do not suffer for suffering itself."

But he told her she could not know if he had done that work. If he had changed. That it was not her right to forgive him.

He closed his eyes and listened to the wind in the cypresses. He told himself not to think of his father. He told himself not to think of anything but the trees and the sea and the sound of the wind, but he thought of her sitting in her own house, and he thought of her father out on the sea, staring down into the darkness of the depths. He thought of a boy looking up at him in the snow and another standing before him in a ruined city, and he kept his eyes closed and told himself he had come to this place by his own will, and though he knew she thought she had called him here, he would not let her keep him where he did not wish to be.

But when he opened his eyes, she was gone.

XII

When she closed the door behind her, she stood awhile with her back to it, looking up the stairs to the terrace. She drifted halfway up and then sat down suddenly and leaned back against one of the tapestries. It was older than the house and all the furniture in the house, and she closed her eyes and smelled her father's smoke in it and tried to think of what was stitched in it: a horse rearing back into the darkness, its rider carrying an empty cage in one hand, a falcon on the dark glove of the other. She had run her hands over it so many times, so many nights, climbing the stairs and descending them, and sometimes if she couldn't sleep she would climb to the terrace and back down again, and when she'd lain in her bed she'd felt the shapes of the tapestry still in her hands, and she'd let them shape the things that came to her in her sleep and then shape the things she drew, with the wind's help, at her desk in the mornings. *We suffer our changes*, her father had. When he had died, they'd carried her desk into his room and she'd sat at it a long while and tried to draw the horse in the darkness, but when she'd drawn the empty cage she'd folded the paper slowly and curled on the bed and listened to the wind in the cypresses, as though someone were making their way through them in the dark.

She sat on the stairs now and looked down toward the door to her room. It was not possible. You remember it, don't you? That face. Not from the papers. Before. Say it. You remember how he looked at you on the docks by Santa Maria. He doesn't remember. And neither do you. No, you do. Look. You do. If that is his voice, then you are going to do something stupid with your life. Shut up. Think of the things he said. Yes, exactly. Think of the things he said.

She did think of them, and she thought of him wounded in the mountains and then she thought no, he's not wounded at all. He lied once and he's probably not wounded at all. Even if he tells you he is, it will be a lie. And it won't matter. You won't pity him because he's a lie. Everything is a lie and that's why your life is your life. If it hadn't been a lie then why would you think this is true? It was a lie just like his wound was a lie. No. You know that isn't true. No one's wound is a lie. You know that. Not anyone's and not your own, either. It's written in everything you do.

She stood and made her way to the terrace and closed the double doors behind her softly and sat on the stone railing looking out to the sea. Tomorrow at noon she would make her way through the piazza and down along the sea wall and up past Santa Maria Maggiore and left on the Via Ferrini to the shipworks, and she would stand on the scaffolding and put on her mask and do the work of her life. The work of your life. Say that. It's good work, and you love it. You know that. Say it again. It's good work and you love it and you know it, but it's not the work of your life.

She slid from the railing and sat on the terrace and threw her hair in front of her and kneaded the muscles of her neck, sore from her long hours on the scaffolding. You don't know what you're doing. If you think you can make anything with your own hands, you're wrong, just wrong. Least of all your life.

She leaned on the wall beside her and looked down through the curtainless window into the dark of the house, its rooms where her mother and sisters were probably already sleeping, where certainly he was not. The wind from the sea came strong against her shoulders, and it smelled of the sirocco blowing north across Sicily and the iron of the shipworks, the olives unloaded in the harbor and the almond he'd placed in her hand. No, she thought, it doesn't smell like that at all. You know that. Look at your hands. Look at them. Nothing is in your hands.

She stood and opened the double doors and made her way down the stairs and stood before her mother's door, laying her hand on it slowly. She stood there a long while, smelling the heavy tapestries in the house, listening for her sisters' footsteps in the darkness, telling herself she'd knocked on the door, softly. But she had not.

XIII

He had stood and paced the room and then looked out at the dark trees in the garden. You could go. You could climb right out and go. Then he felt himself sit on the bed and close his eyes. Where would you go? You can't go back there. Not now. You know that. Not until you've done what you have to. Remember what she said. Not until you know.

When his father flashed before him, he stood again and paced the room and tried to let it pass. Don't, he thought. Not now. But he closed his eyes and saw his father walking along a river in an Alsatian night, and he heard the words his mother had said, and he tried to understand what was happening inside him. It can't be, he'd said to his mother. Yes, my son, it is. It always was. This is the world.

He sat back on the bed and laid his face in his hands and tried to think. The room was spinning. No, that was not your father. Don't believe it. Why did she tell you? She was trying to comfort you, that's all. Why would that comfort you? You know why. No. He did it and that's not what I am. That's not what I did. I have my own ghost to carry and he can't lay this on me now. Not here. Not now. I won't pick it up. He set it down in his own way and I'm not going to do that. We've been through all that already and we've decided. Haven't we? Yes. We've decided. What did we decide? To keep going. Remember. Remember how you said it in Bologna. You don't know anything anyway so you may as well go back. Back. But you can't. You can't go there. Not now. Not ever. What did she say? Think. What did you say? We make our lives, don't we? No. It wasn't supposed to be this way. And it isn't. It isn't this way. Say we make our lives. Even if it ruins you. Say what she said. Say we make our lives. Say it.

He stood again and paced the floor, looking up at her drawings.

They were boats in various stages of construction, some of them with the vast tines of their ribs exposed, some of them nearly completed. The workers were not there. He made his way to the largest of them and stood under it, looking up at the sea she'd drawn. The ship far out on the horizon. You have no idea where you are, he said. You never did.

He looked at the door. Don't, he thought. Don't bring this into anyone's house. Not your mother's and not her ghosts' and not anyone's. Not hers. Not this one. Don't ask anyone to carry anything at all. Don't. You've done enough, haven't you? You've done enough.

He reached up and touched the drawing and smelled his fingers. Charcoal. The fires in Sarande, in Bologna. The horses burning in the mountains. He felt an old ache in his thigh and his knees softened and he sat back on the bed and then let himself lie down on his side. Just for a minute, he thought. Just until the bombs wake you. Just until the end of the world.

XIV

He had slept through the night, as he'd trained himself to do, and he could not remember his dreams. All he could remember was a woman sitting alone in a cathedral, her face swaying in her hands, and when she'd turned toward him, there was only the night where her face had been.

The light was flooding through the curtains, and he sat up and slid off the bed and found his shoes and folded the sweater on the linens and opened the door. Very quickly he closed it again and stood alone in the room, listening to the birdsong in the hedges, the bustle of the morning far out in the piazza. He could hear voices in the garden, out past the cypresses, but he could not understand. He slipped the mask from his pocket and held it to his face and lowered it again. The door opened behind him, and he heard her.

He turned and saw her full in the morning light. The door was still open behind her. He lifted his hands to his face, but she rushed to him and clasped his wrists and pulled his hands down and looked at him.

"Stay here," she said. And he knew they had come.

They didn't know, she told him. But Russo had arranged for a *festa* in the piazza—today, now—because Russo was Russo. Carlo—that *pettegola*, Carlo—had told his father about the one called Vinetti, and Russo's eyes had welled up with gratitude. *Un miracolo.* It was as though his own son Salvatore had come home.

A thought darkened her face, and she shook her head.

"Clara," she said, "Clara was there with mama—yesterday. She's always talking. She always has to talk."

"What?" he said. "Tell me."

Clara had told Russo, she said, Clara and Carlo. Carlo had spoken of his father pacing all night like a madman, *un estatico,* and finally Russo had told them all that this man in their village was none other than all the dead who had paid the greatest price of all, the dead who have no names but only the face of their sacrifice. Language like that. A madman's language. A mourner's. And now he was here. In the garden. In this garden. In this house. Waiting to embrace all the dead who have no names.

"*Cristo,*" he said. "No."

He looked at her and asked her with his eyes if the son was here. The other son. The one he was telling her with his silence he knew.

"Matteo. *Gesù,* you do know him."

He said nothing, and it seemed she was going to slap him, but she did not.

"He'll kill you."

"I know."

"He will kill you."

"*Sì.*"

She looked over his shoulder through the cypresses.

"What are we going to do?"

"Me," he said. "Me. Not you."

He turned and tied on his mask and looked out the window through the cypresses. He could see no one, but he could smell smoke through the trees, and he heard a voice—low at first, then sharp, hardened—steady and resonant as it had been in the halls of San Pietro, and he knew it was a voice from his youth. He knew it was Russo, Matteo Russo. *Cristo,* he thought. No.

When he turned around, she was locking the door.

She looked at him, and he told her to leave him and go out into the garden and tell them he was gone. *Gia andato.*

"Yes," she said.

She turned toward the door and turned back and grabbed his arm. Very slowly she let him go.

"You've done this to yourself."

He closed his eyes. Then they heard the Signora.

She was calling through the door, and they knew she had heard them. How much they could not say.

"Alexandra," she said. "Come."

He shook his head. She could see the silk pulsing with his breath.

"Stay," she said.

She ushered him back to the bed and told him to lie down and turn toward the window. He could feel her lingering over him a moment before she left.

When she'd closed the door behind her, he turned and looked at it. Then he looked out the window. They were standing on the garden path just behind the cypresses, and it was no use. It was no use. You came here to die. You didn't know that's what you wanted, but it's what you wanted. Say it. No, he thought. You don't know that. You don't know anything at all.

He lay back and looked up at the ceiling and laid his hands over his face.

You can say you're sick. You can do that. You liar.

No. They're not going away. They're never going away.

Va bene, he thought. You liar. Now you have to lie for your life.

XV

She led him out to the garden by his arm. He saw Matteo first, and she knew he had seen him. She slid him closer to her and watched him adjust his mask, and they walked on.

Her mother was standing with Russo, and his two sons were on either side of them. The Signora was wearing a bright red dress with flounces down its sleeves, a sprig of laurel in her hair, and Russo turned from her to look at him.

"*Cristo*," he said. He opened his arms. "*Mio figlio. Nostri figli.*"

Carlo grabbed his father.

"Easy, Papa. Let him come."

"Nonsense. Look at him. Matteo, look at him."

"I see him, Papa."

Alexandra looked for her sisters, but they were not there. She was holding him close to her, and when they'd reached the others, Russo embraced both of them together. He had tears in his eyes.

"*Bellisimo.* I tell you, if this is not a miracle. If this is not a sign."

"Easy, Papa."

"Easy? Nonsense. Come, Signore. How did you sleep? Lunetto has a feast for you."

Alexandra touched Leo's chest.

"Sindaco Russo, Signor Vinetti has woken ill this morning. He has talked himself sick last night, I'm afraid. He has traveled far, very far, and his voice is not with him."

"Water." The Signora waved her arm toward the house. "Beatrice. Bring us water."

"Grazie, Signora." Leo's voice was merely a whisper when he said it.

The sons were wearing suit jackets and thin, dark ties, Carlo standing broad-shouldered, slender, a black ribbon pinned to his lapel. The younger was tall, taller than Leo remembered him from the schoolrooms of San Pietro, his cheeks sunken and his eyes heavy, and it seemed that he had not slept at all.

Russo was shaking his head at Leo.

"Ah, my son. My boy. *Il mio soldato.* You have suffered. How you have suffered."

"Shall we send him back to bed, Alexandra?" The Signora made her way toward him and touched his forehead. "Signore, you have suffered enough. Alexandra, take him to bed."

"Nonsense," Russo said. "This is a great *soldato* of the war, and he will not be treated like a child. Like a sick child." He waved her away and touched the medal Alexandra had restored to Leo's pocket. "Signore, you have met my son Carlo." He turned toward his other son and touched his face. "Now. Now you may meet my son. My son who has come back to us. From the dead. From the wreckage. From the ruins of this world. My Matteo." He kissed him. "Matteo."

Leo had lowered his face. He'd watched Matteo consider the medal on his chest, but their eyes had not met. "*Piacere,*" he heard, but no hand was extended to him.

Russo clapped loudly.

"Come, boys. Come."

Bea was shuffling up the path with a carafe of water in one hand, an empty glass in the other, but her mother waved her away.

"Beatrice, you come," Russo said. "And Clara. *Dov'è Clara?*"

"I'll fetch her, Signore Russo."

"Good. Very good. All of us." He kissed Alexandra and shuffled her away, throwing his arm around his guest.

"Come, my son. Come."

XVI

The piazza was full. Russo had laid out three long tables from the edge of the Via Madonna to the catedro, and someone had pinned fresh white linens all down their length. The tables were laid with wine and bread, little dishes of oil in the sunlight, and Leo could smell fresh genetti in the air. But all he was thinking was one thought. One thought. Let her not be here.

They sat him at the head of the table nearest the catedro, and Alexandra sat beside him with her hand on his knee. Matteo was pacing strangely through the piazza, glancing at him now and again, for only a moment, as though he had told himself no, told himself there were questions he would no longer ask, questions to which he did not want the answers. But always he looked at him as he'd done since they'd left the garden, and always their eyes met strangely, and always Leo lowered his eyes and straightened his silk.

The sea wind was blowing up from the waves, and it lifted the edges of the linens, a flurry of hands smoothing them down again in the sunlight. He told himself not to look at their faces. Don't look, he thought. Whatever you do, don't look.

But he did.

He saw Valentino Parri and Umberto Parri and Luca Bombasi, and he saw others from San Pietro. Though he knew the village had run off Giordano and the *fascisti*, he saw Brindi and Del Amici from the Balilla, and he felt his face burn in his mask when they looked at him. He saw Giuseppina Ferrari and Maria D'Angelo, whom he had kissed behind the sea wall when he was a boy, their breath heavy with the peppers from the market stalls. He knew there were other boys who had kissed them and then died while thinking about them in strange places—Tobruk,

Durrĕs, Alamein. Or had died trying not to think of them. *Giuiseppina, Maria, casa mia.* He saw them all, and he knew he had come home to find his death.

He checked for his mother, but he did not see her. The campanile was tolling, and he looked at Alexandra, but he did not know what he saw in her face.

The crowd had stared at him, gossiping—the Parris, Bombasi, others he couldn't name—but it seemed Russo's ecstasy had the sway of them. The campanile tolled, and Russo stood at the far side of the table opposite Leo and clapped his hands. Children were running past him, ducking under the tables, and when he turned toward his sons one of the children crashed against his leg and slumped to the ground and began to cry.

"My son," Russo said, stooping down. He wore a small holster in the small of his back. "Look how all our sons come back to us. Look how wild they are to come home."

The crowd laughed. A woman hustled forward and scooped up her child and scolded him. Alexandra looked at Leo. She had not blinked, and he knew she was trying to imagine his life.

"My sons," Russo said. He clapped again. "My daughters. My mothers and fathers. My countrymen. My Lunetto." Someone clapped Leo on the shoulder, but he did not turn.

"We have here with us today," Russo boomed, "a great testament to the sacrifices our sons have made for us in the terrible years since we were led into suffering. Led into suffering by men who know nothing of how to govern or how to love." The crowd murmured. "We have here a great recompense at the end of a long night of trial." He reached forward, and someone handed him a glass and splashed it with grappa. He closed his eyes and breathed the sea air and smiled.

"Grazie, Carina."

He raised the glass. "We have here not only my son, my beautiful son Matteo." He stilled his voice. "My beautiful son, Matteo."

"Ti amo, Papa."

"Ti amo," Russo mouthed. "Ti amo, Matteo."

The crowd cheered, and Russo gathered himself and lifted his glass higher into the sun.

"Not only my son but all the sons who have come back to us. You know their names. Bombasi. Gallo. Brindi. Lastra." The crowd cheered. "As you know the names of those who did not come home. Those for whom we hang our heads now for a solemn moment in recognition of their peaceful and abiding silence that is with no end." He lowered his head. The crowd settled into a silence, children bickering at its edges. Russo wiped his eyes furtively and then lifted his head.

"And not only do we have with us these honored sons and the losses for whose mothers and souls we pray eternally, not only do we have these sons, these men, but we have with us a great guest whose sacrifice, whose great wound, cannot be named, and whose name then is the name of those sons whose faces we cannot again lay our lips to and comfort and bless with the love of the living. This man who is their emissary. Their testament. And who, then, can sit here among us and be received by us all with gratitude for the soul that he is. The soul of all those who have gone off to foolish wars to prove what need not be proven. That they are sons of Italia. That they are lives like any lives and are worth more than the blood of tyrants. That they are men. Lunetto, I give you Signor Andreas Vinetti."

Leo saw the sunlight flash in the glasses raised suddenly around him. The crowd cheered once more, and a small band began assembling a song in the doorway of the catedro behind him. Alexandra grasped his knee.

He sat as still as he could as some of the crowd patted his shoulder or kissed his head or whispered a blessing in his ear. The Signora was laying out Clara's genetti in the sun. Russo had come to sit beside him, patting his hand as he sang along with the music.

He was looking out across the piazza when he saw his mother. She was wearing her black dress and black veil, and he leaned toward Alexandra and tried to tell her, but she did not understand. Children were crashing against his chair, one of them leaping up and poking at his shoulder. He reached for a piece of genetti and leaned down to the child and held it out for him. The child looked at his mask and stared a moment and hurried away.

He knew it was going to happen before it happened. He could not have said how he knew, but he knew. A child had climbed onto the chair behind him, and he did not feel the ribbon being pulled until the knot had come undone and the mask had slid down and away in the wind and he was fumbling to catch it as it fell.

Russo was staring at him in astonishment.

No, someone said. No. But he could not have said if it was him or Russo.

Russo stood up and grasped the table. Matteo was making his way through the crowd, and Leo watched him the whole way. Stand up, he told himself. Get up. But he could not.

The crowd had begun to understand slowly. It did not matter who knew him. It did not matter. They were being told.

Alexandra was still grasping his knee, but when he turned to her he saw she was looking steadily out across the piazza, and he knew.

He turned slowly. His mother was standing in the wind.

"No." It was Russo who had spoken. "No."

Matteo seized his father and shuffled him aside, and in one liquid motion he slid behind Leo and grasped him around the neck and dragged him back from his chair and threw him down against the wall of the catedro.

The band stopped playing.

Matteo was standing over him, and he could hear the others coming.

"You are already dead."

Matteo had said it very calmly.

"I know."

"No. You don't know. But I'm going to show you."

He fell to one knee and struck Leo hard on the jaw. A sound like a key falling into a well. Leo had raised his arms slowly, and he slumped back against the stones and told himself to get up. Get up.

When he opened his eyes, they were all there. He looked at his mother. She was kneeling behind them all, and he tried to tell her he was sorry. He tried to mouth it to her, to say it with his eyes. But he did not want them to see her. He did not want them to know.

Russo had come and stood beside Matteo. He seemed unable to understand.

"How? How?"

No, Leo wanted to say. There is no meaning.

But he said nothing.

Matteo was saying something to the crowd, but it was lost in their voices. When he turned back again, Leo's eyes flashed, and he knew he'd been hit again.

When he opened his eyes, he saw Russo grappling with Matteo.

Matteo shook away his father and stood straight and brushed down his shirt. He took off his jacket and flung it behind him and lowered his necktie.

"Yes, Papa. *Hai ragione.* To hang him is better." He turned back over his shoulder. "Carlo."

Leo still had not said a word. He slumped down to his side and tasted the blood in his mouth and looked at his mother.

Someone was kneeling beside him. He smelled her rosewater, and he knew.

"Alexandra," the Signora was saying. "Don't touch him."

"Don't," he said. And then, softly, "She didn't know."

"Alexandra, come."

"No," someone was saying, "No."

He felt himself being lifted, and he did not fight them. He closed his eyes and let the blood slide back into his throat, and he swallowed it. So this is what it feels like, he thought. So this is what it is.

Children were crying, and he heard women calling them away. Someone plucked his medal from his breast, and he heard it clatter on the stones below. His head was swaying, and he did not know where they were taking him, but when he felt the coolness of the catedro pass over him, the heavy scent of censer, of oil, he knew.

Suddenly they stopped. He could hear them fumbling with a lock, and then they were calling for the priest to open the stairwell. Others were shouting outside, some for mercy, some for blood, some for something he could not name. He felt a leather belt pass over his face and cinch around his neck, and he knew.

Then he heard his mother's voice.

She had pushed her way through the crowd and was wrestling for his shoulders.

"Nardo. Nardo."

He opened his eyes. Matteo was carrying his feet. He looked at him, and he saw his lips quickening, but he could not understand what was being said.

Matteo dropped his feet and began to struggle with his mother. He could hear Alexandra working through the crowd, and when she reached them she grabbed Matteo and he turned and lifted the back of his hand and brought it down across her face. Hard.

"Nardo," his mother was saying, "Nardo."

Alexandra was lying on the ground. In an instant the crowd seemed to sway. There was a hush and then a clap and he knew someone had fired a pistol in the air.

"No," Russo yelled. "No."

Matteo shoved the others away from him and stood breathing. He looked at his father.

"No?"

"No."

"Why, Papa? No."

Russo shook his head. He looked at Leo.

"No."

He made his way to the woman in the black veil and touched her on the shoulder and told the men to let him go. Let him go.

"Come, Signora."

"*Mio figlio. Mi figlio.*"

"I know, Signora. I know."

They led him up through the pews, and Alexandra walked beside him. He could taste the blood in his mouth, and he reached up for her face, but she lowered his hand and turned away.

He let them sit him in the front pew, and Russo stood on the altar and gestured for them all to come in and sit.

Matteo had stepped up and was whispering something in his father's ear. In a flourish of cassocks, the priest slid out of the sacristy door and seemed to understand, with a glance, that this was the world. This chaos. This rage. He was looking for one person only, and when he found her he helped her stand upright and straightened her black veil and led her into the pew beside her son. He sat with her and she gathered his hands in her hands.

"Lunetto," Russo was saying. "Lunetto."

He held his hands in the air, but it was only himself he was quieting. The catedro had lowered their voices almost without their will.

Leo turned to his mother and let her touch his face.

I'm sorry, he wanted to say. I am.

"My son. My son."

Matteo was pacing on the altar behind his father. His father turned back and held him and whispered to him a long time. Leo turned back to Alexandra, but she was sitting with her head lowered, Beatrice laying a hand on her shoulder. Her mother stood behind her, crossing herself and crossing herself again.

"Lunetto," Russo was saying. "Lunetto."

Matteo stepped down from the altar and stood in front of Leo and stared at him and spat once in his face. He said something Leo did not hear, and then he looked at the woman and said something to her that Leo did hear. Then he marched away through the pews and was gone.

"Lunetto," Russo was saying, "we have suffered. You have suffered. Who has not suffered these many years? And now we come together on a day like this, a day that would have been a feast for our sons come back from the dead, the very dead, and instead this is what we have. This. We have among us one who laid our sons in the grave. My son." He turned and looked at Leo. "My son." He closed his eyes and opened them very slowly. "You. Traditore. I look at you, as I have looked at you, so often, in my sleep, in every place, and I see your face, and I know what that face is. That face. I know my son saw it, too, at the end. And it grinned at him. And it offered him no mercy." He took a handkerchief from his pocket and touched his face. Like someone touching the face of a stranger. "And I told myself, in all my nights, if I saw that face, just once, just for one moment only, there would be no end to the wrath I brought down upon it. No end." He stepped down from the altar and stood in front of Leo. "And I don't trust myself not to bring down that wrath. Not now. Not entirely. Not even here." Someone shouted out, but Russo raised his hand and waited for quiet. He stood there heavily a long while. Then he turned to the woman in the veil. He shook his head and lowered his hand and waited for something to pass through him. "But I look at this woman, and I look at you, traditore, and I see a killer, yes, I see someone who has hid in the bosom of forgiveness too long." He looked at the priest, and then he looked at no one at all. "But I look at you, and I am lost. I am lost."

From the back of the crowd, a woman came hurrying forward, her skirts bunched in her hands. She stepped up on to the altar and threw her arms around Russo, and Leo knew who she was. He knew she was holding her husband tightly, so she would not turn, so she would not look.

"I am lost," Russo said. "Because I want to see that face that has haunted my life these years. And I do see it. I do. As my sons see it. My sons who would slay you with their own hands. My living sons and my lost son the same." He whispered something to his wife, and she shook her head. Again he waited for something to pass him by. As though there were a hand on his shoulder. As though there were some invisible figure whispering him some counsel not even he could understand.

Finally he spoke.

"But I see something else," he said. "Something I cannot abide. I see a boy. I see a boy who has gone wrong in all the ways, a boy who has thought that in making things worse, he might be done with them. But you are not done with them." The woman turned and looked at him, and then she buried her face in her husband's shoulder. Russo touched her hair. "You are not done with them." He closed his eyes and then opened them very slowly. "Traditore. Gemetti." He shook his head. "I don't know if you can make right what you've done, not in this world, and not in any other. But I look at you, and I look at this mother, and I look at my sons"—he glanced at the doors through which Matteo had left him—"my only sons." He breathed. "And I know it is not our work to finish it for you. But I know you cannot do it among us. Not among us. Do you understand?"

Leo nodded.

"Say it. Speak to me."

"I understand."

Russo's wife let out a yelp, and her husband stroked her back as he whispered something to her. She nodded and turned away and sat in a far pew with her other son. Like a world of shadows. Like something the depths of which could never be measured.

"You cannot finish it among us," Russo said.

He stepped forward and leaned down over the rail and gathered the woman toward him and whispered something into her veil. Then he stood upright again and looked at the one before him.

"I cannot protect you from my son. Nor can I keep him from his own idea of justice, not here. Kiss your mother, as my boy cannot do with his." He looked at her again. "Woman, what you do with your life is your business. I give you my word we will not harm you, as we have not done. You did not make this man's life." He turned again. "Stand, man. We walk you out of here. Now."

XVII

His mother had held him a long time before the priest had ushered her away and sat with her in one of the apses, swaying her in the silence of her clothes.

The whole way to the station, he had looked for Alexandra in the crowd, but he told himself even if he saw her he would not speak with her. They do not know, he told himself. Hers is not your story to write. In the dizziness and the heat he'd tried to remember what she'd said about a story written between two lives, and he looked for her once more, but she was not there.

He was still looking for her when they stood with him on the platform, and he was still looking for her when they walked him into the train car, and he was still looking for her when he laid his face on the window, and when the train shook and started away from the station, and he was still looking for her when he closed his eyes and lowered his head and laid his face in the coldness of his empty hands, to smell in them the silk mask that wasn't there.

I

After the catedro she had gone home with her mother and sisters, and they had tried to speak with her, but she'd locked her door and lain awake all day and all evening with the muslin curtains blowing over her body and the swallows flying in and out in the dark. Deep in the night she'd risen and opened the door to her wardrobe and stood a long time before the mirror. Fool, she said. You are going to do something stupid with your life.

She'd sat at the little desk she'd used since she was a child and smoothed the newsprint and written her note in the moonlight. Mama, she'd written. And then she'd told her mother what was in her.

She'd left the note on her bed, weighed down with stones, and then stood looking up at her drawings. Slipping off her shoes she'd carried the chair around the room and climbed onto it and taken down three of the smaller ones and folded them neatly into her bag with the clean newsprint. Then she'd climbed out the window through the cypresses and made her way to the station and curled on a bench and told herself not to think, not yet, not at all. In the morning a conductor had woken her and asked her if she knew where she was. She'd thought it was a strange thing to be asked, but then she heard how she answered.

She did not know where he'd gone, but she guessed what he'd done when he'd taken the same train on the same tracks with the same questions inside him.

When she'd gotten off at Palma he was curled asleep on a bench beside the platform. She'd knelt beside him and touched his shoulder and said his name until he'd woken.

"Don't do this," he said.

"I'm not doing anything. I'm just here."

"What are you going to do? They'll know where you are."

"I told them somewhere else."

"No. Please."

He touched his jaw.

"Let's just walk," she said. "You have no clothes."

"I can't let you do this."

"Is that why you think I'm here, because people let me do things?"

He looked at her cheek that had swollen.

"I'm sorry. I don't know. I don't know anything anymore."

"Stop. You sound like a fool. I'm just here until you get some clothes." She waved toward Palma. "I want to see it, too."

He sat up.

"Let me carry it," he said.

"Stop. Let's walk."

"Where are we going?"

"To find you a bed. Get up."

They made their way down the cliff roads to the sea, and they did not speak. The sea wind soothed her face, and when they reached a grove of palms that opened to a small cove, she told him to let her go ahead, and he sat in the sand and watched her walk out and stand before the first of three tremendous rocks in the water. She looked back over her shoulder, and he rose and walked off to the far side of the cove and did not look back. By a long dock at the northernmost point, before the cliffs, he took off his shoes and rolled up his pants and waded out into the surf. In the distance he saw her step behind the rocks, and he leaned down and scooped the salt water into the cut along his jaw and scrubbed it hard. He had been afraid the bone had broken, but it hadn't. It had swollen and settled and swollen again, and when he walked back up and lay down in the sand, he felt her coming toward him, and when he opened his eyes she was standing over him in the wind, and she shook her head and tapped her own face and said if he was still wearing a mask, she would kill him herself.

He walked alone up the cliff roads to the village and made his way to the *ufficio postale* and picked up the receiver and waited for the exchange. Evening had fallen, and he looked out at the lamplight in the empty streets. He told his mother he wanted her to be at peace. That was all he wanted for her. *Pace.* He asked if she would leave, but she told him she had her home, and his life was his life to make now, and if he had found someone who would go to him with all he had done, with all he had undone, then he did not need an older woman who would do the same. *Verrai a stare con me*, he told her. I'll take care of you. But she told him to call for her only when he'd understood what a home was, when he knew what he had to know, and he hung up the phone and stared out at the lamplight and knew one life had ended, and the most difficult part had only just begun.

II

They'd found an empty villetta that night in the cove, and she'd sat on the sill of its front bay window and watched someone coming up the beach with a lantern. The lantern crossed under the window and climbed the stairs along the south side of the house, and then the back door opened slowly.

They'd talked the owner down to as low as could be done—he'd considered their faces and shown them a few tins of cannellini in the kitchen—and when they were alone again she told him the bed would be for her. They carried it from the rear of the villetta to the southwest corner, where they set it under the curtainless window that looked out to the cove and the sea. They did not speak. On the second night she'd lain in it and watched him where he was curled asleep on the bed of blankets they'd made for him by the long driftwood table. He had not changed his clothes. She rose and went to him and knelt down softly and touched his shoulder.

"Come. You can't sleep here."

He rolled over and rubbed his eyes and looked at her.

"You're sure?"

"We don't know what we're doing anyway."

He'd risen and lain down on the side of the bed where the wind came in from the cove through the window. It was a big, full bed, its linens smelling of the palm groves, and when she'd lain down on the other side, he'd shaken his head and slid himself down to the foot of the bed and stood. He looked out into the shadows of the villetta, and when she asked him where he was going, he walked away and sat at the table facing away from her.

"I can't," he said. "You shouldn't do this. You can still go back."

"You're going to tell me what to do?"

"No. But I'm not going to lie to you. I can't do it."

"You're already doing it."

She'd sat up with her back on the coolness of the wall and drawn her hair forward over her shoulders.

"We don't know what we're doing," he said. "You said it yourself."

"Look at me."

He didn't turn.

"Look at me," she said.

Very slowly he ran his hand across the table, as if to wipe away something that wasn't there, and then he turned and sat sideways in the chair and looked at her.

"You think it's easy for me to just go back?"

"No," he said. "But I can't make it harder for you."

"You don't know—"

"Just let me say this. In Bologna, after everything happened, I couldn't—I can't explain it—I couldn't breathe. I never knew it would be this way, but it is. Some nights it's nothing and some nights it's all there is. I don't know if I can do it." He looked away. "You don't want to live the way I do."

She lowered her head and kneaded the back of her neck, her shoulders, the muscles still tender from the double shifts in the shipworks.

"He tells me what I want and what I don't want," she said.

"Alexandra."

"He tells me what I want and what I don't want."

He stood and made his way across the room and crouched down and laid a hand on the bed.

"I'm not telling you anything."

She did not raise her head. The wind was slipping in through the casements. He closed his eyes and thought to lift his hand from the bed, but he did not.

"We haven't done anything at all," she said. "We're just here. You don't have to stay. But I want to."

"Why?"

She looked up and pushed her hair back and kneaded her temples with her thumbs. He told himself not to look away.

"I can't tell you why."

"Because you won't or because you don't know?"

"Because that's not what we're doing. We're not doing anything that makes any sense at all."

He lifted himself and sat on the bed facing away from her. He could feel the wind on his shoulders from the dark of the sea.

"They'll know where we are," he said. "He'll know."

"I told them Milano. I told them you'd go—"

"—It doesn't matter what you told them. He'll find me. I don't want that for you."

"He won't. His father's spoken."

"What does that matter?"

"With him, everything. And with Carlo. He'll have no home if he does anything."

"*Senza casa.*" He'd said it almost to himself.

She waited for him to speak, but when he said no more, she looked out the window to the sea and heard her own voice come to her.

"We're insane, aren't we?"

"Yes."

"Why?"

"Because we're insane, that's all."

The villetta was quiet. The waves broke softly on the stones of the cove.

"Look at me," she said.

Her eyes were clear when he turned to her.

"It's not a tragedy that I'm here," she said, "is it?"

He shook his head.

"*Va bene,*" she said. "Then let's rest."

He looked at his hands.

"Promise me something," he said.

"What?"

But he only shook his head slowly, as though he'd forgotten what he would ask her.

"Listen," she said. "I promise."

III

The village was not far from the cove, and they woke early in the morning in their tired clothes and started out by foot along the roads. She'd woken before him and rolled to her side and looked at his face in his sleep, his high cheekbones and his heavy lips and the cut in his jaw from Lunetto. The swelling had gone from both their faces in the sea air, and she'd lain on the other side of the broad bed and closed her eyes and run her thumb softly on the linens, sketching the lines of his face until he stirred. They could smell the *pane di pescatore* carried down to the harbor from the village, and when he'd turned to her he'd let himself look at her a brief while before he knew he'd woken. She'd sat back against the window and watched him blink the light from his eyes, and they'd looked at each other a moment before she'd turned away.

"Come on," she'd said, "we need to eat."

They climbed up the winding roads of the cliffs, passing the caves and the ruined stone places that had been the homes of people deep in the Bronze Age and long before. They passed the ruins that had been destroyed by the Byzantines, and they passed the old stones of houses that had been spared in the great earthquakes before the war, and when she turned to him and said something about what can be built up again, he thought he could feel the Basilica again in Bologna, the swallows flying up there in the dark.

The wind followed them from the sea, cooling them all morning along the open roads, and when they reached the village he looked for faces from Lunetto, but he told himself they were far enough, *abbastanza lontano,* that no one came up to such a place without the hotel, that Palma was just one more place in which to have no name at all.

He told himself she was right, that Lunetto had spoken, and when the wind whipped his face he told himself that it had been a long war, that Italia wanted to forget, that the faces in this place seemed to say the same blank thing to all their passing ghosts: no, we cannot see you; we do not want to know.

She sat on the beach when they'd returned, looking out at the rocks and running her fingers through the sand, making and unmaking the rocks, the waves, and when he went to her she asked him to tell her when he'd been there, when he'd swum there when he was a boy, with his brothers, but he only told her it was not a story that mattered. She walked out to touch the three rocks her mother had dreamt of, and he followed her and asked her to tell him, and she did. He asked her if she wanted to go back, and she told him if he ever accused her again of not choosing her own life, she would choose differently.

When he'd gone off to the villetta, she lay alone on the beach, listening to the waves. This is what you wanted, isn't it? To see this place again? To have something other than Lunetto? *Va bene*, what do you have now? You have the blankness of those pages and all of Palma and then you can go anywhere you want. You can make anything you want. You were going to leave it anyway, and so maybe he just helped you do that. Maybe that's why anyone comes into anyone's life at all. To help them out. To help them in.

She closed her eyes and listened to the water sifting into the tidepools through the stones. Then it sifted back out again. You can come and go. You can come and go any time you want. You always wanted to be somewhere else, didn't you? Now you're there. Aren't you? Think of what he said. You were born a long way from home. Both of you. Maybe you can just stay for a little while. Separately. Both of you here but separate. Right? Yes. Just to help each other in. To help each other out. And then you can go. Then you can go back home.

IV

In the morning they walked the roads and found the Tempio di San Fantino il Giovane, who had spent his days a thousand years earlier eating nothing but bread and honey and kneeling in his wild visions of heaven and hell. His remains lay in the stone walls, and they were the oldest of any Saint in Calabria, and she stood before it and told him how Fantino had received a vision telling him to go to Thessalonica, where he gave the blind sight and blinded those who thought they could see. She crossed herself, although she did not believe, and said sometimes we are called to places we do not understand, and he nodded and said here was someone who had lived on both sides of the war he'd fought when he was a boy, and that maybe both countries are in us, somewhere, whatever they are.

She'd brought the money she'd saved from the shipworks, and he'd still had the last of his leave pay stuffed into his pocket when they'd put him on the train in Lunetto, and they bought new clothes at the market in Palma, where the merchants came down from Taurianova with their wool and their linens, their silks spun from the *bachi da seta* that fed on the mulberry groves high up in the mountains. They bought 'nduja and fresh bread and the catches the fishermen had brought up along the same roads that morning: turbot, anchovies, sardella. They bought bottles of grappa and verbicaro bianco, and they bought tropea onions and *clementine* and sott'olio, and when they told themselves they were spending what they couldn't spend, anyway, they bought the black liquorice they both discovered they must have loved once, with its taste of the sea and the troubled intensity of a bitterness they could not name.

The villetta had been built before the Great War, but its lender owned the ships that set out from Palma and the coastal towns, and he had run it with electric power and filled it with driftwood furniture and rebuilt the weathered planks of the stairs that ran up along its side and that were soon to be weathered again by the salt air from the west winds of the sea. It smelled of the dark pine of its rafters and the clear water that came down from the wells of the village, down through the volcanic rock, through the granite, down through the cliffs where the ancient Roman fistulae had been and up into the tin sink by the back and only door, where they scrubbed and cut the onions and rinsed the fish and laid out the liquorice to dry and warm on the kitchen sills.

She hung muslin for curtains, and she gathered bougainvillea from the shoulders of the cliff roads and potted them along the wooden stairs into the palm groves, saving the largest for the villetta itself, where she carried it from corner to corner until she settled it by the small desk that looked out the smallest front window to the sea.

In the first week she lay awake after he'd fallen asleep and looked at her hands, her fingernails she'd scraped of charcoal, of soil, of dust. On the seventh night she slid from bed and found the drawings in her bag and took them out and looked at them. They were three figures of the same ship, the one she'd helped raise in the spring in Lunetto, and she lifted them and felt a hollowness in her she told herself would pass. What are you going to make, she thought. What now? She laid her hand on one of the drawings and asked herself again. While she was riveting the ribs on the scaffolding she'd looked down and told herself to remember every detail, every rivet, every sound the voices made as they clanged off the iron and filled the shipworks with a strange singing. She had never been able to explain it, but somehow even the voices were a part of the drawing, a part of anything you made. If you could hear the voices, all you had to do was listen to them, and the drawing would be there.

She sat at the big, driftwood table and laid the drawings aside and took out a clean sheet of newsprint and looked out the window into the dark. Then she breathed. As she had done in any room, in any place she'd ever been, she closed her eyes and tried to see each thing, each shape, each shadow she had dipped a finger into as she'd made her way among them alone; when she couldn't see something, something she knew was there, she opened her eyes and made her way to it and touched it again, until she felt it was in her hands. Then she sat at the table and tried to bring it all to mind: the wine-dark frame of the back door; the door itself, scored and weathered by the sea air; the white frames of the big windows at the front of the house, freshly painted, it seemed, with those two small moths barely visible in the brushstrokes—olive moths, no doubt, which must have come south in the wind and fed on the jasmine that could still be smelled in the walls. She kept her eyes closed and saw the white-papered walls of the kitchen, the olive-green cabinets that hung on either side of the tin sink, the little fisherman's tin that they'd learned, when they'd brought the fish back from the market, was no icebox at all. She saw the dark-papered hall, with its faded places where other faces must have been, and she saw the chestnut soffit open up to the moonlit splash of the front room, the only room, with its dark rafters and sun-bleached floor; its great bay window and broad, bench sill; its driftwood table and standing lamps and heavy bed under the southwest window. She saw the spareness of the room—nothing else but the little desk, in which someone had begun to carve a name; a half-mended net hanging on the northern wall; a two-doored armoire standing dignified behind the table—and she saw the little hymnal someone had left inside the armoire's only drawer, next to a single copper button and a faded railway ticket and nothing else at all.

She opened her eyes and ran her hand across the page, but when she thought of something rising from its depths, she could see nothing. She could hear the sea laying itself down on the stones of the cove, and she closed her eyes and thought of her mother's dream, of what her father had said in it, of her father's voice in the dark. Just hear the voices, she thought. Just hear them. She opened her eyes and looked at him asleep on the bed, curled there like a child in the place where her warmth had been. You know what this man has done, she thought. Then she thought, Don't call him this man. You are here, aren't you? And what did they do to him? The Balilla. The others. The same ones who were there in Lunetto, carrying him. Carrying this man. No. Don't call him that. You are here, aren't you? Yes, you are here. And you can leave any time you want.

Then she thought, see, you are just like him. You can lie to yourself any time you want.

Sometimes she'd find him lying awake in the morning, and she'd know he was thinking about his dreams. Sometimes he told her. There were just shoes in a room, he would tell her. Or there was just an empty train.

They would rise and walk together up the cliff roads, and she would tell him to say more. The shoes had names in them, he would tell her. Or there was a figure on a train carrying something I couldn't see.

When they'd counted out the money on the driftwood table, she'd shaken her head and walked out to the beach, and he followed her and sat down beside her in the sand.

"I worry about my mother," she said. "My sisters."

Though she'd told them she was elsewhere, and they could not write to her, she told herself she would write to them soon. She would leave the envelope blank except for the address in Lunetto and a little sketch of three forms—they could be tall rocks, they could be burning ships—and she'd stay the hand of the clerks at the *ufficio postale* when they were sure to lift their pads and their stamps and their inquiring eyes.

"But they have Angelo," she said. "And Carlo."

"Still?"

"Yes."

She was picking through the stones between her feet, and she tossed the smaller ones back into the waves and slipped the larger, smoother ones into her pockets.

"What are we going to do?"

"We could get work on the boats," he said. "They need hands always."

"No," she said. "These men here don't take women on their boats. They don't understand." She shook her head. "No."

"What don't they understand?"

She was quiet a long while.

"I don't mean that. My father did their work. It's honest work, and they understand plenty. How can I say anything against them?"

"You're not."

"No," she said, "I'm not."

He felt a silence had entered her when she'd spoken of her father.

"Tell me," he said.

She looked at him and said she knew he knew. Then she spoke of her father. How he had woken in his last nights and told them about his days in the Strait, hauling up the nets. She told him her father would have understood him. And he her father. That her father had had his own wars.

He looked down and sat sifting the stones.

When her father was old, she said, he'd felt the chaos of the world breaking in upon him, and his only answer was a thirst for order. A wild thirst. He was not unlike a boy standing on a crate in a town square, shouting down what he took to be the chaos of the world.

"I never blamed him for it," she said, "but then one night I did. I can't have back what I said to him. And I won't say it again."

"You don't have to."

She smoothed the sand in front of her.

"He was just asking me to listen," she said.

"And maybe you did."

She searched his eyes.

"How?"

"Maybe he said everything he had to."

She shook her head, smoothed the sand between her feet.

"We don't get to be foolish forever," she said, "do we?"

The sun was setting between the rocks, and it seemed to her, as it always did, like ships burning far out to sea. She closed her eyes and listened for the whisper of burning oars thrown down into the water.

"I do miss them," she said.

"I know."

"You must miss it, too."

"Lunetto?"

She turned to him.

"Lunetto."

He pressed his palm into the sand and lifted it, then wiped away the shape his hand had made.

"I didn't know if I'd ever go back, after everything happened."

"But your mother—"

"*Sì*. And then when I was there, just waiting in that house, something came over me. I can't explain it. I had to leave that house. I had to."

"And you regret that?"

He looked at her.

"We're here now," he said. "Let's just be here."

A gust came up from the west and rose up along the southern cliffs of the cove and crashed down behind them, shivering the shadows from the palm groves.

"Tell me about being here with your brothers," she said. "When the hotel was here."

He shook his head.

"It wasn't much of a hotel," he said. "Just a place for a poor woman and her boys to swim, to be in another world. We were here an hour, just an hour, and she turned us right around and we took the last train back. It made no sense at all."

"She doesn't like to leave, does she?"

He looked at her.

"No."

His voice had wavered, but he looked down and lifted a handful of sand and let it slip through his fingers.

"How much do we have left?"

"*Diciottomilia*," she said.

"That means two a day and we can make it to October. Maybe we could talk Bonanno down on the villetta."

"Maybe you could."

He grinned.

"Let's leave it as it is," he said. "He rents it cheap because he knows we're in trouble."

"We are in trouble, aren't we?"

"No. Not any more than anyone else."

"You really believe that?"

"I don't know what I believe anymore."

"Yes, you do."

He looked at her.

"They won't come?"

"No. Not Matteo. Not when his father's spoken. And Carlo. Carlo will help us. I know it. We just—we just can't go back yet. Not yet."

"We could go anywhere. Puglia. Roma."

"I can't—"

"What?"

"I can't leave, not yet."

He shook his head and looked at the sand.

"And what about money?"

"I don't know."

"What about your drawings?"

"What about them?"

"I don't know. Maybe we could trade for them."

"We?"

"I'm sorry."

"Say it."

"It's just that maybe people like this could use something like that in their lives. If they're anything like me."

She looked at him.

"Let's talk about that later," she said. "Please."

"I don't understand."

The water took one of the stones soundlessly where she'd tossed it. She'd not turned toward him, and she thought to tell him how it was with her drawings, how they were something she'd look at, time and again, so she did not have to look at her life, into its windows, into its rooms, that there are rooms in the shadowy house of any life no one needs to look into, but she knew if she said it aloud it would mean nothing. She was here because she had looked.

"Please," she said, "later."

They were quiet awhile. Mastic and oleander grew in the cliffs behind them, and the scents sifted down on the wind. She raised her hands vaguely into the breeze.

"Two a day."

"Two hundred."

"I know."

"We could do that. We don't need wine."

She knew they had bread and vegetables, and they could buy the scrapfish or the little bait-squid in the market each day at one hundred fifty lire a pound, and they would keep them for a day at a time in the kitchen tin, and they would be fine. Fine. She looked out at the waves and thought of her father so young and poor out on the Strait of Messina, looking down into the depths, his hands in his pockets, wondering what would be the shape of his life.

"Leonardo."

"Yes?"

"Nothing," she said. "I just wanted to say it."

He shook his head.

"*Diciottomilia*," he said. "Two hundred a day. We could do that."

She looked out at the sea and ran her hand through the sand and tossed a stone into the waves.

"Yes," she said. "We can."

V

He woke in the night and saw her sleeping. When he lay back and looked up into the rafters, he told himself not to think of it, but he heard his mother speaking of his father. No, it couldn't be. It can't. But yes, it is. This is the world.

He closed his eyes and saw his father walking alone through an Alsatian night. You were alone, weren't you, father? What should I call you? Papa? Father? Léonard, I should call you. No, I should not call you anything. Stay where you are. I should not call you. I will not call you at all.

He tried to remember what his mother had said in Lunetto, the words exactly. Not to tell something is the same as a lie. Not to tell yourself. But he only lay awake and listened to her breathing beside him. What did you do with it, father? Where did you set it down? You didn't, did you? You didn't set it down. You found that other way. Well I'm not going to do it that way. I'm not going anywhere. Now I have it and it's mine to carry. You didn't want to give it to us but you did. Mama's right. You did. You thought you were taking it away but you weren't done with it and so it never went away at all. She's right. It lives in us until someone is done with it. Until someone sets it down. Well I won't do it that way. I won't.

He looked into the shadows of the villetta, the wind rattling the weathered wood of the back door. I shouldn't call you here, should I? But you're here, aren't you? It's not true what she said, is it? That you were never there. You were. You are, damn you. You are.

He looked at her lying beside him. What did she say in Lunetto? Not mama. Alexandra. Alexandra. Jesus Christ she's beautiful. Why don't you tell her that? Because. Because she doesn't need to hear it. She knows. That's why you're here, aren't you? No, it's not. You can pretend it is but it's not. It's more than that and you're in it deep now and even if you wanted to go you couldn't, could you? No. What did she say? There's only one hell and it's for those who believe they haven't made their lives. Yes. I won't do it. I won't say anyone did it. Anyone but me. No one else at all.

He stood and walked to the back door and laid his hand against it. Then he turned back and saw her asleep in the moonlight. What did she say? In Lunetto. Even when we take ourselves away, we are the silences in someone else's story. Yes. How did she know that? How does she know? You know how she knows. You know damn well how she knows. Well now you have to live it and you're not going anywhere. No, you're not. This is exactly what you want and that's why it's hard. Everyone knows that. Even you. No. You're not doing what he did. You're not going to take the easy way. You're not going to give it to anyone else. You're not going to pretend to set it down.

VI

In the last half-moon of July they lay on opposite sides of the big double bed in front of the open windows looking out at the water. She'd tried to draw the pigeons scattering from the belltower in Lunetto, but she'd crumpled the paper and taken it down to the water and torn it in pieces into the waves, the waves that always gave things back to her. When she came back to the villetta she told him she was sorry she hadn't looked at him in the catedro, that she was sorry she hadn't gone with him to the station, and he told her he understood.

"No," she said, "You don't understand. But neither do I."

"When are we going to start understanding?"

She smiled. He'd slid to the side of the bed from which she'd risen, and she sat on the linens and then lowered her head to the pillow and tapped his forehead.

"Right now."

"Really?"

"Sure."

"And how are we going to do that?"

"Shut up," she smiled.

"She says such beautiful things. My God such beautiful things."

She looked at his eyes, the honey flashing in her cellar in Lunetto.

"Idiota. Just kiss me."

They woke in the night and walked to the south end of the cove, where the cliffs rose up into the moon through the fog. A figure was casting his line in the surf, and he turned toward them and lifted a hand strangely and then went right on casting.

"Come," she said.

They walked up the cliff roads in the moonlight, and they sat high above the sea and listened to the fisherman singing in the surf.

"What is it?"

"I don't know," he said. "It's French."

She turned to him.

"Like your father."

He worked a pebble from the rockface and tossed it out into the moonlight. They could not hear it strike the sand below.

"Please," he said, "let's leave him alone." He looked at her quickly and then looked away. "I'm just thinking about my mother. I want her to be happy."

"I know, Nardo. We don't have to stay here forever."

"He's not going to just forget. Matteo."

"We don't know. We don't know what time will do."

He listened to the song lose itself and find itself again in the waves.

"*Dimmi,*" she said again. "Tell me."

"She had a favorite song. Enzo was always giving her things for Natale—he was always finding money—and one year it was a gramophone. Where did he get the money for that? We'd just sit by it and listen to that song to no end."

"What was it?"

"Madame Arthur. She would listen to it again and again—it was Guilbert, Yvette Guilbert—and I'd just sit there with her while Nico and Paolo laughed. But for me it was another world. I'd love to hear that song again, just once. It's ridiculous, I know."

"Why did your brothers laugh?"

"Nico. He was the joker. He would sing along with that record and act it all out like a *cabaretista,* with one of my mother's scarves over his head. She tried not to laugh. All those years I didn't have any idea why she was so moved by that song, that silly French song. Or why I was."

"Nico sounds beautiful."

"He was." He closed his eyes and thought of his brother, Nicola Pierre, who had such clear eyes and seemed to understand the great joke of the world.

"Is it a joke?"

"Maybe," he said.

"*Dimmi.*"

He lay back on the cool stones and listened until the singing faded, the waves crashing softly on the cove below. Then he told her how it had been, a long time ago. How his brother had taught him how to roll his tongue into a circle and hold it out as far as he could, then balance a cube of ice on the tip, as long as he could, until it melted, as though everything depended on it. As though everything depended on it in the world.

Then he was very quiet. He told her he had thought of Nico when he was up in the mountains, how he'd thought of him when he'd held a boy in his arms for so long in the cold, and he told her he'd looked out at the guns flashing in the distance and then down at the boy's eyes and he'd been ashamed.

"Of what?"

"Of thinking it was beautiful."

She leaned over him and laid her lips on his forehead and curled against him as the fog rose up from the breakers.

"That, too," she said. "You can remember that, too."

Sometimes she would wake in the night while he was still sleeping, and she would wake him gently, as gently as she could. She had asked him, in the first week, if perhaps the papers had reached these people, too, if perhaps they would know his face, but he had only looked out into the dark and said no, no one remembers anything if they don't have to. Then she told him she had dreamt of the boy on the peach crate in Lunetto, saying the things he had said.

"Tell me about that boy," she said.

He looked at her a long time, his eyes fresh from sleep, and told her he couldn't remember him. Then he closed his eyes and told her no, that was a lie; he could remember him very well. The hardest part was that he could remember him.

"Do you believe in what he said?"

"I believe he did," he whispered. "And wherever he is now, he might still believe it."

"But he's not here now, is he?"

"No."

"And he's not coming back to us?"

"No."

Sometimes she would wake in the night and not wake him. She would leave a note for him and walk down to the stones of the beach and think about what he'd said about the boy in the snow. He'll tell you when he wants to, she thought. When he's able. If you're able—if you're able to want to know.

When the nights were clear, she would sit looking out at the three rocks in the surf. You can remember that, too, she told herself. The rocks and your mother's dreams and your sisters. The worn, sad hands of your father. But she knew she wasn't remembering anything at all. That we make the world afresh in each remembering, and if even the great myths are alive in us, they are only alive because they change. She looked at the sea and the moon, and she thought about her mother's dream of the burning ships, and she thought about the moon sliding up to the beach like the burning ruins of the ships, the broken oars, and she knew we do not put down our sorrows but only carry them a long time until they are changed. We use them, she thought. And although she thought she would feel cold and alone when she thought it, she did not. She felt her father's hand on her shoulder, smelling of fresh bread and deep nets from the sea, and she thought of her mother lying in her bed in Lunetto, of Clara straightening the house. She thought of Bea rising to tend the garden, and she thought of her own heart rising in the darkness, like a wild thing, a broken thing, a common horse swaying for the daily yoke and the good, brief weight of the world.

That, too, she thought. You can use that, too.

VII

By the middle of September the money had gone. She took work mending the nets at the fishing shacks on the North end of the cove, and he went out from the harbor by morning and came back in the evenings, smelling of squid and baitfish and the open winds far out in the Tyrrhenian Sea. "You come back to me," he'd told her, on the first morning, and when she told him it was not she who was leaving, he smiled at her and turned toward the ship and raised a hand and called back, *maybe, maybe so.*

On the third day he was away, she woke in the morning and hurried to the bathroom and held her stomach a long time. Twice now she had not bled, but she'd told herself it was only that they were not eating as they should, and her body had never known what to do with her, or her with it. But when she sat back against the cool steel of the washtub, she knew she had taken herself far out into the depths, where no one could help her. This is your life, she thought. Just wait. Don't tell him until you have to. Get up and work.

She took herself down to the beach and stood looking out at a storm roiling far out to sea. She could see the gray clouds billowing up from the horizon, and she felt the sea at her feet, swaying with something far inside it that it could not tell of, and she shook her head and said, no. No.

She went alone to Bonanno, who lived in a cascina on the South side of the cove, where he managed his ships and his villetta, and she told him she was going out the next day on the Graciela, the same as her husband. He asked when they had been married, and she said they didn't need to be, because the sea is for everyone, the same as the dead and the world. He leaned back in his chair and looked at her, his eyes asking if she was *pazza*, crazy, and when he tried to sign her on for lower wages, she shook her head and said he was a disgrace to his country and his family and himself. He raised his hands and then opened his book and signed her on for the full wage, and he said if she wanted to drown in the autumn storms, it was her life to drown.

They worked together on the ten-meter boat that left each morning from the harbor north of the cove, and the others on the ship, and especially the captain, listened to her with deep attention when she told them how the great ships were welded and riveted and rigged out and launched into the sea. The smell of the baitfish turned her stomach, and when she was sick some mornings she told him not to follow her to the back of the boat, and when she came back she told him it was only the wind and the waves; she had never had a stomach for the sea.

They trolled for the little silver fish called *hake* that lived far out in the depths of over four hundred fathoms, and they used a broad net, twice as wide as the boat, its mouth held open by ten-meter staves of cypress wood and fastened of ropes made of the palm fronds that an Empire had brought back from its conquests, and from which Palma had taken its name.

She was happiest when she was working, as she'd been in the shipworks of Lunetto, and she told herself not to think of home as she stood on the port side of the ship and leaned back into the ropes that ran over one half of the pulleys and hauled up the net from countless fathoms down.

This is your home, she told herself. Deep down in the coldest depths, it is there.

The first day they'd gone out together, they'd looked at each other on either side of the net as they'd hauled it up with the others, overhanding the ropes and coiling them slowly on their shoulders, and she had mouthed to him for the first time *ti amo. Ti amo,* he mouthed back. Then she said that she could not believe her life. Her cotton collar had blown up over her mouth, and the wind had taken her voice away, and she knew he had not understood. But she thought that probably it was best that way, and sometimes the wind does what it has to do, because she did believe it. She could believe her life.

That first evening they'd come back, tired as children, and lain on the beach of the cove, looking up at the half moon. He'd fallen asleep and seen a boy in the snows of Klisura, but at the moment the boy had turned to him, she'd said his name and he'd woken.

They lay together listening to the sea that had carried them. She told him it was like when you were a child and you'd swum in the waves all day as they tossed you, and when you lay in bed at night, even afterward, you could feel the waves still swaying you, and when you fell asleep, it was as though you were the waves themselves.

"What do you think of when you look at it?"

"At what?"

"The moon," he said.

"I think of the times I've looked at the moon."

He felt himself smile.

"What else?"

"That's plenty," she said. "I think of the times I've looked at it."

"Tell me one time."

She knitted her fingers behind her head and arched her back in the sand. They were wearing grey knit sweaters they'd bought in the village, in late August, when they'd known the winds would grow cold. She could smell the kelp in the sand as she hadn't before, but it was sweet and clean and it did not turn her stomach as she'd feared it would.

"I remember we were here," she said, "me and Clara and Mama and Papa. We hadn't cut my hair since I was born, and I wore it down to my waist. Almost. When I waded out into the water, it floated out around me, and I remember being scared by that, but I can't say why."

He hummed.

"When it was dry," she said, "you could still feel the soft ends of it, and I thought about how that could have been my first hair I'd had even inside my mother's body. And I'd lie awake some nights holding it to my face in the dark. I remember we were here in the moonlight when he cut it."

"Did you ask him to?"

"Yes," she said. "But who knows what we ask for? I cried all night like a *bambina*."

"You were."

"I know. Clara told me."

"Clara," he said.

She sat up and wrapped her arms around her knees, knitted her fingers and looked out over the water.

"She'll be all right."

"Yes," he said. "She will."

They were quiet a long while. They could hear music up in the town above, old songs blowing down to them on the wind.

"I used to help her wash the smoke from her clothes, so mama wouldn't know."

"And yours."

"No. I didn't need that then, and I don't need it now."

He hummed.

"*Può essere*. I guess there are a lot of things we find out we can do without."

"Not forever, Nardo. We might need help sometimes."

"Why?"

She shook her head.

"We just might."

She turned to him and then looked away.

"Say it," he said.

"No."

"Say it."

Her hands smoothed the sand in front of her.

"I still don't believe you," she said.

"What?"

"That you never saw me. That you never sat with those boys on the docks and watched us walk home."

He looked at her.

"Of course," he said.

She squinted at him and smiled.

"*Diavolo.*"

"I wasn't sure it was still you. But then I was sure."

"When? When were you sure?"

"In your room, when you told me about your drawings."

"I didn't tell you anything."

"I know. That's when I knew."

She picked up a stone and threw it at him softly. He lifted it from the sand and slipped it in his breast pocket and smoothed his hand over it.

"Why didn't you ever go out with the others? You missed all the *feste* down by the harbor. Even Enzo went to those."

"I was working," she said.

"Not all the time?"

"Close enough. I was fourteen when Papa—when everything happened, and then there was no other way. If I wasn't working—" she looked at him quickly and then looked down at the sand—"I was working."

He shook his head.

"Why don't you draw anymore?"

"I do, sometimes."

"I wish I could do that, anything like that. I don't think anyone in my family even picked up a book ever."

"That can't be true."

"Listen. They were smart, all of them. My mother is. But they were—I don't know how to say it—practical people. Enzo would have been your manager at the shipworks, for all I know, if he'd come back. He was that way."

"Better than Piccolo."

He watched her shoulders rise and fall slowly.

"Do you miss it?"

"It's hard to say," she said. "It's like I told you in Lunetto. I miss something about it, but I just need to find a different shape for it. It's hard to explain."

"A different shape," he said.

She plucked a stone and rolled it in her palm and slipped it into her pocket.

"What time do you think it is?"

A last blaze still smoldered on the horizon, and he saw a valley in flames on the far side of a mountain, horses pulling that fire up into the snow. He shook it away and lay back again.

"I don't know," he said. "Maybe eight, eight thirty?"

"Two fools, and not a watch between them."

The breeze came softly from the palm groves, and he thought of his father's watch he'd found in Lunetto as a boy, its glass face cracked, its minute hand slowing in the snow and the winds of Klisura Pass.

"It's good not to know," he said. "Maybe we can just stay like this for a while."

"I had a dream Clara came to get me."

He lifted his head.

"Would she?"

"No. Never. Even if she knew where. She's too proud." She swiped at the sand between her feet and drew two lines in it with her fingers. "Tell me more about your brothers."

He sat up and pressed his heels into the sand.

"They were *molto pratico*. Nico, with his little tricks, though. I keep thinking of the things he would have done with his life. And Paolo. It's like they'd barely started to be anything at all. They were boys and then they were gone."

"I'm sorry, Nardo." She touched his cuff and looked at him. Then she looked down into the sand and sketched something slowly. "Nardo?"

"*Sì?*"

"I saw you, too."

"What?"

She looked at him.

"More than once. You were there on the docks more than once. And I saw you."

"Why didn't you tell me?"

"Because I didn't know what I'd seen."

He shook his head, and she reached into his pocket and tossed the stone into one of the tidepools and watched the ripples undo the moon.

"We can't stay here forever," she said, "can we?"

"Why not?"

"You know why." She was dragging her fingers through the sand again. Very slowly she looked at him. "But we could stay awhile. You could make anything you want."

"Who said I wanted to make anything?"

She looked down. "I don't know. Let's just stay awhile."

"To draw it?"

She nodded.

"I still don't understand," he said. "No one taught you."

The wind lifted her hair, and she laid her palm flat on the sand and brushed away what she had sketched in it.

"My father taught me. He would get on these little obsessions. Who knows where they came from, but he'd just hear about something and come home thrilled about it and want to show us all. Even now I don't know where he learned about making something like that—a man like my father, making charcoal—but he was like a child when he figured it out. He cut these pieces of grape vine and brought them home and burned them in a tin can until they blackened, and then he just gathered us all around and drew a big circle on the kitchen table and looked at us with this incredible smile. Then he handed us pieces and we all started drawing. My mother came in and it was like we'd burned down the house."

He hummed again. He told himself, as he had told himself many times, not to think of his father. He told himself not to hear his mother's voice. Not to hear what she had told him in the catedro.

"And then he taught you?"

"No. He was done with it the next day. That's the way it was with him. I don't know, I think sometimes it was that he'd find these things that would open up his whole world—open it up like that circle was open, like some tremendous—some window into another world, and then he'd just stare down into them and have to go back to his life the next day. And then what? He'd have to close it up again, that window."

"I can understand that."

"I know you can. I don't want that to happen to us, Nardo. I don't want to have to close up anything in me just so I can live my life."

He touched her ankle and waited for her to turn to him.

"We're not going to."

When he lifted his hand to her face, she laid her hand in his hand and lowered it into the sand and the stones and told her she had something to tell him.

He tucked his hands under his armpits and searched her eyes as she spoke. She told him what the soldiers had done to her in Lunetto, and she said it slowly, and coldly, as though it were something that had happened not to her but to a stranger whose name she had forgotten. Then she told it again as though she were that stranger. She asked if she could go on, and he said of course, he was there.

"I know," she said. "We're here."

She told him she had seen their faces, but she had not seen the face of the one who had grabbed her and carried her and held her against the stones. She said she woke sometimes in the night, even now, and lay beside him listening to him breathe, and she wondered if that man had been him. She asked him if he understood.

"Yes," he said. "I understand."

She said she knew it was impossible that it had been him, that *pazzo britannico,* but that didn't matter. It was a thought she had had, and once you have a thought, you either think it fully or it becomes your life. He said he understood that, too.

"I know," she said. "I thought I would hate every man, but I don't. I've thought about it a long time, and I've thought of how to say it to you. To myself. I have to know what you are capable of. Truly know it. And if I've stayed without knowing it, then I can't stay at all."

He told her of course he would never do such a thing, *mai in questo mondo,* but she only shook her head and said again it doesn't matter. We have these things in us, and we will have them until the end of the world.

He bit his lip, and she knew she had never seen him in real anger. Let's see what it does with him, she thought. Let's see what it does.

He told her he could kill a man who did that to her, and he knew she was going to ask it.

"Why don't you talk to me?"

He shook his head and looked down. Then he looked at her again. She had not turned away.

"Maybe I haven't changed," he said.

"Only say what you believe."

"Maybe I haven't changed."

He stood and walked to the edge of the water, and he held his hands on his hips and shook his head. He did not want to look at the moon, and though he stood for a long while, he felt only an old rage that had always emptied his mind, and he could not get straight what he was thinking about the half moon and its light and its shadow, about his mother's words in the catedro, about what the barber had said in Bologna about the Colosseo so long ago. *Pensi,* he thought. Remember. But when he turned back to her, she was gone.

He took the path up through the palm trees to the villetta, and he climbed the wooden stairs and went in through the back door and found her sitting on the sill of the window that looked out to the sea.

"I'm sorry," he said.

"I just wanted to tell you," she said. "Just let me tell you."

He sat with her on the sill, and he told himself not to look away. She told him he did not have to talk to her about it, not now, but she knew there were things they could not do until they'd spoken of it all. Even if they did them now, they did not do them. She asked him if he understood.

"*Sì.*"

"I know you do. I don't want it to be this way. But this is how it is."

The wind rattled the window, and she lifted a finger and drew something on the glass, something they could not see.

"I'm sorry," he said. "I don't know how to talk about these things."

"They're not these things, Nardo."

He nodded and laid his hand on her shoulder, and she pressed her head against the glass as the wind shifted the villetta.

"I hate it, Alexandra. I hate what people do to each other."

She hummed.

"You can tell me any time," he said. "I'm here."

"I know," she said. "But let's just breathe."

"You're sure?"

"Sì," she said. "Not now. Please."

Her fingers drummed against the glass, and she pushed herself back and sat looking out at the darkness of the cove.

"Maybe you should work on your pictures tonight," he said. "I could go help Ricci with the lines."

"Let's eat well tonight. We need to. He has Aldo to help him."

"Aldo."

She shook her head and breathed deeply.

"If I ever have a boy," she said, "I'd want a boy like that. He knows what work is."

"Yesterday he almost went down with the whole rig when no one was looking. He snagged his ankle and went right up with the line and swung there like a *tonno*. If I'd done a better job unknotting the lines, he would have been thrown over."

"*Cristo*. Who got him down?"

"You know who."

"The *vecchio*."

He nodded.

"Thank god you don't know what you're doing."

She was sketching something on the glass again, but he could not follow it.

"Sì," he said, "Thank god."

"You know you're a fool, right?"

"I do."

"As long as you know."

"Come, you should eat. We have plenty."

She reached over and touched his wrist.

"*Aspetta,*" she said. "I'm not done telling you."

When she'd finished sketching something silently on the glass, he'd thought to guess what it was, but he did not. He only waited for her to turn to him and tell him. They'd cut her hair on this beach, she said, when she was a child. Right here. She hadn't cut it since what had happened in Lunetto. She turned to him and asked him if that was something he could understand, and when he'd said no, he wouldn't pretend to, she asked them if they could do it together, with their own hands.

"*Sì,*" he said, "if you want to."

She turned and looked out over the sea and closed her eyes and opened them slowly.

"I don't know," she said. "How do you ever know?"

VIII

They cut her hair on the beach in the moonlight, where they knew the wind would come up and blow the clippings away in the morning. They had brought no mirror, and she took it up, one handful at a time, and cut it to her shoulders. She held up the scissor in the moonlight, and he stood behind her and cut the back even with the line she had made, and she ran her hands through it and messed it and told him to look at her.

"*Più bella.*"

"*Di cosa?*"

"*Più bella del mare.*"

She held up the scissors.

"And yours?"

"Should I?"

She shook her head.

"No," she said. "I like it. *Per favore.* A little longer."

They stood and brushed the sand and the stones from their knees and watched the wind begin to shift the clippings toward the water.

"Come," she said.

They walked to the South side of the cove, where Bonanno's dock ran out into the shallows, its weathered pilings lashed together with hemp and salvaged cables, and when they saw him sitting on the end of it they turned back and made, as they had begun to make, a joke between them without words. Something about power, about the owners of the world. About themselves. The wind was slipping down the cliffs into the cove, and when they'd walked back to the place where they'd knelt in the sand and the stones to cut her hair, the clippings were gone.

"So soon," she said.

"Like everything."

"Come."

They sat together in the old, volcanic stones between the tidepools of the cove, and she was speaking of her father.

"I think it can happen when we get old," she said. "We can feel the chaos of the world breaking in on us, and then we just start to feel there's no other way. We just sit there looking at the water, like a Bonanno."

"Your father was no Bonanno."

"No, and he wasn't *fascista*, either. Not in his heart, but he was afraid. I think of him out there on the water, looking down into all that darkness, and he didn't know any other way. He had to give it shape. I can't explain it. I don't think he could, either. But it was like the wolves were at the gates of his life, and he wasn't going to let them in. He wasn't going to let them get the feast they didn't earn." She shook her head. "How could anyone tell him what the wolves were? But I didn't have to tell him, and I didn't have to understand. And even when I marched out with the workers, when they'd lowered us to *tremila* a week, I went up to his grave and asked him what to do. As though he'd be on my side. I never understood it. He was a worker himself. Why wouldn't he be on our side? But then I think I've never been old. And I've never been in the Alpini, watching my friends die."

"That doesn't change everyone in the same way."

"No, it doesn't, does it?"

Her eyes found his, and he knew she was going to ask about his father.

"*Per favore*," he said.

She plucked at the stones between her feet, and he told himself no. He told himself not to enter a dark house in some Alsatian night, not to look at it, and then he told himself there was no house to enter.

"Did he like Panunzio?" he asked.

She closed her eyes and thought of her father, his hands as he cut her hair in the moonlight. Then she thought of the waves lifting her in the harbor when she swam out in his nightshirt in the darkness. No, she thought, you don't have to swim back yet. Not yet. Or to find the same world waiting there when you do.

"Alexandra?"

She turned to him, and her eyes asked him if he wanted to talk about the mountains, about the Alpini, but he only shook his head and turned away and asked her again.

"*Sì*," she sighed. "Panunzio. And Olivetti. And Corradini. Especially Corradini. And D'Annunzio. I'd wake sometimes in the night and find him shaking my ankle, sitting at the foot of the bed with a copy of *Il piacere,* or *Il trionfo delle morte.* I was fourteen, Nardo. But he was near the end, and he just had no way to say it, and no one to say it to. He needed something heroic, I think." She breathed. "It's enough to crush you forever. He'd just never found a way to love the questions of his life, that's all. Can you imagine it?"

"*Sì.*"

"And look where that kind of language got us. Look where it got us all."

"No," he said. "We have to choose."

She searched his eyes.

"How can a child choose? A boy?"

"No," he said again. "He can. I could have."

She looked at her hands.

"What were those meetings like? The Balilla?"

He lifted a handful of stones and let himself think of the young *fascisti* meetings in Lunetto, the lecturer with his upturned mustache, Enzo sitting proudly in his dark-collared shirt, the boys resounding the words they were told: *credere, obbedire, combattere.*

"I don't know," he said, "it must have made sense to us once. But then everything happened."

He let the stones fall and plucked the darker ones, mindlessly, and tossed them out into the surf. He told her how it had been in Bologna, when he'd lain in his bed on the Via Ugo Bassi and listened to the bombs falling on the far side of the city, the floor beneath him rumbling as the raids came closer. He didn't know how to say it. It was like the floor was everything he'd ever known, holding him up above whatever lay below it. That's how he'd come to think of it. We're given that floor—what is it? some words, a map, a story—and then, when it falls apart, what can we do? There's only that silence where the story was, that blackness opening up, and we have to choose. We can cling to the walls, or we can fall.

"And then what? What if we fall?"

"Then," he said, "then we can't hide in that house anymore."

She looked at him.

"The Balilla," she said.

"I don't know how you did it. Not going even once."

She'd reached over and plucked the last of the black stones from between his feet and slipped it into her pocket.

"You know Lunetto," she said. "What they pity they leave alone. No one cared enough about us girls even to poison us with all that. They tried to bring all that into Santa Maria, but I had a good teacher. Always."

"I didn't."

Her voice lowered, as though someone were listening.

"*È tragico.* I'm sorry, Nardo."

"*Dimmi.* Tell me about your father."

She breathed. "He didn't know what he was saying. I just keep thinking of him out on the water when he was so young, and then after, when Clara came, and he had to borrow from his brother in Bologna. It crushed him, I think. He never said it, but it crushed him. Have you ever watched a man fold dough as though it were every enemy he ever had? As though he could remake the whole damned world with his own two hands?"

"My mother."

She looked at him and ran her knuckle along his jaw. There was no scar from the wound they'd given him in Lunetto.

"I know you know," she said. "It's all the same."

"No, it isn't. It's different every time."

"She had her boys."

"She had Enzo. He was the good one. He did it just the way he was supposed to."

"How do you think they know? The good ones."

"It's not that easy."

"No, how do they know? The ones who do it just the way they're supposed to."

"I don't think it's easy for anyone," he said. "I think they fight it the whole time. They're just wise enough to know there's no winning that fight."

"You don't think we can be something else? Something other than the way it's supposed to be?"

"Look at us," he said. "Of course I do."

She brushed something from her foot and then reached for a place below her shoulders where her hair had been.

"And there's no winning that fight?"

"That's not the fight." He thought to say he'd lost that fight a long time ago, and he was glad he'd lost it, but he didn't say it. Instead he leaned back with his elbows in the stones and crossed his ankles and said, "Enzo kept my mother alive. There's no other way to say it. I think we owe everything to him. When my mother lost Nico and Paolo, she lost her *bambini*. But when she lost Enzo, she lost her world."

"And what about you?"

"You think she's lost me?"

"I didn't say that."

"No, tell me. Tell me what you think."

"Nardo, stop. I don't think she's lost you. I broke my mother's heart, I know it, but she knows the *selvaggio* she raised. Your mother must know."

He shook his head.

"It's difficult to say. I always felt like we knew each other least of all. She had her *bambini,* and she had her *eroe,* and she had—I don't know how to say it."

"Her *leone*."

"No. She had a boy who could never do anything except all the way.

And it drove her *pazza*."

"Nardo, I know one thing, and that is there's always one son who's most like his father."

"Don't say that."

"And the mother is coldest to that one. Because that is the one she loves most."

"Don't say that, Alexandra."

She leaned back beside him, but she did not turn to him.

"*Per favore*," he said. "I don't want to talk about my father."

"I'm sorry."

"Don't say you're sorry. Let's just not talk about my father."

The tide was falling back from the stones of the cove, and they could hear the wind shifting in the palm groves behind them.

"It smells like rain," she said.

"*Sì*. I saw it coming a long way off today, out by the canyons."

"Were we out that far?"

"No, but you could see it building out over the canyons, where the rifts go down to god knows how deep. You don't even look sometimes, do you?"

"I work. I focus."

He smiled.

"That's why Ricci loves you."

"Is that why?"

He laughed softly.

"That had better be why."

A smile faded from her face. "He's the only one who's asked our names." She closed her eyes. "Our full names."

"They don't need them here."

"Why?"

"What's a name next to all this?"

"All what?"

"All of it. The ships. The sea."

She gathered her hair in her hands and twisted it up above her head and let it fall to her shoulders. Very softly she laid a hand on her belly that had not yet begun to show.

"Imagine it," she said.

"Imagine what?"

"Falling off, way out there. Just going down into the rifts, in all that dark."

"I don't think there's anyone who's ever been out there who hasn't imagined it."

"You too?" She opened her eyes.

"Of course. Same as your father did. As you. Same as Aldo and the boys."

"Aldo."

"He's a good boy. And a thief."

She laughed.

"Sometimes those things are the same."

"More often than not."

She turned to him and walked her hand up his chest and laid her lips on his jaw and bit him softly.

"*Sì*," she said, "more often than not."

IX

In the last week of October, she woke in the early morning and breathed away the ache in her breasts and watched him sleep. His face was clean-shaven, and his lips were full, and he parted them as though he were speaking with someone in his dream. She heard the birds calling in the first light, the terns and the gulls and the shearwaters, and when she laid her hands on her body and thought of the dark passage of small birds over the open water, she knew she had to tell herself about the child in her.

She waited until he woke to tell him.
"You're sure?" he said.
"Yes."
"What do you want to do?"
"You know what I want."
"I want that, too. I want this, too."
"Then let's work."

They fished for another month out in the Tyrrhenian Sea. The autumn winds brought driftwood onto the beach, large and small from far out in the current, and by evening they would walk through the tidepools and gather the smallest, cleanest pieces and carry them up to the house and lay them out by the windows. The November wind came from the Northwest, and though neither of them, all autumn, had taken any caffè like the others, they bought fresh beans now in the village and ground them and made their coffee in a little samovar on the open range in the kitchen. It tasted of almonds, of the tin of the samovar itself, and they carried it to the ship only on mornings when they could not talk the tiredness out of their bones, and they threw the dregs of it into the surf when the ship listed suddenly in the wind and needed all hands to unmoor it safely.

They wore dark wool coats they'd bought in the village, with double buttons down the breast and collars that turned up nearly above their ears against the winds. They sat together below deck, each morning, on the way out to the fishing grounds, and sometimes he would go up and speak with the captain about an advance on their wages. The answer was always yes, and he stood sometimes alone on the deck after he'd spoken to the captain and thought about that. About the word yes. He looked over the gunwale and down into the sea. On clear mornings he could watch the sea floor as it fell away suddenly down to four hundred fathoms, but as winter came near, the water shone with a gray light, and he looked down and thought of the war. How he'd looked down into the waters as they'd crossed over to meet the Greeks in the mountains. How he'd looked down and tried to see shapes in the ship's wake in the water. Someone's face. The body of a woman. The bridge in Rome. But always the water shifted and erased the shape and made something else. Like shining cities built on the ruins of ancient ones. Like Roma. Like ancient things dismantled to raise up something new. Which would only be torn down again. He looked up from the water and tried to remember where he was. In which war. In which life. He thought of her swaying in the hull below deck, of the soldiers who had carried her into the shadows, and he closed his eyes and told himself they had walked through the ruins of too many cities, too many kingdoms, and their life would not be one of them. Their life. He looked down at the water again and tried to see the face forming in the wake. But the water scattered and crashed, and he could not see what shape it made.

Sometimes she stood at the aft of the ship and watched the cliffs of Palma recede into the distance, and she would close her eyes and try to remember the way morning happened in the walls of the villetta, the way the light broke against the ancient face of the stones. When the winds blew hard, she sat below deck with the others as they sipped their caffè, and there was a silence between them all that she came to understand was the silence of those who had spent many hours looking down into the depths. She had felt it growing in her, too, and she knew it was the surface of a silence that, once broken, would be difficult to close again.

The others were young, only boys, and she would smile at Leonardo as they swayed back each evening toward the harbor and he sat with them and taught them to roll their tongues as his brother had taught him, in Lunetto, before everything. They were never tired, the boys, but each morning she glanced at the old man sitting with his eyes closed on the farthest end of the bench, deep in the shadows of the hull. The boys would fight the sway of the ship, righting their shoulders and jerking their legs, but the *vecchio* would only close his eyes and let it happen to him, and it was as if he was a part of the ship itself, something that had been assembled by other hands, or a part of the shadows it carried.

He worked the starboard pulley with Nardo and three others, and Alexandra watched his bright blue eyes, and she watched his body working, and she tried to mimic it with her own. "Don't pull if they're heavy," Nardo had told her, but she'd only shaken her head and said nothing is heavy if we do it together, if we do it with hands that are not our own.

At the beginning of December, the storms came up. There had been no great autumn storms, as the ship's owner had promised, but now there were the storms that led to winter, and they were worse. To be in them, Alexandra thought, was not so bad, but to ride out in the early mornings and feel them coming, to be half in one world and half in another, that was the most trying time of all.

In the second week of December, she climbed up from the hull in the early morning and held her belly, shrouded in her wool coat, and leaned over the gunwale. Nardo came up and laid his hand on her back and steadied her as the swells rolled.

"We've saved enough," he said. "This is the last day."

She wiped her mouth with the back of her hand and looked at him.

"No," she said. "You know that isn't true."

"We can go anywhere."

"Let's just work today," she said. "Let's just work."

X

That night she told him she would mend the nets again, and he would go out to sea.

"These storms," he said. "I wouldn't leave you alone with our *pesce piccolo.*"

He laid her hands on her belly, the bump that had worried them with its smallness but that showed now when the wind pulled at her clothes.

"Our *pesce piccolo* is fine," she said. "*E il mare in cui nuota.*"

She walked with him the next morning up the path and around the cliff road and down again to the harbor. The surf was rough, and the ship swayed at anchor behind him. He looked at her, and she touched his face and said she touched it in the night sometimes, and she thought she was trying to remember it, but really there had never been a time when she hadn't known it, never in this world.

When he was gone, she turned up the collar of her coat and walked back up the cliff road and around the path and down again to the cove. There was a padlock on the door of the bait shack where she mended the nets, and she knew one of the boys would come and unlock it when the sun had risen.

She slipped a blade from one of the aprons hanging on the door, and she sat on an overturned hull beside it and looked out at the sea. She took a small piece of driftwood from her pocket and began to carve it. Someone was standing, waist-deep, in the water, casting a line into the surf, and by the way he moved with the swell of the sea, she knew it was the old man.

She slipped off her sandals and made her way to the water and realized she didn't know his name. He cast his line a long time, and when he'd caught nothing, and the sun had risen up over the cliffs behind them, he reeled it in and turned around and walked out of the waves.

He bowed to her, solemnly, and stepped away and laid his rod against the bait shack and turned up his collar against the wind.

"Come," he said.

They walked up the path and the cliff roads and stood high up on the rocks, looking out to sea. He'd walked very slowly, but without complaint, and although he had not given her his name, he told her he never went to sea on the feast day of Santa Barbara, because that had been the name of his daughter in some other life.

She'd asked him if he meant this life or truly some other life, but he'd shaken his head and asked how they are not the same.

They stood on the cliffs, and he told her about the Saint for whom he'd named his daughter. Her father had tried to keep her from the world, he said. Her father had built for her a tower of stone, and she did not know anything other than to be grateful for her life. As though it were her life. Her father could not believe in any God who could write the book of the world with mercy in it, but in her heart she had already betrayed him. Betrayed her father. For she already believed such things.

The old man said he did not understand how some people come to believe such things as mercy when they have not even seen the world. When Alexandra had said it was perhaps because they had not seen the world, he merely shook his head and said no, some are simply fortunate. Some are just given to believe these things no matter what they have seen, no matter what they have not.

He told her this other father had kept his daughter in that tower, not so much for her penance but as a vengeance against the world, which he felt did not deserve her. The old man looked at Alexandra and said this is where a man can go wrong. By revering someone, we deny their life. She nodded, and he told her how this father had found a husband for his daughter, but in her heart she could not accept him, this man, because he did not believe. This was in another time, the old man said, so the father had raised his sword to slay his own daughter. The old man said he did not know which time was worse, a time when people slew each other in the daylight, or a time when they did so quietly in the darkness of their own hearts. Then he shook his head and said no, he knew which was worse.

He told her this father had tried to slay his own daughter, but because she believed in a world of mercy, a world of mercy was there for her. She was spirited away, as can only happen in the old books, and she was brought among shepherds who she thought could hide her. She hid herself among the flock, but the first shepherd saw her and cast her out, as though she were no better than a wolf. Because she had things in her heart she would not say. Which is the mark of anything that destroys.

Alexandra said maybe it was not that she would not say, but that she could not, and the old man nodded and said yes, this is the difference.

The daughter, he said, had taken herself away, and she knew even in this other world, her father was pursuing her. That his fury was the fury of one who had had to become something that the young will not have to be. When she came to the second shepherd, she saw his face that was so fair, and so kind, and he took her in and sat her at his table. He laid out a great feast before her, and he told her whatever was his was hers, and he went out again, and this daughter heard him lift one of his animals over his shoulders and walk away. She had had a vision, then, that it was her own heart that he carried, and she did not know what it meant. She fell asleep with the heavy feast in her, and when she woke, the house was dark, and there were two men standing over her, and she knew without looking at their faces that the shepherd had betrayed her. She knew one of them was her father.

His wrath, the old man said, was the wrath of those who feel they have been betrayed by what they have tried to protect. Which is a wrath more terrible because they know, in their hearts, it is a wrath against themselves, for wanting to protect anything at all against the truth of its own self. Which is a sin for which there are few atonements.

This father, the old man said, this father commended his own daughter to the king, who would abide no such believers in his land.

None who believed in any god above him, who was the truth of iron and not the wool of mercy. On the third day, they brought her out of her prison cell and bound her to the stake and tried to give her to the flames. But the flames were extinguished when they came near.

There are men who can do things, the old man said, with their own hands, and there are men who cannot. And it is not clear which are worse. Alexandra had thought he would shake his head again and say he knew which were worse, but he did not. He merely said the prisoner's own father had offered to take up the axe himself and had done it with his own hands, and that even to this day, when we eat our bread on the feast day of this saint, this daughter, we are reminded that every love can be a betrayal as much as a faithfulness. That even to love each other can be a betrayal. If we love each other for what we are not.

Alexandra looked at him and asked him why he had named his daughter for such a tragic figure, and he said for exactly that reason. Because he was of a time when people still believed they could see things in advance. And his mother had told him his eyes were clear blue because he would look down into the depths, and he would see things he should not see. Which could not be unseen. Until the end of the world.

She asked him what had happened to his daughter, and he said you are not listening. He said he believed that story of the saint was true, every word of it, but it was not what had happened to his daughter. He said we relive the same stories again and again, but that does not make them the same stories. No more than any daughter is the same as her own mother, any father the same as his own son. But the stories are in us, he said. Always.

She looked out at the sea and saw the storms far out on the horizon. She did not see the ship.

"Your husband," the old man said. "He has this shame."

She shook her head, but he nodded and said, "Yes, he does." He said he could tell it in the way someone carries himself, in the way this man had hauled up the ropes from the depths, as though there were something at the end of them he wished not to see. No, she said, but the old man said he knew she knew such things, too, about the way men carry themselves, because he had seen her watching him as he worked the ropes of the great net. She said it was merely because she was trying to do as he did. That she was trying to learn. Yes, he said. Yes. Learn.

She asked him where he had learned, but he said she was not listening. About no two being the same. Even though they are the same. If she tried to be his body, she would be pulled down into the waves alone and drowned. Not because she was not strong, but because they were not her actions, they were not her life. He asked her if she understood. She nodded.

"*Credo di sì,*" he said. "I think you do. We may bring up from the depths the same thing, but we must do it in a different way. Each time. Each life."

She told him she had forgiven her child's father, and he told her it was not hers to forgive.

"Yes," she said. "It is."

"Half of it," he said. "Precisely half." He said we are split down the middle in this world, because we do not know which work is ours. We do not know when to be powerful and when to be powerless. We do not know what to forgive and what to leave unforgiven. What to protect and what we destroy by keeping safe. We do not know what we do to the world and what we do to ourselves, and perhaps our greatest tragedy is that we call those things by different names.

She said she understood, and he said no, there is a great mystery in that. For it is just as wrong to think they are the same, those things, as to think they are different. But those are questions no one can answer. All we can do is ask them. All we can do, like the chaos of the deep sea, and like the rage of those who try to have dominion over it, all we can do is find a harmony between them. The depths and the dominion. All we can do is be the battle between them that has no malice in it nor end. No violence in its heart but the violence of creation. Which is pain but is no violence at all.

When he was done talking, she told him she was afraid. She had not heard herself say those words in a long time, and she had not expected to hear herself say them.

He said of course she was. So was he.

She said she was not afraid for herself but for a child. And for him.

The old man knew of whom she spoke, and he held his hand over the waves, where the ship would return. He said she was afraid the child would not have its own story, and she said yes. She was afraid this is what he thought, as well, the child's father.

The old man shook his head.

"I know nothing," he said, "but I know you must cast this fear out of your heart. Because it is only our fears that shape the lives of our children, and the shaping is all the more lasting if the fears are not spoken. Especially to our own selves."

She said she was afraid the child's father would never be done with his shame. She knew he woke sometimes in the nights and paced the floor, and he thought what he'd done would never be forgotten.

The old man said perhaps it was so, but although he did not know much, he knew what we truly fear is often the shadow of what we think we fear. That the child's father is not afraid something in him will be remembered, but that he will vanish without it being known. Is not afraid the remembrance of him will be lost forever in the hearts of the living, but that he will be saved. And only he can do that.

He said perhaps this fear of being forgotten is why some of us make our shames at all. Our deaths.

She looked out over the waves and held her body a long time. At last she whispered, slowly, as though the words were not her own.

"What do I do?"

But he only shook his head.

"You ask," he said, "as though the answer were not your life."

He wiped his hand over his face. "You know what you must do," he said. "Ask yourself what you must ask. When the ghosts go from the face of the one you love, who will be there? Who has been there all along, in truth, and what would you do if you had to face them?" He looked at her. "Who would we lose if we forgave them? Who would we lose if we forgave ourselves?"

Oil rose up in the wind from the harbor, and she felt on her fingers the chill of her mother's rings she'd worn once in the shadows of Lunetto. *No,* she thought, *not yet.* When the old man turned to her, she said she understood. He closed his eyes and told her he thought she did. That we cling to our imprisonments, but there is a place where the law and the freedom are the same. Where the listening and the telling may be one. We say we wish to be heard, he told her, but we hide in our own stories. In the telling. And to want to know is to want to be known. And to listen is to tell. And to open is not just not to be closed.

They'd stood for a long while looking out at the waves, the gulls rising up from the harbor. Finally she shook her head and asked him how he'd known that she needed these words.

He said he had looked long enough into his own eyes to know the sadness of those who possess a story they have not yet told themselves. He had looked at hers, and at her husband's eyes as he'd lifted the nets from the deep sea, and now, he told her, now you must know. Both must know.

"Yes," she said. She lowered her head. "But he is not my husband."

He waited for her to lift her head.

"Don't," he said. "Don't imagine you are ashamed of your own life. When you are not. When your life is not a crime but a sentence of joy you cannot accept."

They stood beside each other as the gulls hung in the winds before them. She asked him of his home, and he said home for him was so long ago. But he spoke of the dead, and he spoke of the living who come back to their first worlds and stand in empty rooms and know what worlds could have been theirs if they had not been afraid. What faces. What hearts. Some fears are right, he told her, but it is hard to know which in this life. He told her the truly blessed are those who have stood in their first worlds and woken. Those who have stood in the ruins and have had one brief vision of what the fear is for.

"It's painful," she said.

"There has always been pain," he told her. "But we merely called that our lives. Our joy."

She closed her eyes.

"It is the only way," he said. "To admit into your heart the one thing you have gone in fear of. It is terrible, terrible. The true fear behind the false ones. The dark vision. The abyss of it." She knew he was holding his hands toward the sea. "But salvation lies within it. You know this."

Her eyes were still closed.

For there has always been pain, he told her again. There has always been pain written in faces, and we took those faces as part of our story, when really they were trying to be the face of the story they were. Or the face of no story at all. Which is the hardest to abide. For it is the radical fact of the other that we have been afraid of. All of us. That they are what they are. Wholly. And alone. And to see that is to see it is so with ourselves. And to risk that no story will hold us. As they must risk themselves. Must admit into their hearts that terror also. And be changed by it. Be delivered from their forgivers into their own hands. And stand trial there on the dark shore alone.

He searched her eyes.

"You must risk the infinite distances between," he said. "Which both must choose to cross in their own time, in their own hope, in the small and perilous boats of their own souls."

She could taste the salt of the sea on her lips. A silence slid between them like the current in the deep channel beyond the waves.

"But that is the only way," he said. "That is the only way to begin the story you are trying to tell. The only story. Which is no story at all."

She could hear him breathing steadily in the wind, and she waited a long while for him to speak again. She knew what he was going to do. The waves crashed below, and very softly he laid his hand above her chest and held it there. "To admit it," he said, "is all. You must admit it all."

A ship's horn blew on the South side of the harbor, and she opened her eyes. He was rinsing his hands in the wind.

Yes, he told her, there has always been pain. But the penance we suffer is merely pain if it is the wrong pain. It is merely conceit. But we can waken. We can. Perhaps, he told her, perhaps we have needed the horrors of our time, and of all times, to make that story visible. To see in our own faces the faces of those who had no story. Or whose story could live again in our own. Or is waiting to be seen. If we choose to look.

He waved his hand over the land. Like a healer over the sick. Over something that did not know it was broken.

"If we choose to look," he said again.

She watched him closely, and when he spoke again he'd lifted his hands and opened them in the wind.

"Soon there will be no secrets anymore, *mia figlia*. The world will know all that can be known. But what wisdom will it have?"

"None."

He shook his head. "You have no faith. We will only know what can be known. But the work remains."

"What work?"

He looked at her and then looked away. Very slowly he lowered his chin to his chest and then lifted it again, sniffing the wind. After a long while he spoke.

"What do we know of love in our time? I was young once, too, *mia figlia*. I loved in such a way that I did not know what I did."

"The mother of your daughter?"

He shook his head.

"It is impossible to tell. We were secrets," he said. "We kept each other secrets to ourselves."

She felt the wind slip into her collar, and she watched the gulls hang above the cliffs before they turned and dove down to the water. The old man looked down into the water, and when he spoke again his voice had freshened with the sea breeze.

"Who knows what the great work is?" he said. "But it all begins with this. With the smallest things. Each day."

Though the wind shifted toward the village behind them, he did not move. He spoke once more of the father and his daughter. Of the life others wish to choose for us as though we could be protected. But that what this father had not known is that a life that can receive another life is a life with dignity. A life that can choose. Then he spoke of the daughter's vision. Of her heart being carried like a black lamb. He said that like most of us she did not have time to live her visions. But she knew, she knew. No one can carry it for us. No one. And if someone stood before us with open arms, if they asked for all our sorrows, our trials, if we gave them up, even if we gave them freely, that would be the worst theft of all.

She nodded and looked down at the harbor below the cliffs. She asked him again how he'd known to speak with her, and he shook his head and said she found him. She looked at him and tried to smile.

"*È un mondo difficile*," she said.

The old man shook his head. "It is a harder world that does not wake us," he said. He said life has always been hard because it is difficult to hear the voice of truth in our sleep. He said the young perhaps have inherited a world with more voices in it, and he did not know if they would be better or worse at hearing their own voices in the chaos. Because perhaps that chaos drowns them. But perhaps it teaches them how to swim. He looked out over the water like a man who has spent many hours in it alone, far from shore. Then he said he had one more thing to tell her, and then he would leave her alone. He said he had not said clearly what he had wanted to say about the harmony. Between chaos and order. Between a life and the world. Between the sun and its shadow.

He said he did not know much but he knew that each life has one thing. One thing. It is always wrong about everything else, but about this one thing it can never be wrong. One.

He raised a finger and lowered it slowly.

He said we know when we have come into times of greatest affliction when we are split precisely in half. When the heart is exactly broken. When a people severs itself and there is no place between, no home, because they cannot abide the mystery a moment more. In such times, he said, we come home and we find we have no home, *senza casa*, because we have destroyed the mystery in our own hearts. We have forgotten. Forgotten the mystery is our only home.

"You see?"

"Yes."

He said he was no *fascista*, but what they had done to Il Duce in the Piazzale was not a remedy. Not at all. He said by making us believe there is only strength, a tyrant can deprive us of our lives. For our weaknesses have secrets also. We think we begin to speak the language of tyrants, he told her, but really those tyrants come from the language we have spoken. In our own hearts. In the darkness. He said we worship such men because they keep our darkness for us. And they tell us it is light. And in that way they can do no wrong. Until they can. He said we see in such a life only what we wish to see in ourselves, and so we see anything that is not him as a betrayal. Of him. Of ourselves. But in truth we have already betrayed ourselves in our own hearts. For turning our back on our shadows. An act that can only destroy and not create a world. For if you deny your shadow it becomes your tyrant. And the heart, he said, the heart is the worst tyrant of all.

He turned to her and smoothed down the grey wave of his hair. The mystery is our only rest, he said. The work of it. For we think we can erase the past, but this is the greatest danger of all. And the cause of all our misery. Because it cannot be erased. Not the past. It will only be transformed. It will show in other ways, he told her, according to the law that cannot be broken. The law of change and sameness. It will show in our works. In our hands. In our laws that are false. So it had been in the heart of any tyrant, and so it had been in the Piazzale. Then he said we think we must choose between a tyranny of fire and a tyranny of stone. Between chaos and law. Between death and death. Law, he said, is death if it is our law only and not the law of nature, which can only be followed if we admit that it is change, if we admit that it is permanent. He said we find the shape of our lives and then we believe the shape is the life. But it is not. It is not. We must sway with the changes, and yet be master over them. Both, he said, raising his hands over the sea. Both. We do not know what moves us, he told her, as the sea cannot know it is the moon that moves the sea. But the moon is not in ruins. The ancient things await in us to awake.

He lowered his hands and looked at them. They were scarred from many years on the waters. He closed one over the other and then lowered them slowly.

"There is no harbor," he said, finally. "There is no shelter from ourselves."

She nodded and said she was grateful.

"For what?"

For the people of that place, she answered. For him. Who'd received her without question. And for what they'd given.

He asked her if she could feel this wind. This wind moving up the cliffs from the sea. Moving through us. Like the voices of the dead. As though it could take something away from us. Even our own lives. He said our lives are not the price we pay but the gift the world is owed. And anything given is not taken away. That if we give away the right things, and only those, then our lives will be there for us to receive. As they have always been. As the forms have always been there for us to feel when we lay our hands on the chaos of our hearts. On the hearts of others. Waiting to become what they already are, by the mercy of our own hands. As all things have been that have the grace to change, all things that cannot last, all the things beneath the stars.

He reached out toward the sea and closed his hands. "For to love is not to win," he said, "but to listen. The song of the world is not love, *mia figlia*. It is savagery and wildness. It holds us with its hands of wind and darkness, its terrible questions, and it harms. It harms. But we can remake ourselves enough that we feel even that touch as the touch of love. If we know the questions are here to wake us. If we know they are still meant tenderly."

He shook his head, as though waiting for something to quiet in him. Then he said there were always the questions. We are the questions.

He closed his eyes and let the wind play against his face. "Grazie," he said.

She looked down. But she had spoken of her shames, she said. To a stranger. Who had no reason to help her.

He said there are no strangers. Except the one in the glass. For we are secrets to ourselves. We lay up our lives in us like harps in the willows, and our loves come and touch those harps and ask where is the place where these were once a song. For we are banished from our own selves, and though some secrets are shameful, the mystery is not. Not the mystery. But there is still time. We can take down that weight. We can lift our hands into the branches and touch the dark harps of our losses and lower them to the earth and make them sing. For the country in which we sing that song is no one's, no one's at all, if the song is true. If the singer admits their own heart. Like these waves. Like the wind. Like the secret of the world.

Then he looked at her and said if you think there are reasons, *mia figlia*, you are lost enough to be found.

She walked with him down from the cliffs, and before he left her, she asked him if she could tell her the dream she had dreamt each night since she'd told herself of her child in her, and he nodded solemnly. She did not know if it was a gesture of understanding, or if he was merely humoring her. As an old man would humor the village fool. Out of politeness. But she did tell him.

He looked out at the sea.

"I'm sorry," she said. "It's just a dream."

But he merely shook his head and said that was a serious dream.

He said there are some among us who hide behind the mask of their own faces, and in being no one they dance, in turn, with each of us, and against our will they let us show the world what we are. Because we think we too are wearing that mask. But we are not. We never were. Each thing is written clear for all to see.

He asked her if he had spoken too much, and she said, "No. Please."

He said when one of these masked ones comes among us, he will move with each of us in turn, and in turn he will unmask us. Because we will believe our treating him is an act, his act, and we will act it out for all to see. But in truth it is what we do. It is our act. It is how we treat our loves, unknowingly, in the secret of our own hearts. Our loves, with whom we act so differently, and whom we treat as though they could not be anyone. Which is why our treating them is an act. Is the real performance and not the truth of our hearts.

She looked out at the waves, and then she looked at his clear, blue eyes, and she asked if her life was an act. Still. And if the masked one in the dream was yet unmasked.

"I'm sorry," she said. "It's foolish."

No, he said. He said no one can tell anyone that. The answer to her first question. About her life. Because the answer is her life. Then he said the second question is easy. The one in the mask was the least masked of all.

She looked at the sun flickering in the deep lines of his face. She asked him if he would lunch with her that afternoon, but he shook his head and said no, he must be alone with his feast on this day. Then she thought she saw his eyes say *and each day. Each day.*

He bowed to her again and took up his rod from the wall of the shack against which the sun had risen. He turned to her, and she asked him if he would look over Nardo.

"I will do my half," he said. "Precisely my half."

When he'd left her, she turned down her collar in the winter sun and lifted the padlock the boy had unfastened and slipped it into her pocket. She thought about what his eyes had said afterward. To be alone with your feast. Each day. Each day until you understand it is not yours alone. She sat in the shack and looked up at the waves and took up the broken nets and began to mend them.

XI

All day Leonardo had hauled up the nets from the sea, and the captain had taken the ship far out past the trade lanes and north to the canyons that went down to nearly to five hundred fathoms. When the skies were clear, they could see the point of Torre Faro far off to the southwest, on the far side of the Strait, past which the sirocco sometimes brought up the dark rains mixed with the sands of Africa, the warm gusts that lifted the fish from the depths, but all morning the skies had darkened, and he knew the time of the true storms had come. He hadn't known that he missed the old man when he wasn't there, but now when he hauled up the net with only the boys again, he understood the silence among them was different than it had been, and he wondered what the old man had seen in his own time, with his eyes as blue as the shallows but his gaze as deep as the sea.

When they'd found a place where the sea bed had not been touched and the schools had taken shelter in the deep rifts of the canyons, they brought up net after net and spread the little silver fish on the deck and sorted them along the length of their forearms, throwing the juveniles back into the chop of the sea. When the storm came from the south, they told themselves that it was just another storm, but it wasn't. All morning the winds built, and by noon there was no peace to speak of. They slid the great net up onto the deck and lashed it down and pulled down the yardarms with the massive pulleys that had been turned from the pines high up in the mountains. The captain came down from the flying bridge and hunkered at the helm in the forecastle and drove the ship head-on into the waves. *Il soffio di Persefone,* he yelled. *Soffiaci.* Some of the boys said their prayers into the wind, and the wind took some of the prayers away.

He lay below deck with the others, far in the shadows where the old man had been, and when the ship listed as it had never done and crashed back down into the waves, he rolled to his side on the cabin floor and turned up his collar and cradled himself like a child. I can't do it, he thought. But he didn't understand what it was he couldn't do.

He tried to think of her voice, of the things she'd said to comfort him when he'd woken in the nights from his dreams. *Your eyes are like a harvest. Like the golden rolls of the vineyards in the hills. Like young wine in an ancient place. Carried down from an ancient place in the mountains.* But it was no use. He thought of her holding him, and he felt the waves crashing against the hull, and he told himself there is only one thing this life deserves to be held by. One thing.

He could hear the boys moaning in the dark. He laid his hands over the wool of his collar and pressed it to his ears, but he knew he would hear them. Other voices from long ago. Then he opened his eyes in the dark and knew if he closed them again he would see them. The faces. Thirty. Every one.

You have to look, he said. He did not know if he'd said it aloud. But he said it again. You have to look. They do not even get to look at them again. Not in any mirror. Not in the eyes of any stranger or lover. Or brother. Nico. Paolo. Enzo. You have to look for them. No, don't fool yourself. You are not looking for them. You are not looking for you. You are looking only because you have to look.

He was standing before the *caporale* in Bologna, and they brought the thirty to him one by one. One by one. One by one he read their sentence. The same sentence for each. *Perché hai tramato la morte, devi morire.* He looked at their eyes as they received it, and he knew there was a word for how they received it, but he did not want to think it. Then he did. *Dignita. Dignita.* They received it with dignity, and it was their dignity that crushed him then and that crushed him now. Let it crush me, then. Let it. But he knew it was not that easy. Nor should it be. He knew it was not over. One by one they came to him, and he held himself in the belly of the ship as the waves rolled, and he let them come. One by one, until the last. The youngest. He was so young he was not yet different from his life. His hair was the color of common wheat, his eyes as dark as the fresh polish of a groom's shoes, and what vow his eyes spoke with the world and the world with him had never yet been broken. *Dì il to nome.* Say your name. In the belly of the sea he heard the boy refuse to say it, and he told himself he had not known then what a name meant, any name, but he knew if it is a curse worse than any curse a man can say to himself in the dark, then it is the first word of the world. Any world. And it will be the last word the world has over us. No matter what we do with it between.

The boys were still moaning, and he kept his eyes closed and made himself look at this last boy before him in Bologna. No more than a child. He brushed the dust from the boy's collar and he watched the boy flinch and then stand straight again. I touched him like that, he said. As a mockery. I told him with the gentleness of my touch that there is no gentleness in this world. None that was not taken away from him the moment he shouted his first thirst into being. The moment he was born.

My son, he thought. What did I do? He slid his hands down to his chest and then slipped them under his armpits and cradled himself as the waves came and the ship rolled. You do not deserve to be held by these hands. Yes, you do. That is exactly what you deserve.

He looked at the boy they had hanged and told him, *Listen. Things were done to me also. Things I cannot even tell myself. In the beginning. My life was taken away before I even lived.* But he knew it was like telling the dead they owed you pity because you were not dead. It was like telling the drowned to pity you because you were thirsty. It was like telling the nameless to pity you because you had a name.

He kept his eyes closed and let the sea rock him. All your life, he thought. All your life you thought you were being guided. But you were the guide, you.

Thirty. He counted them and counted them backwards and then looked at them again. Those who had been killed because they would have killed. As though we can save the world by slaying it. As though we can slay it enough that it can never suffer being saved. Look, he told himself. You are not done looking.

He had tied the ropes in Bologna with his own hands and watched them stand before him. Unhanged and yet already dead. Their eyes looking at another world beyond him. Because what they saw was not worth their breath.

The ship listed to its side, and something crashed against his chest and moaned. He opened his eyes, and he knew who it was. Very slowly he slipped his hands from his armpits and wrapped them around the boy and held him. The ship shook and rolled and then pitched back as though it had been called back from one god to another. From hell to fresh hell. And no rest between. He held the boy with one arm and thrust his other out into the darkness to brace against the far wall when it came. It did come. He felt his hand slam against the beam, and he braced the boy's back with his other palm and did not let him strike it. A chorus of stowed oars rolled down upon them, and he covered the boy and told him something in his ear that even he did not understand. About patience. About it being a long way. He thought of the oars far down in the canyons from ships that had gone down in another time, and he told the boy he had nothing to fear. That this is how it always was. That men hurt men and the gods are just men, the gods are just us. But he knew these were no words to speak to a child. He told him nothing ends, that is the blessing and the curse. But he knew these were no words to speak to a child. To a son. He told them some are spared, and if the wicked are spared it may at least be so that they can suffer the sparing. But he knew. He cradled the boy and said to him none of what he'd thought he said. He said what a man might say to a child only after he has let that child go. I know, he said. I know.

The ship listed again, and he closed his eyes once more and thought of her. Of their child. Of a child in the belly of a sea. He told her he did not know. He did not know if he should ever again be held by anything but the darkness and the cold, but it was not his right to decide. That this life in her needed two, and if he could not be one, he would let her tell him what he was. To shine the light in the depths. Then he told her he would not go. That he should not have come to her but now that he had it was not his right to go. Even if it slew him. Her touch. Her gentleness. In the dark of darks now he let her look at him and read to him the sentence of his life. But he could not hear it. He could not hear it. Tell me, he said. Tell me. But he told himself. He told himself everything was the question. And maybe we only have one chance to answer. And maybe that was your answer. Maybe that was. Then she said tell me, tell me. And he did. He said each sentence was the same. Yet not the same. Each answer the same and yet each of the sentenced his own terrible question. And our only work to be the question. Our only work to let their question live.

He cradled the boy and rocked with him as the ship swayed. The boy was struggling against him now, and he did not know if he was guarding or harming him. Finally the boy slid up his arms and pushed him away and rocked himself alone in the dark.

He lay back on the oars and looked up into the darkness of the beams. The lanterns had crashed down from the hold, and he felt the glass in him and listened to the wind as the ship listed. When he thought of her hands on him he pressed his arms down into the dark and the glass and the splinters, and he and let the pain shake him. He lifted his hands and lowered them over his face and rocked with the sway of the sea. *Padre*, he said. *Puniscimi.* But he knew he'd spoken the words into the belly of the deep.

XII

When she'd finished her work, she tucked the nets into the wicker basket inside the shed and lowered the lid and fastened it with twine so the birds wouldn't nest in it. She locked the shack and looked out at the sun still hanging through the broken clouds on the western edge of the world. *Forse no c'erano tempeste*, she said aloud. Maybe there were no storms. Maybe.

She took the path up through the palm groves and entered the villetta by the back door and hung her coat on its peg among the shadows. The front room was quiet when she entered, and she stood a short while at the table, staring into the wooden bowls they had brought back from the market in September, carrying them in their arms as though they'd held some unseen life to come. She touched one now and then shook her head and carried herself to the bed and tried to stay awake as she listened to the wind.

When she woke, it was evening, but he was not there. She'd heard something in her sleep, and she lay back in their bed and lifted her cropped hair to her lips and smelled it. In the first nights after they'd cut it, she'd lain awake and held it to her lips and smelled the heavy scent of his hands, the palm oil from the ropes of the ship that ran down smoothly into the sea. It was strange, what she felt when she smelled it, but she told herself it was only some passing trouble in her, some thought of what he'd done with those hands, something that had come and swayed her in the night, and which it was not her work to explain.

She sat at the driftwood table and laid down a sheet of her newsprint and smoothed it down. The chair on which she sat was hand-lashed with leather, and she'd touched it when they'd first come, sleepless, to the villetta, and she'd said hands that could make such a thing could understand more than any thinker in the world. Why, she'd asked him, why does anyone need to understand anything when they could just make things like that with their own two hands, when they could just be what they make, when they could just make things right?

The wind slid in through the casements and rattled the glassware, and she felt an ache in her she did not understand. She lifted the charcoal to her nose and smelled the grape vine and the cherry laurel against which it had once rested in her room in Lunetto. *Don't make them of the laurels,* her mother had said. *Sì, mama. Sì.*

She opened her eyes and looked down into the gray expanse of the page. Very slowly she touched the charcoal to the surface and drew a large circle and looked down into it, as though something were there. *No,* she said. *No.*

She rose and stood before the window and looked out at the last light over the sea. They must have gone a long way out, she thought, turning north through the trade-winds after they'd run the sun up along their westward cresting through the waves. She leaned forward and laid her forehead against the window, and when she saw the slightest light of a ship on the horizon, she closed her eyes and shook her head and breathed.

She turned and sat on the sill and looked into the house, the shadows pooling in the two bowls on the table. *Va bene,* she told herself. She leaned forward and cradled herself and rocked a long while, but it had not passed her by, that strange swell rising in her, that heavy swell that had carried her from sleep and left her there on the shores of her life. *Che cos'è,* she thought. What is it?

She stood and drifted through the villetta, touching each thing in turn. Table. Workshirt. Linens. Someone had begun to carve a name in the soft wood of the desk, and she made her way to it and touched it, as she'd done when they'd arrived—just two letters, nothing more—and she felt the room move. She closed her eyes and tried to breathe, and when she thought of the old man she heard him speaking again of fear, of the worst theft of all, and when she thought of Nardo she felt a curtain brush against her neck and she saw the manes of great lions in the darkness and she opened her eyes and breathed a long time where she stood.

She closed her eyes and crossed the room and listened to herself breathe. Then she sat on the bed and opened the drawer and lifted the scissors with which they'd cut her hair. She felt the dark swell rising inside her. The villetta was still, and she closed her eyes and lifted the scissors to her nose and smelled them, letting the dark swell rise in her again until she was standing beside the bed where the casement had blown open and the wind had opened her eyes and the scissors were lying beside her where she'd dropped them.

Nardo, she thought. *Che cosa hai fatto.* What did you do?

She knew it was madness not to tell him, but she sat at the little desk looking out over the cove and pulled out a fresh sheet of newsprint and wrote to him. She told him she did not know what was in her, that she had woken and heard a strange voice like the wind in the trees, like an old man, like the sound of the scissors whispering as they'd cut her hair. She'd thought that sound was nothing, she told him, when they'd cut her hair; she'd thought it was only the sound of something falling away, something leaving, but now, she told him, now she could hear it as something else, something calling, something arriving; now she could hear it like the sound of someone's voice, a child's, a stranger's, a woman's—she couldn't say—and when she'd closed her eyes that afternoon and listened for it again, she'd heard only the sound of broken ropes swinging in a city square, the sound of agony, of people sobbing, and she was sorry, *Mi dispiace, Nardo, ma ti dirò dove sono,* but she would tell him where she was. There are things we have to do alone.

She folded the note and left it on the bed and stood at the table again looking down into the circle she'd drawn. She picked it up and folded it into her bag, then stood listening to the sea. Then she unfolded it and laid it back on the table.

She found the canvas bag she'd brought from Lunetto. It still smelled of the cypresses in their garden. No, she thought. Not there. Not yet.

She looked at her wool coat on its peg and closed her eyes and thought about him. In case he needs it, she thought. In case his is not enough.

When she'd gathered her second pair of sandals and her new, cotton clothes, she arranged them neatly and laid them in the bag with her newsprint, the palm fronds throwing their shadows across them. *Pulita,* she thought. As though she were packing for someone else—a child, a stranger, a lover. As though she knew where she was going. As though she knew where she had been.

She hooked the bag over her shoulder and took the path down through the groves and up the cliff road to where the pavement began on the Viale San Paolo to the village of Palma. When she turned back, she saw the villetta below and the three rocks standing steady in the tide, the place where the old man had stood, casting his line into the waves. She was wearing her loose, wool sweater so that no one would know, but she cradled her body and said a word to the child in her, then said she would not let it be afraid. She tried to remember his words, the old man, but she could not get them right. To betray by being faithful. To forsake the ones we try to save. To hide in the deep fleece of the sea. She closed her eyes and shook her head and said his name into the wind and then turned back on the dim-lit road to the village.

She'd not gone far when the first car came. The driver was a young boy in shirtsleeves, and he'd sold them their new clothes and the 'nduja and the wooden bowls in their first days in the market.

"Ciao, Signora Bianchi." He'd rolled down the window and knocked his palm, lightly, on the car door. "Let me take you."

"You don't know where I'm going," she answered. She'd meant it as a joke, but when she heard the words, she waved them away and turned from him and walked on.

"It gets dark, Signora."

"It's nothing."

"Georgio," the boy said. "It's Georgio."

She turned and looked at him, his thin arm dangling from the window, the big grille of his harvest-yellow Fiat steaming in the last light.

"Georgio," she said. "Of course."

They drove slowly along the narrow roads, between the ancient cliffs, and she held her bag over her lap and closed her eyes as if the strange, dark swell in her would settle.

"*Non è costoso?*"

"No, Signora Bianchi. This car is very cheap. *Molto economico.* My father has people who cannot pay him. That is the cheapest way of all."

She opened her eyes.

"You're not going to the market, are you, Signora? It'll be closed."

"No, Georgio. Only for a ride."

"A ride. I can take you for a better ride than this, Signora. Have you been to the cliffs of Tauriana? *Incredibile.*"

"No."

"No you haven't been or no you can't go?"

She turned to him.

"Do you think I have nowhere to be?"

She could tell he was trying not to smile. He flicked on the lights of the Fiat and laid both his wrists over the wheel and turned left toward the village.

"*Non lo so, Signora.*"

"Tell me. Tell me what you think."

"Signora, *mi dispiace.* I think nothing. I can take you home, if you like."

She brushed something from the dash before her and looked out the window at the lights of the villages up the coast.

"Tell be about Tauriana."

"There's nothing to tell. It's something you have to see, Signora. But not now. Those roads are dangerous." He considered it. "*Non così peri-coloso.* I drive well, Signora. I've been driving since I was *quattordici.*" He held up four fingers, as though it were the number he'd spoken. "I can drive anywhere. But I choose not to. *Me capisce?* I'm no coward."

She nodded.

"Tauriana is a good place to drive in the day," he said. "But not now. Because of how I choose."

She watched him slide his wrists down either side of the wheel and begin to hold the car steady on the road with only his knees.

"You see, Signora. *Sono un maestro.*"

"You were born here? In Palma?"

He slid his hands onto the wheel again and shook his head.

"No, Signora. That is a sad story. But I don't tell sad stories. Not anymore."

He blew the Fiat's horn at a figure standing in the darkness, and the figure waved them on.

"Taurianova, Signora. Not far. But my father, he doesn't want to stay. This is a sad story, Signora. It can ruin our drive."

"You don't have to tell it, Georgio."

"Good. Grazie, Signora. Then I won't. A man cannot always stay in a place."

He'd said it as though he were speaking of himself.

"You know what makes it more sad? Even more sad?" He tapped at the horn again. "The *torrone.* Have you ever tasted *torrone,* Signora?"

"*Sì.*"

"Ah, then you'll understand Taurianova. We have the best *torrone* of all. Famous *torrone.* Sugar and honey, with hazelnuts from the mountains. I can get you some, Signora."

"That's fine, Georgio."

"You're lucky it was me who came by, Signora. You can't know who's on these roads. Bad drivers. Drivers *senza maestria.*" He looked at her quickly. "You were fishing, they say. Out on the Graciela."

She nodded.

"Madonna. I knew it was true. My father won't let me fish. Not out there like the others. Like Aldo."

"Aldo is very brave."

"You don't think I'm brave, Signora?"

"Of course, Georgio. It takes a different bravery."

"*Che cosa?*"

"Your life."

"*Ma dai.* My life. How is that brave? We sell cotton."

She looked at him and thought to smile, but she did not.

"*Ogni vita deve avere il suo coraggio,*" she said.

He touched the horn again and waved at something in the shadows. The light had bled out over the village and the coast and the sea.

"I don't know, Signora. Some are braver than others. I wish I could be out there. He's lucky, *mio padre,* that I respect him. I'm not one to disrespect. Not anymore." She shook his head. "But that's the sad part of the story, Signora. And I won't tell it."

"Grazie, Georgio."

She'd leaned back in the seat and rolled her head to the side and closed her eyes. She felt the road rocking her like the waves of the sea, the big swells far out in the current, and she cradled the bag close to her and told herself not to think of it, not to think of any life that was in her, not to think of anything at all.

"You're tired, Signora."

"A little, Georgio."

"We have a room, Signora, *Papa e io.* You can stay with us on your ride. That's easy. Wherever your ride takes you."

She looked at him.

"Grazie, Georgio."

He cradled the wheel with his knees again, listing the Fiat slightly to the left as the road turned down into the village.

"*Molto bene,*" he said. "In the morning we go to for the *torrone.*"

She closed her eyes and tried not to think of the sea, the villetta, of the door opening to the empty bed and the empty bowls and the darkness and his face when he stood alone in the moonlight, his hands as he lifted the note in the cold. *Nardo,* she thought. *Nardo. Just for a while.*

Then she thought about what she'd said to him, to this boy, this child. *Ogni vita richiede un coraggio diverso.* Every life takes its own bravery. Well, she thought. We'll see. We'll see.

XIII

She woke and rolled to her side, but he was not there. When she opened her eyes, she saw the low, dark ceiling of the room she'd fallen asleep in, and she smelled the *pane di pescatore* wafting from the rooms below her. She'd slept in her clothes, and she stood and made her way to the little basin by the bed and looked at herself in the mirror.

Mi dispiace, she said. But she couldn't have said what life she was saying it to.

She freshened herself and changed into a dark blouse and white, cotton pants, and she stood in the room and felt her belly and then covered herself again with the sweater.

She found her second pair of sandals in her bag and bent the soles in her hands until they were softened. Then she slid them on and stood in the room listening for the waves of the cove. But they were not there.

She ate with the boy and his father at a small, weathered table in a room behind their market stall, a sharp scent of iodine wafting from the little *ospedale* across the alley, where a young man leaned against a crutch in a doorway that no one left by, no one hurried through.

The boy told his father to let her eat in peace, that she was on a ride, *un viaggio*, and sometimes a journeyer has no need to speak at all. The father had only waved the words away and asked her if it was true, if she'd gone out with the others on the big skiffs into the great storms far out in the fishing grounds, and she told him there were only some who could do that without speaking of it, that some things must be done alone, and after that the father had only mussed his son's hair and lifted his own bowl and gone off to eat in his market stall as the customers came by in the morning air.

The boy took her inland to Taurianova before the sun had risen full over the cypresses along the roads. He knew every stone, he told her, every stone, and he drove her into the frazione of Donna Livia, far on the barren side of the town, where his mother had sold her *torrone* for a price, he told her, that even a thief would not permit her.

"I don't tell sad stories anymore, Signora. Remember?"

He parked the Fiat with two wheels on the curb of the Strada Provinciale, and he told her he still could not believe her luck, *la sua fortuna,* that she had set out on her ride with a driver who was *un maestro,* among all the drivers who could have found her, and that this *maestro* had such a place to offer her, a place that his father could not, ever, let go of, a place where his mother had made the great, big bins of her *torrone,* a place he made her promise she would stay in as long as she liked, *finchè doveva,* so long as she didn't ask him any more about it, any more at all.

"I don't tell sad stories, remember? Not anymore, Signora."

"Grazie, Georgio. Grazie."

XIV

When Leo stepped into the villetta and called her name, it was as though he already knew. He saw the note lying on the bed in the moonlight, but he did not read it. He walked down through the groves and then up the cliff roads and down again to the little shack on the far side of the cove. The door was locked, and he sat in the lamplight on the overturned boat and looked out at the waves a long time. The air was cool, and he could see the imprints of the nets in the sand where she'd worked with them that afternoon in the lee of the boat, where the wind had not blown them away. He thought to lean down and touch them, but he did not.

When he went back to the villetta, he stood before the table and lifted her drawing. Without thinking he folded it and slipped it into his breast pocket and sat on the sill looking out into the dark.

He made himself a bowl of white rice and sott'olio and sat eating it at the table, staring at the bougainvillea she'd freshly watered in the corner. The palm fronds were shifting in the shadows. *They do smell like almonds,* he'd told her once. *Sì,* she'd said. *They do. Sometimes they do.*

She had closed the windows and the casements so the wind would not blow the note or the drawing, and he felt the stillness of the house and a sudden silence that seemed to hold him by the shoulders. He set down the spoon and stared at it a long time. *Non ha affatto senso.* It doesn't make sense at all. Then he rose slowly and made his way to the bed and picked up the note.

XV

The house was no more than two rooms just off the Via Frances-co, its dirt-floored kitchen looking out, through a single window, to a shadowed alley where the Via della Fiera met the Via Catenzaro, and in the mornings she could hear the bells of the Chiesa di Santa Maria on the far side of the village center. A radiator stood near the threshold between the two rooms, where someone had scuffed the bedroom floor as they'd pried up the first of the kitchen floorboards, and she stood by it in the mornings and thought of what kind of man would heat a house in which no one lived, what kind of child. She warmed the blankets on it in the evenings, but when she opened the cabinets in the kitchen she could feel the cold at the heart of the house.

She woke on the fourth morning and laid her hand on her belly, its bump that she hid when she wandered, each morning, to the piazza's markets in the heavy wool of her sweater. It still smelled of him. She had thought she could feel the child kicking in her sleep, but though she waited a long time for him to speak to her, he did not. *Il mio pesciolino, il mio dormiente, don't be afraid.*

She rose and washed her face in the kitchen sink and then scooped some water into her hands and drank. The pipes tasted sour, and she closed her eyes and rested her head on the faucet and waited there a long time. As though someone would come and touch her on the shoulders. As though they would tell her what to do.

She shuffled out and around the house into the alley and took down her clothes from the pegs on which she'd dried them in the cool air. Children were playing on the Via Aspromonte, and she thought of the name of the street and the guns far up in the hills of the same name when the British had come across in the autumn of her twentieth year. Then she thought of what he'd said—*I could go all my life without hearing that again.*

I know, Nardo. Io so. But you have to do it. You have to do it yourself.

The boy had told her about Taurianova before he'd gone back to Palma. The Piazza Italia, Signora Bianchi. *Tell them you knew Maria Lombardi. And Georgio, her son. They will help you.*

She was carrying her small canvas bag along the Via Triangolo, and she cinched tight the collar of her gray sweater against the cool morning wind that blew between the old, stone houses, its heavy scent of spices from the market stalls, the ancient grains of salt, of work, the silences of empires mixed, inseparable, with one another. When she pressed her nose into the wool, she smelled him; she smelled the sea, the beach, the east winds, and she told herself to go wherever she was going, and if the child began to kick in her and ask her, she would tell it we are going where we have to, *il mio bambino,* and not even the gods in their wandering can ever say, without lying, that they know.

She'd told herself she was not taking from him if she took the last wages she'd earned in mending the nets, but she slipped the bills from her pocket now and looked at them quickly and slipped them back, and she asked herself if it was a theft if you've already given it. Then she asked herself what can be given. Then she asked herself why we are given what we can't be given at all.

She'd eaten very little for the first three days, and when she'd dreamt of an empty cradle on the waves, she'd woken and told herself no, no more. She drifted through the stalls of the market now, and she bought a small, burlap sack of short-grain rice and slid it into her bag with the two *melanzane* and the guanciale she'd bought for full price on the Via Maggio. *No, Signora,* the girl at the stall had tried to tell her, *it costs nothing,* and she'd thought then that perhaps even her sweater was not loose enough at all. *No, signorina,* she'd told the girl. *We can't all starve.*

She was walking back to the Via Catanzano when she saw she was being followed. He was a tall, slim figure who had turned right with her along the Via Triangolo, then left along the Via della Fiera, all the while whistling a faint song she'd never heard of, his hands in the front pockets of his waistcoat and a shock of copper hair lifting in the wind. He carried an olive-green cap under one arm and a rolled newspaper under the other, and when she looked at him a third time he stopped and bowed to her softly, and she shook her head and walked on.

She sat alone on the bed and ate, the children in the alley throwing their rubber *palle* against the outer wall and singing when they won. *Vinco,* they sang, *vinco, non c'è altro mondo.*

There was an old radio in the far corner of the room, and she sat staring at it as she finished the rice and scooped up a piece of the guanciale with her fingers and chewed it a long while. She knew the boy and his father would have taken the radio if it were not broken, but she set down the bowl and knelt before it and flicked it on and rolled the dial. Nothing, she thought. *Hai perso, hai perso. Non c'è altro mondo.*

She warmed three pots of water on the small stovetop in the kitchen and climbed the little stepstool in the bathroom and poured them, one by one, into the basin above the shower. Then she took off her clothes and stood beneath it and pulled the lever and let the water try to do what it could do.

XVI

She woke in the night and sat up in the bed in a panic. No, she thought. She'd dreamt of him packing up his things and setting out on a ship and then a train and then a great, vast freighter, and she'd seen the villetta burning in the cove and the palm fronds tossing in flames, and she'd seen him staring down into the waves in the winter air. *Tell yourself,* she thought. *Know what you do.*

She stood and paced the floor a long time. When she'd thought about it for as long as she could, she made her way to the kitchen and unscrewed one of the cabinet doors with her fingernail and carried it back to the bedroom. She took a sheet of newsprint from her bag and sat on the bed with the cabinet door across her lap and smoothed the sheet in front of her. Then she reached down and slid a piece of charcoal from her bag and stared into the blankness.

She would tell him where she was, wouldn't she? Or no. She would tell him to give his letters to the Lombardi boy. To Georgio. She would tell him she was only there for long enough for them to know, *per certo.* They had to, they had to know.

But when she laid her hands on the child in her she thought of the words of the old man, and of the depths of the current, and of the swallows in the Basilica, and she said Nardo, Nardo, no, I cannot make this child with fear in his heart. I cannot make him a secret from himself.

She touched the charcoal to the page and drew for a long time— first the fountain of Taurianova, then the chiesa, then the face of the child on the Via Maggio who had sold her the rice, the *melanzane.* Something rose in her, a feeling she remembered from childhood but could not name, and she rode the thrill of it as she drew and redrew these places in which she had never been, these places that had their own, unnamable riches, these places to which she knew she had been called. But when she lifted the drawings into the lamplight, the feeling withered. She laid the charcoal lengthwise on the page and dragged it from left to right and back again. Then she slid the piece over her ear and worked directly in the charcoal with her fingers, dragging it up and down into shapes she did not understand. When she'd worked awhile, she leaned back and cocked her head and saw nothing. No, she said. She cinched herself forward and nudged open the little window into the alley and let the wind slip through from the Via Catanzano. The sheet lifted slightly at its edges, and she closed her eyes and felt the charcoal with her fingers and began to work again.

When she'd worked for over an hour, scrubbing the charcoal with her hands and then working with the piece she'd taken down from her ear, she lifted the drawing and saw it was her own face. She'd drawn her hair blowing across it so that she could only see her eyes and a faint sliver of her lips, and there was a scar on her forehead that she did not have in life. She reached up to her own face as if to check. Then she blew on her fingers and scrubbed at the black smear of hair across the woman's face until it was no more than a shadow. She reworked it with the hair blowing back across the neck and down over the shoulders until it was as long as it had been before they'd cut it on the beach at Palma. She lifted the drawing and looked at it a long time. She'd not drawn the pupils of her eyes. *Later,* she said aloud. *Those come last.*

She'd slept the rest of the night without dreaming. At first light she rose and dressed and set out along the Via Catanzano. When she reached the end of it, she shook her head and turned back and unlocked the house and sat on the bed a long while, eating the rice and the guanciale slowly.

She was on the Via Triangolo when she saw him again, the figure in his same, three-piece suit, his shoes as polished as his eyes where he sat back against a fender in the morning air, smoothing down his newspaper in the wind.

There is only one way, she thought. *Solo un modo.*

When she stood before him, he lowered his paper very slowly, but he did not look at her.

"*Tu mi segui.*"

"What makes you think I follow you?"

"*Tu mi segui,*" she said.

He'd pushed his cap back on his head, but he lifted it now and tucked it under his arm and looked at her.

"You are new in Tuarianova."

"That's not a reason to follow me."

He raised his eyebrows.

"I think you believe I'm someone else."

"No. I take you for you."

He nodded.

"*Veto.* Why are you here in Tuarianova?"

"Why? *Ho bisogno di un motivo per essere da qualche parte?*"

He raised a hand, as if accused.

"You don't need a reason, no."

"*Va bene,*" she said. "*Allora non sequirmi.* Then don't ask."

XVII

Leo had moved the bed to the center of the room, before the largest window, but when he'd tried to sleep in it, he kept waking and staring out into the darkness, and he did not know where he was.

On the fourth morning he'd woken and sat at the little desk and not gone out to sea. He was wearing a white linen shirt they'd bought in the market, in summer, and he'd taken off the top and only button, so that it did not rub her when they slept. You can't find her, he thought. Even if you did, she wouldn't be there.

He lowered his head to the desk, as he'd done when he was a boy in the bright schoolroom of San Pietro, in the smell of fresh-pressed shirts and peasant bread and hymnals, and he thought of her crossing the Via Borghese with the others from Santa Maria Maggiore, her books pressed to her chest like the stories of all the lives she had yet to open.

Ciao, a boy would call to them. *Cosa hai imparato oggi? What have you learned today?*

Non per parlare con te, they would always answer. *Not to talk to you.*

XVIII

She was still sick sometimes in the mornings, and when the scents of the streets slipped in through the windows, but she told herself it was the sour water and the cold, and if the child had come to them in late July, then it was nearly five months now, and the hardest part should have been behind her. But when she thought those words, she closed her eyes and said, *Scema, non hai imparato niente su questo, vero?* You haven't learned anything about this at all.

She'd woken early sometimes and walked the streets until she thought she understood the town. The Piazza Alessandro, the Piazza Italia, all the franzioni: Amato, San Martino, Pegara. She'd walked to the fountain sometimes and sat on it and stared at the buildings, the ancient buildings, that had been spared by the war. Spared. What is it to be spared? In the chill wind she'd closed her eyes and listened to the waters of the fountain and tried not to think of the waves laying themselves down on the little pebbles of the cove, of Palma, of Lunetto, of the little volcanic stones washed up from the ancient sea bed of the harbor, from the days when the gods had shaped the world. Had they? Had they made it? She'd laid her hands under her breasts and held herself very still, and very calm, and she thought if they had, if the gods had made this world, they have long since remade it with their abandonment, and who can say which world is more merciful, who can say which world you would prefer to come into at all?

On the first Sunday of January, she sat in the back of the Chiesa di Santa Maria and closed her eyes and smelled the heavy censer, the wax candles in the children's hands as they passed her. You were not even with him for *Natale*, he told herself. *Che cosa hai fatto, Nardo.* What did you do?

She had told herself not to think again of Lunetto, not there, but in the warm scent of the church now, she let herself think of it. She thought of the cypresses in the garden, standing tall and dignified as her sisters, and she thought of her mother lighting the candles and laying out the gifts on the table, one for each daughter, one that went unopened before an empty chair. She thought of her mother unrolling the drawings she had given her, each year, and then the stories her mother would tell after the Natale feast was over, each year, even if, in the lean years, the feast had simply been their being there at all. *Mama,* she said aloud. *I'll come home soon. Not yet, not now, but soon.*

She closed her eyes tightly and tried not to see them, but she heard her mother and father speaking in hushed tones, in the kitchen, her mother asking her father if perhaps things had not gone astray, if perhaps it was all wrong, if perhaps these new laws from Norimberga were what they were said to be. Alexandra had sat on the stairs, against the tapestries, and watched them. *Nonsense,* her father had said, as her mother had nuzzled him for comfort. *Nonsense, la mia bambola. I fascisti, they care. They care.*

Alexandra opened her eyes and looked at the light through the stained-glass windows. A beast of burden. A saint slaying the coiled question of a dragon. She closed her eyes and thought of mother telling her sisters of her dreams, each morning, of Clara waving them away and of Bea leaning in to whisper, *Dicci, mama. Tell us more.* She thought of Clara, Claretta, holding her own body all those months ago, in those last nights of summer, asking herself if she was carrying a child, if Angelo would come back across the waters from Messina, if anything comes back at all. Claretta, she thought. *Potresti farcela.* You could do it alone.

When the mass had ended, she stepped out onto the Via Toscano, and she saw him again. He did not wait for her to speak with him.

"It's a small town, Signora."

"*E allora?*"

"We find each other again and again."

"*Non credo proprio.*"

"I do. I think so."

She was walking swiftly, her gray sweater turned up against the chill. She could hear children playing on the far side of Piazza Alessandro.

"I think you mistake me for someone else."

"*Chi?*"

"I don't know," he said. "Someone who means to hurt you."

She stopped and turned toward him. Her hair had begun to grow to her shoulders again, and she flicked it back and shook her head.

"And you think I need help?"

"I don't know. I see you alone. With this child."

He had not had time to close his eyes before he knew she had slapped him. Very slowly he stooped down and picked up his cap and said something to himself she did not hear. Then he closed his eyes and bowed to her, very slightly, as he turned from her, his copper hair lifting in the wind.

XIX

The old man was standing at the door when Leo opened it.

"I can't," he told him.

"*Sì*, Leonardo. You can. You must work."

He shook his head at the old man and then waved his hand back into the shadows of the villetta, as though to show him what was there, what was not. He had laid out his clothes on the bed and folded them into the linens and cinched the bundle together with a belt she'd left behind.

"Where do you go?"

"To Roma. To Trastevere."

"No," the old man said. "*Non ancora. Aspetta.*"

"For what?"

"For her."

He shook his head. He told the old man it was no use. That he had waited these many days, and he had asked himself many times if she was coming back. But he knew in his bones she was not.

"*Non lo sai,*" the old man said. "You don't know."

But he only shook his head again and said he knew in his bones what she had decided. As she had written in her note, in her own words. That she could not raise a child with fear in its heart. Of its own father. Of his hands.

"It's not what she means," the old man said.

"No. You don't know what she means."

"But it's not—"

"No."

"It's not what she fears, Leonardo."

No, he told him. It is. It is what she fears. And neither he nor this *vecchio* nor even she herself could tell her what she fears.

"*E perché Roma?*"

"Because if she doesn't come, at least I'll have that. At least I'll have Rome."

"And what would you have then?"

"*Perché mi torturi?*"

The old man stared at him a long time, his clear, blue eyes set deep in the lines of his heavy face. As if it were the face of another life, not his own. Or as if he had worn it in another time. Or as if it had so become his own that it could not seem real.

"*Perdonami,*" he said.

The old man turned down the stairs and pulled up his collar against the cold. The palm fronds were tossing in the wind, the shearwaters bickering in the shadows. When he turned around on the path, the door was still open, Nardo still staring at him in the cold.

"Come," he said. "*Ancora una settimana.*" One week more.

XX

By the second week in January, there was no money to speak of. She sat on the end of the bed and spoke to the child in her.

Today, do you know what today is, il mio bambino? Sì, today your zia Clara will wake and say she is old. But she is not, is she? No. Sì, we will tell her. I will write to her today, I promise. No, I will, I truly will. Maybe she'll have the gelato, like mama and Bea. It's my favorite, you know that. We'll get you an icebox, I promise. Sì, any flavors at all. Il mio preferito? You know, don't you? Sì, oranges. Clementine di Gioia Tauro. Always. No, there's no icebox there, either. No, and not here. But we'll get you one, I know it. Dimmi, zia Clara, what should we write to her? That we have everything we need? Sì, we will start there. And what else? That we have done this to ourselves, as she knew we would? That we don't even have an icebox? That we need her help? She would like that, sì? She would. She would like to help.

Come, let's talk about the gelato. Talk to me. Which one will be your favorite? Which one?

She sat on the floor and lifted her sweater and ran her hand down the dark line on her belly. As though it were something she had drawn. Something that another hand had made. Something the maker could undo.

She covered herself again and spread her drawings around her. She had picked up the first of them often, its scent still heavy with the sea, but always she'd rubbed her thumb over the places where the eyes should be and said no, later, *non ancora*. She had drawn the ships of Lunetto and the shore; she had drawn the shipworks, all of them, on fire, and then, when she'd tried to draw the child, she'd rubbed it away and drawn a net floating on the waves, the edges of it torn by something from the depths. She picked it up and looked at it and felt her child move in her. *Molto bene,* she said, *ora lavoriamo.* Now we work.

She shouldered her bag and made her way back to the Via Maggio and spoke with the girl who had sold her the rice, the guanciale. *Hai bisogno di aiuto?* She asked her. *Sì,* the girl said. We need help. *Tutti noi non moriremo di fame.* We can't all starve.

She knew he would come, and he did. It was a Tuesday morning, and he came in his three-piece suit again, his morning paper folded under his arm.

"*Riso,*" he said. He hadn't looked at her.

"Only rice?"

"*Sì.*"

She scooped the short grains into a small, burlap sack and tapped it down and leveled it with her palm and cinched it closed.

"*Duecento.*"

"*Come stai?*"

He still hadn't looked at her.

"What?"

"How are you feeling?"

"*Sto bene,*" she said. "*Grazie.*"

He nodded and lifted his rice and tucked it in his arm and turned to go.

"Signore?"

He waited until he'd reached the other side of the Via Maggio before he turned around. He looked at her, his eyes calm as the sea wall in Lunetto.

"*Sì?*"

"You haven't even asked me my name."

XXI

Leo was throwing one arm over another to free the net, but it was caught in the pulley above. Aldo had tangled his ankle in the line again and gone up to the yardarm, his eyes wide as he dangled upside down over the water, the wind barely swaying him as he called out. The men were laughing on the deck.

"*Non è divertente*," he was yelling.

The water was calm, and the old man had knelt down before Leo and cupped his hands and told him to stand. *E facile,* he said. *Possiamo risolvere questo problema.*

Leo nodded and set a heel in the old man's palms and let him boost him up and then wrap his foot in the rope and cinch it tight to hold him up near the boy's foot. The men were laughing behind him, but he only looked down at the boy's face and reached down and grabbed his belt and lifted his weight off the snag. *Va bene,* he told the boy, *va bene.* Then he widened the net with his teeth until the boy came loose, and very slowly he held him by his belt, swaying over the waves. *Adesso ti ho. Non ti lascerò cadare.* I won't let you go.

XXII

She was sitting in a small, covered garden where he'd taken her on the Via Due Franchi. She'd told him she hadn't wanted to go inside, and he'd said yes, of course, the garden is warm, come.

He'd led her back through the house and into the garden where a table was laid out with bread and olives. She saw that the third wall of the garden was open to the Via, and she sat in a chair at the table and set her bag beside her on the stones and waited a long time for him to come back. She was wearing a thin wool sweater she'd bought in the market, a scent of *melanzale* stitched into its umber. *Cosa stai facendo,* she'd thought. What are you doing? But when she heard a child calling out in the parlor, she stood and pushed her chair back against the ivy, squinting into the shadows of the house.

A girl came running out in a cream, satin dress, chasing a ball that had escaped her. She stopped short at the threshold of the garden and stared at the woman in front of her. The child's eyes were tired, her red hair pulled back into a French braid that she swung around suddenly to look into the shadows.

He came back carrying three glasses by the stems in one hand and a green, glass bottle in the other. He stroked the child on her head with his elbow and gestured for her to sit at the table.

"*Aida, questa è la Signora Bianchi. Siediti.*"

She slumped her shoulders and shuffled up to the table and slunk herself into a chair.

"*Piacere, Signora.*"

Alexandra looked at him, then at her.

"*Piacere, Aida.*"

"Papa, can I play?"

"No, Aida. Eat. Don't you want to talk with us?"

She was squinting at Alexandra's arms crossed over her belly.

"I don't know."

"Well, then the answer might be yes. How could you know?"

"Papa."

He broke a piece of bread and held it up in the air until she asked for it. Politely. She sat gnawing at the center of it, brushing the crumbs from her dress.

"Aida was at *una festa*. She goes to more *feste* than her father. Don't you?"

"I should. *Le feste non sono per gli adulti.*"

She reached forward for the olives, and he pushed them toward her.

Alexandra still had not sat. "Signora Bianchi," he asked. "Do you like *spigola*? They catch them right out in the *Tirreno*. Whole big nets of them. *Sono i miei preferiti.*"

She looked at him and took her seat slowly. *Sì*, she thought she'd said. But she'd said nothing.

"They're my favorite," he said again. "They catch them out there even now, in winter, them and those beautiful *gamberetti*, which Aida loves so much. Don't you, Aida?"

"*Un po.*"

"*Un po. Ridicola.* You love them."

The child was looking at Alexandra.

"What's wrong with your hands?"

"Aida," her father said, "is that any way to ask?"

Alexandra laid out her hands on the table. She'd scrubbed under her fingernails, but the charcoal still dulled her cuticles and blackened the small cracks in her fingertips, and her knuckles were raw with winter.

"*È magico*," she told the child.

The child's eyes brightened.

"Magic?"

"*Sì.*"

Aida looked at her father.

"Go ahead," he said. "Ask her."

"Can you do magic now?"

Alexandra held up a finger and reached down into her bag and tore off a corner of one of her last pieces of newsprint. She searched until she came up with a piece of charcoal and held it up in the air as though it were a thing of great wonderment.

"What is it?"

The child slid herself from her chair and stood beside Alexandra, waiting. Very slowly Alexandra laid the charcoal lengthwise on the page and drew it across, left to right, right to left, up and down. Then she breathed on her finger and scored three lines, slowly, in the charcoal.

"What is it?"

"Read it."

"It's an A."

"For Aida?"

"Why not?"

The child frowned.

"That's not magic."

"Aida," her father said.

Alexandra laughed.

"No, you're right, Aida. Because you didn't make it. It's only magic if you make it yourself."

"*Va bene.*"

"Would you like to try?"

The child nodded.

"Papa, can I try by myself?"

"Of course, Aida. Sit with us."

"But I have to do it by myself. Can I borrow it, Signora Bianchi? *Posso portarlo dentro*? I'll give it back."

"You don't have to give it back, Aida."

"Grazie, Signora. Grazie."

Alexandra handed her the charcoal and slipped the rest of the sheet of newsprint from her bag and told her it was for a big picture, something she could think about a long time before she made. "Do you understand?"

"*Sì.* I think so, Signora. I'm going to start thinking about it right now."

She took the sheet and hurried to the door, but her father called after her.

"*Cosa, Papa?*"

"Aida. Where are your manners?"

"But I said thank you. Grazie, Signora Bianchi. I'll bring it back."

Her father shook his head and waved her away, and she was gone into the house, the stairs rattling as she climbed up hurriedly into the shadows.

"Mi dispiace, Signora. This one has no manners." He reached forward and tapped the hollow crust of bread his daughter had left on the table. "*Sì,* Aida," he said, as though she were still there. "Go. Play."

He sat back against the ivy and lifted his glass and smiled.

"You didn't think I had a daughter."

"No."

"Why not?"

"I don't know."

He shook his head.

"It's not easy."

"You have no help at all?"

"Come. Taurianova is a small town. I told you. Everyone helps." He seemed to consider something. "A small town, *sì?* Like your own?"

"Lunetto."

He nodded. "*Sì.* We're even smaller. And that's our blessing, no? The bombs ignored us, all those years. We were not even important enough for that."

She crossed her legs under the table and leaned back.

"I know," he said, "what you thought of me. Maybe you still do."

"What do I think?"

He smiled.

"Why would you not think it? But that's not the way I am. I know what it is to do this, to raise a child like this." He looked at her. "*Perdonami.* I'm a plain man. I speak plain."

She shook her head.

"Go on."

"That's all. I saw you, and I know what this world is. It's *difficile*."

"There are things we must do alone."

He cocked his head and ran his finger around the rim of his glass.

"Like this drawing of Aida's. That was clever. I haven't seen her like that in quite some time." He raised an eyebrow. "You're an artist?"

"I'm a shipwright."

"A shipwright?"

"*Sì*. Since I was fourteen. It's good work and I'm proud of it."

He nodded. "Of course. But that's not an easy life, is it?"

"Nothing is."

"Maybe. Maybe. But what can we do? We can make it easier."

"And you think this is what's easy?"

He smiled a long time, but he said nothing. Finally he reached for the breadcrust and broke it and laid the two halves beside each other on the table.

"No," he said. "I don't."

He looked up at her. His eyes were green and clear, his copper hair streaked with silver.

"I don't suppose you'll tell me," he said.

"Tell you what?"

"What happened."

"*Ovviamente no.*"

"Of course," he said. "Nor should you have to."

The child laughed once in the house as he sipped from his glass and set it down and ran his finger once around its rim.

"Small towns are small towns. I tell Aida not to worry what people say. About her mother. But people talk. People talk."

"They do, don't they?"

"Who can blame them? Who among us is satisfied with their own story?" He lowered his eyes and thumbed some dust from his glass. "Calabria is a simple place. It can't keep everyone satisfied."

A slight breeze shifted the ivy. He touched his dusted finger to his tongue and shook his head, and when he'd waited a moment he leaned back against the ivy and sighed.

"She's the smartest in her school. *La nostra Aida.* I shouldn't boast, but it's not me she takes after. I thought she'd lose everything if I had to fight. Everything. But the war forgot about us. The boys have to fight."

"They aren't boys."

He looked at her and tightened his lips.

"You're right. Of course you're right. Don't think I don't understand soldiers. The things they have to do."

"You've fought?"

Something like a smile flashed across his face. "Would you believe me if I said my grandfather fought with Carmine Crocco?"

"No."

His smile widened and then fell away. "My great grandfather. He was only fifteen years old. *Un ragazzo.* They fought up in the hills, in the orchards, everywhere. In Basilicata, in Campania." He laid his hand flat on the table. "In Calabria."

"My father used to talk about Crocco," she said. "How they betrayed him."

"Who betrayed him?"

"His own men."

He looked at the brick wall of the garden, as though he were looking out to sea. "Betrayal means nothing. It's just a word the rich get to say. When Garibaldi came across the Strait with his thousand men, he knew he could get the starving to join him. This is what it is to be Calabrese. You fight for the ones who put bread in your hands. That's all. It has nothing to do with right or wrong. With principles."

Alexandra shook her head. "No. Some have principles. Some fight for principles."

"Maybe what we call principles are only our hungers by another name."

He touched the bread again and looked at her, but she said nothing.

"These boys," he said, "these men—they come back from war and we ask them to sell guanciale." He lifted his glass and considered it. "I worry about this world we leave to Aida. *Per i bambini.*"

She could smell the fish from the shadows of the house, the censer from the church beyond the tall walls of the garden.

"I have a cousin in America," he said. "New York. I think about Aida. About a life over there. *Una vita nuova.* What would that be?"

"It would be a life. Same as here."

"A life." He mouthed the word again. *Una vita.* "I don't know, Signora. Would it be the same?"

She said nothing.

"I tell you, though," he said, "I would never let her forget her mother tongue. No. Never. You lose that, you lose home forever."

"And what's in New York?"

"Everything." He opened one hand. "*Qualunque cosa.*"

"And you think it would be easier?"

"Who can say? These are difficult times. For all."

She looked at her glass and lifted it and then set it down again. She hadn't taken a drink.

"Let me tell you what I think," she said. She reached over and lifted one of the halves of the crust he'd broken. "I think it is not meant to be easy. If it were easy, it would be for everyone."

"Is it not for everyone?"

"Yes. But not all of it. Only for those who earn it."

When he'd mouthed her words slowly, as if to himself, he reached across and opened his palm and lifted his eyebrows. She dropped the bread into his hand, and he leaned back and took a bite.

"Those who earn it," he said. "I agree. But how do we do that, Alexandra?"

"Signora. *Chiamatemi Signora.*"

"Of course. How do we earn it, Signora?"

"I don't know," she said. "It's different for each of us." She paused. "And betrayal means something. If you're poor enough you know that."

He nodded and considered the empty crust of his daughter's bread. For a long while he leaned back and seemed to stare into its hollow as the wind turned. Finally he spoke.

"I agree. I think perhaps you think I want something I do not want. I offer you *amicizia*. Friendship."

"I think you're a man who follows women in the streets."

"Women. A woman. Who knows?"

"My life, Signor Vergamo, is not a game."

Very slowly he set down the last of the bread and looked at her.

"No, Signora. It is not."

He stood and brushed the crumbs from his cuffs and went off into the house with a bow. She did not know if he was coming back. The wind had picked up in the Via Due Franchi, sifting past the open wall of the garden. She reached for her bag and lifted the gray wool sweater and pulled it on over her clothes and shut her eyes, the ivy whispering around her. *Aida*, he was calling in the house, *mangerai da solo? Vuoi mangiare da solo?*

A car passed slowly on the cobbles, children ringing their bells at it from their bicycles, and she thought of Georgio and Aldo and the boys on the Graciela, then of Aida in her room, staring down into the torn, blank page, then of the sharp-eyed figure of this child's father. *Perchè,* she thought. *Dove siamo?* When she opened her eyes, he was there: beaming, green-eyed, his copper hair waving down his temples, a platter of *pesce* in either hand. *Pesce,* she was thinking. *Nasello.* Each of them like its own wild secret that had been pulled up from the depths of the sea.

XXIII

When they'd eaten, he walked her back along the Via Gemelli and up the Via Catanzano to her door that was set deep in the old stones of the Via della Fiera, its black-painted wood chipped and dented where years of shoes had pressed or held it open on their way.

She led him inside and took his coat and hung it on the kitchen door and stood back against the sink, her bag still slung over her shoulder.

"This is it."

"This is plenty," he said.

She'd tucked her drawings away in the kitchen cabinet before she'd left, and when she stood in the kitchen filling two glasses of water she thought of them, of the woman with her hair across her face, of the empty net frayed and swaying on the waves. She shook her head and ran the tap and then thought of the pipes.

"*L'acqua*," she called back. "It's not good."

She heard him huff from the other room.

"I don't ask for much," he said.

They sat on the end of the little bed, and she was thinking of the boy's mother who had slept there, of the boy himself who had probably slept on the cold floor of the kitchen, who had probably been brought into the world in this very place.

She turned to him and asked him if she thought it was fair.

"*Che cosa?*"

But she only shook her head and asked again.

"Nothing is fair, Alexandra."

She shook her head and looked at the cabinet door she'd leaned against the far wall, its edges blackened with charcoal. Her hands lay open in her lap, and she looked at them, one at a time, in the dim light, her fingertips still roughened by the nets she'd mended, the charcoal blackening the split skin, her palms still scored from the first days out on the sea. She asked him if he thought it was possible for someone to love someone without reason; to love someone so much that they could only hurt them, again and again, to see if it was not a love they could wake from.

"No," he said. "*Non credo sia l'amore.*"

She looked at him, his clean face in the lamplight.

"*Non lo so,*" she said. "I think we can do things like that. I think we can do things we never thought we could do."

"And then what?"

"And then we know."

She touched her hands to her face. Very gently. Then she asked him how it had been with the girl's mother. Aida. If he had survived that.

"*Sopravvivere?*"

Yes, she said. If he had survived it.

They were quiet a long while. Finally he laid his hand on her thigh.

"*Parli senza senso,*" he said. "You speak nonsense."

She lifted his hand and laid it in his lap. Children were playing against the outer wall again, and she heard their mothers calling them home in the darkness. She shook her head and looked at the open door to the kitchen, the dirt floor worn down by the years of those who had walked from one room to another, as though they'd had some other place to get to, as though they hadn't been where they had been.

"No," she said.

She turned to him, and he laid his hand on her face and held her and kissed her hard. Lifting one hand only she braced herself against his chest and pushed him back slowly. She looked into his eyes a long while.

"No," she said. "No."

When he'd gathered his coat, he stood at the door and waited for her to speak.

"*Taurianova è una piccola città*," she said. "*Aida troverà una madre.*"

Then she closed the door and locked it and curled on the bed in the lamplight. She heard him knock twice before he left her. The children were still playing in the alley, and their mothers had given up calling them back. She pulled her knees up to her chest and cradled herself and spoke to the child inside her. *Stiamo andando a casa*, she said. We're going home.

I

He woke in the dark of Palma and scratched at the beard he had let happen. The villetta was unwarmed by any stove, but the cliffs on either side of the cove stood tall against the winds and broke the harder rains that had begun to come now from the east, and he thought of how it had been to curl beside another in the mountains and to wait. He had dreamt of a regiment in a valley, their boots moving through a grassland of hyacinths, and when they'd come to a mountain he'd seen soldiers holding out in the ruins of the ancient monastery at Monte Cassino, firing from the Benedictine windows in the hills. When he'd woken, he'd told himself not to think of his brothers. Rolling to his side he laid a hand on the sill, as though to feel that it was still there, and he lay awake thinking about the broken roads up into the winds of Klisura.

"You think it will be rough?" Antonio had said.

"*Fanculo,*" Gian had said. They were hanging to the straps as they sat in the back of the transport, swerving up the snowy roads of the mountain. "What isn't rough? The Greeks want us to come up. Tell them, capitano."

"*Non lo so,*" Leo had said. He'd reached over and touched Antonio's cheek softly. "Don't worry, Tonio. No one knows anything anymore in this world."

Some of the men had laughed.

"Tell them, capitano," Gian said. "No one. Not even the *generali, sì*?"

"I didn't say that."

"Of course not. No one said anything seditious at all." He grinned at the other men.

"Capitano," another whispered, "will we have the *Luftwaffe?*"

"I don't know, Bruni. It's a matter of the weather. They might not make it. Maybe our own will."

"Madonna. If the Germans won't, then we won't. They have the better planes, don't they? Don't tell me. I know they do. Madonna. I hate when we don't have *supporto aereo*, capitano. It's a god damned slaughter."

"Floris," Leo called up to the driver. "How much longer?"

"Who can say, sir? *Tre chilometri* at the next post, but then there's the turn and we might have to push."

"Madonna," Bruni said.

"Floris." Gian was buttoning a letter into his breast pocket. "What kind of a name is Floris for a war?"

"It's a damn good one," the driver called back. "My father was at the Battaglia degli Altipiani with that name, and the Austrians didn't forget it."

Gian laughed.

"*Sì.* It must have sounded sweet on their lips."

"You want me to stop the car?"

"Floris," Leo said, "it's nothing. Just drive. Bruni, stop."

"I joke, capitano. You always liked a good joke. What's this that troubles you?"

"He knows it's a slaughter," Gian said.

"Careful."

"I'm sorry, capitano. I don't say it in disrespect, but *gesù cristo* I can tell it's no good up there. Listen to those guns. Antonio, listen to them. You hear that?"

"I knew it," Antonio said. "I knew it was bad."

Leo had looked at the young caporale, with his oily hair, his eyes as green and worn as the canvas behind him, a spill of freckles down each cheek in the morning light. The caporale had lowered his head and looked into the helmet in his lap.

"Look at me, Tonio."

The boy lifted his face.

"You're going to be fine, you understand?"

He nodded.

"Give him some time to piss himself, capitano." Bruni slapped Antonio's shoulder, and the others laughed.

"Tonio," Leo said. He hadn't taken his eyes from him. "You hear me?"

The boy nodded. The others were still laughing.

"Say it, Tonio. Say you're going to be fine."

When his mother had written him in Bologna two years later, asking him what he had done with their name, he had paced the streets each night in civilian clothes, his thigh healed and his hair cropped short and a burning in his stomach he did not understand. Finally, in the second week of his sleeplessness, he'd walked down the Via Ugo Bassi under the broken lamplights and stood before the Fontana del Nettuno, staring a long time at the inscriptions before he looked up at the bronze-cast figure of the god himself. Perhaps he was like any of the gods, that god; perhaps he would not outlast the wild tides of this war. The bombing had begun in earnest only in the summer of that year, when the British had come up from Algeria with their long-range planes and dropped their hell on rail stations and citizens alike. Citizens. Leo had looked down at the inscription on the Fontana and nearly touched those words. *Populi Commodo. Built for the people. Senatus Populusque Bononiensis.*

Now, in the villetta at Palma, he remembered how he had sat back against the Fontana in Bologna, a world ago, and looked out at the city, the curtains drawn, the streets emptied by the curfew. The worst raids had come in September, when the Germans had disarmed the *Regio Esercito* and taken prisoners, and Leo had stood before the others and taken his oath with the Repubblica Sociale Italiana, swearing he would fight on with the Germans until the end. He had hoped to go to the front—perhaps to Anzio or Nettuno, perhaps to the Garigliano River or the Sangro, perhaps down through Roma and back home again, pushing back the waves of *il Britannico e gli Americani* that were still sure to come—but the colonello had ordered him to stay in the city with his command and occupy the city against its own people, its own ghosts, the partisans rising up against the Esercito as they'd done in Napoli, raiding the depots and the armories and sniping from behind the fresh-washed linens in the gardens. *Bella ciao,* they had sung, *e se io muoio da partigiano, seppellire lassu in montagna, sotto l'ombra di un bel fior.* But what was a song like that to the Germans? *Vernünftig handeln,* the *Wermacht Generalmajor* had plastered on the walls of the churches—*act reasonably, and you will enjoy my protection. Every German wounded will be avenged a hundred times.*

Avenged. Leo had sat back against the fountain in Bologna and tucked his knees against his chest and listened for planes in the night sky. Already he had heard of what had happened in Napoli, after the resistance. Already he had heard of the burning of the Biblioteca Nazionale, of the men gathered like cattle into the *stadio,* of the trains in the night taking people away to places from which no one returned. Already he had lain awake in the small bed of his quarters on the Via Ugo Bassi and tried to tell himself it could not be so, that *il motivo dell'Italia* was a cause and a true cause, that it was never about the ruin itself but about what the ruin could do, and they would not take away what it could do and leave the ruins alone. They wouldn't do that. Not to my brothers. Not to me. Not to the women and the children, *i civili.* Not to these ruins. He thought of who they were, but he could not get it straight. They. *Essi.* Who were they and where was he? Where did the cause live? In the bodies? In the bullets? In the snows and the winds themselves? He thought of that word, cause—*motivo*—and he tried to tell himself the cause for which he'd fought was not a cause that did such things, that he did not do such things, that these hands had not done such things, that no one did any such things to anyone at all on this burning earth except those who wished ruin on his country. But when he'd thought it, he knew he had no idea what the words meant. Ruin. *Patria.* He had told himself to think of that boy in the snows of Klisura, to think of his brothers, Nico, Paolo, Enzo, to think of his mother alone in the cellar in Lunetto, to think of everything, then nothing, then of his father—yes, think of him, think of your father, whoever he was, your father who you may as well say feels like everything in this whole damned war itself.

*Bella ciao, bella ciao. Seppellire lassu in montagna. If I die as a partisan,
bury me, bury me up in the mountains.*

When he'd risen from the Fontana he'd made his way at last to
the piazza where the thirty partisans had hung no more than a month
before. No one was there. He closed his eyes and felt the wind blowing
back from the Via Rizzoli, and he heard the first of the planes far off in
the darkness and then stood alone in the piazza as the first bombs of the
night fell on the far side of the city. He did not take shelter. When the
sirens had ended, he'd walked back to his quarters and lain alone in his
bed, thinking of the shore of Lunetto, thinking of the wind, thinking of
nothing but the darkness itself until the figure of Nettuno rose up from
that darkness with his trident and his stone face and his hand waving
over the chaos of the deep. Let the bombs come, he'd thought. Let the
waves wash over us all.

II

She did not know if he would be there. She woke at first light and took up the bag she'd packed in the dark, her drawings folded neatly into her clothes, and she reread the note she'd written for Georgio and his father. She took up the charcoal and wrote something for the mother, as well, and she knew Georgio would understand. *Grazie,* she wrote. *Suo figlio è così coraggioso.*

She left her thin wool sweater on the bed and locked the door behind her and set out down the Via Catanzano. Her sandals were still heavy with the dirt floor that had held them, her toes cold in the winter air, but she walked the warmth into them down the Via Aspromonte and stood on the corner of the Via Francesco and waited for a car and told herself not to think of his face, not yet.

III

He woke in the dark of the villetta and listened to the waves of Palma. No, he said. Today is the day. Roma. You will go down to the damn water at first light and ask Ricci for what he owes on the week. If he says yes you'll take the damned train and not look back. You can do that, can't you? You can do that for you and for her and for the one you know you have to do it for, can't you? Just relax. You could always do it before, couldn't you? You could always do what you told yourself you had to do.

His shoulders were sore from hauling the ropes, and he reached down and kneaded the muscles of his thigh that had seemed to heal so perfectly. *Ricci*, he thought. *Hire your boys.*

He had dreamt of his brothers, and when he'd woken he'd understood why. Enzo had come into this world, like him, like their mother, in the first week of summer—he thought now of how he'd spent his *compleanno* in Milano, alone, thinking of Enzo, of their *madre turbada,* before he'd gone back to Lunetto—but Paolo and Nico had howled themselves into this world, one year apart, in this first week of *gannaio*. How could it have been otherwise? That was the same week, they'd been humbled to discover, of their father's birth, the date printed in faded, gray ink in the papers they'd found among their mother's things, years later, in the shadows of Lunetto. *È ufficiale,* they'd always said, *ufficiale. Siamo eroi,* heroes—*but we just don't know how.*

He lay back now trying not to think of his brothers, but he closed his eyes and saw them on the landing craft at Durrës. Paolo. Nico. He said their names aloud and pushed himself up and sat looking out into the dark. Very slowly he laid his forehead on the coolness of the window and said their names.

He did not know if they had made it through the landing all those years ago, when the Albanians had fired their 75s. All day Guzzoni had thrown his men at the shore, and though the resistance had been light, it was only the third wave that broke through. Paolo. Nico. He said their names again. He thought of the boys crossing the sea with their *compagni*, talking about their lives as though they still had them. Then he thought of the silence that always began before it began. Nico, no. Then he opened his eyes and looked out into the dark of Palma and said you were only boys. What were you doing there? What did I tell you to do?

He held his palms against the glass and then closed his fists on the sill. As though he'd taken something from the night. Pieces of driftwood still leaned against the window, and he stared at them a long time and tried to think of where they'd come from on the far side of the dark. Then he closed his eyes and watched his brothers walk up from the sea, their carbines on their shoulders, their dark boots shining in the moon. Paolo, he said. Nico. He called them forward as though he were the city they had come for, all its streets in ruins, all its doors in flames. Come, he said. Come. He knew they would make it to him if he called them on, and he called them very steadily, and very softly, as though they could hear him through the barrage. The sun had not yet risen over the sea, and though he tried to see their faces through the dark and the smoke, he could not. Paolo. Nico. He waited a long while, and when he felt them come close he said their names and held his breath and opened his eyes, but there was only the night and the wind and the waves.

He lay back and told himself it was over. Don't, he thought. Just don't. But he knew he could hold it off no more. When he closed his eyes, he saw his father walking along a river in the moonlight, three rifles slung over his shoulders, and he tried to see his father's face, but he saw only a flash of black like the dark side of the moon. He opened his eyes, but he made himself close them again, and when he'd rolled to his side and cradled himself he saw his father standing before a dark house on a summer night, and then everything was still, and the garden was dark, and then his father kicked down the door and stepped inside and the windows blazed with light.

He opened his eyes and looked out at the darkness of the cove. He was holding himself tightly now, and it felt as though he was carrying himself over a thin bridge to the other side of the dark. The wind shook the villetta, and he closed his eyes and heard it climb the stairs and rattle the door behind him, and then the room was very still, and very calm, and he knew his father was standing over him. He knew the chill he felt on his neck was his father's hand, and he took it and tried to say something into the night, but his father leaned down and laid his lips to his ear and told him to wake, just wake. He shook his head and told his father he would like to stay where he was, just a moment more, but he only felt his father's hand on his shoulder and then the coldness of the house and then there was a voice he had not heard since another world.

There is only one way, Leonardo. Do you know what it is?

No.

Yes, you do. Tell me what it is.

No.

Tell me.

He opened his eyes and turned back and saw only the darkness of the house. Rolling onto his back, he looked up into the rafters and thought of the sea, of his mother. Then he laid his hands over his face and said I know, I know.

IV

It was mid-morning when she reached Palma, and she told the driver to take her as far as he could along the Viale San Paolo to where the pavement gave way to the broken roads toward the cove. She closed her eyes and waited for the smell of the sea, the palm groves, the spray of waves lifting up along the cold winds of the cliffs.

"You've been gone a long time?"

"*Sì*," she said, but her eyes were still closed, her fingers crossed over her belly.

When they'd gone as far as the pavement would go, she reached forward with the last of the coins she'd earned on the Via Maggio, but the driver lifted a hand and waved it away.

"No, Signora. Keep some."

When she'd walked down the cliff roads and down the path to the villetta, she stood at the back door a long time. She laid her hand on the latch and turned it open, but she knew he was not there. The wind was cold from the sea, and she left her bag at the door and walked back up the path and down again on the far side to the harbor. Two of the younger boys were perched on the docks, casting their long lines into the coldness of the waves. She crossed her arms against the cold and climbed up to the dock and knelt down between them.

"Is he here?" she asked.

"Who?"

She looked at their eyes and then rolled her tongue into a circle as his brother had taught him once, in Lunetto.

"*Sì*," they smiled. "*Sì*. He's here."

V

She was standing on the dock when the ship came in. A fine rain had begun as she'd waited, but she knew he had seen her a long way off, and he'd gone down into the hold and waited for the others to leave. Some of the boys greeted her softly, but the others passed by quietly and then the old man stood before her and held out his hands and gathered hers and lifted them.

"*Mia figlia*," he said. "You misunderstood me."

"No," she said. "I did. I did understand."

When she saw him, he was standing against the rail with his day bag over his shoulder. He had not shaved in a long time. He came to her very slowly and stood before her as the rain fell and weighed his hair and laid it down over his forehead in the cold.

"Don't say you're sorry," he said.

"No. I won't."

She reached up and pushed his hair back and felt his beard.

"Is it warm?"

He nodded.

"Cold out there," she said. "It must be—"

He was watching her lips as she spoke. Then he looked straight into her eyes.

"It is," he said.

She laid her head on the cold wool of his coat and waited for him to hold her, and he did.

VI

That night they sat together at the driftwood table, and she did not know how to tell him. In the nights to come, she would tell him of the boy who had helped her, that he was a good boy, a boy who was only trying to help. *Non essere arrabbiato con lui*, she said. But he only shook his head and looked out at the waves and said no, there was only one boy he was angry with, only one. She told him she'd come back, that she did not come back to little boys, but he only lowered her hands from his beard and said *Io so, Alexandra*, but I know there are still things I must do. I know there are still things we must do.

She'd told him about Tuarianova, of the *torrone* the boy had spoken of, of his mother who had spent her years in dirt-floored rooms off the Via della Fiera, with her only windows looking out to the shadows of an alley where no one came.

"But she had them."

"Yes," she said. "She had them."

"What do you think will happen to him? A boy like that?"

"He'll find his way. You should see him drive. *Molto coraggioso.*"

She'd waited for him to smile, but he only looked down at the scuffed floor of the villetta and spoke softly.

"Alexandra, how do you know?"

"Know what?"

He looked at her.

"How do you know?"

She laid her head on his shoulder and sat breathing the *pane di pescatore* drifting up on the wind from the houses over the cliffs by the harbor.

"I don't."

"You don't."

She lifted his chin. "Nardo, I don't think you're supposed to know. I just think you're supposed to be in it."

"And that's where we are?"

"That's where we are."

They'd sat together on the sill of the bay window in the first night, and she'd told him she wanted to show him something. She made her way to her bag and took out the drawings, all but one, and laid them out on the floor in front of them, the wind from the sea playing with the pages.

"I knew it," he said.

"What? What did you know?"

"That you were working. Every night I wished it for you."

She looked at him and then at the drawings.

"Working," she whispered.

"They're not finished."

"No."

"Tell me about them."

She turned toward her drawings and waved her hand over them. Her hands were thin, and strong, and always they had brought to his mind, for reasons he could not explain, the foal he'd watched come suddenly from a draught-horse in the ruins of Sarande, those hands somehow like the foal and its shadow and the startled mare standing beside it.

"I can't tell. Maybe not yet. I just know I think something's changed, Nardo, something I can't explain."

"How?"

"Because I found out something else."

"What?"

She breathed and thumbed back his hair that had grown heavy at his temples.

"Later," she said. "I'll tell you later."

She touched his hands. They'd grown raw from the ropes and the cold, but he'd worked the oil into them, each morning, and they were not cut. She laid them on her belly and told him to wait. A soft rain was sifting against the windows, and when the child fluttered, he looked at her and shook his head and then lowered his ear to her cotton.

"What do you think?"

"A boy," she said.

"*Sì*?"

"*Sì*. What do you hear?"

But she knew what he heard. She knew.

They'd moved the bed back to the southwest corner, beneath the window, and when they lay together he sat up and looked out toward the cove, as though he were listening to something a long way off. She was tired as she'd never been, but she'd woken and seen him and sat up until he looked at her in the moonlight.

"I'm here, Nardo."

"I know."

"I can't keep my promise."

"What promise?"

"That I won't say I'm sorry."

He looked away.

"You don't talk to me," she said. "Talk to me."

He nodded, and she lay on her side and looked up at him and listened. He told her about his days at sea when she was gone, how he would look down over the waves and think about where she had gone, as though the waves could tell him. As though the world were here to tell us what to do. He told her he had understood hopelessness. That she had taken a child from him. Their child. Then he told her about the boy hanging in the net above the sea. How he'd climbed up with the old man and freed the boy and held him swaying over the sea. Swaying there, over the sea. He asked her if she understood.

"I want to," she said. "I want to understand."

"I know. Me too. But not now. We should rest."

"*Dimmi*," she whispered. "Tell me what you're thinking."

"I don't know." He looked at his hands. "Is it true what you told me in Lunetto? That we'll never be free of it? That once we've ruined ourselves somewhere, we've ruined ourselves everywhere in the world?"

She looked at him and laid her hand on his chest and shook her head.

"No," she said. "Not at all."

"But you said it."

"I said it, and I meant it. But you don't have to mean a thing forever. You know that."

"What does that mean?"

"Nardo."

He looked away.

"I'm here," she said, "you have to tell me."

"I don't know what there is to tell. You're right. Of course you're right. We don't have to mean a thing forever. But I think of that damned *idiota* in me saying the things he said in Lunetto, and it's more than words. It's not just words."

"*Dimmi.*"

"I tried to make it right in Bologna. But how do you do that? By the time winter came I may as well have been a partisan myself. I would get my orders, but I wouldn't do anything but give them to Luca. I told you about Luca."

"No, Nardo."

He shook his head.

"Jesus."

He was quiet awhile. Then he leaned back against the wall and laid his palm on his forehead and drew it down across his face and spoke quickly.

"Luca was a runner. I gave him the orders I'd been given and in ten minutes the partisans had them, the Corpo di Liberazione. They stayed one step ahead of us, of them—I don't know how to say it—and nothing ever happened again. Not that I saw. Not until it was over."

"Couldn't you have been shot for that?"

"So what?"

"Don't say that, Nardo."

"I don't mean it now. But I meant it then. I just wanted the whole thing to go away."

"And then you went up to the Basilica?"

"Yes." He breathed. "It's a mess, Alexandra. I thought I was doing the right thing. I thought I was doing what my—I thought you do what you have to. I thought about my brothers. About things that happened. I don't know how to say it."

She sat up and leaned her shoulders against the cool glass of the window.

"I know," she said.

"No. I didn't do more. I just didn't do more."

"You could do more now."

He shook his head.

"It's not that easy."

"I know," she said. "I can't imagine it."

He closed his eyes.

"Yes, you can," he said. "You told me once you wouldn't pity me. Don't do it now."

"I don't. I'm not."

"Good."

"You can't stay like this, Nardo. And not just for your sake. Do you understand me?"

"What am I supposed to do?"

"How many times will you ask me that?"

"None. No more times. I'm done asking."

"Nardo."

He shook his head.

"Time, Alexandra. I just need time."

"I won't say I understand."

"Please don't."

She lay back and lifted her hair across her lips.

"I won't say I can understand. But it wouldn't kill you, Nardo."

"What?"

"To be understood."

When she'd turned away from him, she stayed awake awhile running her finger through the dust on the sill, tapping her thumb on the glass to the rhythm of the waves laying themselves down on the shore. Don't think that, he told himself. Don't. But when he lay back looking up into the rafters, he knew he had already thought it. Nothing will rinse it away but what you do.

VII

The next week the big storms came up, and she'd taken the nets up to the villetta where she sat on the big sill looking out at the waves. *Non preoccuparti*, she sang to the child, *tuo padre capisce il mare*. She worked on the nets until her fingers bled, cutting away the edges of the broken twine and then tying the slip knot at one end and doubling it and tying an overhand on the other side, cinching it with her teeth and cutting away the dross. When she'd run out of twine, she'd take out the drawings and work at them on the driftwood table, lifting each in turn and holding it upside down, into the light, as she'd learned to do in Lunetto. *No,* she always said. *Non sei tu.*

She worked on all of them except one. With the woman whose hair she'd drawn across her face in Taurianova—first across her face and then back behind it and over the glint of her shoulders—with this woman she could do nothing. Or she would do nothing. She laid her down and slid her across the table and covered her with one of the wooden bowls and said *no, aspetta. Later. Non adesso.* Then she would lift the drawing she had come to miss, when she was away from it, and she would shift the broken net on the waves, mending it and rending it again with her strokes of the charcoal, letting the wind drift in and take it out of her hands.

On the fourth night of a big southern wind they lay together in bed, and he did not know how to tell her about the storms. She'd touched the small cuts in his arms from the glass of the lanterns, the chill of the splinters, but he'd only said he'd cut them on the tough gills of the hake as he'd laid them along his arm to judge them. To give them back or keep them. She looked at him and shook her head and said the words back to him until he heard them.

He rose and showered alone with the light off and then turned it on and picked the last of the splinters from his arms and washed his face a second time. Then he looked at the beard on his face and lifted his hands to it, as though he could take it off. *Don't,* he told himself. *Don't run. Don't be proud.*

When he came back to bed, she was working at something in her hands, but she saw him and laid it on the sill and drew the curtain over it. He asked her what it was, but she lifted it and slid it behind the pillow and said nothing, something to make for them, a surprise. He smoothed the linens between them and said he was not sure if they needed any more surprises, but she only smiled and asked him about the old man.

"They say he fought in Abyssinia, and his son at Caporetto. But he doesn't say."

"Caporetto."

"*Como tuo padre.*"

She breathed. "Have you talked with him?"

"Yes."

She shook her head.

"But he's silent on the sea," he said. "Like all the old ones."

She looked at him.

"Do you think we'll be old?"

He laid his palm between her shoulders and felt her ask it again. He told himself not to think of the boy in the snow, nor of the boy in the piazza in Bologna, but he knew he would think of them in the night.

"Of course," he said.

He touched her face and told her he was sorry she had to work with the nets alone. "I hate it," he told her. "I wish you were out there with me."

"Nardo," she said, "I know."

After a while he thought she was sleeping, but she lifted her hand and laid it on his stomach and drummed her fingers.

"We have to eat more," she said.

"I know. I can get an advance. Ricci will give us one."

"Again?"

"Let me ask him tomorrow."

He ran his hand along her arm and laid his fingers in the crook of her elbow and began to knead her muscles down her forearm. Then he kneaded the other one, slowly, down through her palms and then out through the tips of her fingers.

"Nardo?"

He hummed.

"Don't say hate. Not anymore."

He closed his eyes, and she reached up and touched his face. With her other hand she felt down along his body until she felt, through the soft cotton of his pants, the heavy scar that stretched up his left thigh from his knee to the blade of his hip. She had touched it, sometimes, in the first nights, when the moon did something with it she could not explain, and he'd let her lay her hand on it and ask him.

"Clean through," he'd said, the first time.

"Then why did they open you?"

"To be sure. It's good to be sure."

"You hide it well."

"There's nothing to hide."

She'd lifted her hand and drummed her fingers on his chest. "What about your medal?"

"No."

"We could get a new one."

"No."

She'd waited a long while. Then she'd shaken her head and laid her hand on the scar again.

"It must have hurt. But you don't limp at all."

"No, not with one like this. With the knee, maybe. But not like this. They made it worse when they opened it."

She'd looked at him.

"But they had to."

"Maybe. *Sì*. But I walked around on that crutch forever."

"Not forever. Not you. You threw it away, didn't you?"

"After a while. I was done with it."

"Brave of you."

"No. I was just done with it all."

She'd shaken her head again. "You're lucky."

"It's ugly enough."

"Not ugly. They just opened you up a bit. That's all. Sooner or later it happens to us all."

He'd laid his hand between her shoulders and rocked her.

"You can ask me about it."

"No," she'd said. "This not something you ask. This is only something you tell."

They were lying now in the bed again, and he was trying not to think of the storms, of the sea, of the snows that had risen up from the valleys at this time of the year when they'd gone up the mountains to meet the Greeks.

"Have you thought about the spring?"

"What do you want to do?"

"We'll stay here," she said.

"With what school?"

She hummed.

"We can go up to Scilla," he said.

"No."

"Farther?"

"Catanzaro. Maybe Catanzaro."

"Why not Roma? Maybe we're not peasants, and we just don't know it."

She smiled.

"I wanted to go there after the war," he said, "but I never did."

"Why?"

"I don't know. I had to go home."

"Did you have any idea? About this."

"No," he said.

"Neither did I."

"Liar."

She smiled.

"Did you really never have it before? Like this?"

"Not this bad."

She told herself not to laugh.

"I don't need to know," she said.

"There's nothing to know. There were the girls at the *feste* in Lunetto and then nothing."

"Not even in Bologna?"

"No."

"Not even the nurses?"

"No."

She laid her hand on his thigh, and then she touched her belly.

"I'm so big, Nardo."

He laid his hand over her hand. "Just here," he said. Then he tapped between her breasts. "And here."

She rolled her eyes and touched his thigh again, but he lifted her fingers and touched them to his lips.

"I like it when you draw," he said. "They smell like smoke."

"Look what it does to my hands."

"It's better that way. Why would anyone want anyone whose hands don't look like their life?"

"Nardo."

"I mean it. You'll show me, won't you?"

"Show you what?"

"The one you won't show me."

She lifted her head and searched his eyes. Very slowly she laid her head on his chest and felt the house grow cold.

"What will we do in Roma? Isn't it a mess?

"We could live in the Trastevere," he said. "I don't think they did much to the Trastevere."

"Say it again."

"Trastevere."

"What does it mean?"

"Beyond the Tiber."

"That's plain enough," she said. "Say it again."

He did.

"Yes," she said. "That's it."

He closed his eyes and told himself what had led her away was over, that what had happened in the storms was over. But he knew they were not.

"Nardo?"

"*Sì?*"

"What did you want, when you were a boy?"

"To not be a boy."

She smiled.

"What did you really want?"

"That's easy. What everyone wants. To see things."

"I don't think that's what everyone wants."

"I did." He breathed. "We had a map at home. I can still see it. Something my father left. I spent more time with it than I did with anyone. Sometimes I'm not sure if I had any real friends at all."

"Even the boys of the Balilla?"

"Especially them."

She touched his thigh.

"I used to dream about—"

"Say it."

"It's silly."

"Say it."

He breathed. "I used to dream about these two horses—two horses coming to get me in the night. Dark horses. One of them had a rider but the other just a saddle. They'd come and stand under my window, and the rider would always whistle to me. I knew what they were, but I never saw them. I never saw the rider."

"Where were they taking you?"

"I never saw that either. But I always woke and looked out the window. Like—I don't know—like I told you in Lunetto. Like I had somewhere to be."

"Did you ever think you'd get there?"

"I sure as hell tried."

She laughed.

"I loved that map," he said. "I can still smell it. I would look at it all day, just to think about what places were like. Cina. America. Messico. Even Bologna. Roma."

"Roma," she said.

"*Sì*. I remember the Piazza del Campidoglio and the great fountains. Di Trevi e dei Fiumi. And the Ponte dei Quattro Capi. You walk over it and you feel two thousand years old." He shook his head. "Two thousand years."

"I thought you said you never went?"

"I said after the war."

She leaned on her elbow and looked at him.

"There's still so much we don't know." She thought of the old man, the words he'd spoken into the wind. Then she laid her hand against Leo's beard and looked at him again. "I want to know."

"Ask me."

"Il Vaticano. What was it like?"

He closed his eyes.

"Like a fortress. I don't know what they were keeping in and what they were keeping out, but it was a fortress. We went through in the fall. You would have liked it." He felt her breath come near. "You would have liked so much of it. The others didn't. They were just there. I was only a *caporale* then. I wanted to see Il Vaticano, but the others had no interest in that. Only the things men do in Roma."

"And you didn't do those things?"

He opened his eyes.

"No."

She saw in his face it was not a joke.

"*Dimmi*," she said.

"I was alone. I was looking for the gate, but I went the wrong way.

As I always do. I walked the whole length of the wall before I could find my way in. And then when I got in, I didn't want to be there. I just left."

"I know that feeling."

"What feeling?"

"Wanting something so bad for so long and then standing in it."

"You mean us?"

"No."

"You're sure?"

She straightened his sleeve.

"I don't mean us, Nardo."

He closed his eyes. He knew she was still looking at him, and he opened his eyes and told her to tell him.

"Nardo? Do you want to know?"

"I should give you time."

"No," she said. "That's not how it works. You have to ask."

He cinched his arm around her and sat them both up in the bed and looked at her.

"Sì," he said. "I want to know."

She told him about all the mornings in Lunetto she'd woken from the dream in which she'd said a name. She told him of her dream in Taurianova of sifting the dark grain from the light. And then mixing them again. And the bread that came after. She told him of how she'd gathered golden fleece in a dream and woven new clothes for their child, how she'd climbed to high places and gathered water with no light in it, then crossed a river and given it to a queen. And in the queen's face, she'd seen her life. Until she drank and was released. She told him how she'd dreamt of him falling into the sea, looking up from the depths at a vague light that closed itself slowly, like the eye of a child. Which he could not reach. By which he could not be seen. He shook his head and told her no, that shouldn't be why, but she only touched his hand and said wait, listen. She told him of the drawings she missed when she was away from them, the net on the sea and the waves themselves, and she told him yes, there was one, or part of one, she would not touch. But she did not speak of it. She told him, instead, about her mother's dream of the ships burning far out to sea, and she told him of her own dreams of a light on the water, a flaming chariot scattered on the depths, empty nets floating on the surface of the sea. *Dimmi,* he asked her. *I will,* she said. *No,* he said, *about the drawing.* She shook her head and said *later, Nardo. Please don't ask. Sì?*

Sì.

She told him instead about the nets she'd mended with her own hands, about a child carrying a torn page up into the shadows, and she told him what she'd thought about the wind, how sometimes it does things for us, sometimes it has a hand in what we make.

She placed her hand on his thigh and rubbed away the faint smudge of charcoal she'd left there, and she told him about Scilla and the factory and the young man with his falcons and his grey eyes and his manners from another world. A world that had passed and would not return. She told him about the festival in Lunetto with the empty cradle, and when she asked if he'd been there, he said she didn't need to ask, and she laid her hand on his chest and listened. She told him about her days raising the great ships, how she stood among the great ribs of the ships, and it was as though she were standing in the belly of the whale from the old stories, going down into the depths of her own life. And that she had been the one to make the thing that would take her down, and the thing that would lift her up again. Both. Because she was the heart of that thing. She remembered the words of the old man, and she asked him if he understood.

"*Dimmi,*" he said.

Then she told him how it had been with her father. How there were things he had never spoken of. How he called out about them in his sleep. And maybe that's all we ever do, any of us. Maybe all we do is call to each other in our sleep. Maybe our ghosts call out to each other.

He closed his eyes. She asked him if she should stop, but he only kept himself very still and said no, please, go on. Then she said he had spoken in his sleep. Some nights. That there were words he said that did not belong to her. Words he spoke about trains to strange places, about something being a long way away. About cities burning. She told him he could tell her when he was ready, *o quasi pronto,* but that perhaps what the old man had meant was that we never arrive. That we are never ready. That all we have is the setting out. The way itself. If we do it in earnest.

She could see his eyes were far away. She asked if he wanted to talk about Roma, about the swallows in Bologna, but he said no, please, tell me. She laid her chin on his chest and said there was nothing more to tell. "Please," he said. When she closed her eyes she could smell the bougainvillea, the palm fronds wafting like almonds, and she rolled her ear onto his chest—like the sound of the great chains of the ships, singing under the waves of the harbor. Then she told him. She told him she knew what does the calling, and when she'd seen his face again in Lunetto, she'd known if it is really our lives we call, then the answer will not be easy at all. As it hadn't been. She'd known it, she told him, even as she wanted to run from him. Even as she did. Although she didn't yet have the words for it, she'd known. And it's the having no words that makes a life. A life is not what we tell. The story, yes, but not the life. There are no words for that. Like the secret of the world.

She held him a long time, and she told him she could never love a man who couldn't weep. He tried to say, as a joke, that she had made sure he was not that man. But when he said it, he knew it was no joke. He knew this was his life, and we know perfectly well what we do.

After a long while, she stood and kissed him on the head and came back with two glasses of water. They sat in the bed, and they laid the empty glasses on the sill, and she told him to tell her more about Rome.

"Are you sure?" he said. "We're here now."

"Yes," she said.

He told her he'd seen as much of it as he could. The *divisione* were there three days, and then they had pulled out for San Marino. It was a long way, he told her. He'd thought they were going up to Ferrara, but they'd swung around and crossed the water to be with the Alpini, in a place he'd never seen. They'd spent Christmas in Albania, he told her. In Sarande. All he could think about was Nico and the others. He didn't know where they were, not then, not yet, but he knew they had lied about their age and disappeared in all that chaos. He knew what he'd told them to do.

"Were you afraid?"

"For them. Yes." He breathed. "And for me."

He was quiet a long while as she stroked his chest, and when he spoke it seemed as though his voice had gone away and come back to him.

"Do you think we keep death inside us?"

She looked at him.

"What?"

"Someone told me that once."

"That we keep death inside us?

"Something like that," he said. "That that's what we're supposed to do."

"What does that mean?"

"I don't know. That we have things inside us, and we're supposed to admit them."

"Yes. I think that."

"And if we admit them, they're not death?"

"Nardo," she said. "These storms are not good for you. For us."

"I can stay here tomorrow."

"We need the money, Nardo. The three of us. And the storms have passed. Haven't they?"

He looked at her.

"I don't know."

"I'm listening," she said. "You can tell me about the things inside us."

"Let's rest," he said. "I'll ask Ricci tomorrow for this month and next."

"He'll think you'll run. No one wants to be out there in winter."

"He won't think that. And we're not running anymore, remember?"

She laid her head on his chest.

"I do," she said.

When he'd fallen asleep, she stayed awake thinking about what she'd told him. Sometimes it is not real until you tell it, she thought. Then she thought yes, yes it is.

She thought of Scilla and what could have been her life. Of those falcons coming and going and landing on another man's wrist. The lightness of it. The weight. Like a life. Like a child's heart. Like fate. She thought of the long ride to Tuarianova and the longer ride back, the smell of censer in the Chiara di Santa Maria and the smell of the wax on the hands of the children as they passed by, the brave boys who held the wax so steadily and firmly although it burned them. Of his brothers so young and troubled, wherever it was they'd been told to go. Of him. Of him in the snows.

She rolled to him and laid her hand on his chest, but he did not wake. Rest, she thought. Let's just rest. She closed her eyes and thought of a woman standing on a dirt-floor and then very slowly falling to the ground because her child was calling itself into this world, her only child. Then she thought of the girl in Taurianova—Aida—of her father's lips so cold and thin in the shadows, and she opened her eyes and watched Leonardo in his sleep and thought this is what it is; it's not supposed to be fair. The villetta smelled of him, and when the wind slipped up the stairs and rattled the back door she closed her eyes and said her name to herself. Then she said this one. This name.

She thought about what he'd said about death. About the things inside us. Then she thought about the old man, waving his hands over the waves. The boats of our souls, he'd said. In the darkness now she thought of someone making a boat in a field, in the summer sun, the bindweed snagging on the ribs of it. The sun was hot, and silent, and she thought of her own hands sanding the heartwood, the knots in it, like all the nights of childhood. Then she watched herself lift the boat on her shoulders and carry it down to the sea and climb inside. And lock the oars. And hold them close. And choose.

She rolled onto her back and laid her hands on her belly and listened to the waves crashing down on the stones in the cove. It's true, she thought. Of course it's true. Nothing can deliver us from ourselves.

VIII

They woke once more in the night, and he rolled to her and watched her until she felt his awakeness.

"Nardo?"

She'd propped herself up on her elbow, and he reached up and touched her face.

"*Il mio mare?*"

"I didn't mean what I said, about you not asking."

"What?"

"When I told you not to ask about the drawing."

"You want me to ask?"

"No," she said. "But I didn't mean you can't ask. You can. You have to. But just once, *va bene?* Then the other half is me. Precisely half."

"What are you talking about?"

She looked out the window and then turned back. Her thumb was making small shapes on the linen between them, shaping something he could not see.

"Do you think it's safe here? Still?"

"He won't come, Alexandra. That's all over. If he was going to come, he would have come."

Her hand stopped moving, and she tucked it under the pillow and lay down and looked at him.

"Maybe he doesn't know where we are. Maybe no one does. How would they know?"

"We're not far."

"That's exactly why he won't know."

She tried to smile.

"Yes," she said, "no one would be as foolish as we are."

He shook his head.

"What's wrong, Alexandra?"

"Nothing. *Dimmi.* What happened today? Were the winds very bad?"

"It's a good ship." He smiled. "Aldo was very brave."

"Aldo," she said.

She rolled onto her back and laid her hands on her belly.

"Those boys. What's a boy doing out there on those waves?"

"The same as us. Only worse. His mother and father have nothing. And they know it."

"Calabria has always been poor. You'd think we'd have learned how to be poor."

"He has."

She turned and laid her head on his shoulder and smelled him.

"Every day you smell more like it."

"Like what?"

"The sea."

"Good," he said.

"Once it's in you it never leaves you."

"Good. Very good."

She laughed, and he slipped his fingers into her hair and lifted it and let it fall.

"Does it feel lighter still?"

"Yes," she said. "And heavier. Ricci likes it."

"You like it?"

She nodded against his shoulder.

"We're safe, Alexandra. I promise."

She nodded again.

"*Dimmi,*" he said. "Tell me what's in your mind."

She told him she was not sure if it was best to be safe. That perhaps there were things in their life that they had only thought they were done with. In their lives. That she wanted them to be safe from harm but not from themselves. Not from each other.

"Do you understand?"

"I think so," he said.

"I don't want us to run from anything anymore. Ever."

"But we are."

"I don't mean we go back. Maybe there's nothing to go back to. I don't know. But I don't want this child to run. Do you understand?"

He looked at her, and then he lay back looking at the ceiling, the dark rafters raised by other hands. In another time. Another world.

"And you think I'm running? Still?"

"Yes."

Very slowly he closed his eyes and rolled away and sat up on the bed and left her. She heard him take his coat from the peg and walk out through the back door, and then she heard him walking down the wooden stairs in the dark. Then she heard nothing but the wind and the waves.

She lay there a long time, laying her hands on her belly. She closed her eyes and saw an empty cradle alone on the water, and she felt dark waves breaking over her. She thought of something lifting her and carrying her through the dark and laying her down in a strange place. Alone. She told herself to think of it. Fully. What he had done. Then she told herself a war is a war. No, she thought. You know what he did. There is not a night of your life you have not seen it. And yet you are here. Don't ever tell yourself you haven't chosen.

She lay in the dark thinking about children. About cities burning. About young men and what they did when they were afraid. After a while she felt the child quivering, and she thought of the swallows high up in the darkness of the Basilica, and she shook her head and said the fool, the fool.

She took her coat from the peg and walked down to the beach. He was sitting by the tidepools looking out at the waves. She told herself the strong are the ones who go to the weak. Then she said no, it is the other way around. Then she said whatever world that language is from, the weak and the strong, it is not this world.

She stood behind him, and he stood and walked to the edge of the sea, the waves small and breaking in the starlight. She could hear the wind through the three rocks toward the south end of the cove, and she looked for the moon like ships burning far out on the water, but it was just the moon.

She walked to him again and stood behind him.

"You don't know that," he said.

"Then tell me. Tell me what I don't know."

He shook his head. He was quiet a long while, the waves running up over his ankles. Then he told her he wasn't a coward.

"Is that what you think? That I would think that of my child's father?"

He said nothing. Finally he looked out at the horizon and said he knew she did not trust him. That she never would.

He knew what she was going to say before she said it, and she did say it. She said she would never pity him, not him, and that if there was still one thing standing between her and her trust, it was exactly what he knew it was. It was that there was still one thing he would have to do before she could trust. One thing only he could do. One.

He looked at his feet in the darkness of the water, and he thought of what his mother had told him about his father. But he could not get the words right. It seemed like another world. Don't let yourself think that, he thought. That world is right here. Right here. Until you do what you have to.

He tucked his hands into his armpits, and then he thought of her in the coldness of the wind. You haven't changed, he thought. Look at the breaking of these waves, and tell me you've changed. No, he thought. No. But when he turned around to see her, she was gone.

When he'd spoken to himself in the cold and heard nothing he hadn't heard before, he walked back up to the house and saw her turn away from him in their bed. He took a pillow very softly and curled on the kitchen floor and fell asleep. When he woke, as he knew he would, he lay back on the cool floor and listened to her breathing in the other room. He closed his eyes and opened them, but he was still where he was.

He stood and changed quietly into his cotton trousers and the blue shirt he'd worn when he'd met her, from which they'd washed his own blood into the sea, and he pulled on the grey knit sweater and buttoned the wool coat and stepped out the back door and down the stairs and took the path to the sea.

He stared at it a long time. The waves were dark with the quarter-moon in them, and the tide was low. He left his sandals beside one of the tidepools in the fine-pebbled sand and walked out to the first of the three rocks standing taller than the villetta at the edge of the sea. The face of it was wet with the sea-spray, but he worked his toes and his fingers into the crevices and climbed up the gentle slope of it and curled on top of it under the moon like a child. After a while he lay flat on his back and looked up at the stars.

He knew she was right. If you don't think it fully, it becomes your life. Maybe it already has. Maybe that's what your whole life has been. The silences. Shut up, he said. Coward.

He closed his eyes and opened them and the stars were still there. As they'd been when he was a child. They are not for me anymore, he thought. No, he thought. Yes they are. That's what you're afraid of.

When he closed his eyes again he knew he would see him, and he did. He saw the boy in the snows of Klisura Pass, and he looked down into his eyes that were nearly as dark as his brother Nico's. Nico, he said. Nico. But he knew it was not him.

He'd let his eyes open again, and he lay back on the rock and let the waves shake him. Just be the sea, he thought. Like she said. You have been stone long enough. Try something different. Try it.

He closed his eyes tight and held his hands over them. The sea was crashing against the east face of the rock, and he could hear the wind in the palm trees up the beach toward the villetta. After a while he let the wind do what it had to, and he was lying in the snows of Klisura Pass, and the wind was gutting, and the boy was moaning beside him.

He rolled to his side and laid his hand on the boy's chest and pulled him toward him. We have to go, he said. The boy shook his head and pointed to his legs, but he did not look.

He lifted his own leg with his left hand and slung it over and rolled himself onto his knees. He felt a pain in his thigh he could not imagine the world would permit. Not yet. The wind was blowing him forward where he knelt, and he slid himself behind the boy and tried to lift him by the shoulders. It was then that he saw the boy had no legs.

He reached down and pulled the boy toward him by his belt buckle. The boy said something he could not hear. Then he did hear it.

He sat back in the snow and pulled the boy into his lap and cradled his face.

"They're gone," the boy said.

"No one's gone. They're coming back."

"They're gone."

The boy opened his eyes wide.

"They're not looking."

"What?"

"They're not even looking."

A cold had entered Leo he had never before known. He looked away from the boy and squinted into the storm, but he could see nothing but the wind lifting the snow and the small flashes of artillery down in the valley. Then he heard horses hauling the guns up in the dark.

He looked back over his shoulder and then down at the boy. His lips were blue, and the top lip was trembling with a brown wisp that had never been shaved.

"Help me."

The boy had closed his eyes, and Leo had slapped him. He patted his shoulder for the carabina, but it was not there. He took out his pistol from the holster at his hip and blew the snow from the barrel and pointed it up in the air and fired. Then he fired again. He looked back up the pass for an answer, but there was only the snow.

"*Non spararmi*," the boy said.

"I'm not going to shoot you."

The boy closed his eyes. He slapped him again.

The wind was driving up the slope, and he watched the boy and listened to the guns working up into the pass. He thought the boy was listening, too, but after a while he saw him slump his head to the side, and he could not see his breath in the cold.

He lifted him by the shoulders and shook him.

"Papa," the boy said. "Papa."

He had not opened his eyes.

"No," Leo said.

"Papa."

The guns were flashing far out in the dark, and he closed his eyes and felt the boy breathing. He thought for a long while before he spoke.

"*Dimmi*," he said.

"Papa, *mi dispiace*. Papa."

"I know."

"Papa. Papa."

He rocked forward and held the boy hard, and he did not know what to do. He pulled back the hammer of the pistol again and heard it click and then let it fall in the snow. He was rocking the boy from side to side.

"Papa," the boy moaned. "Papa."

The wind was matting the snow against their bodies. He turned and saw figures moving in the snow higher up in the pass. In the wind he could hear the language they spoke.

"Listen," he said. "Look. No one is gone. *Te l'avevo detto*. Didn't I tell you?"

"Papa. Papa."

The boy said it once more and then opened his eyes. Like endless wells deep into the heart of the world. Into which even this child had not been permitted to go.

"Papa," he said. "*Mi dispiace*."

He leaned forward and laid his lips to the boy's ears, and he told himself to say it. Just say it. The wind was lifting the boy's hair and laying it down against his face. Finally he did say it. I forgive you, he said. I do.

He held the boy's face to his chest, and he waited until he could not feel his breath. Then he slid him down into the snow and began to crawl away toward the voices in the dark.

He opened his eyes. The stars were there. He could hear the waves again and the palm trees and the tide rising into the tidepools in the small stones below. He held himself and rocked himself in the sea wind, and though he was alone he knew he had crossed over to a place he had never been. Or had always been. The stars shone in the darkness, and he told himself the life he held was his life, and though he could not tell if he had carried it or it had carried him, he knew he was there. And no one would carry it for him. No one. Léonard, he whispered. Leonardo. He had thought he was going to think of Bologna, but when he closed his eyes again he saw only an emptiness where the piazza had been, and he knew there were limits to penance. To the justice a man can mete out even to himself in his own heart. And that those limits were perhaps why such things happened and would happen again. To the end of the world. Think of it, he told himself. Think it fully. Don't ever tell yourself they were only orders. Don't ever tell yourself the orders didn't let you do what you burned to. What Nico and the rest of them—No. Think it. Think it fully. But when he tried to think of it, he heard her voice calling to him through the wind, and he opened his eyes and looked at the stars, the stars that had gone out long ago, and he knew in his bones that the penance can be nothing but another crime. If it is a way to hide from the world to come. All that matters is that you know. Say it, he told himself. Say if you know. He told himself he did know. That he knew it as much as he would ever know, and that if he did not look at it again it was only because there was a world to come. Which knew his face. And which knew his name. He listened to that world calling him, and he told himself you will know by how it holds you. You will know if that world knows. Knows if you have seen it. If you have looked. If you have held what you have to hold in the darkness beyond end. And admitted it. Admitted it all. And if that world chooses your life you will know that your life has looked enough at the past that it can have a world to come. Without fleeing its own heart. Without forsaking the past without which the future is nothing. Without which the present is nothing. Without abandoning the past which is merely the future unready to be changed. In every moment. Without end. Look, he thought. It is calling your name. Even yours. Even these stars are for you. Even this sea. It is calling your name and listen and listen and you have done what you have to and tell me it is not enough. Enough. Tell me. Listen. This is your name. This is your life. Alexandra. Alexandra. The only atonement is openness. The only redemption is attention. The only atonement is to be here.

IX

She steadied her belly and climbed onto the rock and sat with him and held him.

"I'm sorry," he said.

"I know. I know."

They walked back to the villetta in the moonlight. The sea had taken his sandals, and they made their way slowly over the stones and climbed in through the open window and lay on the bed as they'd done in Lunetto, the curtains blowing over them in the dark.

"It's over," she said. "All that is over now."

"Even though it's not over for them?"

"Yes," she said. "Even though."

X

That night his mother woke in Lunetto from a dream she could not explain. She'd seen her three sons sitting at a table in a small house, nothing but a single candle between them. The wind shook the candle-light in the rafters, and when the eldest had begun to speak, they had turned their faces toward the door, and the candle had gone out in the wind, and in the darkness she had heard someone telling her sons to stand, stand.

She rose and laid her hand on the night table and watched the first light shift in the picture frames. She heard her mother speaking. There are those who go deep into cities and strange places to find their lives, her mother had told her, but they stand alone in some shadowy house years later, their children's clothes folded away in their rooms, and they understand what they found in those bright eyes and that handsome face was perhaps joy and perhaps bliss, but it was not a life. It was not their life.

She turned and took herself down the sconce-lined stairs her father had torn down and remade in some other time, past the relics, past the gilt-framed portraits of her parents, her elder sister, the three of them so still and dignified and lost together in the great influenza of 1918, leaving her in that house with only their silences and their clothes and her sixteen years.

She sat alone now at the kitchen table, and although she stared at the gramophone in the parlor, its dark dials like the waves in her youngest son's hair, she did not switch it on. The house was cold, and she stared at the black flash of the telephone her eldest son had brought her, one autumn, when he'd stood so tall and noble in his uniform of the

Bersaglieri, his collar stiff and his boots polished and that dark promise of capercaillie feathers blooming from his brim.

–*Enzo, siamo poveri, poveri.*

–*No, mama. Non più. Sei ricco come il sindaco.*

Enzo. Enzo. The dark bloom of those feathers. Where is the Dnieper river, anyway? What does it mean, Petrikowka? What was it your nonna told me, so long ago? Darkness is a promise the world shall not break. But between the darkness and the darkness, there is some light; there is what we make; there is the brief, sweet word of our life.

She opened her hands and laid them on the table and closed them again. The bread she'd made in the evening lay covered on the sill, in the worn copper pan her father had bought her mother in the autumn of his twenty-fifth year, when he'd come back from Abyssinia—a scar in his side he would never speak of—and taken her mother up to Volterra and beyond, drifting through the markets where merchants sold wares from the ancient Etruscan mines in the hills. *Papa,* she thought. *What was your life?*

She smelled the bread now and thought of children running through a house, children's hair tousled from sleep, children tugging at a woman's hems and asking for a taste, just a taste. My sons, she said. Laying her hands flat on the table, she lifted her fingers one by one and counted off the months to the birthday of her second son. *Cinque. Quasi cinque.* You know now, Nardo, don't you? Only you can do it. Only you. With your life. Then she shook her head and sat in the parlor and switched on the gramophone. My son, she said. Go. Keep your word.

XI

The mistral winds came down from the Rhone Valleys of France and past Sardinia and into the Tyrrhenian sea, and when the skies were clear the boys of the Graciela spoke of the ancient winds whose names had been lost after the Empire had fallen, whose names they had been told were gods' names, whose names they'd wished they'd known.

By February she was seven months pregnant, and he had fished through the winter storms, and although it was cold, there were calm days now before the true storms came. She sat sometimes at the driftwood table, and sometimes at the small desk before the westward windows, and when she thought of the old drawings she'd brought from Lunetto she shook her head and told herself she did not need to look at them; she knew what they were. Then she'd think of the drawings she would make if she did not have to make her life. No, she'd think. That's ridiculous. There's no other way. When she'd think it, she'd take out her new drawings and stare at them and shift the charcoal like the sands in the winds of the cove and let them show her what they were. But always the woman she'd begun in Tuarianova sat unfinished, and always she would think of her and drag her own hair across her own face, her own eyes, and though she knew what it was like to be so unfinished, so undone, she'd kept her tucked away and never lifted her and never let her see the villetta or anything in it.

She sat with the old man on Sundays, when he did not fish, and they spoke of children and of the days to come. They listened to the wind in the cliffs behind them, and he spoke to her somberly about the old days, when the village was so poor and there were no motors to push the boats out beyond the break. He said that work had broken many, but maybe that was what people had forgotten. Maybe we are meant to be broken into this world.

She was walking back up to the villetta, on the third Sunday of the month, when she saw someone on the north side of the cove. She knew it was him. She made her way through the tidepools and crossed the sands and found him sitting in the stones by the dock of Bonanno.

"Nardo."

When she'd settled herself beside him, he told her he'd walked the cliffs all day, that if the old man could have his days of rest, then maybe he could, too.

"Of course, Nardo."

He shook his head.

"It's strange, Alexandra. I've lived with it so long. I don't remember how to live without it."

She nodded.

"The first time you know those shots are for you," he said, "something happens."

"Leonardo."

"There's what happens right away and what happens after." He kicked at the shell flints. "What happens right away is you wake up. I don't know how to explain it. You can smell everything. You can't die."

"And then?"

"And then you do."

"No."

He shook his head.

"It's just that everything gets all mixed up in you, and after it's over you're not sure if all the pieces will ever go back to where they were. You're not even sure where they were."

"Nardo."

"It's just that maybe I'm starting to remember. Remember where they were. And that's hard."

She cinched herself toward him and laid her head on his shoulder. Through the palms they could hear the shore birds nesting again in the cliffs, trilling in the fistulae behind them, and she laid a hand on his thigh and waited. After a long while she spoke.

"You know, we haven't swum here ever."

"It's cold."

She rolled her head and rested her chin on his shoulder and stroked back his hair.

"What isn't?"

He felt himself smile, and he looked down and picked at the stones.

She stood and brushed off her pants and slipped off her shirt and laid her hands on the fullness of her belly.

"You're crazy."

She nodded.

"They'll see us," he said.

"And?"

He shook his head and stood slowly and unbuttoned his heavy wool shirt. When he'd rolled up his pants he saw her standing naked before him, and he shook his head and slipped off his pants and let her take his hand and lead him down through the tidepools.

The waves were small, and the tide was low, and they waded out beside the dock and let the chill take their breath away.

"Careful," he said.

"I'm always careful."

He held the pilings of the dock and guided her out to the end of it, and they stood where the swells lapped their shoulders and the current began at their ankles.

"Always," she said.

Then she pushed back her hair and winked and pulled him down into the water.

XII

The morning of her twenty-third birthday, she woke late and he was not there. She sat at the little desk that looked out the front windows to the cove, and she wrote her mother a letter, as she had done in the first months they'd been there. She told her about the old man, with his weathered face and his true hands, and she told her about her days out on the current where the bottom of the sea fell away to four hundred fathoms or more. She asked her mother to tell her sisters she would write to them, and she asked her if perhaps one day she might be able to understand that this man was a good man. That he was not a secret to himself. She wrote the words and looked at them and then looked out to sea. He is not a secret to himself.

She ran her fingers over the characters someone had carved in the desk, someone who had not finished a name, and she touched her fingers to her lips and listened to the wind and the sea. Then she ran her hand over the soft wood and felt the ghosts of the words others had written there, the voices in her father's body the last time she'd touched it, the silences in her own. We are the silences in each other's stories, she wanted to tell her mother. But she didn't. Instead she took up the pen and asked her mother if she had known she'd had a daughter who would leave, if she had ever done anything so thoughtless in her own life, and if she had, perhaps she could understand that it wasn't really thoughtless at all. That if we did not do the things we felt called to do, we would resent forever the ones we had chosen over our own lives. She looked at the words and shook her head. She knew her mother would think she was saying she had chosen not to be with her. It didn't matter if it was true. It was not something her mother would understand, and in that way it was not true. A truth belongs to everyone or no one at all.

She crossed out the words and wrote the letter a second time, asking her mother if she could understand that she had chosen her own life, even if she did not know what she was choosing when she chose it. But that her mother had been her guide, like the guides she had spoken of in the old days, from another time. Like Russo's wife. Like those who can show us, with the dignity of their lives, the dignity of our own. She told her mother that this was the life she chose each day. She woke and looked at this man and said Yes. Yes. And the only task of a life is to unmask each other and ourselves and see what we are saying yes to. To know.

She folded the letter and sealed it in an envelope and drew the three rocks on its back flap and ran her hands through her hair. She looked at her hands and saw the fingertips roughened from the nets. I'm working, she said. If tomorrow were the last day of the world, I would wake and do the work of my life.

She closed her eyes and breathed the air and thought perhaps it was not true what she'd thought about a truth, that it was for everyone or no one at all. You can have your own, she thought. Yes. You have to risk it. You have to risk the distances between.

She looked out at the waves and closed her eyes and laid her hand on the largeness of her belly. Then she laid her hand on the envelope. She knew she had not said what she'd hoped to say. She had wanted to tell her mother how it really was, how this man had come into her life and done the one thing she had been so afraid of. How he had refused to love her for what she was not. And in so doing he had taken from her the dream of her life and given her the truth. That she was who she was. And not the endless chaos of the sea. But that those are the moments, mother. Those are the moments of beginning. When we find someone who takes off the mask of our vastness and sees us for the one, still living mystery we are. As we do for them. In them. With them. As we admit and are admitted. And that seeing is not a diminishment. And that form is our freedom. And that unlasting is our vastness. And that place of our changes is our rest.

She looked at her hands and closed them tightly, but there was no pain. When the wind rose and the light shifted in the window, she told herself it did not matter if she was late to start mending the nets. If you get the work done, what does it matter how it happens? No, she thought. That's not true at all. All that matters is how.

When he came in through the back door, he was carrying a radio he'd bought in town with a turn-table on its top, and she shook her head and said his name.

He smiled and set it on the large driftwood table between the empty bowls and set down a paper bag he'd carried under one arm. He unspooled the thick black cord from his shoulder, as she'd seen him do with the mooring ropes of the ship, in late summer, and he plugged it in and turned the dial. The villetta filled with music. He clapped his hands once and opened his arms and smiled.

"Come," he said.

She shook her head and rose and went to him. She laid her arm over his shoulder, and he lifted her left hand and laid his palm in the small of her back and swayed her.

"You're a fool," she said. "We're broke."

"You thought I forgot."

"No. I knew you forgot."

He smiled.

"I thought you were fishing."

"Which one is it? I forgot or I was fishing?"

"Both," she said. "Nardo. Tell me you didn't steal it."

"*Traditrice.*"

She shook her head.

"Ricci," he smiled. "It's from Ricci."

He swung her off the floor and then dipped her slowly and raised her up and kissed her. She touched his face and said he was a fool.

"I know. Your fool."

The wind came in through the window from the sea, and she saw a brief sadness flit through his eyes, but she saw him shake it away and smile and go on dancing.

"I have a day planned for you. For us."

He grinned as he lifted her again, but she shook her head and roughed his hair.

"It's Friday, Nardo. Ricci will fire you. We'll have nothing."

"No," he said. "We never have nothing." He dipped her again.

"Careful," she said.

"I'm always careful."

When he raised her up, she took his face in both of her hands and kissed him a long time. Then he held her out at arm's length and looked at her.

"Play."

"My fool," she said. "*Il mio bellissimo stolto.*"

"*Aspetta.*" He held up a finger and made his way to the paper bag and slid out a record. He placed it on the turn-table and flicked off the radio and lowered the needle.

"What is it?" she asked

"Yvette."

She shook her head and smiled.

"Where did you get that?"

"Georgio. Georgio can get anything."

"Georgio."

"*Aspetta,*" he said. "*Non finito.*"

"*Ma dai.*"

Sliding the bowls apart on the table he laid down the bag and slipped out a small vial of rosewater. Then he lowered his nose to the bag and sniffed deep and pulled out four *clementine,* two in each hand, and pretended to juggle them. When he'd set them on the table, he raised a finger and pulled out a heavy ream of fresh, white paper, the glint of it wrapped lengthwise with a black, silk bow.

"Anything," he said.

She went to him and brushed his hair back from his brow. She hadn't looked at the paper.

"Nardo."

"Come," he said. "The wind is good."

"*Aspetta.*" She held him by the belt and sat back on the table, holding the back of his neck as she kissed him. She felt her breasts rise under her cotton, and he bit her ear softly and asked, as he always asked, if it was not bad for the child. She told him what she always told him—*nothing is*—and then she slipped off his belt and laid it over his shoulder and shuffled herself free of her clothes and placed her palm in the small of his back as she helped him into her.

XIII

The water was calm, the wind listing softly from the east. He'd borrowed a three-meter skiff from Aldo, and he rowed them out from the harbor in the winter sun, their heavy sweaters pulled up to their chins. They'd packed 'nduja and the *clementine* in rolls of newspaper, and he'd brought a bottle of verbicaro bianco that he said was only to wet their lips. Yours, she said. Your lips.

He lowered the anchor no more than a kilometer out, where the winds were soft, and they could see the cliffs of Palma swaying in the distance. She said February was a dangerous month, when the storms could come suddenly, and he smiled and said he was a sailor now, and he knew the sea. She laughed and said he sounded like an old man, and she thought she could see the same sadness flit through his eyes before he smiled and checked the knot of the anchor rope as the boat swung out into the current of the deep.

They ate the 'nduja on biscotto di grano, and he sat back in the bow, sipping the verbicaro. He asked her what else they could possibly want.

"We don't ask for much," she said.

"You could ask for more."

"All I want," she said, "is no storms. And then the spring. And then our life."

"This is our life."

"I know."

He took a sip and looked over the gunwale at the horizon. It was clear.

"I don't think we'll have storms."

"Don't say it."

"I mean this winter. All winter."

"I know. Don't say it."

"I'm sorry," he said. He set the bottle down and took up a *clementina* and scored it with his finger.

"Remember?"

She reached out both hands, and he gave it to her. On the skin of the fruit she scored the shape of their country with her fingernail, and then she made a small X in the heart of it.

"Roma," she said.

"Roma."

They ate and talked as the sun warmed. They'd bought the biscotti at the market in Palma, and they'd left it out for three days in the big wooden bowl on the driftwood table, so they knew it would taste of the sea. She'd lifted a piece to his nose when he'd carried the boat on his shoulders down the cliff roads, her hair still wet against her shoulders, and he'd breathed and she'd said, "Like Palma. It smells like home."

He reached back and lifted a jug of water they'd stowed in the bow, and they wet the ancient grains of the bread and softened it and spread the 'nduja with their fingers. The crust was hard and fine, its scent like almonds in the sea air. She watched him take a bite as he sat in the prow, and she waited for him to smile.

"Good?" she asked.

She reached over and lifted his piece and smiled at him as she chewed. The wind was soft and cool, and they drank from the jug and passed it very carefully between each other when the boat swayed. Just once she took up the bottle of wine and sniffed it and touched the rim to her lips and said soon, soon.

They spoke of Clara and Angelo and Messina on the far side of the Strait, from which the real winds came, and they spoke of her mother, who called each of her daughters a dove, as though they carried her dream of some wild peace in their own hearts, but always they spoke again of the storms.

"They name them after men here," she said.

"What men?"

"Lost ones."

"It's probably to be less afraid of them. They're not afraid of the dead here."

"In Sicilia, I think, they name them after women."

"We're all storms," he said.

"Sì," she whispered. "*E mari.*"

The sun had come up full over the cliffs, but the chill still slipped into the open sleeves of their sweaters, and he asked her if she wanted to go back.

"No," she said. "It's warm. It hasn't been warm in so long."

"It's not true just because we say it is."

She closed her eyes.

"Yes it is," she said. "Yes it is."

When they'd eaten, he took up a long wooden rod from under the gunwale and baited a hake through its eyes and tossed it into the swells. He sat up on the prow with his legs braced on either gunwale, and he swayed as the old man had done, and she watched him with pleasure as he fished. He was not fishing long before the rod bowed, and he tightened the drag and let the line swing over her head to the other side and then up toward the prow, where he kept it clear of the anchor rope. They knew it was something big, and when he'd fought it for a few moments he let the drag out and plucked the line like a piano string.

"Aldo," he said.

But they knew the boy had no money to buy strong line, and that everything they'd borrowed, including the boat that held them up over the fathoms below them, was stolen. Stolen or borrowed, she'd thought, as they rowed out. This boat. This body. This bread.

He tightened the drag again and the fish made its leap. It was a sea bass no longer than his arm, but it was strong from its time fighting the current all the way down from Scilla and beyond, fighting it for the run up in the winter months to find its mate. When he'd brought it to the side of the boat, she leaned forward and took the rod from him and he asked her not to pull. She held it very tight, with the line palmed against the rod, and he felt down along the line and bent down over the gunwale and came up with the fish, its broad tail swinging in his hand and his thumb hooked in its mouth as wide as two of the *clementine*.

"*Chiedi,*" he said, "*e riceverai.*"

He knelt and kissed it on the head and watched her smile.

When he rowed them back, he was singing *Madame Arthur. Madame Arthur es tune femme, qui fit parler, parler, parler.*

"What does it mean?"

"The others talk and talk about her," he said.

"Why?"

"*Pourqui? Elle avait un je ne sais quoi.*"

She lay back with her feet toward the open sea, her hands on her belly as she looked up at the clouds.

"Did your mother sing it?"

"No," he said, "she just listened." His breath was heavy as he rowed. "But sometimes I sang it for her. When she was upset. It always worked."

"Can you sing it now?"

"From the beginning?"

"Yes, from the beginning."

He sang it slowly as he rowed, and she thought about the boat the boy had stolen. How do you steal a boat? she thought. Do you go in the night with others and take it from the house of the ones who built it with their own two hands? Do you do such a thing with your own brothers, your own father? You must have carried it a long way, Aldo. A long way so that the one who made it would not know. Down along the road with the gunwales over your shoulders. And your own voice echoing to you in the hull when you told the others where to go. A long way from its maker. As we all are, Aldo. As we all are.

Aldo. She thought of his clothes frayed at the hems and sewn with new buttons and passed down from brother to brother. Perhaps from father to brother. And then to son. She thought of his older brothers gone off from this village, this sea, to find their lives. As she had come here to find her own. Because we never know. She felt the waves sway her from side to side, and she felt the child in her, and she thought of Nardo's brothers, the older and the younger—how they, too, had worn each other's clothes and lain alone, sometimes, in those clothes, asking which life was theirs, which life another's. We never know, she thought. Then she thought of a boy carrying a boat on his shoulders through the dark with one thought, one thought only, and she touched her lips and said his name aloud and then to herself she said *yes, sometimes we know enough. Sometimes we know.*

"Nardo," she said. He had finished his song. "What am I like when I'm sleeping?"

"I thought maybe you were sleeping now."

"Maybe I am."

"No, you don't talk in your sleep."

"*Ma dai.* I don't talk?"

"Sometimes. But they're just dreams."

"*Sogni.*" She opened her hands and closed them. "Why do you think we dream?"

"Us?"

"No. Anyone."

"I don't know."

"He says such beautiful things."

The wind had turned, and he was rowing faster now.

"Maybe we're not supposed to know things like that," he said.

"No. I don't think so. I think it's because there are things we don't know we remember. There are things we don't know we are. And maybe you're only supposed to know if you want to know."

"I think sometimes I could do without them."

"*Ay.* Just like Clara."

He laughed.

"Nardo," she said, "what would you say if you were me?"

"What?"

"Right now. The first thing that comes to your mind. But as me."

"As you?"

He had stopped rowing, and she waited.

"I want to go home."

"Are you saying it as me or as you?"

"As you," he said.

"Good," she said. "Say more. I'm you."

"You're ridiculous."

"I know."

He laughed.

"*Va bene*," he said. "I'm afraid sometimes."

"Of what?"

"Of the same things you're afraid of." He paused. "Not having a home. That you took me from my home forever."

She breathed. Very slowly she ran her hands over the gunwales.

"I won't say I'm sorry," she said.

"Because you're stubborn?"

She laughed. "We're still playing, right?"

"*Sì.*"

"Well then I'm you," she said, "and yes, I'm stubborn sometimes. And that's not the worst thing in the world. I like that I'm stubborn. And so do you."

"So what?" He'd started rowing again.

"And I didn't take you from anywhere, Alexandra," she said, "and we're on our way home. We always were."

"Good," he said. He was rowing hard now. "I like that. Because look at this sea, Leonardo. I thought you knew all about the sea, you sailor, but look at this chop now. You didn't know about that, Gemetti, did you?"

"I don't know everything," she said.

He laughed.

"No," he said, "you don't. I shouldn't even ask you questions. But I'm going to. One last time," he said. "I'm going to ask you one last thing, Leonardo."

"*Sì,*" she said.

"Why on god's earth do you have that awful beard?"

She cradled her belly as she laughed. The wind shifted the boat, and she lifted a finger and drew it along the edges of the clouds above.

"Nardo," she said. "I don't think I could draw you."

"You're you again, aren't you?"

"*Sì.*"

"*Perché?* Why couldn't you draw me?"

"I don't know. Not yet. I wouldn't want this to be any different than it is."

"Why would that change anything?"

"It always does."

"Maybe every time but one. Maybe you were doing it wrong the other times."

"Or maybe they were doing it wrong, the ones I drew."

"I don't know. Can it be wrong if you just sit there?"

"*Sì.*"

He stopped rowing.

"Of course," he said. "Of course it can."

The boat rocked slightly as he lowered the oars again unevenly and began to row.

"Nardo?"

"*Sì?*"

"Nothing. I just wanted to hear you say yes."

The waves swayed her, and she braced her hands against the gunwales and then laid them over her chest. When the swell had passed she thought of the great ship far out in the sea that had made such waves. Of the great ships she had made, which nothing but the sea could carry. *Portare,* she thought. She thought of what it was to carry anything at all. As her mother believed she carried a wild dove in her heart, as though we could carry for someone else their dream. As if we could carry the dream they call the world. She laid her hands over her belly and thought of what it was to be carried. She thought of the boat carrying them on the sea, and of what the old man had said about the battle between the depths and what mastered them. Like the hand waving over the chaos of the deep. She closed her eyes and asked him what he thought chaos was.

"You," he said.

She asked if he was joking.

"Of course," he said. "I'm the storm. You had your life, and then I came."

"Nardo," she said. "No more joking. You know this is my life."

"I know."

He looked out over the swells.

"Alexandra?"

"*Sì?*"

"What do you think it is? Chaos."

She thought about it. She told him she thought it was different for everyone. That each of us has her own law. And we learn to break it in different ways. And where we break it, we have our lives.

He asked if there is not a law common to all, but she shook her head with the sway of the waves and said she didn't know. She said she'd thought there was, and now she wasn't sure, and maybe when she was older she would think so again, but she said she knew it would be a different law she believed in, whenever that time came.

The waves were lifting and swaying them as he rowed hard.

"I think there can be both," he said. "Ours and everyone's. I think both can happen at the same time."

She said she'd spoken to an old man who'd thought the same thing, but she did not tell him who the old man was.

"I think he's probably very wise," he said. She knew he was smiling as he said it.

"Yes," she said. "He was. He is. But the same thing can be said by different men. Wise and unwise."

"And you think I'm unwise?"

She lifted her hands from her body and opened them and spread her arms over the gunwales.

"Unwise enough to marry me."

Very slowly he stopped rowing, and she heard him lean forward and lay the blades of the oars on the prow behind him and lock the oarlocks. He came forward on his knees and leaned over her and steadied her belly and looked into her eyes.

"Yes," he said. "I will."

XIV

That night he lay in the dark after she'd fallen asleep, and he thought of her dream, the one she'd told him about the burning ships in the waves, the oars thrown in the harbor. Maybe it was her mother's dream, but it was her dream, too. If we remember it, it's always our dream, too. It always is.

He thought of the night he'd spent by the Fontana in Bologna, looking up at the stone face of the god. Let the bombs come, he'd thought, let the waves rinse it away. No. Nothing can rinse our lives from our lives. No one is those waves. As it was with my father. Even if we are rinsed of our lives, our lives remain. In the worlds we make. The only way is to know what you do. It is the only way, Leonardo. If you die not knowing, your life will be lived again and again, in the hush of others, until it knows.

He thought of walking with her beside the sea of Lunetto for the first time. How they'd spoken of the great shipworks gone up in flames, how he'd told her that was something to go in fear of even in your dreams, all those ships burning in the dark and nowhere to go. He thought of her drawings, the nets and the birds and the currents, the steel and the ropes and the harbors, and when he tried to think of the child he thought instead of the face she hadn't touched on the page under the bowl on the table. Then he thought of the shipworks again, all of them in great flames in the darkness, the ships and the hands that built them with nothing, nowhere to go. He closed his eyes now and breathed the sea air, the scent of the dark pine of the rafters. No, he thought. He rolled to his side and laid his hand on her shoulder and felt her breathing. No. This is what we have. This place where the rowing is the privilege. Where the way there is the place. Where to go and not to go are sometimes one.

XV

That night her mother had stood in her room in Lunetto and opened the wardrobe and stared into the mirror. As though it were her daughter she might see there. As though she could tell her the things she had forgotten to tell.

She sat at her daughter's desk and looked up at the drawings she'd left behind, the ships unfinished and the empty seas, and then she looked out at the cypresses in the wind, the moon in the room with her like the empty dresses of another. Very slowly she took out a blank piece of paper and lifted it to her lips and smelled it. Like the wind in the foothills. Like the hills themselves. Like the laurels. She laid the page in front of her and placed one hand on it and dragged her other hand across the heavy silver of her rings, in which the years had written their own fair share of names.

She lifted a pen and touched it to her tongue and thought about what she would say to her daughter, if she could write to her where she was. *You have a home*, she thought to write, *always*. But when she thought of the words on the blankness of the page, it was as though she had scrawled them, for no one, in the ashes of the moon.

She stood and made her way to her daughter's bed and lay down in the linens, the muslin curtains blowing across her body. She was wearing her dark cotton blouse and her blue, wool coat, and she had come a long way through the winds down from the cherry laurels in the foothills. *Do you remember?* she'd thought to write, in the moonlight. Do you remember whose room this was? Do you remember that this was the day?

The wind was cold in the cypresses, and she rolled to her side and reached for the latches and pulled the windows closed, the curtains settling on her shoulder. She lifted them and tucked them between the bed and the sill and then brought them to her face again and smelled the rosewater of her daughter.

You remember, she said. Of course you do. And may the remembering be the yes of your life.

XVI

The sirocco brought up the warm winds, all March, from the des-
erts of Africa, and she'd see him off from the harbor in the mornings and
then return to the villetta and stare at her pages, her blackened hands,
the drawing she would not touch. Then she'd tuck them away softly, as
though someone were there with her, someone she should not waken,
and carry her sandals back through the groves and down to the south
side of the cove where the nets were waiting to be mended.

He'd sold a string of sea bass at the market and bought her a cream
organza dress with sheer, cream sleeves, its loose fabric that would settle
comfortably over her body, and she'd bought him a broadcloth suit and a
new, black tie, and then she'd gone to Georgio and his father and asked
them what they would like for a used pair of shoes. Georgio had slid out
quietly from behind the stall and gone to her and cradled her around the
hips and said, *Io sapevo. We will get you the torrone, Signora. Il migliore
del mondo.* Then he'd looked at her again. *Io sapevo,* he'd said. *I knew.*

On the first Saturday of April she'd placed a small sandstone pebble
in each shoe and taken them out and asked him to try them on before
he changed, and he'd stood in his cotton pants and looked at her and
said, "*Che cosa?* What did you put in them?"

"Nothing is easy," she'd said. "Remember that."

"How could I forget?" he'd smiled.

"Good."

All morning he'd sat on the bed polishing the shoes. When he'd
looked up and seen her in her dress in the doorway, he'd laid the shoes

on the night table beside him and then sat down before the bed as he'd done in Lunetto.

"What do you think D'Annunzio would say about this?"

She laughed.

"I don't remember a single thing about those books."

She sat down on the floor with him and straightened his necktie.

"He'd say something about death, that's for sure."

"You're ridiculous."

She reached up for his shoes and laid them on the floor beside her. The villetta smelled of the oleander and mastic that had begun to bloom in the cliffs above, a faint scent of vanilla and almond, the sea grape climbing the wooden stairs toward the windows.

"You know that's bad luck. New shoes on a table."

"I know."

She breathed.

"I wish my mother were here, Nardo."

"We could wait. We don't have to do it now."

"No," she said. "I don't want to wait. Not anymore." She looked at her hands. "But I wish she could be here."

"I know. We could still tell her. We could tell all of them. We have time."

"She wouldn't have it this way. Look at me. None of them would."

He shook his head.

"Maybe we're wrong about all that. Maybe we have no idea."

He helped her up, and they sat beside each other on the bed, her palm on his thigh.

"We can't tell anyone, Nardo. Not yet. Not until we're in Roma."

"And then?"

"Then we hide in the *forteza*."

He laughed softly.

"Be serious," he said. "What will we do?"

"Then we'll just be Romans. Not Calabrese."

"No one could make us not Calabrese."

"You mean *idioti*."

His laugh was loud, and lay back on the bed and placed his hand between her shoulders and steadied her as she lay back beside him.

"What do you think we'll be like? As Romans?"

"I can't even imagine it."

"But you were there."

"It doesn't mean I can imagine it."

She turned to him.

"Nardo, we can hide in a city, can't we? Anyone can hide in a city."

"Alexandra. It's over. All that is over."

She looked up again into the rafters and folded her hands on her belly.

"Nardo."

"*Dimmi.*"

"We haven't seen a newspaper in months."

"That's why we're here."

She smiled.

"*Dimmi,*" he said. "What do you think will happen?"

"Just what you said in Lunetto. The Democrazia Cristiana will have their way."

"And then what?"

"And then we won't read the news ever again."

He hummed.

"Maybe we can do better than that."

"Yes," she said, "we can. We won't *be* the news ever again."

He smiled and laid a hand on her belly.

"Did he swim today?"

"Of course," she said. "He's always moving." She looked at his eyes. "He's fine, Nardo. He's strong."

"We haven't bought clothes for him yet."

"I know."

"Why?"

"You know why."

"Because it's bad luck."

She nodded.

"Alexandra, we don't need luck anymore."

"Yes we do." She rolled her head to him. "Tell me about your dream."

"What dream?"

"You were talking in your sleep again. This morning."

"*Ah, Cristo.* What did I say?"

"You don't remember at all?"

"No."

"Think about it."

He rolled his head to her and then looked up at the ceiling.

"Something about Roma?"

"No."

"About the storms?"

"No."

Very slowly he sat up and laid his hand on her thigh and turned toward her.

"About the swallows," he said. "In Bologna."

"Yes," she said. "Tell me."

XVII

They were married in the April light in the chapel of Palma, where the old man stood as witness. The pastor of Palma had refused to wed them—*sei perso, you have never needed us before*—but the old man had gone and spoken to him a long time, and when he had returned to their villetta, he'd said he had had no luck, but luck was no part of this. He would get them another priest. A good one. Who could understand that the laws of God are not on earth to keep us from changing. From being the great sway of our changes.

They stood in the chapel together, and Aldo and some of the others had come. They exchanged wooden rings they'd bought each other the day before, and they'd told each other that they would buy real ones when they were able, but when they stood together in the chapel and slipped the rings on each other's fingers, they knew there were no other real ones. They whispered their vows to each other, softly, her lips grazing against his close-cut beard, and when Aldo said he couldn't hear, they turned to him and smiled and then said the vows again.

They walked back from the village together, and when cars stopped to ask them if they wanted to be driven, she only ran her hands over the child in her and *said no, grazie, abbiamo ciò di cui abbiamo bisogno.* We have what we need.

The old man and the boys walked with them, and when Georgio passed by in his car he slapped the door and yelled *mi dispiace, Signora, stavo lavorando,* and when she turned and looked at those beside her she thought perhaps they were in another time. But then she looked at him and thought no, we are in this one. This one and the old ones both.

This world is the other.

Ricci and Nardo carried the driftwood table out through the window of the villetta and down to the beach, where they laid it with anchovies and sardella and sott'olio, 'nduja and small bowls of liquorice for the children. The old man had carried down the radio and plugged it into the generator of the bait shack, and Alexandra danced with him slowly as the boys howled. He looked at her straight with his clear, blue eyes, and he told her it was as though she were his own daughter. She told him she was proud of that. He, too, she said, had a chance to remake his story. He nodded and said it was not good to make an old man tremble. He reached into his pocket and held up a small wooden box, and he told her he did not have many gifts to give, but he hoped this would be a small blessing for the years to come. She thanked him and asked him if she should open it now, but he laid his hand on it and said no. For you both. For later.

The priest who had wed them was very young, and he sat at the table drinking wine and grappa and speaking with the *fidanzata* of one of the boys. Sometimes he touched her leg, and she lifted his hand and laid it on the table and went right on talking.

He'd asked them their name for the *certificazione*, and when Leo had said Gemetti, the priest had paused and looked at both of them. Then he leaned down and wrote it. She looked at Leo and asked him something with her eyes. He said they were not running anymore. Not now. Not ever again.

When they'd eaten and danced, they sat watching a storm passing far out in the south winds, the first stars rising behind it, and some of the boys had drunk much wine and were asleep in their chairs at the table. The priest had gone back up to the village with some of the others, and the old man came and kissed Alexandra on the hair and shook her husband's hand. They asked him where he had found such a priest, and he said there were always priests to be found for anything, anything, but that this one had simply been there. They said they could not pay him back, but he waved his hand over them, as if to ward off the thought. *Per la nostra felicità,* he said, *dobbiamo altri.* He grinned and said he had found the priest asking for grappa, and he'd known he was the one. Alexandra smiled and asked him where he had come from, and the old man had said not far. Lunetto. He bowed again and told them it was a foolish world, but they had made it less foolish with their promise. Which could never be broken without breaking the breaker. Until the end of time.

They looked at each other, her eyes as they had only been once before. We're fine, he told her with his eyes. We're here.

He offered to walk the old man home, but the old man refused. *Go,* he said, *tonight we do the work.*

They lay together in their bed, her drawings tucked away beneath the radio, and she told him she was uneasy.

"This is our home," he said.

"Nardo."

"No one knows."

He laid his hands over her face. Gently. Like a mask. Very slowly he lifted them.

"We're done running," he said. "Even in Roma. We're done."

"I don't know. And there were so many in the chiesa today, Nardo. How do we know what they see?"

"Let them see."

"Why, Nardo? Why?"

He let his hands play over her face again, and when he lifted them, she saw in his eyes what he was going to say.

"Because you know," she said.

He waited for her to smile, but she did not. She looked at him a long time as the windows whistled, the casements open to the spring winds, a distant singing somewhere in the darkened cliffs above them. Finally he spoke.

"What do you see?"

She brushed back his hair that had grown longer since their time together on the sea, his hair that smelled of salt, of wine, of the palm oil that eased the ropes over the pulleys and down into the canyons of the deep, and she kissed him and pointed up to the darkness where they knew it was the old man who was singing.

"Later," she said. "Let's listen."

XVIII

When the priest had gotten back to the chiesa in Palma, he'd spoken awhile with the pastor who had refused them—about the reprobates, about the ones who have no contrition—and when the pastor had told him he had drunk too much and that perhaps he was just like them, the priest had gone off into the rectory and sat down and looked up at the ceiling. Stains in it like patterns he could not explain. Strange shapes and mayhem. A stain of chaos in the clean wool of the world. When he'd closed his eyes he'd said the name to himself again and again. Gemetti. He heard girls' voices and the voice of a boy's fidanzata, a poor boy who was nothing, *niente,* and then, very softly, he heard the voice of the son in Lunetto who had said that name to him, again and again, in the shadows. Gemetti.

He licked his lips for the last taste of wine in them and rolled something up from his throat and spat it out on the rectory floor. The one who had said that name to him. His hollow eyes. His questions. Then he rose and made his way across the room and stood by the telephone on the pastor's desk. They shall beat their swords into ploughshares. Yes. But it is for the cowardly and the liars and the sorcerers that the lake of fire has been prepared. Only them. Let the dead bury the dead.

Sindaco Russo, he said. *Ricco bastardo.*

Then he laid his hand on the desk and steadied himself with the wine in him and picked up the phone and waited for the exchange.

XIX

They fell asleep in their wedding clothes, and when they woke in the night he asked if she was sure it was a son.

"I know it is," she said.

He said he would like to have a son and a daughter both, and she said she wanted the same. But we must start here. Everything has a beginning, she said. Just begin, she said, and the rest will follow.

"We should pay him back."

"We will. Somehow."

"He won't even say his name."

"Maybe he can't."

She shook her head.

"Nardo. Do you think it will ever be easy?"

"No."

"You don't think it's supposed to?"

"I don't know."

She reached up and brushed something from his face that wasn't there.

"Tell me about the storms, when you can't see the shore."

"You know all about that," he said. "*È lo stesso per tutti.*"

She shook her head against his chest and told him no, it wasn't the same for everyone. Perhaps we could understand, each of us, but it was never the same.

"I'll go out there again with you, Nardo," she said, "after."

"What about Roma?"

"Let's stay."

"Really?"

"I don't know. Just a while." She turned away and then looked at him. "We won't be there forever, will we?"

"Who knows? Do you think he'll want to be a *pescatore*? *Un marinaio*?

"*Può essere*. We can teach him."

"Not in Roma."

"No. We'll come back. We'll visit."

"What will he be in Roma?"

"*Un gladiatore*," she smiled. "Whatever he wants."

He gathered her hair and drew it out so that it touched her shoulder in the moonlight.

"We have time," he said.

"*Sì*."

They were quiet awhile, the wind shifting the palm fronds in the groves of the cove. Finally she laid her hand on his thigh and asked her if he'd known what the storm had been called. Its name.

"No."

She lifted her palm and laid it on his chest. She told him how she'd stood as a child on the beach of Palma, feeling the little waves on her feet, the little waves from far out where the storms were, and she knew they were the waves of some great thing passing far out there in the darkness.

"*Non lo so*," he said.

I don't know either, she told him. *Ma penso che non avesse nome.* But I think it had no name.

They'd fallen asleep in their clothes, and when the child kicked in her in the night, she sat up in bed and waited for him to wake.

"*Stai bene?*" he asked.

"*Sì*."

He laid his hand on her.

"*Sta bene?*"

She shifted his hand until he could feel the child. Like a small swell from a ship passing far out in the darkness. They could hear the waves laying themselves down on the beach, a wind picking up in the palm groves.

"Do you want to work? I could make caffè."

"No," she said. "Grazie."

He looked at her and asked her if they were really *sposati*.

"Of course," she said.

He said if he woke to find it had been a dream, she would have to kill him. She laughed and said his name until he believed it. Until she did. Until they knew it was the same thing she would have said in any dream.

XX

He woke before first light and stood at the table and laid his hand on the stack of blank pages and watched her sleep. She was still wearing her dress. *Let's not change yet*, she'd said. *Not yet.*

He went to her and pulled the sheet up over her shoulder, but she did not wake. No one was left on the beach, and he stood looking out the window to the moon on the three rocks in the shallows. He closed his eyes and smelled the rosewater in her hair. Then he made his way to the bathroom and took the razor from beneath the sink and shaved for a long time.

He stood before the mirror looking at his face. His jaw had healed early the past autumn, where he'd been struck in Lunetto. He ran the water and washed his face, and then he looked at himself again. His breath against the glass. His hair they would cut by morning. He lifted his hands and held them over his face and spread his fingers and looked through them. As though his own hands were a mask. Of his own acts. Through which we have to show the world our life, its very face. As though our life and our acts were not the same.

He turned back and opened the door and saw him standing before him. A pistol in his hand. They said not a word. Very slowly he looked down the hall and saw his wife asleep in the bed, and he looked back at Matteo.

"Come," he heard.

Matteo walked him out through the back door and closed it quietly and took him down the path and out into one of the palm groves. He told him to kneel down, and he did. This figure standing before him with a pistol. Russo's son. His hair lifting and settling in the wind.

He said he had waited for this moment a long time, and now he would have to hear him speak.

Leo nodded.

He said he had thought perhaps he could forgive him, but all through the winter he had heard rumors of Gemetti and the Bianchi daughter not two hours away, and he had told himself that only a mockery like that would make him give up on forgiveness again. He said he'd thought no one could be so foolish, no one, but now that he saw this fool before him he knew he was wrong. They can. He told him priests have loose lips and drunken priests drink because they cannot forgive. Even themselves. He spat on the ground and asked why a man would so mock another man's life.

"No," Leo said. He told him he would not mock him, but Matteo only shook his head and said sometimes we do not know who we are trying to harm. Until it is too late.

He took a small towel from his back pocket and wrapped it around the pistol and looked at him. "Say it," he said.

"Please."

The wind shifted the palm fronds. He told him to stay there on his knees because he had one more thing to say. He told him of his mother in Lunetto. The woman in the veil. He said this woman died in the winter. In the streets. Like a dog.

Leo shook his head and said it was not so. He said he had phoned his mother every month to hear her voice. Just to hear it. He had never spoken, he'd said. Because he wanted her to be done with him. But he'd wanted to know.

Matteo shook his head and said no man knows when he is speaking with a ghost. With a memory. As perhaps he might be now. Because there is always the hope that the world is our dream. Or that it is not the dream we have been powerless to keep in our hearts. Then he shot him.

He slipped the towel into his pocket and cleaned the pistol on the dead man's shirt and dragged him out to the beach, where he would be found. He laid the pistol in his hand and then thought about that. No, he thought. Like a dog. He took up the pistol again and slid it into his own belt at the small of his back and looked at the villetta. He thought about her. No, he said. Let her know. Only in the hearts of the living do the dead stay dead.

XXI

The old man found him first. When he had helped the boys clean away the feast, he had walked the cliffs above the cove and kept walking as night fell. He'd sat a long while looking out over the waves, his songs growing softer in the moonlight, and when he'd looked down onto the beach, he'd seen him. He'd taken himself down along the cliff roads, down through the willows, and when he'd come to the cove he'd waited in the palm fronds before he'd gone to him. The moon was full, and there was no wind. He knelt over him a long while, looking down at his face that seemed like the face of a boy in his sleep.

When he went up to the villetta he stood a long while before the back door and then went in. She was sitting up in the bed at the far side of the house, the windows open behind her, and she was still wearing her wedding dress. She looked at him, and he made himself walk to her very calmly and then looked at her eyes. Searching his for an answer. She said her husband's name, and he shook his head slowly and said there were no words for what he'd come to say. No, she said. But she had not said it. Merely breathed it. Like a promise. Like a vow. Then she howled it as though it were the birth-pang of the world.

XXII

She had tried to go to him, but the old man had held her very hard and pressed the window open and called out to the beach until one of the boys came. It was Aldo, and the old man spoke to him quickly and harshly and told him what to do. She was thrashing in his arms, and he told her he would take her there, *lo prometto, lo prometto,* but she would have to understand it was not something she could unsee.

Nardo, she said. *Nardo.*

Aldo had gone off and was calling for the other boys in the wind. The old man stood with her and clasped her and walked her to the back door and then steadied her when she fell. They sat together on the threshold, the wind shifting in the first light in the palm groves, and she slapped him hard with one hand and then the other. He did not move. She looked at her hand and told him her husband had just gone off a moment as he sometimes did and all they had to do was wait. He would return.

Sì, he said. *Sì.*

She stood very slowly and made her way down the stairs and looked out at the cove. The boys were kneeling near the tide pools, and when they turned toward her she knew she must have spoken. She knew she had fallen to her knees, and when the old man lifted her slowly she knew where she was. She knew the old man had let her go, and she knew no one was carrying her through the darkness, and she made her way forward in the moonlight and let herself down onto her knees again and looked awhile at the boys' faces in the wind.

XXIII

They buried him high up in the hills looking out to the sea. She walked up the cliff roads every morning to visit him, and then she walked down and sat at the shack mending the nets until the light fell. The old man visited her often, but she did not speak with him. He sat on the boat beside her, and they watched the true storms of spring building far off on the horizon, and only once she turned to him and said she should not have let them stay, she should have known. But then she only shook her head and looked at the nets and heard her own words she'd spoken when she'd woken him at the station of Palma. No, she thought. No.

She rose and walked back to the villetta and saw the food the boys had brought her, and she lay down on the coolness of the kitchen floor and wept a long time. She told herself not to think of his hands. His smell. She told herself not to think of the one who had done it, of the place in the palm groves where she knew it had happened, of a young man riding a train through the night and the door opening and a woman asleep in a bed as though she could keep on dreaming her world. No, she said. Then she let herself see their faces. Both of them. Each of them afraid. No, she said. She laid her face in her hands and let herself think of a figure running off into the palm groves and the darkness, and when she'd watched him a long while she did not know which one he was, which one was fleeing, which one was left alone in the cold. No, she said. You know. You know.

She pushed herself up and laid her shoulders against the tin in which she still kept their *clementine* and sott'olio. The child kicked in her, and she told herself not to think of the mothers of Palma, the mothers of Aldo and the boys of the Graciela, the mothers who lived in their villetti above the cliffs and had never once spoken to her, not once, the mothers who passed her sometimes on the roads and looked at her body and shook their heads and walked on. No, she said. She cradled the child in her and said it aloud. You are not a secret to yourself.

She would not sleep in their bed. She carried the pillows out to the beach and curled there as she had done as a child. In the moonlight. When they'd cut her hair. She cradled her belly and spoke to the child in her, and she told him about his father. About his war. About his time in the mountains and the snows. About how she had seen a man in a black mask standing in the market of Lunetto. Lunetto, she said. She told him about her sisters and her mother, and then she told him about his grandfather, how he had spent so many days out on the sea, staring down into the depths, as though he could see the shape of his life to come. She told him about his father's brothers, the older who had vanished in the snows, and the younger who had been lost, and the youngest of them who had never begun. The youngest, with his dark eyes and his heavy hands, who had made his brother laugh even long afterward when the world was no joke at all. She told him that the world is hard, but it is hard for everyone, and that is how we find each other, in the ache. She held her belly and told him about the old man, about his stories, how he had taught her that our lives are stories for which we are only half the maker. But that much. No less. And that he, too, this child, would be given that chance. She told him that we live the same stories again, but that does not make them the same. Then she told him that she would not be afraid. That she would not pass that into his heart. That the fears in us become the lives of others, and that his father had died with no fear in his heart. Because he knew. He knew.

She slept on the beach and dreamt of many things. She dreamt of them dancing in the moonlight, and she dreamt of ships burning far out to sea. She dreamt of oars thrown into the waves, and she dreamt of a child alone on a little boat, a black silk mask laid on an anchor beside him. She dreamt of a woman waking in the night to look out into the cypresses at the moon. She dreamt of a woman saying a name in her sleep, and when she had said it again, she woke and looked up at the moon and asked herself if she could dream again.

She did, and she dreamt of Lunetto. She dreamt of a terrace where she sat with her mother and father, and she dreamt of the sea wall and the sea. She dreamt of the *clementine* in the market and the almonds, and in the dream she held them to her face and smelled them and she asked herself what they smelled like and she said home. Home.

On her last night on the beach she lay awake and knew the child had almost come. She closed her eyes and listened to the waves, and she told herself she had one more dream before he came to her. And she did dream it. She dreamt of a child lying in the shadows of a great Basilica, listening to the swallows fly through the darkness above. She dreamt of a child far from home, listening to the birds in the darkness, and she dreamt of the child closing its eyes and very slowly letting a question begin in it. Of why there is hunger. Of why hunger comes into this world at all. In the dream she closed her eyes very softly, as he had done, and then when the swallows grew very quiet she felt something kick in her, and when she'd woken she'd moaned out in pain, and the old man was standing over her in the light.

XXIV

She delivered the child in the *ospedale* of Palma with the old man at her side, and when it was over they laid the child on her breast and she sniffed his hair, the scent of him like milk in the wind and the clean, fresh depths of the sea.

She gave him the name of his father, and she took him home and bathed him in the sink and changed him on the old, driftwood table, and she turned on the radio and swayed him in her arms as she looked out at the moon on the waves.

The old man had bought things for her, and she found them on the sill and in the dresser and on the bed, and she knew there were things in other places, but she would not look there. Instead she looked at the sea and at the beach and at the child. She looked at his eyes, which were honey-colored like his father's, and she told him about the honey in her cellar in Lunetto and the small, driftwood swallows she had carved for his father, which she had wanted to give him on their wedding night. She told him what a gift was. She told him that one of them was up in the hills now on her father's stone, and the other was here. She touched her chest. Here. I have not yet finished it, she said. My half.

She lay in their bed with him on her chest, and she listened to him cooing. Like a dove, she thought. No, like a child. Like this child.

She did not want to be without him, and she sat on the big sill and fed him while she looked at the sea. She looked at her wooden wedding band, and she thought of the silver rings of her mother. In which the names had been worn down by the ages. Which erase nothing. So long as we live.

He had bought them a bassinet and a child's blankets in the weeks before the wedding, but they had not wanted to set any of them out. *Sfortuna*, he had said. Let things be.

She laid Leonardo down and watched his eyes and soothed him until he slept. Then she made her way into the bathroom and sat on the cool tile and said his name. Her body shook slowly, quietly, and when the briefest howl escaped her, she heard him wake, and she shook her head and stood slowly and looked into the mirror and said no, Leonardo, your mother is here. She will not let this take anything else from you in this world.

She went to him and pulled a chair beside him and soothed him all night as she sang. She sang to him of kingdoms and riches, and she sang to him of the truly poor who have the world. She sang to him of great battles and the peace thereafter, of those who find their vengeance and cannot go home, of those who carry something in them that cannot be named, and when he cried she spoke to him and held him to her breast and told him she was there. There. Then she laid him down again and told him his father was there, also. She touched his face and said his father was there.

XXV

She had not wanted to look at the fresh paper he'd brought home for her, and in the second week after his death she'd carried it out to the beach and stood staring at the sea. Then she'd carried it back and tucked it under their bed and told herself not yet, not yet.

In the third week she woke from a dream of him. He was alone on a train in his uniform, and he was curled up like a boy with his collar turned high, as she'd seen it when they'd fished together in the autumn winds. He was rubbing the warmth into his shoulders, and though he looked out the window time and again she knew he did not know where he was going.

She woke and sat up in the bed and fed the child, his hair like milk in her palm, his eyes unhurried as honey, and when he cooed she ran her thumb across his brow and then swayed him until he filled the villetta with his voice that had never been.

When he'd fallen asleep again she knelt and pulled the papers from under the bed and laid them on the driftwood table and sat staring out at the waves, the black silk ribbon between her fingers, her dark hair loose over her shoulders.

She drew as she had never drawn before. She worked all night and into morning, and when the child wept she fed him, and in the days to come she carried him along the cove and told him of what she was drawing. She drew a high, wind-swept place in the mountains, where the laurels were blown down to reveal a stone, and she drew a man carried by other men into a cathedral, dark birds scattering around them. She drew a woman walking through a narrow street beside a cathedral, and she drew her hand against the stones of the catedro's wall and then she brushed away the hand and drew the woman walking on into morning.

She drew Palma. The palms in the groves and the great cliffs that rose up on the Southern edge of the cove where the mastic grew in the fissures and the winds spoke their own tongue as they lashed it. She drew the winds themselves, the voices in them, the songs. She drew the Graciela in the harbor and the boys waving from its railings and the great net casting itself out into morning, and she drew the sight of the cliffs from the ship itself, the houses small and humble in the cliffs and the village of Palma behind them, the houses that the boys would always point out as their own and that the old man would wave away when he was asked of them. She drew the three rocks in the water, tall and dignified, and she drew the moon in the tidepools of the ancient sands that had rinsed away and risen again in the great storms. Then, when she had drawn it all, she drew the storms themselves. Wild, rising, they lashed the white silence of her pages and lifted the ship and left it, and the figures knelt on the foredeck, and sometimes the ship would vanish, and sometimes the ship sailed through.

When she'd told Leonardo of the storms, that they had no names at all, she laid the pages down and told him she had only begun. She drew a boy standing at a window, two dark horses beneath him, and though she dragged her hands over the horses' bodies she did not know where they were going. Go on, she almost told them. Go on. She drew an empty train and a room full of shoes, and she drew the names in them and said the names aloud, and when she woke as though she had heard his voice beside her she drew the things he had spoken of in his sleep. She drew a boy kneeling alone in the snow, and when she'd finished it she returned to it often, sometimes by morning, sometimes by night, and then she drew a figure cradling the boy in the snows, and she let the wind trill through the page as though they were speaking with one another. She drew their own child as he slept, and she let her fingers shape and reshape his face, and then it seemed as though he was telling her how to make what she made. When she was through with the charcoal she'd brought from Lunetto, she cut fresh willow and cypress from the cliffs and took a tin from the bait shack and made a kiln on the beach and swayed Leonardo and told him how her father had taught her, long ago, how his eyes had been so like a child's when he'd drawn that first circle on their kitchen table and her sisters had laughed and spoken about what they'd drawn. Horses and great ships, vast armies marching in the dark. She placed the willow and cypress and a shard of the Graciela into the kiln and then, very slowly, a handful of the driftwood they'd gathered in the autumn before the storms had come. When she'd let the fire die she carried Leonardo up to the villetta and spoke to him as she drew. She drew cities ravaged and cities restored, cities raised up from the ashes. She drew the old man looking out from the cliffs, and then she drew a woman in a tower, a woman among flocks, a woman standing dignified with a dozen torches approaching her where she was bound. Then she drew the villetta itself, the willows and the oleander blooming in the cliffs behind it, an empty bed glinting through the moon in an open window. When she rested, she lay on the bed with the child on her chest and drew with her finger on the linens beside them. She drew without looking—an anchor; a wave; a stolen boat; and then, very slowly, she closed her eyes and spoke to her child and let her finger draw the face of his father, every touch of it, every breath.

When she had worked on every piece but one, she laid her child down and paced the room and lay down on the floor where his father had slept in the first nights, curled like a child. She could hear the wind in the palm fronds, the bells of Pasqua in the campanile, a singing from the village above. *Sì*, she whispered. *Sì*. Then she'd risen and found the drawing under the wooden bowl and smoothed it on the table and stood over it, running her hand across the page. The villetta was still. The songs were gone. *Sì*, she whispered. *Sì*. Then she took up the charcoal and worked. She worked quietly, without rest. She worked as the wind shook the villetta, and she worked as evening fell, and she worked until she saw a face made of shadow, a face made of light. When she'd stared at her face a long while she turned and looked out at the sea and then turned back and drew the eyes very carefully—first one, then the other, each one as cold and open as the sea itself, as wild as the lost and their voices, as deep.

She rose and fed her child and sat with him at the driftwood table. In the lamplight she laid aside the page and lifted a blank one and smoothed it down. The villetta was quiet, and she lifted the charcoal to her nose and smelled the sea in it for a long time. When the wind lifted the paper, she knew she would have to draw it, and she did. She drew a man standing in a square with the black flash of a mask across his face, and when she was finished she lifted it and sat with Leonardo on the sill and told him about his father. About his war, about a boy in the mountains, about a boy on a peach crate in a town square saying things he thought he could never have back. When the wind shifted the page in her hand again she told him sometimes the voices never die but sometimes they do, and there are voices that the wind takes away and there are voices that come back to us on the wind, and then she laid down the drawing and carried him to the turn-table and lowered the needle and played his father's favorite song. This is not your father's voice, she told him, but sometimes if someone loves something enough, though they cannot say why, especially when they cannot say why, their voice is a part of it, and all we have to do is listen, and it will be there.

XXVI

In the first week of May, she sat at the desk rocking the bassinet with one hand and finishing a sketch with the other. When she was done working, she stood and kissed the child and then leaned out the window and called down to the beach. She ran her fingers along the letters etched into the desk, and when Aldo came up through the palm trees, she leaned down over the sill and handed him the page and kissed him on the head.

"My shipmate," she said. *"Il mio compagno di bordo."*

"Maestra d'ascia," he said. "My shipwright."

She packed their things slowly. She laid out two tight-woven fishing nets on their bed and placed in them the radio, the charcoal, the blank pages of paper. She folded her drawings and tucked them into her organza dress and then slid one out again and left it on the table. She folded her sandals into her cotton pants, and she looked out at the sea. Then she turned and walked to his blue shirt he'd folded on the sill and that she'd never since touched. She lifted it and took out her drawing he had folded into his breast pocket and opened it halfway and then folded it and tucked it back again. She found the record he'd bought and slipped it inside his shirt and then she placed it in the net with his shoes and his suit and the letters he'd written for his mother. When she'd let herself remember the words of the song he'd sung to her, she took out his suit again and lifted the driftwood she'd carved and tucked it into his breast pocket and then folded the suit and placed it in the net. She looked out once more at the sea. When the child woke, she slipped into her pocket the gift the old man had given them. Which she had not yet opened. Then she closed the nets and heard Ricci and the others climbing up the stairs.

XXVII

They loaded her things at the station, and the boys knocked on the glass of the *cabina telefonica* until she hung up the receiver and stepped out onto the platform. They kissed the child, one by one, and then Aldo handed her a folded note and told her Georgio, it was from Georgio, he'd almost forgotten.

"Aldo," she said, "*Stai attento al mare.*"

"I will. I'll be careful."

"I left something for you. *Una sorpresa.*"

"For me?"

"Go. See."

"You made it?"

"Go ahead," she said. "*Non farmi piangere.*"

The old man came to her last. He told her he was ashamed of what he'd brought to her, of what the priest he'd brought to them had done, and she told him he could not have known. Then she told him it was not hers to forgive.

He asked her if it was not foolish to go back and she said no, *non adesso,* we can go back but we don't go back, that an old man had told her many things, but the one thing she remembered was that no two stories were the same. Remember? she asked.

He held her a long time. Then he laid his hand on the child and said he had spoken too much already for an old man, and he had no wisdom or knowledge of her life to come. She told him no one did. No one.

She sat on the train with her son in her arms and watched the sea and his eyes the whole way there. She thought of the shipworks and of the great, unfinished ships waiting in the sunlight to be made. By human hands. By anyone's. By hers. She thought of the house yet to be raised by the edge of the sea, the open windows through which the swallows could fly all evening, and she thought of the blank pages and the work she would do by morning. The large works that would fill the rooms and more and then the whole expanse of the sea. And the small ones that would be truer because they knew. She thought of a son wading out to swim in the sea. To sway with it. As though he were something the sea had made. And the light. As though he were the depths and the dominion both. As though he were the secret of the world.

When she was not far, she reached into her pocket and pulled out the box the old man had given them. She did not open it then, nor any time after. It was not for her, she thought. It was not for her alone.

When the train reached Lunetto, she looked at Leonardo's eyes and then she looked out the window to the platform.

Her mother was there. *La mia colomba,* she was saying, *my dove.*

She looked down at her child and then unfolded the note Aldo had given her. *Don't forget,* Georgio had written. *It takes a different bravery.*

Joseph Fasano is an American poet, novelist, and songwriter. His novels include *The Swallows of Lunetto* (Maudlin House, 2022) and *The Dark Heart of Every Wild Thing* (Platypus Press, 2020), which was named one of the "20 Best Small Press Books of 2020." His books of poetry include *The Crossing* (2018), *Vincent* (2015), *Inheritance* (2014), and *Fugue for Other Hands* (2013). His honors include the Cider Press Review Book Award, the Rattle Poetry Prize, and a nomination for the Poets' Prize, "awarded annually for the best book of verse published by a living American poet two years prior to the award year." His writing has appeared in *The Times Literary Supplement, The Yale Review, The Southern Review, The Missouri Review, Boston Review, Tin House, Verse Daily,* the *PEN Poetry Series,* and the Academy of American Poets' poem-a-day program, among other publications. His work has been widely anthologized and translated into Spanish, Lithuanian, Russian, Ukrainian, Swedish, Chinese, Italian, and other languages. He is the Founder of the *Poem for You Series,* and he teaches at Columbia University and Manhattanville College. His latest project is a "living poem" for his son that he is live-tweeting at twitter.com/stars_poem

Ingram Content Group UK Ltd.
Milton Keynes UK
UKHW011815230323
419066UK00005B/357